Prai

"With insightful and skil

"An exotic and detailed w~~orld, peopled by~~ characters that I'd love to be friends with . . . and some I'd never want to cross paths with."
—Robin Hobb

"A fantastical, richly drawn, poignant take on a classic coming-of-age story . . . a vibrant tale told with surety and grace."
—Leigh Bardugo

"*Pantomime* has long been one of my favorite queer reads that showed me how books could challenge the world's narrative. In this author's edition, Micah Grey shines on center stage with a twisting plot encased in stunning worldbuilding. Do not miss this series!"
—Linden A. Lewis

"A lyrical, stunningly written debut novel, which set my heart racing with every lift of the trapeze. In Micah we have one of the most original—and likable—protagonists I've read in a long time. An author to watch, without a doubt."
—Amy McCulloch

"Welcome to a world of shills and showmen, fading tech and circus freaks, where nothing and no one is what it appears. An absorbing, accomplished debut."
—Elspeth Cooper

"Set in a vividly imagined world . . . *Pantomime* is a fablelike story as beautifully unique as its main character."
—Malinda Lo

"Who hasn't dreamed off running off and joining the circus? Lam's Micah does just that, discovering a world of clowns and acrobats, con men and tricksters, corruption and incompetent doctors . . . I look forward to more from this author."
—Brian Katcher

"Well-written and intelligent fantasy with characters I loved and a wonderful protagonist, in a fascinating world. I really enjoyed *Pantomime* and I can't wait to re-enter Elada and continue to unravel its secrets"
—Fantasy Faction

By L. R. Lam

THE MICAH GREY TRILOGY

Pantomime
Shadowplay
Masquerade

THE DRAGON SCALES DUOLOGY

Dragonfall
Emberclaw

SEVEN DEVILS
(with Elizabeth May)

Seven Devils
Seven Mercies

STANDALONE

Goldilocks

THE PACIFICA SERIES

False Hearts
Shattered Minds

MASQUERADE

L. R. LAM

DAW BOOKS
NEW YORK

Copyright © 2026 by Laura Rose Lam

A version of this book was first published in 2017 by Pan Macmillan

All rights reserved. Copying or digitizing this book for storage, display, or distribution in any other medium is strictly prohibited. For information about permission to reproduce selections from this book, please contact permissions@astrapublishinghouse.com.

This is a work of fiction. Names, characters, places, and incidents are products of the author's imagination or are used fictitiously. Any resemblance to actual events, locales, or persons, living or dead, is entirely coincidental.

Cover design and illustration by Vera Drmanovski
Interior design by Fine Design
Maps by Anthony O'Mahoney
Edited by Aranya Jain

DAW Book Collectors No. 1997

DAW Books
An imprint of Astra Publishing House
dawbooks.com
DAW Books and its logo are registered trademarks of Astra Publishing House

Printed in the United States of America

Library of Congress Cataloging-in-Publication Data

Names: Lam, Laura, 1988- author
Title: Masquerade / L.R. Lam.
Description: First DAW edition. | New York : DAW Books, 2026. |
Series: The Micah Grey trilogy ; 3
Identifiers: LCCN 2025049833 (print) | LCCN 2025049834 (ebook) |
ISBN 9780756420314 paperback | ISBN 9780756420321 ebook
Subjects: LCGFT: Fantasy fiction | Novels | Fiction
Classification: LCC PS3612.A543285 M37 2026 (print) |
LCC PS3612.A543285 (ebook)
LC record available at https://lccn.loc.gov/2025049833
LC ebook record available at https://lccn.loc.gov/2025049834

First DAW edition: March 2026

10 9 8 7 6 5 4 3 2 1

To the readers who kept the magic alive.
Thank you.

CONTENT

Note on Editions — ix
Content Notes — x
A Reminder of Shadowplay — xi

1. Fever Dream — 1
2. Recovery — 8
3. Rooftop Secrets — 14
4. Three Chimaera — 22
5. The Burning Spires — 36
6. Infirmary — 45
7. Take Your Medicine — 54
8. The Body Snatcher — 63
9. The Magic Show — 68
10. Flames & Rain — 78
11. The Penny Rookeries — 85
12. The Morgue — 92
13. Street Magic — 102
14. The Shimmering Girl — 110
15. The Lily — 117
16. The Horned Boy — 127
17. The Hospital — 137

18. The Snakewood Palace	*145*
19. A Royal Secret	*154*
20. Forget Your Woes	*163*
21. Ahti's Scion	*173*
22. The Doctor & His Assistant	*182*
23. The Needle	*190*
24. The Gargoyle	*200*
25. Unmasked	*209*
26. The Spark	*220*
27. The Blurred Man	*231*
28. Across the Water	*240*
29. The Kashura	*247*
30. Red Glass	*257*
31. Awakening	*270*
32. Like Clockwork	*281*
33. Homecoming	*291*
Epilogue: Carnivale	*298*
A Conversation with L. R. Lam	*305*
Reading Group Guide for Masquerade	*308*
Acknowledgements	*309*

NOTE ON EDITIONS

Please note: this edition, first released in 2026, is the third volume of the author's preferred texts of the Micah Grey trilogy and is markedly different from the earlier released editions.

CONTENT NOTES

Violence, blood, death, terrorism, xenophobia, medical trauma, manipulation, characters with trauma and PTSD, medical gaslighting, drug addiction, and drug use. There are soft-focus scenes of a sexual nature. Mention of death in childbirth in a character's backstory. The world remains gender essentialist, but a few characters within this volume are outright interphobic or homophobic. Sites like The StoryGraph may have additional content notes added by users.

A REMINDER OF *SHADOWPLAY*

SET THE STAGE

I believed there was no one left alive who remembered the world as I used to know it.

This world was once a very different place where Alder, Chimaera, and humans all shared the land.

At the pinnacle, of course, were the Alder. Those ethereal beings created the Chimaera. They often stayed separate, watching over Chimaera and human alike and occasionally sharing their magic. Our lives were better with them guiding us, perhaps, but there was always that disturbing sense that our lives were not our own. I always wondered what other secrets they kept from us.

Chimaera were a step in-between the human and the Alder. I was and am a Theri Chimaera—a blend of Alder and human features, but with dragonfly wings rising from my back. There had been Theri Chimaera with manes like lions or tails like fish. A glimmering of scales on flesh or nails sharp as thorns. Eyes that glowed blue, purple, or green in the darkness. I had a friend called Matla who once flew in warmer skies with me, her wings like a giant owl's.

Anthi Chimaera appeared entirely human but for gifts bestowed by the Alder. In the time before, Chimaera and humans lived in verdant gardens strewn throughout the world. When a Chimaera's mortal body grew old, they could leave it behind, yet they would not truly die. The mind and soul could transfer to an Aleph or a body of metal and gears until a new body of flesh was ready.

Humans were lowest on the hierarchy—though that does not mean they were poorly treated. I had always found humans fascinating and frustrating by turns. They lived one life and either left their mark or were forgotten by the fog of time.

My role for the Alder had always been that of protector. My partner Relean and I had raised Chimaera whose powers could become dangerous. At the end of our last lifetime together, Relean and I had two charges: Dev and Ahti. We loved both dearly.

Ahti was a Theri: scaled and more powerful than any other Chimaera I'd come across. Only Dev, an Anthi, could absorb the other's powers and bring him back to equilibrium. Ahti's powers made him a target of the Kashura, an Alder sect that believed all Chimaera were a threat and the world would be better without them. We were captured and Ahti taken where Dev could not help him. Ahti lost control.

Once, I'd had an entire people that looked like me. Once, I'd had a home. That world is gone in soot and flame. My protection was worth less than nothing. The Alder could have helped put our world to rights, but instead, they left us all to burn to ash.

●●●●

I lived on in my Aleph. I slept for a long time, my metal disc buried deep underground. Eventually, I was unearthed. For years, I rested on mantelpieces in fancy houses. Occasionally, I'd half-awaken from *slumber, listening idly to human conversations. If I reached out to them, no one heard me. I drifted back into hibernation.*

Eventually, I ended up in a circus. They called me the Phantom Damselfly and kept me in one of their funfair tents.

For the first time in centuries, I felt a call. Chimaera were unknowingly reaching out in the darkness, their powers re-emerging. They were dim, but present and growing. I was limited in my Aleph form. Eventually, I reached out in subtle ways. It took patience, but I had plenty of it. I dreamed of a blurred man who wished to destroy all Chimaera. I knew I must stop him, whoever he was. I had been created to protect my charges, and there was a chance to rewrite the mistakes I had made centuries earlier.

My Kedi, Micah Grey, joined the circus as an aerialist's apprentice, just as I knew he would. When Micah came to my tent the next night, I spoke to him. He heard me, and all was set in motion. Of course, his time beneath the big top was brief and ended in disaster.

Micah and Drystan next took to the magician's stage, and I continued to lay my plans. Fifteen years earlier, Jasper Maske lost a duel against his embittered rival, Pen Taliesin Spectre. Since then, the disgraced magician had lived in his dusty, rundown Kymri Theatre, tinkering away in his workshop to create grand illusions he could show no one. This man owed Drystan a life debt, and the pale jester, with my little Kedi at his side, demanded a séance and a chance to collect on that debt.

The spirits whispered to Micah Grey during the séance, showing him visions of a woman in a red dress and her child, both of whom would prove important. Maske allowed our fugitives to stay, giving them space and time to recover from the ruin of the circus.

Micah, upon learning of the duel and meeting Cyan, the tarot reader formerly of Riley & Batheo's Circus of Curiosities, convinced the magician to teach all three the tools of his trade. Eventually, they aimed to challenge Taliesin to a rematch, and Maske also hoped to regain a certain bit of Vestige he'd lost in the initial bet. They visited Twisting the Aces, a magic store in Imachara, and Maske struck up a friendship—and later something more—with one of the shopkeepers, a widow named Lily Verre. Micah had another vision that showed him flashes of the magician's duel, the woman in the red dress, and also the mysterious Timur leader of anti-monarchist party the Foresters. Was he the blurred man who wished to destroy all Chimaera?

At first, Drystan and Micah were suspicious of Cyan and her motivations. At one point, they even followed her but only found her sneaking off to meet her beau, a sailor named Oli. Micah was plagued by dreams that were memories of my own life: of Dev, Ahti, and my Relean.

Eventually, Micah discovered what Cyan truly was: another Anthi Chimaera, with the ability to read minds. She shared that Shadow Elwood, who had dogged Micah's footsteps for months, was after her, too, and they agreed to team up to take him down.

Maske grew confident enough to challenge Taliesin to another duel through their respective apprentices. This time, he even wagered the deed to the Kymri Theatre in return for a chance to win the Spectre Theatre and a lost bit of Vestige that was very dear to him. Taliesin accepted. Three months after they signed the agreement, it was official: Maske's Marionettes and the Spectre's Shadows would perform in the Royal Hippodrome of Imachara.

After visiting the Spectre Shows and meeting Taliesin's rather unpleasant twin grandsons, Drystan and Micah snuck into Shadow Elwood's home while Cyan kept watch. They discovered proof that Elwood was falsifying his findings and cheating his clients. They also found a box that contained three vials of a mysterious substance, and hidden beneath, a Vestige artefact known as a Mirror of Moirai. When Shadow Elwood returned unexpectedly with a woman named Leda, Drystan and Micah only narrowly escaped detection.

Their attempt to give their proof to the Constabulary a few nights later did not go smoothly. They had touched the Mirror of Moirai, unwittingly allowing Shadow Elwood to narrow down their location. He found them and held them at gunpoint. Cyan and Micah used their powers to overwhelm him, but Micah almost lost control. Cyan learned that, with enough power, she could command others to do her bidding. Together, with Drystan's non-magical help, they managed to subdue the Shadow and left him tied up in front of the Constabulary steps with proof of his wrongdoings. Elwood was imprisoned, and Micah hoped his past life as Iphigenia Laurus was well and truly behind him.

Maske and his Marionettes were invited to the noble Elmbarks' residence to hold a séance on the Night of the Dead. There was, of course, a wrinkle: two of the other guests were none other than Micah's adoptive mother and his brother, Cyril. While Micah was beyond surprised, he and Drystan wore Vestige Glamours to disguise their appearance, and the show must go on. Cyan performed the séance perfectly, perhaps actually channeling the spirits to bring others comfort. The night was not through with them yet, however: after the show, the cynic—a doctor with a Vestige clockwork hand—revealed himself to Micah as none other than Doctor Pinecrest, the Royal Physician, the man who had given Micah to the Lauruses as a babe. He was the one who had likely employed Shadow Elwood.

Doctor Pinecrest insisted Micah must come for an examination, for if his powers were allowed to continue unchecked, he could become dangerous. Micah reluctantly visited the doctor in his personal quarters near the Royal Snakewood Palace and learned some of the *secrets of his past. The Royal Physician also suspected Micah was Chimaera and urged him to come back if any of his symptoms worsened. I roused myself and began Micah and Cyan's long-delayed lessons in magic.*

Just before the grand duel, an automaton Maske had built for the finale broke, and his hopes of victory cracked alongside it. I borrowed Micah's body to help him fix it, before revealing myself to Maske. I had a surprise of my own: that the Vestige artefact Maske had lost to Taliesin in the duel was another Aleph, and it might have housed my long-lost love.

The night of the duel arrived. Both sides performed well, but we should have realized Taliesin never liked to leave things to chance. Beneath the stage, he sent his burly bear-like Theri Chimaera guard to attack Maske. Micah managed to stop him, and Cyan and Drystan finished their performance.

After the Collective of Magic's deliberation, Maske and his Marionettes emerged the victor. Nicolette Snakewood, the Princess Royal of Elada, congratulated them. It was as if everything had finally settled into place for young Micah and his newfound family. Yet Micah did not realize there was a second Shadow darkening his path.

I had to let the inevitable happen. Micah discovered that Lily Verre, the woman who worked in the magic shop and had begun courting Maske, was the woman in the red dress and also a Shadow working for Pinecrest. Lily's son was a Theri Chimaera, his skin covered in a gleam of scales, with horns emerging from his forehead. He was the very picture of Ahti, and Micah was so very like Dev. The two circled closer, caught in each other's orbit. History was repeating itself, and my heart broke in both fear and hope.

Micah fell ill with a fever. This, I did not foresee. His fever dream contained many hints about what happened long ago and what was to come. And now we arrive at the next part of his tale: rising dangers, a collision of fate; false magic on a royal stage, and true magic that would decide the fate of the world.

I wonder if he will ever be able to forgive me for what is to come. My little Kedi. My newest ward. Our last chance.

1

FEVER DREAM

"A fever may burn a man alive. Some of the wise men who called themselves seers or mystics would deliberately kindle a temperature in the body. They said the fever dreams showed them their fate and the fate of those who followed them."

"MYSTICS AND SEERS," FROM A HISTORY OF
ELADA AND ITS FORMER COLONIES,
PROFESSOR CAED CEDAR, ROYAL SNAKEWOOD UNIVERSITY

When my eyes finally cracked open, echoes of a dream of the end of the world swirled in my mind.

The phantoms, the parts in this play to come, walked across the stage. I saw the woman in the red dress whose son was eaten from the inside. I had to hope the world might yet fall into place the way I thought—hoped—it would.

Anisa's voice echoed in my head as if I were still dreaming. I blinked the last of the sleep from my eyes. Drystan held my hand. Judging by the white silken wallpaper, we weren't at the Kymri Theatre.

"Where . . . ?" I managed, my voice a croak.

"Pinecrest's apartments," Drystan said. His blond hair crowned his head in a messy halo. He had dark circles under his blue eyes. "You've been out for four days."

Four days. I let out a shaky breath, pushing myself onto my elbows. The room was pristine as a hospital, but the walnut furniture was far too sumptuous. The floor was softened with rugs, but there were no paintings on the walls, making it feel impersonal. The bed's linen was so crisp it crinkled.

"Where are my clothes?" I asked, clutching the front of the plain, unfamiliar tunic I wore.

"They're here." Drystan nodded to a chair in the corner. "I've been coming every day. Don't worry, I was the one to change and attend to you."

My relief was palpable. I lowered my voice. "Where's Anisa?" The Aleph had been in my pocket when I'd fallen ill. Drystan took Anisa's disc from his coat. I held my hand out, and he dropped it into my palm. My fingers closed around the metal. Swirling Alder script was etched into the sides, the Vestige metal shining green, purple, and gold in the light. It thrummed in my hand, but Anisa was silent.

I'd found the Phantom Damselfly in R.H. Ragona's Circus of Magic; or, rather, she'd found me. I had taken her from the ruins of the circus, and she had sent us visions of the past and her life. I'd learned about the Alder, the Chimaera they'd created, and the Vestige they'd left behind. She said she needed me for a plan to save the world. I never knew how much to believe.

On my arm, where the syringe had pinched me, was an already-fading bruise. I touched the scab of the needle mark and winced at the pain. What had Pinecrest given me?

"What happened after . . ." I trailed off. *After I said I loved you and you said you loved me?* I was almost afraid to say it aloud in case it had, too, been a fever dream.

"After you fainted, I took you straight to Pinecrest. I didn't want to, but figured he was the only one who could help. He didn't seem particularly surprised to see you."

"He didn't?"

"No. It was like he'd been already expecting us at any moment." His lips thinned, and he lapsed into silence. I felt stronger, but still not much better than a piece of meat pummeled by a hammer. My head ached. Drystan drew me closer, resting his forehead against mine.

"I had the strangest dream . . ." I said.

"What was it?"

I pulled back, my eyes darting to the door. "Not here," I mouthed, even though the details of the dream were already fading—Anisa at the end of the world, the threat of a bright light before darkness.

A knock sounded at the door. Without waiting for an answer, Doctor Pinecrest entered. The Royal Physician was cool, collected, and impeccably dressed, as usual. His clockwork hand caught the light, the brass Vestige within covered with translucent skin as if trapped in amber.

The doctor with the clockwork hand appeared onstage, smiling a self-satisfied grin, though he was as ignorant as all the rest. He did not even know what he truly wore against the stump of his arm.

"Micah," he said. "So good to see you awake." The slightest pause, the smallest look at Drystan. "There's a fresh pot of tea in the lounge, Drystan, if you'd like to help yourself." The use of his real name rather than his stage magician name, Amon, was deliberate.

I didn't want Drystan to go, but he reluctantly pulled the door shut behind him, Anisa's words still whispering in my mind. *The pale jester, who, despite his lack of power, could yet change everything.*

I pulled my covers up to my neck.

"You gave us all quite a fright," the doctor said.

"What happened to me?" I asked, scrunching the coverlet so hard I feared tearing the fabric.

"Your body turned against you, I'm afraid. It's happened to some of the other Chimaera I've studied."

My mouth tightened.

"Your extrasensory abilities grew too quickly," he continued, pulling on a pair of white gloves. "A spike or a storming in your mind, if you will. You're lucky you were able to see me straight away. Much longer and you might not have made it."

Gooseflesh pricked my arms. He was confirming I could have died. Growing up as the daughter of a noble family, I'd always been stronger and faster than my friends. I'd never grown ill. Even when I broke my arm the night Drystan and I fled the circus, it'd healed weeks faster than it should have. It felt strange to no longer be able to rely on this body. It was hard not to think of it as a betrayal.

"So, what? Have you cured me?" I asked.

A small shake of the head. "I've only alleviated the symptoms, for now." He opened a plain cabinet in the corner and brought out a metal tray, setting it on the bedside table. On it was a flask made of Vestige metal, glimmering in the light like oil mixed with water. The top was an uncut emerald polished to smoothness. Next to it was a filled syringe. He picked it up, and the dark green substance shone in the light from the window. I shivered. It looked a match to the liquid in the vials Drystan and I had discovered in Shadow Elwood's apartments. The lacquered box was hidden in the loft of the theatre beneath my bed.

I blanched, gripping Anisa's Aleph even tighter beneath the covers.

—*Be careful*... I heard the barest whisper.

So far, Pinecrest had claimed to have my best interests at heart. I still didn't trust him. After everything that had happened to me, I was understandably beyond wary of doctors and their cures.

"What's this?" I asked, gesturing to the vial and syringe with my chin.

"I dosed you with this tonic of my own making four days ago, but

I'll give you another measure before you head home. After this, you'll need weekly doses to keep the symptoms under control."

"So, there's the sting in the tail. I'm to be reliant on you."

"I'm afraid so."

"Side effects?" I asked.

"Vivid dreams. Possible increased manifestations of some of your emerging abilities, but without it attacking your body."

I sent him a tentative thought. —*Are you like me? A Chimaera?*

He smiled, but didn't answer.

—*And if I decide I don't want to be reliant on your medication, and I run away to Linde or somewhere . . .* My thoughts trailed off.

—*Then you'd probably die within a month from a seizure brought on by a fever,* he replied.

Well. Shit. My head fell back onto my pillow.

"I agree it's not ideal," he said aloud, "but it's the best option we have at the moment, Micah. In the meantime, I'll continue my research, but this medicine is the first step for a cure. I'm sure of it."

He wiped a drop of sweat from his brow. I guessed it wasn't easy for him to speak mind to mind. My interest sharpened, and my grip tightened on the Aleph beneath the covers.

Pinecrest gestured to the flask. "I discovered this in that jungle where I lost my hand, and I developed it while abroad in Byssia."

"What's in it?" I asked, not bothering to hide my suspicion.

"It's an Alder liquid, though no one knows the ingredients. There are some additives to make it more stable and last longer. It is not unduly dangerous, I assure you."

"Saying something is *not unduly dangerous* is not wholly comforting," I pointed out.

Doctor Pinecrest smiled ruefully as he set the flask aside and picked up the syringe. We both stared at it. "One ingredient is a form of opiate, partly derived from Lerium, but with other additives that suppress the spikes in power your body cannot handle. Another component is ground-up Vestige crystals."

I blinked at him, shocked both by the answer and the fact he had given it.

"I understand this is a lot to take in," he said. "Ask your questions, and I will answer to the best of my ability."

A shiver of foreboding ran through me. I'd seen a few of the small blue crystals inside automatons, like ice-blue hearts. "You're telling me you injected me with a mysterious Vestige substance, actual Vestige, and an addictive drug."

"It's not addictive at one dose a week, but . . . yes."

I made a skeptical sound deep in my throat. "Am I to be a laboratory rat for this little experiment?"

"You're not the first I've dosed," he said.

I stared at him.

"Initially," he continued, "I used it in desperation, when I had to either administer it to a dying child or let them perish. The risk paid off. There are now half a dozen in Byssia and Linde who have taken this medication weekly, for years, without issue. They are stable, and their powers are controllable and don't harm them."

I sputtered, but he only looked at me with that infuriating calmness. I had so many questions about these others across the sea, but I sensed he'd tell me nothing if I pressed the subject.

"What happens if you run out of this mysterious substance?" I demanded instead.

"I've more than enough to last years, never fear, and I expect to find a permanent cure long before then."

I didn't know whether to believe a word he said.

He picked up the syringe and tapped the glass lightly to break the bubbles. "Well," he said. "Are you ready?"

—*Can I refuse?* I asked Anisa.

—*I sense he is telling the truth,* she said, keeping her mental voice quiet as possible. *At least as he knows it. I have no idea if Alder-made elixirs can remain stable over centuries. There seems not to be a choice here, but that does not mean I like it.*

Neither did I, but I hung my head in defeat. I was trapped, and we all knew it. "Yes."

"It will be all right, Micah. I'll make sure of it."

With that, the doctor pulled up my sleeve and, with the prick of the syringe's needle, pushed the mysterious medicine into my veins.

2

RECOVERY

> *"In the smaller Byssian villages, there are many types of supposed panaceas and poultices for illnesses. Many studies have been carried out to ascertain their efficacy. Most are little more than quackery at best, but some, especially those that used Vestige liquids found in the area, proved to be shockingly effective. Yet due to the volatile nature of Alder-age liquids, they are not advised for consumption."*
>
> **FOLK REMEDIES IN THE FORMER COLONIES,**
> **PROFESSOR SHAWN TEAK, ROYAL SNAKEWOOD UNIVERSITY**

"How are you feeling?" Doctor Pinecrest asked.

My head spun as the warm, pleasant dizziness of the drug took hold. My limbs were loose and my mind, which had been spinning with worry like a gear, quieted.

"High," I said.

"It'll pass. Come on, let's get you up and moving about." He held out his gloved clockwork hand.

I took it, cool beneath my touch, leaving Anisa's Aleph hidden beneath the bed covers. The doctor hauled rather than helped me upright. My knees almost collapsed but held. I took a few shaking steps.

"Good, good," Doctor Pinecrest said. "You're taking it well. Why don't you get dressed and then meet Drystan and me in the lounge in a few moments? I've made tea."

I nodded, and he slipped from the room. I dressed slowly, awkwardly. A strange rush of delirium rose in me, and I broke into an uncontrollable laugh. My legs tangled in my trousers, and I almost fell over. Eventually, my clothes were all in their proper place. I slipped Anisa's Aleph into my pocket, willing myself to sober up, with limited success. I glanced about, but Pinecrest had tidied away the flask and syringe when I wasn't looking. I tried the cabinet door. Vestige lock. No hope of breaking into it without Pinecrest's square Vestige key.

Slowly, the doctor led me to the lounge, where Drystan sat on a chaise, sipping from one of the cups from Pinecrest's Vestige tea set. At the sight of me, his worried face relaxed, only for his brow to crease again.

A flash of light on metal caught my eye. The drug had made the colors of the room seem brighter. On the mantelpiece was a disc that looked just like Anisa's Aleph and the empty artefact Maske had won back from Taliesin. Taliesin's disc had turned out to be the Aleph of Anisa's long-lost love, but Relean had run out of power and was gone. I picked this one up, curious, but it didn't hum with power as Anisa's did. It, too, seemed empty. Despite that, it still appeared to glow faintly blue, along with the tea set and any other Vestige in the room. That was new. I stared at the Aleph, mesmerized by the shifting hues.

"Leave that," Pinecrest commanded, his voice sharp, and I set it down, fighting down a surge of annoyance. My emotions were seesawing wildly.

Pinecrest took the Aleph to the cabinet of curiosities. I'd seen it the last time I'd visited. It looked like the spirit cabinet we used for some of our magicians' illusions, except it was topped with a carved and gilded human skull with pointed canines, reminding me uncomfortably of Juliet from the circus.

I staggered to the sofa and sat next to Drystan. He put his arm around my shoulders protectively, then peered into my eyes.

"His pupils are big as saucers," he said to Pinecrest, his voice hard and accusatory. "What'd you give him?"

I half-heartedly pushed Drystan away and picked up my cup of tea, closing my eyes as the steam rose toward my face. I inhaled deeply and took a sip. The herbs burst along my tongue.

"Wait until you hear this," I muttered. "You'll blow your top."

"I gave him a medicine he needs to keep his powers from turning against him," Pinecrest said. "Micah consented to it."

A muscle worked in Drystan's jaw.

"Don't worry, I feel grand. Stop frowning so hard." I put my fingertips to the corners of his mouth and drew his lips up into a smile. He leaned back from my touch, the line between his eyebrows deepening.

I took another sip of tea and ate a caramel biscuit.

Doctor Pinecrest opened the cabinet door a few inches. A soft blue glow emerged from the crack, and then the doctor snapped the door shut. He gave me a bland smile.

"How are you feeling now?"

"Strangely giddy," I said, struggling to focus on him. "Considering the whole almost-dying and now-being-reliant-on-you-every-week thing."

"The euphoria will settle down by the evening. The last twenty-four hours before your next dose, you might feel lower in spirits. That's normal."

"Oh no. My cup is empty." I stared at the bottom of it in dismay.

He smiled. "You should go home and rest. There's a carriage waiting outside for you both. But I'll see you next week, I trust, Micah Grey."

His words punctured some of the fog. "I don't exactly have a choice, do I?"

His gaze was almost sad. —*For now, no, you don't,* he whispered in my mind.

• • • •

Cyan opened the door to the Kymri Theatre before we even knocked. She wore her usual Temnian sarong, and her long, dark hair trailed down her back. She'd redone the braids threaded through her long strands, replacing the turquoise beads with purple. She peered at me in concern.

—*Are you all right?* she asked me telepathically.

—*I feel marvelous.*

She cocked her head at Drystan.

"Pinecrest dosed Micah with something. Says he needs it every week. He's currently off his face."

"I am not," I said, too loudly.

"Maske's been beside himself with worry, but I'm not sure how he'll feel if he sees you like this."

"Ohhh noo," I said in dismay, drawing out the words. Maske should be on top of the world, not fretting about me. He'd won the duel against Taliesin, and he'd just found out Cyan was his biological daughter.

I breathed in the familiar scent of the Kymri Theatre. Wood polish, a hint of oil, and good coffee. The mosaics on the wall seemed to glitter with the effects of the drug in my system. This was the first place where I'd felt truly safe. This was my home.

Even over the last few days, the theatre had begun to transform. The columns, carved with palm fronds, had been freshly painted, the windows scrubbed, and the marble front steps swept. It was being restored to the jewel of architecture it was meant to be, based on the grand monuments of Kymri, the islands of hot sands, black oil, and deep blue sea. There was a newly erected booth outside, though we hadn't started selling tickets yet. Soon, though. Soon.

Drystan tried to usher me to the staircase, but Maske stuck his head out of the kitchen door. "Micah? Is that you?"

"Hiya!" I waved at him enthusiastically.

He froze, looking between us.

"Well, there goes that plan." Drystan sighed and steered me toward the kitchen.

Maske had his usual diagrams spread over most of the dining table. Oli, Cyan's beau and our once-stagehand, wasn't at the theatre. He'd delayed going out on the ship until after our duel, and would only be back in late autumn.

"Micah," the magician said. "Last time I saw you, you were on death's door."

"I'm feeling much better." I stood tall, trying to appear sober and knowing I failed. The world was spinning.

Ricket the cat wandered in from wherever she'd been napping. I patted her head before picking her up in my arms, burrowing my face in the fur of her neck. She allowed it for a second before she started wriggling, and I let her jump back down.

Overcome with a surge of affection for the man who had taken us all in, I next gave Maske a hug. He always welcomed them, even if I knew physical displays didn't come easily. He patted my back awkwardly before I pulled away.

"Victory suits you, you know," I said magnanimously, but it was the truth. His suit was immaculate, his best silk cravat tied and fastened with an opal pin, and his grey-streaked hair was neatly pomaded into place. The largest change was how the worry lines around his eyes had slackened, and how he smiled more easily. The frown returned as he peered at me.

"I'll be fine," I assured him. "Pinecrest said this'll pass in a few hours and I'll be right as rain. Have to go back to him weekly, though.

I don't like that, but dunno how to get out of it without the whole risking-death thing."

"Hmm." Maske let the topic go, fixed us some simple sandwiches, and set out fish for the cat. I drank a giant mug of coffee, the warmth settling in my stomach. I wolfed down three sandwiches, barely even listening to Cyan, Drystan, and Maske's conversation. My body hummed with energy. It was a little like being drunk, but . . . enhanced. I was as focused as a beam of light. It was elating. It was terrifying.

I drained my cup and stood, and the kitchen tilted alarmingly.

"I think I need a lie-down now," I announced.

"That's an excellent idea," Drystan said, gently taking my elbow. "Come on, you."

3

ROOFTOP SECRETS

> "Lerium's origin is debated. It grows well in the hot climate of Kymri, but its first recorded use might be in Linde. The flower is similar to poppy, but the petals are a brilliant purple and the drug made from the sticky sap is far more potent than opium. Curiously, they seem to sprout best in a field with Penglass nearby."
>
> "LERIUM," PROFESSOR CAED CEDAR,
> ROYAL SNAKEWOOD UNIVERSITY

I'd thought I wanted to rest, but as soon as I looked at the bed in the loft, I couldn't face the thought of crawling under the covers after having spent four days in bed.

"Wait," I said. "First, the roof."

Drystan sighed but dutifully escorted me to the terrace. Spring would soon turn to summer, and the afternoon air was warm. I stared over the rooftops of Imachara. Doves cooed softly from the dovecot we'd installed for our magic tricks so we didn't have to rent them each time. A woman hung washing out to dry from her window. The cobalt blue domes of Penglass dotted through the granite buildings twinkled in the sun, casting their shadows over the stone. In the distance, we saw the dark and white twin spires of the Celestial Cathedral, one topped with gold and the other silver.

"My favorite view," I said, gesturing at it like a magician on the stage.

"Stay well away from the edge," Drystan warned. "I don't trust your balance just now."

My mind still felt heightened, like I could do anything. I closed my eyes and focused inward. After several long breaths, some of the strangeness faded into the background.

"There you are," Drystan said, relieved, when I opened my eyes. "You're back a little, aren't you?"

"Think so." The wind whipped up, and I shivered. Drystan opened his arms, and I went to him, huddling against his warmth.

Cyan joined us on the roof terrace a few minutes later. We sat on one of the benches we'd brought up recently, with me in the middle, and it reminded me of sitting on the tightrope with Aenea and Arik not long after I joined R.H. Ragona's Circus of Magic. It'd been a little more than a year, but I missed the circus, and the aerialists, with a deep pang. Drystan kept an arm around me, and I leaned against him, his presence steadying me further.

I took Anisa's Aleph out of my pocket, marveling anew that within this little Vestige disc was a being older than we could comprehend.

Cyan crossed her arms. It was still difficult to believe that she and I were, in a way, like the spirit trapped within Vestige. We were both Chimaera. She could read minds and sometimes glean the future. It'd served her well as a tarot reader in the circus before she'd come to the Kymri Theatre.

"What does Anisa have to say about it all?" Cyan asked.

"Let's see."

I pressed the lever and set the Aleph on the ground. A pillar of smoke rose from the disc, faint in the bright light of day before forming into the Phantom Damselfly. It always gave me goosebumps when she first appeared, her large eyes staring at us with a blend of melancholy and mystery. Swirling silver tattoos twined about her forehead and along her hairline, snaking down her neck before disappearing beneath her plain dress. Behind her, gossamer dragonfly wings rose, flapping noiselessly. Through her transparent body, the darkened outline of the round, stained-glass window of our loft was visible, decorated with a dragonfly of its own.

—*Hello, little Kedi*, she said, her voice echoing in our minds. She rarely used our names, preferring her nicknames for us. I was 'little Kedi' for the being between male and female worshipped in some areas of the Archipelago. Drystan was 'pale jester.' Cyan was 'little bird', from a dream she and I had shared where she had been an owlish woman who had died protecting Ahti, Anisa's charge who later nearly destroyed the world.

I told Cyan and Drystan everything Pinecrest had shared with me.

"Cyan, you've been feeling well? No headaches or symptoms like mine?" I asked.

She shook her head. "I'm perfectly fine. My abilities seem the same." Her own powers had been growing, though. Like me, she'd had visions of the future. On the night Shadow Elwood had almost caught us, she'd been able to command him to do her bidding against his will.

"Hopefully you won't have any spikes," I said. "I don't want us both reliant on Pinecrest, if we can help it."

She shivered. "I'll say."

I turned to Anisa. "Can you tell us anything else about this medicine?"

She rested her ghostly fingers on my face, gazing into my eyes.

—*It is as he says, as far as I could tell. Lerium mixed with Alderage materials.*

Drystan's head whipped toward her, his hand clenching into a fist.

—*There are old elixirs and panaceas that may do as he claims. But it'd surprise me that they survived the centuries. I sense your body and abilities are stable.* She paused. *While it's not ideal, perhaps being near the doctor once a week is helpful so we can keep an eye on him. But you should also continue your training to ensure you can keep control of your magic, even without the use of this potion.*

"If Pinecrest is the blurred man, he could be poisoning me," I pointed out.

—That is true, she admitted. *But if he were, wouldn't he have simply let you die when presented with the opportunity? Either he's not the blurred man, or he wants you alive for some other reason, at least for now.*

I shivered.

"I don't like the sound of any of this," Drystan said, pacing the length of the terrace.

"We have a sample of this elixir, don't we?" I asked. "It looked exactly like what we found in Shadow Elwood's apartments in those vials."

Drystan paused in his pacing, nodding. "I guessed that in the four days you were sick. I've looked at it a few times, but all I could figure out was that it has Lerium as an ingredient."

"Can we, I don't know, study it and figure out what's in it?" I asked.

"I'm not sure who we'd ask," Drystan said. "I wouldn't trust any of my old contacts." He had once helped run Lerium for a crime family in Imachara and barely escaped with his life.

Anisa inclined her head. *—I would not be able to glean much else, either. It is useful to keep at hand in case little bird does grow ill. It'd buy us time before we would have to bring her to Pinecrest directly.*

Cyan wrapped her arms around herself, shivering despite the late spring warmth.

"What do we do in the meantime?" I asked.

—We watch, we wait, and we keep our eyes wide open, Anisa said.

"Bullshit," Drystan said. "Simply sitting around on our arse is a piss-poor plan—sorry, Anisa."

She blinked at him, unperturbed.

"We should try to find other Chimaera," Cyan said. Our heads swiveled toward her. It took my addled mind a moment to catch up.

"If we can find others," she continued, rubbing her left forearm with her right hand, "we can see if anyone else has grown sick—whether this is an actual threat to Chimaera or not. I don't like simply waiting to see if I fall ill, too."

"How would we even find them?" I asked. "What about Lily's son? He's already seeing the Royal Physician."

"Yes," Cyan said. "But if we speak to them, we lose the advantage of surprise. We can watch them from afar, but I don't think we should approach them just yet."

"There's Juliet, Tauro, and Violet, if we could find them," I mused. On Drystan's and my last night in the circus, they said they were leaving to find more of their—our—kind, but we didn't know if they stayed in Imachara or went elsewhere. Had they found any others? I tapped my lips. "There was Lutier, that bear-man I fought at the end of the duel, but I don't exactly want to search him out again."

Cyan shuddered. "Me, neither."

Anisa closed her eyes, spreading her awareness. *—There are others, but it's difficult for me to sense them. If fate wishes you to find them, you will.* Her voice echoed with a certain amount of prescience.

I sighed. Too much to hope for a straight answer from the Phantom Damselfly. Something else niggled at me through the high of the drug. I thought of Maske's empty Aleph, and the one we'd seen at Pinecrest's apartments. That one had been empty.

"Anisa," I said, slowly. "How close are you to running out of power entirely?"

She blinked at me.

"How long?" I whispered.

—*You guessed before I could tell you, my clever little Kedi. I do not know*, she said. *I never had cause for it to grow so low. I should be in a clockwork woman by now and gestating a new body. The Alder had the method of recharging Vestige, but even Chimaera like me don't fully understand how. I hibernated to slow it down, but I have not recovered as much as I hoped. As best as I can tell, I will only be able to come forth three more times for an hour or so each before I run out of power entirely. Or, if I wanted to live on, you would have to join with me forever on the final try.*

I blinked, taking it in. The Phantom Damselfly had, essentially, told us she was dying. Drystan's eyes were wide, and Cyan pressed her hand to her lips. The thought of blending with her forever, of my body and mind not being fully my own after I'd fought so hard for independence . . . it terrified and repulsed me.

"I'm sorry," I said, the words feeling inadequate. "I don't think I would be able to offer that to you."

—*Me, too.* She stared up at the sky, letting herself grow more transparent. *But if I manage to save all remaining Chimaera before my time winds down, then I will go to my death gladly. I must return to my Aleph, but I only hope I can last long enough to see this through. If you call me, I will come, but I ask that you use your three wishes wisely.*

It was like she was a fairy trapped in a bottle offering favors, like in the stories I read as a child. With a sigh, Anisa transformed into mist and returned to her Aleph.

The three of us sat with that, lost in our own thoughts. Eventually, Cyan went back to her room, and Drystan and I climbed down to our loft. The high from the drug had nearly faded, though I still felt the buzzing of power in my veins. Still, it was better to feel back in control, and for Drystan to not look at me with such obvious concern.

"Everything had been practically perfect a few weeks ago," I said. We'd just won the duel against Taliesin and his grandsons. I'd realized I'd loved Drystan. Now, my life had fractured again, and the future seemed more uncertain than ever. Anisa had been strange, and at times frustrating and frightening, but the thought of her being gone forever hurt, too.

Turning on my side, I rested my forehead against Drystan's.

"We'll get through all of this," he said. "We always do."

—*So far.*

Drystan pulled back. "What'd you say?"

"Hmm? I didn't say anything."

"Strange. I swore I heard you say, 'so far.'"

My mouth formed a little "o."—*Drystan,* I thought at him. *Can you hear me?*

He jumped back and swore.

My jaw fell open. "You did!"

"Did you just . . . speak in my mind?" He sounded panicked. "Can you read my thoughts?"

"I don't know. Do you want me to try?"

"No!"

I was a little hurt at that.

"I thought only Cyan was psychic," he said, his eyes still round.

My breath hitched. "No one save Cyan has ever been able to hear me before Pinecrest. Not without Cyan's help."

It didn't take a mind-reader to tell Drystan was perturbed.

"It must be the side effects Pinecrest was talking about," I said. "Maybe my abilities are stronger when I'm on the drug."

He came closer, but we didn't quite touch.

"Are you afraid of me?" I said, my voice cracking. —*Am I still a freak?*

"You're not a freak. Never think that."

I hadn't meant for him to hear that bit.

He embraced me again. The warmth, the feel, the smell, the very presence of him centered me. We'd not been together very long—only a handful of months. It felt so very delicate, and we curled protectively around the newness of it.

"Hey." He put his hands on either side of my face, lifted my jaw, and pressed my lips to his. I tried to forget everything and only focus on Drystan. I'd said those three words when I wasn't sure I'd have the chance to utter them again. I pulled back from the kiss and met his eyes. I was no longer afraid. "I love you, Drystan Hornbeam."

After another long kiss, he pulled back, smiling gently. "Hey. I love you, too, Micah Grey."

I let myself savor the words. If I'd learned one thing, it was that loving him was as natural as opening your eyes after a long sleep. His fingertips left shivers in their wake as he traced my jawline, down my neck, along my shoulders, my collarbone, and skimmed over my sternum and toward my belly button. He hooked his fingers in my belt loops, his pupils dark with desire.

He pulled me to the bed, and I followed.

4

THREE CHIMAERA

"We must rise up against injustice. We must take back what is ours. And we will. No longer will we let the Twelve Trees of Nobility soak up all the water, the sunshine, and the nutrients of the world. The rest of us are hungry, and we will be fed."

EXTRACT FROM A FORESTER PAMPHLET

The next day, the last thing I wanted to do was stay stuck inside the Kymri Theatre.

I skipped down to the kitchen. Drystan gulped his coffee—he hadn't slept much, and I suppressed a wicked grin. My fault.

I skipped my morning coffee for fear it'd make me bounce off the ceiling. I sipped apple juice instead.

Cyan stared at her toast, focusing inward. Ricket meowed indignantly in the corner, and Drystan rose to feed the little calico cat.

Maske entered the room, grabbing his coffee.

"Maske," I said. "I've had an idea for the show."

"Oh?" he said, stirring, coming to the table and reaching for the newspaper.

"I'd like to work in some of my aerialist skills," I said. I'd been thinking about it for a while.

"We've already got our hands full with inventing a new routine before opening," Maske said, opening the paper.

"Can we try?" I asked.

"Might cause someone to make the connection to the circus," Drystan pointed out.

"Not if we're careful," I pressed.

"Ach, we can give it a try," Maske said absent-mindedly, and my heart lifted.

A minute later, he set the newspaper down, and one look at his ashen face made my stomach drop. He pointed to a bold headline that carved itself into my brain: "ARE CHIMAERA REAL AND AMONG US?"

It was *The Daily Imacharan*, a respectable newspaper, not some rag printing rumors in the hope of better circulation numbers. I grabbed the paper, skimming the article, my heart hammering.

"That's already out of date, according to the delivery man," Maske said. "I'll turn on the radio. He said there'd probably be an update on the hour. I was his last delivery, so he was about to race home to try and catch it."

The radio was another new purchase since Maske won the duel. It was not a Vestige artefact, though the inventors had spent many hours taking Vestige apart and putting it back together again to create something similar.

It took him a few moments to find the right station. Eventually, crackling, discordant music filled the room.

The two minutes until the clock in the hall struck nine had never seemed so long. The music faded away, replaced with the announcer's smooth tones. "Good day, Imachara. It is nine in the morning on one of the days that will go down in history.

"Early yesterday, three people claiming to be none other than Chimaera presented themselves at the gates of the Royal Palace, asking for a meeting with the Princess Royal Nicolette Snakewood and her uncle, the Royal Steward."

I sucked in a breath as Cyan stiffened. Maske and Drystan were silent.

"Many assumed that they were simply pranksters," the announcer continued. "The supposed Chimaera claimed they came as a gesture of friendliness and peace, and all three were loyal citizens of Elada. The guard we interviewed was initially highly skeptical, as you can imagine. The cloaked figure lowered the hood, revealing a beautiful, olive-skinned woman. The guard said her eyes glowed yellow as a cat's, and he claimed her dark hair shone purple in the morning light. She shed her cloak, and she wore nothing beneath. Before the guard could even register his shock, those yellow eyes brightened and, right before his very eyes, she transformed into a cyrinx cat."

Drystan and I exchanged a look.

"Violet," I whispered.

The Chimaera from the circus. She'd revealed herself to me on the last night, when she'd transformed in Bil's cart.

The radio crackled. "A moment later, the cyrinx returned to her human form, put her cloak back on, and again, ever-so-politely, asked to come in."

The announcer paused for effect.

"And, Imachara—you'll never believe what happened next. For the Royal Palace did, indeed, open the gates and invite her inside."

My mouth was so dry I had to steal a sip of Drystan's coffee.

"Evidently, today at noon, the Chimaera plan to address the city in front of the Celestial Cathedral. There will be a full security presence, and anyone who wishes to attend is urged to be patient, peaceful, and to listen to what they have to say. We will also be broadcasting their words live should you wish to remain in your homes. Whatever they say, I have a feeling Imachara, Elada, and the Archipelago as a whole will never be quite the same again. We'll bring you more as we know it."

Maske turned off the radio. The silence in the kitchen was deafening.

"Well," Drystan said. "I suppose we know what we're doing this lunchtime."

"You shouldn't go," Maske said, immediately. "It isn't safe. We should listen from here."

"We can't miss this," Cyan said. "It involves us."

Maske pressed his lips together. He loved performing in front of large crowds, but he couldn't stand to be amidst the crush of bodies. After so many years living alone, he was still a hermit at heart. I understood his reticence.

"You can stay here, Maske, but we're going," I said, keeping my voice gentle. "It concerns us."

"Be careful," he said. "Emotions are high. Stay out of the way."

"We'll watch from the rooftops," I said.

He nodded and turned back to his coffee cup. The three of us left our dishes in the sink and almost ran upstairs to get ready. My heartbeat hammered in my chest.

Chimaera were unveiling themselves. How would Elada react?

• • • •

Two hours later, Cyan and Drystan followed me toward the Celestial Cathedral. Imachara's streets were busy. My senses had always been sharp, but thanks to Pinecrest's medicine, I swore I could catch scents from half a street down and hear sounds from even farther away. As well as chimney smoke and unfurling flowers, there was manure, rotting rubbish, stale body odor, and all the other unpleasant smells of a city. The crisp morning was busy, with shopkeepers setting out their wares, paperboys crying the headlines from the corners, and the engines of cabs and carriages sputtering and growling. Horses drawing carts whinnied. The sun emerged, glinting off the mica in the soot-stained granite of Imachara.

My energy was so high that, despite my dread, it was hard not to skip down the pavement. Other Chimaera in Imachara. We would see or maybe even meet them. We couldn't out ourselves, of course, or public scrutiny would fall on us even more than it already had from us winning Maske's duel. The Policiers no longer seemed to be actively investigating Bil Ragona's death at the circus, but we still had to be careful.

There was an hour and a half until noon and already the streets were packed. We threaded our way through the throngs of the crowd. We managed to find a small side street that was less crowded than the others and had a helpful bit of scaffolding.

"Over there," I said, pointing. "We'll have a good view."

We climbed, and Cyan used her powers so people were less likely to glance up and notice us. Up on the rooftops, we had space to breathe. The Celestial Cathedral dominated the square below. The silver- and gold-tipped white and black towers jutted proudly toward the sky. A hasty temporary stage had been erected on the cobblestones before the church's closed doors. The sight of it made me shudder—it reminded me of a gallows.

Anisa's Aleph was cold as I clutched it within my pocket.

The last time I had been here was Lady's Long Night. That night, all had been hushed and peaceful. As the grand clock near the Cathedral ticked closer to noon, the square grew even more crowded. The area behind the temporary stage in front of the church was blocked off, so the three Chimaera might have an escape route if the crowd grew too rowdy.

Though the people surged forward, no one came closer than ten feet from the edge of the stage. Cyan's mouth pursed. "Can't you feel it? They've put up a Vestige Shroud."

My eyes widened. A Shroud created a barrier around a set perimeter. Nothing could go in, nothing could go out. The Royal Family or prominent political figures used one whenever they addressed the public, to stave off any assassination attempts. The fact that the family had presumably given the Chimaera one for their own protection would rankle any who felt threatened by magical beings.

Finally, the Cathedral bell tower began to toll. Twelve gongs sounded out over the square. A hush fell over the crowd as the last klaxon faded. The Cathedral door opened, and three hooded figures emerged. They walked with careful steps up onto the stage and lined up behind the pulpit. As one, they removed their hoods. Gasps and low murmurs rippled through the crowd.

Juliet, the Leopard Lady of R.H. Ragona's Circus of Magic, stood in the center. A sudden vertigo made me grip the top of the scaffolding at the edge of the roof. Juliet had been a friend to both Drystan and I, though we didn't know her well. She'd preferred to keep to herself. The darker rosettes on her skin stood out in stark relief.

Next to her was Violet, her hair coiled into a sleek bun at the crown of her head. Her eyes searched the crowd before rising toward the rooftops, drawn to me as if I was iron to her magnet. Even from that distance, I felt the force of that gaze. I raised my arm to her in greeting, and her lips curled into a smile.

The man next to Violet had short red hair like a horse's coat on his skin. From this distance, I couldn't see his eyes, but I suspected they'd be an unnatural color, like Violet's yellow ones. Orange, perhaps. I wasn't afraid of any of them—how could I be? They were Chimaera, even if they were Theri—with animal aspects—instead of Anthi like me and Cyan.

Juliet took a breath. She'd gone before crowds time and time again, but she'd usually sat on her stool in the freakshow tent, gazing imperiously at the gawkers and hissing at anyone who came too close. She'd never spoken to large crowds like this, as far as I knew. Violet, of course, had only performed as a cyrinx. I wondered where Tauro was—the bullish man had also been a member of the freakshow tent at the circus. He couldn't speak but understood everyone around him. I hoped Juliet and Violet were looking after him and keeping him safe.

"Good afternoon," Juliet said, her voice clearly reaching us even on the roof. I saw a disc smaller than Anisa's Aleph attached to a metal band like a collar around her throat. A Projector. "I am called Juliet. My friends here are Dirk and Violet. And we come to you, today, to tell you a plain and simple truth: we are Chimaera."

Gooseflesh prickled over my skin as the crowd erupted into noise. Some cheered, but too many gave shouts of anger, disbelief, or fear. Faces twisted or slackened. The crowd surged forward, a few knocking against the Shroud.

Juliet gestured to the russet Chimaera, who stepped forward. From his pockets, Dirk took out three juggling balls very like the ones Drystan and the other clowns had once used at the circus. He lifted his chin and, instead of juggling with the power of his hands, caused the spheres to levitate above his head with magic. The crowd gasped at the display. It was no sleight of hand. Even the crowd could see that. He lowered the balls, his expression serene, and put them away.

Juliet held up her hands, her Vestige-amplified voice carrying over the rising sounds of the crowds. "I know some of you may think this is somehow a trick. I assure you, it is not. Others have questions, concerns, and fears. Change can be frightening. I know too well how life can shift at a moment's notice." Her face closed, and guilt stabbed me. At my side, Drystan stiffened, and I took his hand.

"I know our appearance has been widely reported already," Juliet continued, "but we thought that it would be better for you to hear this from us directly. There's less chance of rumors being construed as facts. The Royal Snakewood family has graciously let us speak, and so we shall use our voices." She paused and licked her lips nervously.

• • • •

A man stood at the edge of the crowd on the far side of the square, watching the players move on the stage. He took out his pocket watch and flipped it open, counting down the time. The face of it was strange, made of meteorite-like metal and carved with Aleph glyphs instead of numbers. The hands danced one way, and then another. The man's every breath was labored and wheezing. His fingertips were blackened, as if by frostbite.

• • • •

I blinked, unsure whether I'd imagined it, until Cyan shook her head as if chasing off a fly.

I shot her a look. "Did you see that?" From that man's vantage point across the square, I'd even caught the rooftop where the three of us huddled. It was like a strange double-vision, all undercut by a deepening sense of dread.

"See what?" Drystan asked. "I don't like the look of the crowd." He eyed the throng below us. Even from up here, I could sense their restlessness.

• • • •

Someone passing by caught sight of the man and gasped. The mask he wore on the lower half of his face to hide the damage must have slipped.

He tugged it up, the movement radiating pain through him like a scream. He waited. His Vestige pocket watch ticked softly.

• • • •

"Someone in the crowd . . ." I trailed off. "Another Chimaera? He's injured, maybe." My unease grew, until I was afraid of choking on it.

"Something is going to happen," Cyan said, her hand rising to her throat.

• • • •

The man stared at the three Chimaera on the makeshift stage in front of the Cathedral with such hatred it burned as bright as the pain of his failing body. He'd read the restricted documents in the Royal Archives before he'd left the government. He'd learned his share of secrets, and then, in a twist of fate, he'd discovered so many others that had been long lost to time.

He felt the ancient power rising in him, like transparent wings flapping beneath his skin. He shoved it back down, using the Vestige in his hand to help control it.

The Chimaeras' presence in the world could destabilize everything he'd worked for. They, and the Royal Family, were too powerful, too uncontrollable. If they were allowed to survive, it would change everything. He had been planning this for years. Today, the first domino would fall. He could not fail. He turned, his reflection catching in the window.

• • • •

The shock jolted me back into myself. Anisa's fear infected me. It was the blurred man, but his features were now clear. I'd seen those curls around his head, the mask on the lower half of his face, the intense eyes.

"It's Timur," I said. "As we suspected, the blurred man is Timur, the former leader of the Foresters." We'd heard he'd been kicked out of the movement weeks ago. The rumors said he wanted to go too far. This would certainly count.

Drystan's eyes were wide. "What? Are you sure?"

"Yes, it's him. We have to get down there, now," Cyan said, her voice ringing with certainty. "There is enough Vestige around. Maybe I just . . ." She trailed off, heading toward the scaffolding.

What was Timur planning, and how could we even hope to stop it? We began climbing down the scaffolding as fast as we dared as Juliet's voice rose again.

". . . we can assure you, we are truly Chimaera. We've suspected it for a long time. Though we may look different to you, we are people with feelings, hopes, and dreams. We mean no harm. We only wish to make ourselves known and to reach out to other Chimaera hidden among us to let them know: you are not alone."

The crowd murmured again, heads swiveling left and right, clearly wondering if the person next to them could be anything like the three people on the stage.

"I don't like this," Drystan said. "That crowd is one step away from turning nasty."

● ● ● ●

Timur knew there were only a few minutes left. He'd left his little present in the square this morning, just after they'd erected the temporary stage. A seemingly innocuous bit of Vestige nestled at the base of the stairs, little bigger than the spheres the furred abomination had just moved with his mind. The Shroud was in place. The true humans would largely be fine. But these three Chimaera, at least, could be destroyed, and it would send a message to all the others hidden throughout Elada and the Archipelago: you are not safe here, or anywhere.

• • • •

"He's left something beneath the stage," I said, my voice rising in panic. "My gods, this is an assassination."

After Anisa had warned us so many times, the blurred man was finally here. We knew who he was. What he planned. It was happening.

Cyan started pushing closer. She turned her head toward the Policiers. She couldn't reach the Chimaera through the Vestige Shroud directly, but she could try the next best thing.

—*Policiers*, she sent, as clearly as she could. The ring of officers around the crowd all stiffened at the voice in their head. *There's a weapon beneath the stage. Someone's trying to kill the Chimaera. Please. You must stop it.*

I sensed at the last minute she decided not to say the name Timur, since it would mean the Foresters would be blamed, and we weren't certain he was still working with them. Some clapped their hands to their ears. Others looked around, wondering who had spoken. In the confusion, no one was acting fast enough. Cyan let out a snarl of frustration and shoved her way through the crowd. On the far side of the square where the blurred man hid, I sensed his irritation at our interference, but also slight amusement.

• • • •

No one could hope to stop him. He thought he could have used the Foresters for this, but that bitch Lorna Elderberry had managed to oust him. He'd known they'd never have had the stomach for what must be done, and so he had not told them the full truth. She'd find out what he'd planned soon enough.

But there were others who had believed in his vision, in the need to rid the world of Chimaera and the danger of what they could do without control. He had brought them with him. He'd formed his own movement, and even plucked a name from the past for it:

The Kashura.

He snapped his Vestige pocket watch shut. Time was almost up.

● ● ● ●

The word hit me like a slap. The Kashura had been the name of a faction of Alder who had wanted to destroy all Chimaera.

How had Timur learned of it?

"So, if you are like us," Juliet continued as we finally made it back to ground level, "please, come find us. This is no trickery. No trap. We want to understand why we have returned after so many centuries. We are staying in the Palace. The Crown has invited us to speak with them, to share what we know and to plan a way forward, together."

"Bollocks!" someone cried out in the crowd, and other angry voices rose. But the Policers must have blabbed enough that word was spreading. Panic rose in pockets.

We pushed through the crowd as people began to race in the other direction.

—Get out of the way! Cyan threw the thought at those around her so viciously that they stumbled to the side as she forced a path through. This was too obvious, too bold, too dangerous, but fear had its claws in us. We were running out of time. All was about to change.

Timur, the blurred man, waited from his safe vantage point.

"Please," Juliet said, her voice shaking. "That is all we have to say at this time. Thank you for listening. In the Lord and Lady's Light, we look forward to brightening Elada's star." Her head turned as one of the Policiers said something to her.

—*Beneath the stage!* Cyan yelled in her mind. *Look beneath the stage!*

"You're cursed by the light!" someone from the crowd called, and others took up a chant of "cursed, cursed, cursed."

—*It's an Incendiary, a Vestige explosive*, Anisa said, her voice insistent. *I might be able to stop it if we get there—but there is no time—*

Drystan grabbed my sleeve, trying to drag me back. "Micah, we have to get out of here. Now."

"We can't leave her," I said. "We can't let anyone get hurt."

Cyan had nearly reached the barrier at the front of the stage. The crowd closed around her, and she disappeared from view. The panic of the crowd was rising, people pushing desperately, growing more afraid, confused, and dangerous.

I shook off Drystan, trying to think. My powers were stronger since I'd been to Pinecrest's. I reached for the spark in my chest and tried to alter time, hoping all around me could slow while we moved at normal speed. But my magic had always been temperamental, and time kept on ticking.

The russet man, Dirk, walked down the steps as Juliet thanked the crowd one last time. He paused—had he heard Cyan's message?

The crowd yelled more insults. At the perimeter, Policiers and Royal Guards called for order. We were minutes away from an all-out riot.

For a precious moment, my magic worked. People around me slowed. Dirk, moving normally, reached below the base step of the stairs and drew out the small Vestige artefact. I caught the impression of a sphere with intricate swirls and a colorful sheen as the light hit it.

Yet as soon as I'd grabbed my power, it slipped away. I couldn't *hold* it. Despite my short training with Anisa, I didn't have control. While I could do it by instinct, for self-preservation, the power wouldn't always come to my call. I reached into my pocket, gripping Anisa, hoping she could somehow help without me calling on one of our last three chances.

Though I couldn't see Cyan any longer, I felt her bashing her fists against the Vestige barrier before she somehow pushed her thoughts *through* the Shroud.

"A bomb!" one of the Policiers yelled in alarm, hearing Cyan's warning and recognizing what was in Dirk's hands. "An Incendiary!"

Juliet and Violet recoiled with such surprise that even the panicked crowd must have realized they weren't responsible. The two Chimaera stumbled off the stage, racing toward the escape route.

—Timur is behind this, I thought at them, and Cyan pushed it in their direction. *Timur, the former Forester.*

Juliet's steps slowed, and she glanced over her shoulder in my direction. I didn't know if she'd heard me.

—Throw it! Cyan screamed at Dirk, and his head turned toward her. His orange eyes widened as he stared at her through the Shroud, and I saw them flash as blue as Penglass. He drew his arm back and launched it with all his might, using both his muscles and the power of his mind. He threw it much farther than a normal human ever could. The sphere of the Incendiary caught the summer light as it flew toward the Celestial Cathedral.

The Aleph in my pocket burned hot as an ember. In my head, Anisa *screamed.* The sound was horrible, louder than a Banshee alarm. Around me, people winced. She was more terrified than I'd ever sensed, even when she'd shared the memory of dying at the end of the world.

Time had run out.

I had just enough time to throw my arms over my head in useless protection as the deafening, echoing boom of an explosion thundered across the square.

5

THE BURNING SPIRES

"An Incendiary is a small, handheld explosive Vestige device. They were once plentiful, but many were understandably used in the various wars both within Elada and the other islands of the Archipelago. They are ingenious artefacts. You can easily program when it will ignite, set the radius, and they won't degrade over time in the way more common explosives can. When they are inert, they are also far safer than gunpowder. While a modern bomb must be connected to a detonator, the Incendiary can be set off from hundreds of miles away. It is perhaps for the best that there are so few left these days."

"VESTIGE," PROFESSOR CAED CEDAR,
ROYAL SNAKEWOOD UNIVERSITY

The sudden sound shook the ground and reverberated in our chests. Flames furled from both of the metal-topped cathedral towers, and smoke, black and thick, rose to the sky.

Between the explosion and people screaming, my ears were ringing.

Another concussive blast vibrated through the square. Had Timur set a second Incendiary inside the Cathedral? Drystan and I staggered, nearly falling onto the cobbles.

We gazed up in horror as the Cathedral towers broke, seeming to pause before beginning to fall. Luckily, they tumbled back onto the roof of the church, rather than forward onto the crowded square. The sound of the roof collapsing was deafening, dust and debris rising from the ruin of the church. It was as if my eyes couldn't take in the images and believe this was truly happening. How could such a small thing do so much damage?

My ears buzzed and my vision swam as wreckage rained from the sky. A small piece of stone or brick struck my shoulder, another hit my head, and the world dimmed and quavered. I staggered as more screams rent the air.

Smoke and dust filled the square, swirling motes of embers and ash drifting down like flakes of snow. I coughed, wiping my face, my hand coming away wet with blood and soot. I was still panicked and disoriented. My head hurt. Drystan had been right beside me, but he was gone.

"Drystan!" I called, choking and coughing. The dust stung my eyes. My arms groped out, desperately searching for him. And where was Cyan? Was she all right?

Please, please let them be unharmed. I sent the thought into the air like a prayer, unsure if my magic caught it. *Please let everyone be all right.*

"Micah! Here!" Drystan called to my left. About a dozen moaning or screaming people were between us. Those who could still walk tried to push their way from the square. My feet had already been stomped on half a dozen times. Someone crashed into me from behind, and I stumbled.

Drystan fought his way toward me, his face filthy with soot. Sirens wailed and echoed against stone.

I'd wondered, in the moments before the explosion, if the Shroud had somehow turned off. Yet I realized now that, despite the explosions, it *had* held during the worst of the violence, and it was the only reason all of us weren't dead. The square was filled with debris, but all the largest pieces of rock and rubble remained behind the line where the barrier had been. If the Royal Family hadn't put up that Shroud as a security precaution . . . it didn't bear thinking about.

Where were Juliet, Violet, and the third Chimaera, Dirk? He hadn't been behind the Shroud when the Incendiary went off. I couldn't sense Timur at all anymore. Had he meant to send us those visions to taunt us, or was that the work of the spirits and fate?

Around us, people struggled to their feet. A woman in her sixties slumped against the statue in the center of the square, groaning, her eyelids fluttering, blood staining the arm of her blouse. Her grey hair had come undone and sprawled over her shoulders. She was stout and rosy-cheeked, with a red-splattered yellow kerchief around her neck. The statue above her was of some long-dead general. He had lost his head and half his shoulder. I crouched in front of the woman.

"Are you all right?" I asked. The woman stared up, glassy-eyed, at the Cathedral ruins. The stain on her arm was dark and growing. I pressed my palm on her sleeve, over the wound, and she protested vaguely.

Drystan was already a step ahead of me. He unbuttoned his coat and tried to rip his shirt, but his hands were shaking too badly. I told him to press on the woman's wound and tore it for him, my heightened abilities making it as easy as shredding paper. I wrapped her cut as best I could to stop the worst of the bleeding, but I wasn't sure it was enough, and there'd be a risk of infection. Her head was lolling alarmingly.

—Anisa? I sent to the Aleph in my pocket. *Can you help me heal her?*

She didn't answer. My anger flared. I knew it was important to go after the man who did this, but we both knew it'd be futile. Timur was already long gone. Even so, Anisa saw no need to waste her resources for a "mere" human who had already lived more than half her life.

"Fine," I muttered, placing my hands on the woman's arm and reaching for that spark in my chest. "I'll do this myself."

The power came more easily than it ever had before. I felt lit up like a glass globe. I tried to remember what Anisa had done during my lessons. How she'd pushed her awareness and powers into the body, like *this*, and tapped like *that* into both my power and the innate life force of the person I was trying to heal.

My awareness of the ruined square fell away as my magic flowed into the woman. It was only me and this stranger whose life I was trying to save. The skin of the wound pushed together and began to knit, but I didn't actually know enough about anatomy and how a body fit together to do much more than that. Afraid of doing more harm than good, I pulled back, even as my magic demanded more, more, *more*.

The sounds and smells of the real world slammed back into me. My lungs were working like a bellows, and I felt as though I'd sprinted half the length of Imachara. But the woman's bleeding had stopped. She was pale and needed medical attention. But, like with Aenea the night the circus was destroyed, I'd helped bring her back from the brink, and I was heady with the power of what I'd just done.

The woman blinked, in such shock that she barely noticed we were there.

The ambulances had arrived in the square.

"Can you help her get to a doctor?" I asked a passing man. He was so dust-stained I couldn't guess at his age or hair color, but he looked strong and burly. He nodded and helped the woman to her feet. She could stand, barely.

"Thank you," she said to me, faintly.

I wasn't sure if she'd realized how I'd done it. "You're welcome," I said as they staggered in the direction of the ambulances. Though I was glad I'd helped her, I regretted the delay.

Picking my way through the debris, I tried to reach the remnants of the Cathedral, Drystan close by my side. Blood, warm and wet, still ran down my temple. Drystan tore off another piece of his shirt and told me to press the cloth to the wound. I did it absently, still searching.

"Cyan!" I called, and Drystan echoed me. Before us was an untidy barrier of boulders that had once been part of one of the most beautiful buildings in Elada.

"Cyan!" I screamed again, then used my mind: —*CYAN!*

Some of the peoples' heads turned, as if they'd heard me.

For what seemed an eternity, there was nothing . . . then a faint: —*Micah.*

My knees almost buckled with relief. —*Where are you?* I asked.

—*I don't know. Somewhere dim and dark.*

I stared at the mess of stone in front of me, dread tingling through my limbs.

—*Help me . . .* Her voice drifted.

—*Cyan! Stay with me!*

She didn't respond, but I caught a few images: a small patch of sky, a smudge of darkness in the corner. It was the ruined stump of one of the cathedral towers. I tried to follow that angle, swallowing against my dry throat, terror pulsing through me. To my left was a pile of rubble.

"Oh Lord and Lady," Drystan said as he put it together. She was trapped somewhere beneath it.

—*Cyan, come on, are you all right? Please, Cyan.*

Nothing. Fumbling in my pocket, I drew out Anisa's Aleph, clutching the Vestige disc tightly in my palm.

—*Anisa, you have to help me now. Your little bird is trapped.*

Drystan hovered near me as the chaos swarmed around us. My watering eyes shut tightly. —*I'm using one of my three wishes. You said you would come when I called.*

An aching pause, and then a bloom of magic unfurled in my mind.

—*I should have seen this*, the Phantom Damselfly whispered. *I should have been able to help stop it. Yet I sensed nothing. They were Chimaera. I should have been able to protect them.* Her voice was tight with grief.

—*Cyan sensed it*, I said. *Now she needs your help. Our help. She is your ward, as sure as I am. So don't let us down.*

A pause, a whisper. —*I'm too weak to do it alone. I shall have to take control of your body again.*

My breath caught in my throat. She'd done this twice before, but that didn't mean I liked it. —*All right. Yes. Just find her. Free her.*

—*Say it, little Kedi.*

—*Come to me, Anisa. For the next hour, come to me.*

Anisa rose in a gossamer sheen of blue and purple, shimmering in the air before settling into my skin. Drystan watched, his mouth falling open, but no one else seemed to notice. I curled into a corner of my own mind, a silent witness to Anisa's use of my body and powers.

She raised my hands. A spark in my chest, and the pile of rocks shimmered. Deep in the rubble, amid the pockets of air, I could see the outline of Cyan's body. My forehead furrowed, and then Anisa moved me forward, physically moving some of the smaller pieces of rubble.

"Hey!" a man called behind me. "The whole thing could crumble and collapse! Wait for the Policiers and the firemen!"

Anisa ignored him, continuing to shift rocks with my hands. Drystan tried to help, but Anisa motioned for him to stop. With some of the larger ones, she used a spark of my magic to help move them out of the way. Before long, she'd created a little hole. She reached my arm into it. After a horrible, aching pause, a hand clasped mine, and there was a spark as our magic touched. Cyan squeezed my palm weakly. My body began to pull her out. Drystan's hands came around my waist, helping as best he could.

Gradually, Cyan emerged from the rubble. She was grey with dust, and her eyelids fluttered, but she clung to consciousness. Her ankle was swelling, and she could barely put weight on it.

"Cyan?" Drystan asked.

Her eyes shone with grief. "I can feel them all," she said, her voice distant. "All their pain. All of it, all at once."

With Anisa still in my body, I could sense others trapped in the rubble, their souls shining like burning coals among the stone. Seven altogether.

—*The medics will help them,* Anisa said in my mind.

—*The medics can't sense the stone like you can. They're frightened and hurt. I healed that woman a little, but we both know I don't know how to fix this alone. While you're here, within me, help me help them.*

She navigated my body over the rubble, gently moving the rocks aside to find the pockets of survivors, drawing the victims upright through the dust and debris.

She didn't stop until we'd helped the other seven people under the ruins. Nurses arrived with stretchers and took them away. At least one of them probably wouldn't make it. He was a middle-aged man, and a baker judging by his stained uniform. His leg was crushed to a mangled mess, and his skin had the deathly pallor of someone not long for this world.

The last body we took from the largest pile of stones was Dirk, the furred Chimaera. He was most definitely dead. Anisa's grief echoed through my body as she placed my hand against his cooling cheek. Where were Violet and Juliet? Had they survived?

The worst of the danger had passed. My body stood, unmoving.

—*Anisa,* I said. *The hour is up. Give me my body back.*

There was another reluctant pause. I tried not to let my fear show.

—*Anisa.*

—I could last longer, she said. *Here, within you. Perhaps even for years. By the third call, you'd have to make the decision anyway.*

Her words sent a stab of horror through me. I knew, every time she possessed me, she yearned to stay. To be embodied. To be able to touch, to feel, to taste.

—Anisa, I said again. *I still have those two calls. We'll find a way to give you more power, or some other way to save you. I promise. But you need to let me go for now. This body is mine. Not yours.*

She took the Aleph out of my pocket, turning it over with my hands. Blended as we were, I realized she often thought of this disc as a prison. She'd been trapped in it for so many years. When she was deep in hibernation, time slipped around her like a stream whose current she couldn't catch. I understood her yearning, but I could not offer her what she wanted. Not until we knew for sure there was no other way, and maybe not even then.

Finally, with a gentle, mental sigh, she flowed out from my mind and body and back into the Vestige gripped in my hand.

As soon as she was fully gone, I fell to the ground. Drystan helped me sit up as I settled back into my body. My temples pounded both from the use of magic and my head wound. Despite that, I felt so much steadier than I would have before I'd been dosed with Pinecrest's medicine.

Cyan didn't look much better, but at least she was still conscious. She groaned. "Everything is still so loud in my head."

"You should probably go to the hospital," I told her.

"You, too." She pointed at my temple.

When Drystan realized I could stand on my own, he picked Cyan up with some effort. She curled against his chest. Still dizzy, I had to lean on Drystan heavily as he led both of us to the medical queue. We waited our turn, watching the firefighters scurry to put out the last of the flames. I couldn't tell how many had died. Too many. I felt numb, but now that the immediate danger had passed, my mind swirled with questions. After all of Anisa's warnings about the blurred man, we now had confirmation that he was indeed Timur, the former leader of the Foresters. But why did he hate Chimaera so much, and what was his aim? How could we ever hope to stop him?

Drystan's expression was as mystified as I felt.

When we reached the front of the medic queue, the tired nurse took one look at Cyan and gestured to the next ambulance carriage. We clambered into the back with her, where another equally exhausted nurse began treating some of her injuries before giving me a cleansing wipe for my bleeding temple.

As the ambulance rattled down the rubble-strewn streets, I looked out of the small back window at the destroyed market square. Just a few months ago, Drystan, Cyan, Cyril, and I had gone to the Cathedral for Lady's Long Night. Now there was no children's laughter, no bright streamers fluttering from market stalls. All was instead the grey and black of broken stone, and the red of dying flames.

6

INFIRMARY

"Once there was a sleeping princess, trapped within a castle of fire. A sleeping dragon curled around the moat. Each of his exhales kept the stone aflame. The princess was protected, for she slumbered in an enchanted room at the top of a tower. Many a knight and warrior tried to defeat the dragon, rescue the princess, and win her hand—as well as the dragon's hoard of gold and jewels. Every time a knight approached, the dragon had only to crack open one eye, let loose his flames, and the would-be hero was roasted in his armor.

This is one of those stories you may say does not have a happy ending. For no knight ever came to rescue the princess. She still slumbers in her enchanted room, the dragon twined protectively around the castle. She may never be rescued. But, depending on her dreams, perhaps she does not need saving at all."

"THE PRINCESS, THE DRAGON, AND THE CASTLE OF FIRE,"
HESTIA'S FABLES

The Infirmary was on the cusp of chaos.

Raised voices and frantic footsteps echoed down the corridors. When I'd last been here to ask whether Aenea had survived, the waiting room had been half-full. Just after the attack, it was filled to bursting. The smell of blood and smoke lingered on the air.

Only one of us was allowed in with Cyan, and since I was more injured, Drystan gave me the slot, saying he'd wait for us outside on the steps.

A nurse, so young she must be newly qualified, told us that Cyan was in shock, but she was beyond lucky considering how much rubble she'd been trapped under. I lent Cyan my shoulder as she limped through the hallway. Another nurse sat me down on a chair and wiped the dirt and crusted blood from my face with brisk efficiency, making my cut sting anew. She was a little older, short with a round, pretty face. Her black hair was mostly hidden by her starched hat, and despite how many people she must have already treated in the last couple of hours, her uniform was still pristine.

Cyan's presence flickered in my mind.

—*Are you all right?* I asked.

—*Sore, but I'll live. Can't say the same for everyone.*

—*Did Violet and Juliet survive?* I asked.

—*I think so. But I can't be entirely sure. Everything's muddled.* She closed her eyes. *I felt the third Chimaera die. Dirk. In that moment before he passed, I learned so much about him. Like he was a spirit conjured in a séance.*

She sounded woozy from the pain medicine, but with all the Vestige in the hospital enhancing our abilities, I could hear her thoughts as clearly as a treble bell. —*We're so delicately tethered to life, Micah. It's like we're all walking on a barely frozen lake that could crack beneath us at any given moment.*

I'd learned that well enough. Cyan's thoughts and her vacant expression made me shiver.

—*Anisa took your body again*, she said.

—*I couldn't do it alone.*

The nurse finished bandaging my cut and continued treating Cyan. My body reminded me it was still a body. I desperately needed a piss. I asked for directions, and the nurse gave them. I headed down the corridor.

I tried not to look in the rooms, afraid of seeing something that would add to my nightmares. I did my business and washed my hands for a long time, watching the blood and dirt swirl down the drain.

On the way back, a voice floated to me through an open door: "I'm just supposed to leave her here? There's nothing else you can do?"

I froze. I'd recognize that voice anywhere.

Cyril.

I crept toward the door. My brother was arguing with a doctor. The older man shook his head at Cyril. He wore glasses and a moustache. "I'm sorry, but all we can do is wait and see." Behind them both, a curtain was drawn around the bed, and my heart constricted at the sight of it.

The doctor bid my brother farewell and pushed past me. Cyril caught sight of me in the doorway. His breath hitched. He recognized me immediately this time, even though I must have looked a mess.

"Micah," he breathed, rushing toward me and gripping my shoulders as if to prove to himself I was real.

"What are you doing here?" My mind was racing. He must have come up early before term started at the university.

Instead of answering, my brother—my strong, stalwart brother—threw his arms around me. I gripped him tightly. Beneath his cologne and smoke from the fire, I smelled echoes of lavender soap and Father's cigars.

"Cyril?" I asked. "What's happened?"

He pulled away, trying to gather himself.

"It's Mother," he croaked, his eyes darting to the curtained bed. "She came with me to visit after I'd settled into my university apartments. We were going for something to eat when..."

I reeled. "Oh, stars. You were in the square?"

He nodded, unable to speak.

"Is she all right?"

He shook his head. "They don't know yet. They don't know. She . . . threw herself in front of me."

I didn't know what to say. My mind felt like it was screaming as loudly as Anisa had right before the explosion.

"She tried to protect me, and she shouldn't have. I'm bigger than her, and she's grown so frail. She was hit by something in the head. There was a lot of blood." He heaved in a shaking breath. "And now they can't wake her up."

My lives, past and present, collided in a single moment. First Cyan had been hurt, and now my mother.

Mother had always wanted me to be someone or *something* I wasn't. I'd never forgive her for that. She was still the woman who raised me, though, and now she was lying in a hospital bed.

I'd last seen her at the Elmbark residence when she and Cyril had been invited to an evening of stage magic and a séance. Her eyes had only seen a young, male magician, not her runaway daughter. In the séance itself, she'd asked after me, and Cyan had passed along my messages to her.

Cyril took my numb hand and led me closer to the bed. My palms grew clammy as he pulled back the curtains.

She was tucked into the hospital bed. Her head was wrapped in bandages. Despite her small stature, she'd always been such an imposing figure. How many times had she chastised me for not embroidering enough, or sullying my pinafore?

My mother was diminished. She'd lost more weight since the Elmbark séance, and the skin around her jowls sagged. Rosacea bloomed brighter on her cheeks due to the drink and laudanum. Her bony hands rested on the coverlet. It was strange to see them not hidden by her ever-present white gloves. Was this my fault, or was it her own guilt eating at her?

A nurse bustled over. She was tall and thin, with a pinched mouth. "Only one visitor per patient, please. We're far too crowded as it is."

"Please. I just arrived. She's—she's my mother." My voice was raspy.

The nurse's face softened, slightly. "Ah." She checked my mother's chart.

"How is she?" I asked.

"Broken ribs, broken clavicle, but the most worrying is the head trauma. We're hoping she'll wake up soon."

"And if she doesn't?"

Her eyes filled with pity, and that was answer enough. She ushered us out apologetically. I needed to find Cyan and Drystan. My head still hurt, and my muscles ached. I didn't want to spend a moment longer in this building full of the injured or dying. I wanted to go home, close my eyes, and try to forget everything I'd just seen and done. Aenea had lain in a bed in one of these wards, just after the circus. Which one?

I found Cyan just as the nurse finished wrapping a bandage around her arm.

"Where were you?" she asked. Her eyes widened as Cyril followed me into the room.

"Let's find Drystan first," I said, but I sent her a few mental images to give enough context, and her brow creased in sympathy. Cyan was still limping badly from her sprained ankle, and I offered her my shoulder again.

Outside on the steps, Drystan stood, his face slackening with relief at the sight of us. "There you are." He, too, looked at my brother in surprise.

"Our mother," I said shortly. "She's been injured."

He sucked in a breath. "I'm sorry. Will she be all right?"

"Too early to say." Cyril's voice was strained.

"All we can do is wait and hope for the best," I said. "But me and

Cyan are all right." By tomorrow morning, the cut on my head would probably be gone, and Cyan would heal quicker than normal, too.

"Let's go home," Drystan said.

"Please," I said.

• • • •

Cyril came back to the Kymri Theatre with us. Sirens still echoed as we navigated the twining streets.

As soon as the front door opened, Maske bustled through. "I heard—on the radio—"

"We're fine, Maske," Cyan said. "Just a few scratches, a sprained ankle, and bruises."

"Can my brother stay with us a few days?" I asked, gesturing. "My mother's been hospitalized."

The magician's mouth opened, then closed. "Of course. You are most welcome here."

"Thank you," Cyril said.

I closed my eyes. "Thanks," I echoed. Cyan and Maske went off together, and I knew she'd fill him in on the details. I was grateful I didn't have to. He'd probably go check on Lily, who had likely been working at Twisting the Aces, as she was keeping up that ruse. We hadn't told Maske she was a Shadow. Delaying would only mean it'd hurt all the more when the truth came out. I knew, deep down, that we probably should tell him, but all three of us were too unwilling to break his heart. We were telling ourselves we would once we'd discovered more about her and why she was following us.

Drystan and I showed Cyril to one of the empty rooms. It smelled of dust and a hint of mold, as we hadn't yet started refurnishing the spare rooms. I took the covers off the furniture and Drystan found some bed linens.

"Sorry it's, ah, not in the best shape," I said, brushing away a cobweb from the vanity mirror.

"This is more than fine. It's twice as big as the one in the university apartments I'm sharing," he said, admiringly. "Maybe I could rent it from Maske, if he wouldn't mind me hanging about?"

"I'd love that." The thought of him staying here cut through all the fear and exhaustion. We'd have to make sure Father didn't find out, but perhaps there was a way. I gave him a hug, and he squeezed me until the vertebrae in my back cracked.

Once he was settled in, I headed to the loft and ripped off my stained clothes. Using the ewer and basin there, I washed off the worst of the dust and dried blood—Drystan was in one bathroom and Cyan in the other, so I'd have to wait my turn for a proper bath. Feeling closer to normal, I put Anisa's Aleph in my pocket and headed up the steps to the roof terrace, where Cyan and Drystan soon joined me. Cyan was pale and wrapped in a thick robe. Drystan's blond hair was damp and stuck to his skull.

Anisa seemed to be back in hibernation, but perhaps she could hear us.

The sun set, the sky stained red, orange, and yellow, and I hated how it mirrored the fire of the afternoon. From the theatre, we could see the ruin of the Cathedral. I turned away from it. The full impact of the day hit us like an anvil.

"We have learned a few useful things this afternoon, at least," I said, finally breaking the heavy silence. I counted them on my fingers. "One, which is the most important: Timur is the blurred man Anisa warned us about. Two: he hates Chimaera—Cyan and I felt it without a doubt. Three: while it sounds like he had indeed been kicked out of the Foresters, it seems he still has other people working for him: his Kashura. A new movement based on a very old one."

Cyan shivered, remembering the vision we'd shared.

"Four," I continued, "he had access to Vestige. The Incendiary, and that strange pocket watch that seemed to help him . . . direct power somehow. Anyone have ideas about that?"

Drystan and Cyan frowned, thinking, before reluctantly shaking their heads. I didn't know either. Was Timur Chimaera, but weak, like Pinecrest perhaps was, and this device helped him amplify it?

"Five: there's something physically wrong with him. He was in pain, and his fingers were blackened. His face frightened someone. And six: he knew we were there and wasn't particularly surprised or concerned. He felt secure in his plan."

"Yet we still managed to interrupt it," Drystan said. "Cyan got Dirk to throw the Incendiary. Who knows how many lives you saved by doing that?"

Cyan closed her eyes, features rippling with pain. "Didn't save everyone, though."

I took her hand wordlessly.

"Who will Elada blame?" Drystan went on. "That's the question. I'm going to guess they'll settle on the Foresters, even if he's left them."

Cyan bared her teeth. "I should have pushed against his barriers more. I wish I was strong enough to break into his mind and peel him apart like an orange to find out exactly what he's planning."

"Well, that's a slightly alarming mental image," Drystan said, mildly. "But I agree it would have been helpful."

I sighed. "What do we do now?"

Drystan gazed out over the city. "Find allies?"

"Like who?" I asked.

Cyan shook her head, equally mystified. If we could find Violet and Juliet, that would be helpful, but I had no idea where they'd gone.

"What about Lily?" Drystan asked.

"She's spying on us for the doctor," I said. "I don't think we'll find an ally there."

Drystan put a finger to his lips. "Perhaps not, but it might be worth looking into her anyway. Just in case."

I held Anisa's Aleph in my hand, but it felt almost as inert as the one that had once housed Relean. She was asleep where we could no longer reach her without me using another of my three chances.

We were on our own. We'd get no more answers today.

7

TAKE YOUR MEDICINE

"I lost another one today. My third. I need to do something soon. I have to save them, or there will be none left."

FROM THE PERSONAL DIARY OF DOCTOR SAMUEL PINECREST WHILE ABROAD IN BYSSIA

A week passed. Our cuts and bruises healed.

Cyril went to visit my mother every day at the Infirmary, but I couldn't face seeing her in that hospital bed again. The doctors still weren't sure when she would wake up, but she was stable for now.

Our small troupe hid inside the Kymri Theatre, venturing outside only for food and newspapers. The temporary sign proclaiming "No Shows Until Further Notice" remained on the door.

Banshees and other Vestige security evidently tripled in price on the black market overnight. Food costs crept up further as traders from the other islands of the Archipelago hesitated to bring their wares into Elada's ports. The streets were nearly empty, some of the shop windows boarded. Imachara was holding its breath, wondering if this was a one-off or the first of several attacks.

If Elada looked weak, other islands would use that to their advantage. Elada had, after all, subjugated them on and off for centuries as the former head of an empire. Yet it'd only ruled through the perceived threat of superior Vestige that made any war against Elada useless. If Vestige was breaking down, the other islands were well aware that this threat was now rather empty. Byssia, Linde, Northern and Southern Temne, and Kymri all watched and waited.

While Imachara had always been a little dangerous, it hadn't felt particularly unsafe to me after we'd caught Shadow Elwood. Yet I started keeping a little dagger inside my boot, just in case, and I had Drystan teach me how to use it.

The Foresters were quick to say that they had nothing to do with the explosion. Their new leader, Lorna Elderberry, spoke for them. Unlike Timur, she didn't hide her face with a mask, and her portrait in a newspaper article showed a woman in her fifties with a strong chin and grey hair wearing a high-collared dress. She looked very no-nonsense, and she'd been strong enough to oust Timur.

Drystan, Cyan, Maske, and I listened to her speak on the radio one evening, her voice clipped and confident. She claimed that the Forester's primary aims were still to reform government, and that they had no strong political stance on these so-called Chimaera.

Some believed the Chimaera had staged the explosion—aiming to be martyrs for the cause. But anyone who had been there that day had seen their obvious surprise and fear and witnessed Dirk throwing the Incendiary to save people in the square.

Sirens called more often. Riots broke out in the poorer parts of town. There were accounts of demonstrations in other parts of Elada, too. I wondered if Father had left Sicion or not. Many nobles fled the capital to their estates in the Emerald Bowl. But there had been vandalism even there, I remembered, so even they might not be safe from the unrest.

The Snakewood Crown likewise stayed quiet on the topic of Chimaera. I was sure that somewhere in that Palace, the Steward was having meeting after meeting.

In problems closer to home, Cyan, Drystan, and I knew we should find out more about Lily Verre and her son, but we were too afraid to follow her in case she spotted us. Cyril went back to his apartments to meet his university friends occasionally, but for all intents and purposes, he had moved into the Kymri Theatre, at least until our mother woke up. Maske didn't mind, especially since Cyril had offered to pay a bit of rent. Cyan liked him well enough.

Poor Drystan might have been a little put out—that first week, I spent every spare moment that wasn't magic and séance practices catching up with my brother. He'd guessed Drystan and I were a pair, and he told me about a girl in one of his lectures he fancied. I'd missed him desperately. I left out plenty of key details about my own life, though. I shared next to nothing of my newfound abilities, or Chimaera, or Doctor Pinecrest. I told myself I didn't want to worry him when he was already worried enough about Mother, but the truth was I remembered how he'd looked at me that night we'd discovered my touch could make Penglass glow, and I didn't want to see that expression of awe tinged with fear on his face again.

Cyan was different after the explosion and often kept to herself. Her thoughts drifted to mine more often, as if seeking reassurance. Each time, I'd let her in. She would recover, just as Drystan and I had after the circus, even if the memory of that day at the Cathedral would always be with her.

All too soon, the week had passed. On the last day, my energy took a sharp downturn again. A low fever returned; my bones were heavy, and I could barely keep my eyes open.

Despite my many misgivings, it was time to return to Doctor Pinecrest and his vial of medicine.

• • • •

Doctor Pinecrest tapped the syringe, popping any lingering bubbles, just as he had the first time he'd dosed me. The dark green fluid in the glass was almost black. On the way over to Pinecrest's apartments, I'd had to lean on Drystan because I was so weak.

I forced myself to watch as Pinecrest pressed the needle into my skin and pushed the plunger. Within a few seconds, I felt brighter and more alert. My magic swirled through my veins, under control, and that loose, buzzing high tingled from my heart to my fingertips and toes.

As soon as he took out the needle and applied a bandage, I pushed my sleeve down. Drystan waited for me in the front room, drinking tea. Cyan was still keeping her distance as long as she could manage.

Before dosing me, Pinecrest had asked questions about how I had been feeling over the past week. As I pulled my coat back on, his next words surprised me.

"I heard about your mother."

I stiffened.

"Have there been any improvements in her condition?" he asked.

"Not yet. My brother has gone to see her frequently."

"But not you."

"Not me."

"I know a specialist at the Royal Snakewood University," he said. "I'll write him a letter and have him examine her if he hasn't already."

"You'd do that?" I asked, surprised.

A wave of the clockwork hand. "Of course. I'm not pleased with what she nearly did to you. Yet I remember her expression when she held you in her arms for the first time. There was love there."

I looked away. I wasn't sure she looked at me like that later on. "Thank you. I know my brother will appreciate it." Still, I was wary, certain that any favor came with strings attached. I was already too much in his debt.

I took a breath, changing the subject. "What do you think about the Celestial Cathedral attack?"

"Whoever was behind it, I think it made quite a statement." His tone was unreadable.

"Some say it was Timur, the former leader of the Foresters," I chanced.

"I find that unlikely," he said.

I stared at him, trying to determine if he was lying. If he was somehow working with the blurred man, I'd obviously never forgive him and do everything I could to take them both down. But if he wasn't... Anisa said we needed allies. But could I ever trust him enough?

"Surely you have more of an opinion than that?" I pressed. "A Chimaera was killed. Did you know him? Dirk?" I didn't want to give Pinecrest Juliet or Violet's names.

A shake of the head. "No. They were at the Royal Palace, but I wasn't granted admission to see or speak to them. I did ask, and I expect if things hadn't gone the way they did at the Celestial Cathedral, I would have."

"Do you think they had extra abilities or were at risk of growing ill, like me?" I asked.

"I'd have to examine them. I'd love the chance to."

With my powers strengthening again, I tried to reach out to him with my mind. For a tentative moment, I sensed something just beyond reach before I lost it again. His mind was as inscrutable as his blandly polite expression.

"Whoever was behind it, this attack has upset the delicate balance of Elada and the Archipelago, no question about it," he continued, seeming oblivious to my snooping. "The Royal Family and the Twelve Trees of Nobility anticipate this is just the beginning."

The Twelve Trees were the most powerful noble families in Elada. My own adopted family, the Lauruses, had been nobility on the very outer rings of influence. With the money Pinecrest gave my parents when they adopted me, the Laurus family fortunes had risen again.

"Who do you think is behind it?" I asked.

"I've no idea," he said, spreading his hands. "Those who fear the threat of Chimaera or have a growing mistrust of the monarchy still seem to be flocking to the Foresters all the same. Their numbers are growing."

"The Foresters have remained neutral on the subject of Chimaera so far."

"Very carefully, yes. The Foresters are waiting to see how this goes, even if they weren't behind the attack."

"Many still don't even believe Chimaera are real," I protested. Plenty thought Violet, Juliet, and Dirk's physical differences had been due to Glamour or cosmetics, despite their magical display. "So why do they hate them?"

"It's easier to fear something so far beyond their ken."

"Even if they said they meant no harm?" I pressed.

"Especially so."

I bit my lip. "Do you think there'll be more attacks?"

He nodded. "The Steward has put the Princess in hiding in the Palace. She's not to see anyone she doesn't know. She can't venture out, not that she did often before. They are working on deepening diplomatic ties with the other islands of the Archipelago."

I shook my head. I supposed being a child didn't matter when you were heir to the throne.

Pinecrest tugged at his cufflink. "I'm hoping things calm down and the Steward will allow her more freedom soon."

"That must be difficult for her." I'd had only a taste of that cloistered life as Iphigenia Laurus, and it'd nearly suffocated me. Many said the Steward wanted nothing more than to hold on to the throne as long as he could. I wondered how he treated the princess.

"Indeed." Pinecrest looked me over again. "Have your magic shows begun again?"

The drug took stronger hold. The room was growing fuzzy around the edges, the warmth of my muscles an unpleasant burn. It was growing harder to follow the conversation. I wanted to go to the next room, take Drystan's hand in mine, and leave.

After too long a hesitation, the words broke through. "Not yet," I said. "We'll hopefully be performing tomorrow night."

Pinecrest hesitated.

"What?" I asked, frowning at him. "You're circling something. Out with it."

"You know, your manners haven't improved much since I first met you," he said, mildly.

"That they haven't, especially when I'm drugged." I hoped I wasn't slurring.

"I don't know if such rudeness deserves what I might offer." A corner of his mouth lifted.

It took me a moment. He was *teasing* me. Fine. Two could play this game.

"Please, most prestigious Royal Physician, what, pray tell, do you mean?" I swept my best bow.

He broke into a laugh, and with the influence of the drug, I found myself almost smiling back at him. I hardened. I remembered how cold his eyes had looked when I'd woken from my fever dream.

He steepled his hands together. "I was thinking of asking the Steward if he'd allow entertainment for the Princess Royal. If I vouched for the performers."

It took a few heartbeats before I caught his meaning.

"You'd ask Maske's Marionettes to perform for the Princess Royal?"

"And whatever members of the court are let into her coterie of trust, yes."

"At the Palace?"

"Indeed."

My frown deepened. "Why?"

"You really are a suspicious one, Micah Grey."

"Yes, well, I've had need to be."

He sobered. "That you have. This isn't entirely for your benefit. I remember how Princess Nicolette loved watching you perform at the duel. It was all she talked about for weeks. Keeping her happy keeps the Steward pleased, and that keeps me content."

I'd be foolish to turn it down, yet this was as dangerous an opportunity as it was potentially beneficial. "It's not my decision, but Maske's," I hedged, even as we both knew that Maske would never turn down performing for royalty.

He nodded. "I'll issue him the invitation if the Steward agrees."

"I won't mention it until then," I said. "I don't want to get his hopes up."

"Fair enough." Pinecrest seemed genuinely pleased, but my suspicion still flared bright as a lighthouse lantern. There were rocks in these waters. This was the man who had hired Lily Verre to spy on us for months. A man who had been studying Chimaera for longer than I'd been alive.

Lily hadn't come to the Kymri Theatre since my illness, for which I'd been grateful. But I knew she wouldn't stay away for long. Her son must be ill, like me, which is why she came to Pinecrest for treatment. Was the horned boy as dangerous as Ahti had been, all those centuries ago? My thoughts strayed to Cyan. She said she was fine, but what if her powers started misbehaving, too?

Doctor Pinecrest's human hand rested on my forehead, startling me. "Are you feeling all right, Micah? You've gone a tad cross-eyed."

"I'm fine. Just the effects of the drug." It wasn't a lie. My body echoed with the high, my limbs slackening.

—*As before, it shall pass*, he said in my mind.

"Is there anything else?" I asked, determinedly speaking aloud.

"No, you're all done for today," Pinecrest said. "Go home and rest. I'll see you in a week, Micah."

"Next week," I echoed faintly, pulling on my coat.

8

THE BODY SNATCHER

"Of the Alder way of life, we know next to nothing. Who were their rulers, what were their political factions? Did they live in harmony or fight among themselves? What were the extents or the limits of their power? How did they create Chimaera, and what was their purpose in doing so? If they did indeed leave this world when the waters rose, how did they do it, and where did they go? I cannot publish a paper of only questions without answers."

PROFESSOR CAED CEDAR'S
UNPUBLISHED NOTES

The blurred man drove the simple farm cart through the dark streets of Imachara, flicking his reins across the sloped back of the old nag he had hired for the night. He wore a cloak, the hood pulled up over his face, and two cloaked Kashura, the ones he trusted the most, were perched in the back of the cart. Just after midnight, they reached the cemetery on the outskirts of the south side of the city. The wrought iron gates stood tall and imposing. With difficulty, he dismounted as the other two Kashura tied up the horse.

Timur limped up to the entrance. Pain radiated down his spine with every step he took. The left side of his face and left hand were numb, but his failing body would last long enough for what he needed.

The guard was in the shelter of the gatehouse. The blurred man could just see the guard smoking his pipe, the blue-grey smoke curling around his head, his lantern the sole speck of yellow in a world of black and grey.

Carefully, Timur picked the main lock, looping the chains back slowly so they didn't clink and give him away. Pouring a little bit of oil into the hinges from a little bottle in his pocket, he eased open the gate and slipped through. Keeping to the darkest shadows under the ivy-covered wall, he crept closer to the guardhouse, his Kashura following him like shadows. He reached into his pocket with blackened fingertips and clutched the Vestige pocket watch, an Isochrome. With it, he could control his magic better, even as it always tried to fight back. The spark ignited in his chest.

—Sleep, *the blurred man sent.* Sleep deep, old guard. Dream of what you want the most, and imagine you are far away from this place of death.

The guard's eyelids grew heavy, his head falling to his shoulder. The pipe fell to the ground, extinguishing in the grave dirt.

Timur smiled.

His Kashura caught up to him. One was taller than him, and one much shorter. Timur pointed wordlessly to the storage shed, and he broke the lock with a burst of power. The Kashura darted inside and emerged moments later with a wheelbarrow and two shovels. Timur nodded, and they followed him wordlessly to the freshest grave.

"Dig," he commanded, his voice harsh from his damaged throat. It had grown worse over the last few months, and he could now barely speak.

For a long time, there was no sound but the soft fall of dirt onto a rising mound to the right of the grave. He had wanted to do this alone, but this body no longer worked properly, and to use more magic would only blacken his fingers further.

He had no anticipation of the grisly task aside from what it could ultimately give him. The taller Kashura's shovel hit the coffin with a thunk. *It took them a long time to raise the coffin from the ground. The shorter Kashura held out her hands, magic sparking on her palms. It'd taken a lot of effort to convince a Chimaera to join his cause and arguably work against her own interests. It was better for Timur to use her magic and conserve his. The coffin rose and rested on the ground.*

With another burst of magic, the blurred man unlocked it, the two Kashura pulled open the lid, and stared down at a man who looked dead, but was not quite gone.

The man, in his early thirties, was from a wealthy enough family that they'd been able to bury him quickly. The poor often had to wait. Timur had slipped the Alder-age liquid into the man's drink at a tavern. He would only linger on the threshold for a little longer. They were just in time.

Timur had chosen this man for his strong build and expanse of muscles. He'd been hale as they come. First, Timur had to get this near-corpse back to where he might be able to make best use of it. He reached for the near-dead man's face, turning it this way and that with his half-rotten hands.

"*Take him,*" *Timur croaked.*

The taller Kashura loaded the near-corpse into the wheelbarrow, and the other closed the lid of the coffin and reached for her magic. The coffin hovered over the grave before lowering into the ground. The Chimaera staggered with exhaustion as her companion filled the grave.

Finally, the Kashura finished tamping down the earth. With luck, no one would ever discover it was now an empty grave.

The three made their way back to the cart and loaded the body into the back, covering him with a cloth. With effort, Timur climbed into the driver's seat. The taller Kashura returned the wheelbarrow and shovel and locked the gates. The cemetery guard slept through it all.

The blurred man spat a loosened tooth into the cobbles. The two

Kashura climbed into the back of the cart, next to the body, and they left the graveyard behind.

• • • •

I awoke in the dark, curled around Drystan, gooseflesh prickling my skin. He burrowed closer to me, making a sleepy sound of contentment. The dream was already slipping through my fingers like water. I sat up and took a notebook and pencil from the bedside table, ready to scribble down everything I remembered.

"Micah?" Drystan's voice was murky with sleep.

"I had a dream," I said, frantically scribbling. "Timur stole a body from a grave."

That woke him up. He sat up, running his fingers through his blond hair. "What?"

A knock at the loft door startled Drystan, but I'd been expecting it. "Come in, Cyan," I said.

Cyan wore a robe over her nightgown, her hair wrapped up in cloth to protect the braids hidden in her long hair.

"You dreamt of him, too?" she asked.

"Yes," I breathed, even though she already knew it.

"Well, there goes my beauty sleep," Drystan said, yawning. "Tell me everything."

"Timur's body is failing him," I said. "His fingers are rotten and he's moving slowly. He and two Kashura broke into the Ashen Graveyard, you know, the big one outside of town?"

"Of course I know it," he said. "Plenty of my ancestors are buried in there."

"He made the guard fall asleep and his accomplices dug up the grave of a man he'd poisoned."

"Who?"

I tried to remember the name or the carvings on the gravestone, but it'd either been too dark in my dream or I'd already forgotten. I shook my head. "I don't know. Do you remember, Cyan?"

A line between her eyes appeared. "No. I'm not even sure I'd remember where the grave was."

"Evidently the body wasn't quite dead yet—the poison kept them on the brink," I said. "Brown hair, buried in very fine clothes. Muscled. Early thirties."

"We can look into that," Drystan said. "What's his goal?"

I shook my head. "I don't exactly know. But I suspect . . ." I trailed off, swallowed.

"He wants to use that body," Cyan finished. "The one he's in clearly won't last much longer."

"What, he's going to . . . jump?" Drystan asked. "Is that even possible?"

"I don't know," I said. I clutched Anisa's disc, but I felt nothing. It really was almost as if she were gone.

I looked at them, grimness spreading through me. "I'm pretty sure Timur aims to find out, though, and our best bet is to try and stop him before he does."

9

THE MAGIC SHOW

"No one can convince me otherwise: I think the Foresters were behind the Cathedral attack. You want to know what I think of the growing situation? I think they've the right idea about these Chimaera. There were those three monsters, and the Lord and Lady showed them what they thought of their kind, right in front of their own church. I think the monarchy is a lump of phosphorus, and the Foresters are the rain."

ANONYMOUS UNPRINTED LETTER TO *THE DAILY IMACHARAN*

The next morning, even though I slept terribly thanks to the vision of the blurred man and woke later than usual, all the excess energy of the drug gave me a spring in my step, and my power sang beneath my skin. I had another reason to be ebullient and push the dream aside: we had our first magic show at the Kymri Theatre that night, after all.

I froze as soon as I entered the kitchen. Right next to Maske, Lily Verre was spreading butter onto a slice of bread. Her dark blonde hair was in an elaborate braid, a feather-festooned hat on the sofa at her side. Drystan and Cyan were doing their best to appear nonchalant. Maske was oblivious, as we hadn't told him anything about either Shadow Elwood or Lily being a second Shadow hired by Doctor Pinecrest. We hadn't started our investigations of her, yet, either. I tried to school my features into mild surprise, but I could feel the blood draining from my face as Lily met my gaze. The skin around her blue eyes crinkled as she smiled.

"Good morning . . . Sam!" she said, with enough hesitation to signal she knew full well it was a false name. "Toast? Coffee?"

"Both, please," I said, faintly.

Maske had fallen hard for Lily, or at least the woman she pretended to be around him. They'd met up regularly since the magician's duel, usually heading out for a meal or a show at one of the theatres in town. Seeing her there as if nothing had changed made her betrayal of spying on us for Pinecrest hit all the harder. Would she leave here and immediately report every word back to the doctor? Did she know we'd discovered her secret?

"I say, Sam, are you feeling quite all right?" Lily asked, the knife hovering above the bread. "You look so terribly pale. Amon, Celia, any toast?"

Drystan and Cyan demurred as I sat down, pouring a cup of coffee from the carafe on the table. I took a sip and grimaced. Lukewarm.

"I'm fine. Just a little under the weather, I suppose," I said, hoping my voice was steady. Carefully, I reached out to Cyan with my mind. She'd recovered from the worst of her injuries, though she still limped a little. —*Can you get anything from her yet?*

—*Not a thing. She's still protecting herself with mindless chatter that's impossible to break through. It must be so difficult for her to keep up.*

—*Her whole charade must be. It also means she might already suspect what you can do. Which is . . . not good.*

Cyan nodded, almost imperceptibly, as she took another bite of her toast. I still had no idea what to do: confront Lily, or hang back? If Pinecrest *was* working for Timur, then Lily would be, too.

Drystan looked between us, clearly guessing we were speaking to each other. I reached out and took his hand, thinking at both him and Cyan: —*We'll do nothing for now. But soon, I want to find out what she's really up to.*

He startled at the sound of my voice in his head but recovered. One side of his mouth quirked in agreement.

Lily Verre finished her toast and spoke brightly to Maske, hopefully unaware that the three of us recognized her as a viper in our nest.

●●●●

At lunchtime, we went over to the Ashen Graveyard. It was to the south of the Penny Rookeries outside the city limits. I'd never had cause to go before. I shivered as we walked through the gates I'd seen in my dream. The brightness of the late spring sun was a stark contrast to the gloominess of the previous night.

We couldn't exactly ask the guard to direct us to the freshest grave of a man whose name we didn't know. Many of the headstones had ornate carvings of the sun, the moon, or an hourglass with wings reminding us that the time we all had left was finite. It took close to an hour, but between Cyan and I following the impressions of our dreams, we eventually found it.

The pristine grave showed the name Alfred Deven. He had been thirty-three when he'd died. It was strange to know that the coffin six feet down was empty, and no one might ever discover the truth.

Cyan said a prayer for him in Temri, and Drystan and I bowed our heads.

"What do we do?" I asked.

"We should slip a note to the Constabulary," Cyan said. "I tried to warn the guards about Timur right before the explosion, but I don't know if they necessarily heard or took it seriously."

"Would they listen to this?" I asked.

"If they dig up the grave and find the empty coffin, maybe," Drystan said. "I suppose it's worth a try."

We left the bone garden behind. In town, we paused at a coffee house for a tea. Drystan wrote down everything we knew with his left hand to disguise his handwriting. It was barely legible. Cyan used her powers to get close enough to a passing Policier to slip it into his pocket before strolling away.

The contents of the note and the chicken-scratch handwriting combined made me fear that they'd discount it immediately, but at least we had done *something*.

That afternoon, we scrubbed for hours to prepare the stage for the first magic show since the duel in the Royal Hippodrome.

"We really need to convince Maske to hire more hands to help us out with all this," I puffed as we mopped the stage floor.

"Agreed," Cyan said, her face pink. "I miss Oli." His ship wouldn't be back until autumn at the earliest. He'd done the work of two people without complaint.

When we were finally finished, though, the place shone like the jewel it was. I went upstairs to wash and change into my newest performance suit. It fit me perfectly and felt just right. I put my mask in my pocket. I couldn't wait to be back out on that stage, watching the audience hanging on to every move. We'd come up with a new routine after the magician's duel and were excited to unveil it. Even though we were pretending in some ways, on the stage was where I felt most truly myself.

Cyril agreed to man the ticket booth for us and do some of the easier stagehand tricks. I poked my head out of the window a few times and heard my brother laughing as he took coins and gave out tickets. While he was obviously still worried about our mother, this seemed a welcome distraction.

I was performing alongside Maske, and Cyan was our assistant.

Tonight, Drystan would be the other stagehand. Drystan, Cyan, and I would be swapping roles. But, for the foreseeable future, Maske would perform every night. He had fifteen years to make up for, after all.

I peeked out through a gap in the curtain. Our first show was nearly sold out. This was what we'd been dreaming of for months: an actual audience settling into those seats and waiting for us. Behind the stage, Drystan set the gramophone playing. This last moment would always give me a certain thrill—the violin, the piano, the deep thump of the drums, and the expectant silence of the people on the other side of the curtain. I tied my mask onto my face, adjusting it until it lay just so. The pause, the breath before the magic began. No drug could ever make me feel as good as this.

We always told a story through our illusions. It helped string the acts together and created a thread for the audience to follow. The show where we had beaten Taliesin and his grandsons had been the story of Maske, in many ways: a magician who had let his hubris overwhelm him. He'd had to pay for it before ultimately finding his redemption.

Before stepping onto the stage, I turned on the Glamour around my neck. With the flick of a tiny switch, it could alter our appearance. Initially, we'd shifted our features more dramatically, but now we only changed our hair color. Cosmetics and the masks we wore did the rest. The Policiers had never caught our trail, and the smaller the changes, the slower the Vestige would run out of power. While our fortunes were better, we still couldn't easily afford more.

Maske held out his white-gloved hands. His black suit was sharply tailored, his bowtie as white as his shirt, and he wore a dark red cape that came to his waist. He wore the black velvet mask the three of us had given him for Lady's Long Night, embroidered with a moon and stars. He'd donned it at the duel, too, and said it always brought him luck.

"Welcome, one and all, to the Kymri Theatre. I am the Maske of Magic. You may have heard of me." He gave a wry smile as he paused for the audience clapping. "Once, a great Seer was so impressed by my powers that she gave me this very theatre. And now I have shared my magic with this young man, one of my most talented and trusted students."

I bowed low, accepting the scattered applause. "I won't let you down," I said.

"You never do," he replied. Beneath the lights of the stage, I felt a rush of warmth. The high of Pinecrest's dose had faded, but my real magic was at its brightest. Part of me wanted so badly to unleash it and amaze the audience beyond measure, but I kept it contained. Real magic, after all, would be cheating at the grand art of stage illusion.

Maske held out his hands, and a spark of red light emanated from them.

I recovered from my flinch and held out my own hands, letting them glow an echoing green. The audience gasped with delight as the chime of bells and strings rose from the gramophone.

Maske and I moved to either side of the stage, gesturing to a screen painted with cranes and clouds. Maske told the audience that our powers had recently been challenged by a Temnian princess, and she was here to showcase her skills.

"We'll see whose magic is the most powerful by the end of the night," he promised. "But you will be beyond amazed by us both, this I promise you."

Cyan came onstage, introducing herself as Madame Damselfly. She was dressed in a fine burgundy gown in Eladan style, the skirts voluminous with petticoats, and topped with a black split overskirt. The bodice had black and gold detailing around the corset and a green brooch at the chest. Her mask was molded, dark-red leather reminiscent of flower petals or wings. She wore sheer, elbow-length gloves that showed her dark, claw-like fingernails. Her long hair, unbraided tonight, flowed free down her back.

She raised her arms above her head and rose from the floor, aided by hidden cables, until she hovered six inches above the stage. She held the blue crystal ball we used in seances, and it glowed. I looked away. Even though it was only an illusion—a simple flare of chemicals—the light reminded me of how my touch affected Penglass. I still largely avoided getting too close to the mysterious, Alder-made glass since we'd left the circus, even if it whispered or sang to me when the moon was brightest. Cyan lowered back to the floor, throwing us a challenging look as she made the crystal ball disappear with sleight of hand.

The story alluded to our recent magic duel, but we were making some changes and experiments. We'd decided to integrate some of our acrobatic skills into our tricks. It'd meant long hours oiling away the rust that had gathered in our joints and muscles since we'd left our respective circuses.

"A strong opening from Madame Damselfly," Maske said. "Let's see how Sam the Magnificent compares."

My stage name still required some workshopping. Cyan and I squared off from each other. I echoed her movement, rising a few feet above the stage and striking a pose. The audience murmured appreciatively as I lowered back down.

"And now . . ." Maske said. "Let's see them duel properly!"

—One, two . . . three! Cyan counted in my head.

The wires raised us above the audience at the same time. Behind stage, Drystan and Cyril helped us both fly.

The crowd below us craned their necks, some of them open-mouthed. We'd used the best-quality wires, so even those squinting their hardest shouldn't be able to see the thin supports in the dim lights. Cyan and I swung toward each other, and then away.

At one point, our faces nearly touched, and our hands sparked with ersatz magic. Behind stage, Drystan handed Cyan's wire controls to Cyril before climbing to the gridiron above, dropping down two silken sashes that reached the stage's wooden planks. Slyly, Cyan and I unlatched our wires, which slid back up to the gridiron, before reaching out to grab the silks. We wrapped them around the arches of our feet and ankles as makeshift footholds. We let our fingers alight, blue and green sparks meeting in the middle in another shower of light. It'd taken a few tries to make sure we weren't at risk of singeing the fabric. We flipped upside down, our bodies forming mirrored crescent moons, and confetti and glitter fell from our hands.

The audience applauded, and even though this new trick brought back complicated memories of the trapeze, I couldn't keep the smile from my face. Our circus's past and our new illusionists' present had melded into something new. Each swing reminded me sharply of Aenea. She had taught me the ropes at the circus, quite literally. She was still out there, likely at a vaudeville show in this very city, even if I'd been too afraid to break my word to Anisa and seek her out. High above the stage, I let the performance honor her. It'd taken a lot of practice to pull this off so quickly, but I was so glad we'd done it.

But it was Cyan across from me, not Aenea, and the show painted us as rivals, not partners. The music from the gramophone rose. Untwining ourselves from the silken sashes, we continued our "battle." Cyan put a small pile of white feathers on a table, shrouded it for a moment with a silken scarf, then pulled the silk away to reveal a white dove. The bird cooed as she set it on her shoulder and bowed. Paix, the dove, then flew up to the gridiron, where Drystan had a treat ready as a reward for her returning to her cage.

I responded to Cyan's challenge by flipping through the air and showering her with paper blossoms. She brushed them out of her hair impatiently before jumping into a handstand. Her skirts bunched up to reveal the loose pantaloons favored by Kymri women to make this less shocking for the audience.

I was still suspended above her on the wires. I reached into my pocket and took out a shiny red apple, balancing it carefully on the top of my head.

Cyan picked up a bow and arrow hidden behind the table and pointed it at me. The audience held their breath as she took final aim and then let the arrow fly.

The crowd gasped, and even I had to fight not to flinch. The arrow *thunked* into the apple. It was an illusion, not that the audience realized I wasn't in actual danger. Scattered applause broke out, and I returned to the ground. We both bowed to the crowd. When I rose, I took a large red length of silk from my sleeve.

"I will prove myself the stronger by sending this Madame Damselfly to a world across the Veil and through the mists of time," I said.

After I draped her in the silk and pulled it away, Cyan disappeared into the hidden trapdoor. The audience gave exclamations of surprise. I stood tall, the proud victor.

While I'd collected my applause, Cyan had climbed back up to the gridiron. Right on cue, she reattached her wire and dropped down from the gridiron to land on my shoulders, now wearing a large pair of false damselfly wings, once again holding the blue crystal ball.

"You have returned!" I said, delighted. "We're both so powerful, why don't we declare this a draw?"

"I'll allow it this time," she said. "But I doubt you could survive what I've just seen." She smiled mysteriously at the audience.

We held our arms out, and she gracefully slid down my back. We took a last bow and pose, and headed to the wings as Maske took his place onstage.

Yet just before he began his first act, we heard a loud *boom*.

It was close enough that the entire theatre shook, dust falling from the ceiling.

A beat of silence.

There were a few scattered claps before they trailed away as they realized it wasn't part of the act.

We all heard the distant wail of sirens and the bone-deep sound of a second explosion.

10

FLAMES & RAIN

"The Museum of Mechanical Antiquities proved somewhat controversial during its inaugural year. While Vestige is often collected and celebrated by the nobility, the idea of allowing anyone inside to look at some of the rarer artefacts, even if many of them had long since run out of power, was considered shocking. One of the prominent donors was Doctor Samuel Pinecrest, but while he was abroad on research, other funding dried up and the building had seen better days. Upon his return to take up his post as the Royal Physician, he tried to revitalize the Museum, but eventually, it was closed. Much of the Vestige was sold and split up into various private collections. It had been something to wander from room to room and marvel at past wonders."

"VESTIGE," PROFESSOR CAED CEDAR,
ROYAL SNAKEWOOD UNIVERSITY

The theatre shook again, even more alarmingly. Cracks appeared in the walls of the auditorium. Smoke trickled in through the windows, and I smelled it so strongly I feared something inside the Theatre was burning.

The sprinkler sensors triggered, and the ceiling began to rain. Within moments, everyone was drenched. Screams tore through the air as the audience scurried over the sodden velvet seats, racing toward the exits.

"Everyone please leave the theatre and stay calm. Stay in the middle of the street, as far away from the buildings as you can," Maske's voice boomed from the stage. I was disoriented. Where had the blasts come from?

Next to him, Cyan sent her awareness over the crowd, subtly echoing the urge to remain calm. Her dress was so soaked she looked like a wilted flower. I felt her draw on some of the Vestige in the audience to help enhance her powers. Whether they realized her influence or not, people slowed down so there was less risk of them trampling each other. Their fear remained as palpable as the rain from the sprinklers. Drystan used the hidden passageway to appear on the other end of the theatre and help usher people out of the double doors.

Parents clutched their children close. Strangers lent others a hand if they stumbled. Within a few minutes, the theatre was empty except for Maske, his Marionettes, and my brother.

Cyan and Maske picked their way over the puddles in the alleyway between seats. "I'm going to go upstairs, get Anisa's Aleph, and try to find Ricket," I said. "I'll meet you outside in a minute."

"This building might not be sound," Maske protested.

"The explosion happened a few blocks over, I believe," Cyan said. Cyril didn't know she could read minds, of course, but the rest of us looked at her in grateful reassurance. She'd taken off her mask. Her cosmetics had smeared across her eyes, and her wet hair was glued to her forehead.

"Go help the others," I said, trying not to think of collapsing ceilings. "See if you can find out what happened."

Reluctantly, they let me go. The building seemed secure enough, but the cracks were worse on the upper levels. When I reached the loft, I stifled a sob.

Half of the roof had collapsed. Our belongings were covered with broken shingles and dust. Stumbling and coughing from the smoke, I made it to the bedside cabinet and grabbed Anisa's Aleph, stuffing it into my pocket. I took one lingering look around our ruined room before I heard a frightened mewl.

"Ricket," I said in relief, crouching down. The calico cat ran toward me, and I scooped her up in my arms. She purred in fear, huddling against me, and the cat and I fled the creaking, broken theatre. I assumed the doves in the dovecot above would have fled, but I couldn't risk going up to check on them. I headed back down the cracked staircase.

Out on the street, most of the audience of the Kymri Theatre had stayed together, clustered close in the drizzling rain. I locked eyes with Cyril, and he nodded, letting me know he was all right. The sky was red, black, and purple as a wound. The Kymri Theatre had sustained less damage than some of the other buildings on the street. A few near the end of the block had half-collapsed. My neighborhood. Our home.

Was the fire spreading? On my tiptoes, I craned my neck as if that would help me see through the buildings.

With a lurch, I realized I had a very good guess at the flames' origin: the Museum of Mechanical Antiquities. Cyan echoed my horror. She'd already told the others.

"How bad is it?" I whispered to her.

Cyan closed her eyes, and her awareness brushed across me. I could almost see the purple, blue, and green of the web of her power spreading through the streets before coming back into her. That was new. Was it a result of Pinecrest's medicine? No one else seemed to notice it. She opened her eyes.

—*Bad.*

"No," I whispered aloud. Hopefully some people on that street had managed to evacuate, but how many had been asleep in their beds at the time of the explosion?

—*The fire isn't spreading,* Cyan thought. *The wind is in our favor and the firemen are there. They'll do what they can.* She sent me flashes from the minds of people nearer the attack: the hiss as the water from the hoses hit flames. People clustered next to ambulance carriages, some weak with smoke inhalation and wrapped in blankets as they waited their turn to be carted to the Infirmary. Anisa was still deep in hibernation, and I wasn't sure if this merited using one of my two remaining wishes. I clutched Ricket closer, feeling her warm fur against my cheek.

While the Museum of Mechanical Antiquities had closed to the public last year, citing security reasons, I'd heard there were Vestige artefacts still stored inside and protected with Banshee alarms. How much had been destroyed?

Closing my eyes, I tried to push away the image of the clockwork woman's head burning. In one of her visions from the past, Anisa had inhabited a clockwork body like that while she'd grown a new body of flesh and bone—something so impossible I almost hadn't believed it. The clockwork woman's head had been haunting but beautiful, with gears showing beneath synthetic skin like Doctor Pinecrest's hand. Could Vestige burn?

—*Were Timur and his Kashura behind this?* I asked.

In my pocket, Anisa didn't answer.

—*My guess is yes.* Cyan's face tightened. *Yet again, I didn't sense it in time to stop it.*

—*What could you have done even with more warning, Cyan? This isn't on you, or me. He knows something of magic. Perhaps he learned how to make sure we didn't know of it this time.*

Though I suspected he didn't know I'd seen that dream of him bodysnatching. If the Policiers had ignored our note, would they look into it after this newest attack?

—*There was a lot of Vestige still in the Museum when it was open, wasn't there?* Cyan asked.

—Yes, I said. *All sorts. It was mostly defunct, though, and I'm not sure how much would still be there.*

Her face tightened in unease. —*I have a sneaking suspicion the Policiers won't find a lot of it in the wreckage.*

I echoed her fear. Timur already had access to some Vestige, I knew from the dream, like that strange pocket watch he'd called an Isochrome. If Timur *had* managed to steal something else from the Museum, what was he planning to do with it?

The evening was chilly, and my suit was soaked through. Our audience was dispersing, their shoulders hunched. As soon as the last of them was gone, Maske's head bowed. It seemed one tiny tragedy on top of the much larger one, that the explosion had happened right as he was about to perform again. Cyan put her arms around him in understanding as Drystan, Cyril, and I stared up at the Kymri Theatre. Even in the dark, I could see cracks in the façade and slipped shingles on the roof. The water damage from the sprinklers alone would be significant. The brand-new paint on the columns was smoke-stained. We didn't know for sure how bad it was yet, but it didn't look good.

"Well. We can't go to the insurance office until tomorrow," Maske said, wiping his eyes. He took a deep breath and squared his shoulders. "It looks like it's safe enough to go in and get some things. We'll spend the night at the Spectre."

Maske had already sold Taliesin's theatre after winning it in the duel, but he still had the keys. We briefly went back into the Kymri to grab our money, find a wicker basket for Ricket—who was complaining a lot less than I expected—and whatever undamaged clothes and possessions we could fit into a knapsack or a carpet bag.

Drystan let out a low whistle when he saw the ruin of our loft. The stained glass of the dragonfly had smashed to pieces, the shards scattered across the floor.

"Don't worry," he said at whatever he saw in my expression. "It can all be fixed."

"I hope so."

We shook the dust out of our rain-sodden clothes and packed the rest of our things. Maske waited for Cyan and Cyril to leave and locked the door. Hearts aching, we turned our back on the Kymri, not knowing how long it'd be before we'd return.

• • • •

We walked the twenty minutes to the Spectre. A few people roamed the streets, their body language sad or confused. The fire still stained the sky and the call of sirens echoed against the stone tenements and the Penglass. There were no shouts for justice and no crowds looting. Not yet, at least.

Taliesin's old theatre was dark and cold. It was as ornate and grand as the Kymri, but it was in the classical style and didn't have as much character as our home. Drystan and I chose a small chamber with two sofas, and he started a fire in the hearth. My brother found another room in a far corner. Cyan and Maske climbed the stairs to the second floor. Drystan and I spread our sodden possessions in front of the fire to dry and pushed the sofas together for a makeshift bed. Ricket curled up on it, waiting for us to join her.

Last I'd heard of old Taliesin, he'd sunk further into his Lerium addiction. He was still rich enough, but he was too ill to perform. His grandsons were travelling to the other islands in the Archipelago.

"Maybe Maske can stall the sale, and we can use this place until the Kymri is fixed?" I asked. After having our first performance in weeks, I didn't want to stop.

"I don't know," Drystan said. "I think it'll take at least a few months to fix the Kymri. The new buyers probably don't want to hold off that long."

I sighed. "This is awful."

"I know. It will work out, though. It has to."

The sofa was lumpy and uncomfortable, and I couldn't settle.

"Stop being so restless," Drystan complained after an hour of this.

"Sorry. Can't sleep." I feared dreaming of the grave robber or of the clockwork woman in the Museum of Mechanical Antiquities engulfed in flame.

Drystan sat up, rolling his head side to side until the vertebrae clicked. "Me neither."

We stayed up for a few hours, talking to each other about anything other than what'd just happened. We made up silly stories, taking turns in the telling, Ricket warm in my lap. At certain points, we curled up with laughter until our stomachs hurt.

It was what we'd needed. Who cared what was outside this small room with its warm fireplace? It didn't matter. Not that night. Finally, I fell asleep, and it turned out I had plenty of reason to fear my dreams.

11

THE PENNY ROOKERIES

"The Penny Rookeries refers to the poorest neighborhood in Imachara, little more than a slum on the south side of the city. This is where the poorest people of the capital live, along with criminals or moonshades who may struggle to find accommodation elsewhere. Conditions are overcrowded, with limited plumbing and sanitation. This, combined with the nearby factories, tanneries, and abattoirs, means on a hot summer's day, the smell of it can reach the nicer districts of the capital."

**A HISTORY OF ELADA AND ITS FORMER COLONIES,
PROFESSOR CAED CEDAR, ROYAL SNAKEWOOD UNIVERSITY**

The blurred man stared down at the corpse he'd stolen from the graveyard in dismay. It should have worked. Timur had prepped the body himself. Wires poked from the dead man's veins, connected to a refurbished Ampula tank he'd stolen from the Museum of Mechanical Antiquities.

Four Kashura had helped him this time. The light of the sole glass globe caught on their hooded cloaks and the stone of the walls. Safer if they didn't even know each other's identities.

It should have worked. It almost had.

For a moment, Timur had felt his soul blend with his stolen Chimaera magic and reach toward the body, but at the last minute, the machine had malfunctioned, his stolen magic misbehaving even with the use of the Isochrome. Timur had crashed back into the ruin of his body, and he'd smelled burning flesh.

Timur winced at the singed, useless body before him. What a waste.

"What went wrong?" one of the Kashura dared ask.

Timur shot her a look. "Are you questioning me?" He'd had his moments of doubt about the Chimaera.

"I would never," the Kashura said, bowing her hooded head. "You alone know the way forward."

"It is only a setback," Timur said. His fingers were entirely black. His atrophied heart skipped in his chest. This had been a risk. Next time, there could be no room for errors. He was running out of time.

"We simply need better equipment . . . and another body."

••••

I awoke with a gasp, freezing despite the blazing fireplace.

Drystan heard me and woke.

"Nightmare," I said, my teeth chattering, and he wrapped his arms around me.

"Lord and Lady, you're like ice." He rubbed my fingertips. "Did you dream of him again?"

Up above, I knew Cyan had had the same vision, and that she, too, feared what it meant.

"We were right—he was trying to jump bodies, but it didn't work. I dunno why." I described the dream in broad strokes.

Drystan's brow drew down. "You said Alfred Deven hadn't been quite dead when he'd dug him up."

I shivered. "He definitely is, now." I swore I could almost smell the smoke and cooked meat in my nostrils. "But Timur is definitely going to try again. He'll have to."

"You didn't notice anything that could help trace us back to where he was?"

I frowned, trying to remember. "One of the Kashura is Chimaera. They were all somewhere dark. Cold. It had stone walls."

"I hate this," Drystan said. "Never knowing what's around the corner or what to do. I hate that I can't stop the nightmares for you."

I moved closer to his warmth.

We didn't say another word, but neither of us slept any more that night.

• • • •

The next few days held a parade of bad news.

We went to the insurance office the morning after the fire, queuing with everyone else. Maske managed to hire a surveyor to assess the extent of the damage to the Kymri. By afternoon, we knew it was as we feared; the building was overall sound enough, thankfully, but it wouldn't be safe to live in during renovations. We had no luck with delaying the sale of the Spectre, either; while the new owners were kind enough to let us stay for a few days while we worked out our affairs, they wished to start work immediately to turn it into residential quarters.

The biggest problem was the insurance itself. While nearly destitute, Maske had paid the smallest premium, and since winning the duel, he hadn't yet amended it. The company would barely pay out for any repairs. The sale of the Spectre Theatre would cover most of the damages, hopefully, but in the meantime . . . we were broke. Again.

Maske found us rooms in a tenement in the Penny Rookeries, which was all we could afford or even find at short notice. The walls smelled of mold, and the bed frames were more rust than metal. We had a decent view of the street and the docks in the distance from the grimy window. There were three tiny bedrooms and a box room, and the lounge was little more than a closet. The fireplace in the lounge didn't draw out the smoke properly until Maske fixed it, emerging covered head to toe in soot. There was an ancient stove tucked in the corner and a half-broken chill box, which was as close as we could get to a kitchen. There was only the box room as a workshop, which left Maske grumpy. Our windows were covered with oilskin rather than glass, and we were lucky to have that. Even Ricket turned her nose up at it.

I hadn't spent any time in the Penny Rookeries since coming to the capital, but everywhere I looked, I saw people ground down by poverty. The place was very like a birds' rookery—slanting buildings with ramshackle wooden galleries built haphazardly against stone. Many windows were stuffed with rags. The streets stank with garbage and the waste people threw out of the windows. There were children with bare feet and no coats, and while it was early summer, I suspected in winter they were dressed no better.

After the attack on the Museum of Mechanical Antiquities, the Snakewood Crown enforced a sunset curfew throughout the capital. Those who worked late shifts had to apply for special dispensation papers. Many felt the curfew wouldn't be a deterrent—the attack on the Celestial Cathedral, after all, had happened in broad daylight. The restrictions certainly weren't helping the growing anti-monarchy sentiment. People were afraid, but they were also resentful, especially since the Crown hadn't yet caught the perpetrators.

Cyan had dropped off another note at the Constabulary Headquarters. We'd written that Timur, the former head of the Foresters, was behind both the Celestial Cathedral attack and the one at the Mechanical Museum and told them again to dig up Alfred Deven's body.

After we'd settled into our small, sad rooms, Maske told us in no uncertain terms that we were not to let our skills go to waste. Street shows would be our trade once more, and whatever coin people threw into our hats would be our day-to-day spending money. We built up a new routine, practicing in the cramped lounge.

A few more days passed. My energy faltered. I could barely keep my eyes open after practice ended. I slept later and later in the mornings, until Drystan would pull the covers away and I'd protest at the sudden cold.

All too soon, it was time to visit the doctor.

Maske had asked Drystan and Cyan to test out their routine that morning, and I was feeling brave enough to go to Pinecrest's apartments alone. I walked through the cramped streets of Imachara, dodging the fetid puddles and feeling guilty at ignoring the beggars pleading for spare coins. The buildings gradually grew nicer. When I passed the Infirmary, I wondered if, even now, my brother was in there visiting our mother. We'd all tacitly agreed that the Penny Rookeries was no place for him; he'd stand out a mile with his rich clothes and be pickpocketed in seconds, so he'd taken up his shared room near the university again. I missed him already.

The doorman at Pinecrest's building knew me by sight and let me in. I headed up the grand staircase and knocked on his door, and the doctor opened it himself. I'd noticed he kept few servants.

"Good morning, Micah," he said warmly, welcoming me inside. While we knew Timur was at the heart of this, I tried to remember the build of the men in the cloaks. Did any of them match Pinecrest's size? Pinecrest might not be the blurred man, but that didn't mean he wasn't one of his Kashura.

Pinecrest already had the syringe prepared on the table. My eyes caught on it.

"I'm afraid I haven't been able to ask about performing for the

Princess," Pinecrest said. "The Palace has been in an uproar since the latest attack, as you might expect."

With everything that had happened at the Kymri Theatre, I'd honestly half-forgotten. "That's all right," I managed.

"I'm afraid we'll have to keep our visit short today as well," he said. "I've been asked to visit the morgue at the medical school."

I made a noncommittal noise, my eyes still on the syringe.

"Normally I'd take my assistant with me," he continued, "but he's in a lecture."

"You have an assistant?" I asked, curious despite myself.

"Of course. Helps with some of my experiments. Bright young chap destined for great things, I suspect." The doctor paused, as if something had just occurred to him. "I say. Would you like to accompany me to the university? I think you might find this visit rather intriguing."

"To the morgue?" My fingertips tingled.

"Indeed. They have a cadaver Doctor Maral would like me to take a look at." He paused. "It's the Chimaera who died at the Cathedral."

My ears rang. The thought of seeing Dirk's dead body again filled me with horror, and I was, as usual, suspicious of the Doctor's motivations. At the same time, I had the afternoon free, as Maske knew I wasn't quite myself after being dosed. The high hadn't been as severe the second time, as if my body had grown used to it, so I'd hopefully have my wits about me. This would be dangerous, but I had a feeling I'd learn something useful.

"I'll go," I said.

"Wonderful," Doctor Pinecrest said, his eyes crinkling at me. "I know you have your hesitations about doctors, yet I hope this will show you that medicine is not always something that needs to be feared."

I remembered the sensation of trying to help the older woman after the Celestial Cathedral explosion, and how I'd suspected that if I'd known more about the human body, I'd have been better able to help her.

Doctor Pinecrest picked up the syringe. "First things first. Hold out your arm and roll up your sleeve, if you please."

With a resigned set of my jaw, I did as he asked. Ice soon flowed through my veins again.

12

THE MORGUE

"Neonatal death. Low temperature. Jaundice. Atypical anatomy: tail, caul, ichthyosis. Cause of death: unknown."

UNSIGNED MEDICAL NOTES, ROYAL SNAKEWOOD UNIVERSITY

Doctor Pinecrest defied the current fashion of hiring a chauffeur by driving the horseless carriage himself. I sat up front next to him, the high of the tincture flowing through my veins. The smoke from the exhaust stung my nose.

"I went abroad on sabbatical a number of years ago," he said when I asked why he didn't have a driver. "Much of my early research into Chimaera was conducted in Byssia and Linde. I grew used to doing things myself. Once I recovered from my injury"—he waved his clockwork hand, hidden by his glove—"I chafed at servants dressing me, feeding me, or driving me everywhere like a child."

In this way, I was similar to Pinecrest. As Iphigenia Laurus, I'd been uncomfortable with being treated and dressed like a porcelain doll. I'd preferred climbing scaffolding or trees with my brother. I watched Pinecrest's clockwork hand move the brass controls of the carriage with ease.

"I was grieved to hear about the damage to the Kymri Theatre," Pinecrest said. "Where are you staying now?"

"We've some rooms in the Penny Rookeries," I said.

The doctor clicked his tongue. "Not the best part of town—especially with all the civil unrest at the moment."

"It's only temporary. If we keep to ourselves, it's fine enough."

"Let's hope it stays that way," he said.

"I've been wondering . . . did you lose anything in the fire at the Museum?" I hoped I sounded casual as I steered the conversation.

He gave me a sidelong glance as he fiddled with the controls. The carriage made a right turn. "No, luckily, I took most of the items in my collection back when it closed. But plenty of artefacts that hadn't yet been sold were still stored inside."

"So, the clockwork woman is safe?" I asked, my heart lifting in hope. She'd terrified me, but she'd fascinated me, too.

He gave a little smile. "She is safe," he confirmed. "But I still lost a few treasures." His hands tightened on the controls, his only hint of anger.

"I heard rumors some Vestige went missing," I chanced.

Pinecrest shot another sharp glance at me out of the corner of his eye. "Difficult to tell in the wreckage."

I wished I could ask him what an Isochrome was, but if he was working closely with Timur, it'd give away far too much. Before I could think of what to ask him next, we pulled up to the medical school right across the square from the Royal Infirmary.

He caught the direction of my gaze. "No change in your mother's prognosis, I hear," he said, guessing my thoughts.

"No," I said, shortly.

I climbed down the steps of the carriage, straightening my suit jacket, fighting down my nerves. I'd been to the medical school a couple of times, following the woman in the red dress.

A guard at the gate of a side entrance let Doctor Pinecrest and I into a courtyard I hadn't seen before, filled with lush trees and walkways. A few patients lounged in the sun, some in wheelchairs and others bandaged. The patients were usually poor, or lower middle-class who couldn't quite afford the private doctors' surgeries.

"Come along," Pinecrest said.

I followed Doctor Pinecrest through the labyrinth of corridors. I heard quickened footsteps behind us and turned to see a young man, slightly out of breath. He was little older than me, and a few inches shorter. His build was heavy-set, with an open face and a hint of a goatee at his chin. I stiffened.

"Doctor Pinecrest," he said. "Doctor Maral said you'd be coming by this afternoon, so I asked permission to leave my lecture a little early."

Doctor Pinecrest gave him a wide smile. "Ah, marvelous to see you, my boy." He gestured between us. "Kai Molleson, this is Micah Grey. Micah, this is Kai, my assistant."

I met his eyes, and his widened in recognition. After all, he'd met me once before, dressed as a girl. Kai wore a heavy coat despite the warmth within the operating theatre. His hair was just as brown and curly as I remembered from the day I'd met him, when I followed the woman in the red dress and unwittingly witnessed Doctor Pinecrest welcoming Lily Verre and her child.

Kai had found me, seemingly by chance, and been friendly enough to lead me across the square to the Infirmary. He'd helped me find out whether Aenea had survived the night at the circus. Had that all been some ploy, too?

Kai held out his hand, and I squeezed his palm tightly. He had a strong grip.

"Nice to meet you," I said, firmly, meeting his eyes and shaking my head minutely in warning.

"Nice to meet you . . . Micah," he said, his expression difficult to read.

"Come now, let's not be tardy," Pinecrest said. He led us through the lower levels of the university until we reached the entrance to the morgue.

A young Byssian doctor greeted us. He had deep brown skin and his black hair was shaved close to his head. He was very tall—I had to crane my neck to look up at him, and I wasn't particularly short.

He shook Doctor Pinecrest's hand, his brown eyes crinkling. "Thank you for coming, Royal Physician. What an honor."

"The pleasure is all mine. It's not every day you have the chance to see a supposed Chimaera, after all."

I stiffened, and something flickered in Kai's expression. Interesting.

We entered, the blast of cold air from the room hit my cheeks, and I shivered. Doctor Maral closed the door behind us.

"Before we view the cadaver," Doctor Maral said, "I must, of course, ask for the utmost discretion from your assistants." He eyed Kai and me.

Doctor Pinecrest waved his clockwork hand. "But of course. I promise none of us will go running to the newspapers or anything like that." I noticed he didn't clarify that I wasn't actually his assistant.

"You have my word," Kai said, serious.

"Mine, too," I added. Of course, I'd tell Cyan and Drystan everything as soon as I was home.

Doctor Maral nodded once and pushed open the door. The air was cold, and I shivered beneath my coat. The walls were lined with metal doors, and I knew that bodies lay behind them. Doctor Maral brought us into a back room, unlocking it with a square Vestige key.

In the center of the small, cramped room was something blocky covered with a white cloth. With an almost showman-like flick of the wrist, Doctor Maral took away the cloth to reveal a Vestige tank. I stifled a gasp. It was made of the same type of metal as Anisa's Aleph, crafted in a way that looked almost organic. There were bulbous glass windows on the top and sides that reminded me of bug eyes, revealing a murky green liquid and an impression of the body inside.

"This is a piece of Vestige known as an Ampula," Pinecrest explained to me, as if he were lecturing to a student. "Very rare, of course. Corpses stored within it do not decay. This is useful when we have such a shortage of cadavers for anatomy classes."

Doctor Maral did something to the controls on the side and the top of the Ampula opened. A ledge within rose, revealing the corpse of Dirk—the Chimaera who'd been with Juliet and Violet at the Celestial Cathedral. His russet fur was dark from the liquid.

I'd last seen him pulled from the rubble of the Cathedral, eyes blank. Now, they were closed, and he had a Y incision across his chest. Countless cuts scored the short, slick fur. His stomach was dappled lighter with white and grey. A much larger gash had been stitched shut. The air smelled medicinal.

"Indeed, here he is," Doctor Maral said. He stared down at Dirk's corpse, his eyes sparking with anger.

"He wasn't behind the Celestial Cathedral attack," I protested. Doctor Pinecrest's head swiveled toward mine with too much interest. "I was in the square that day. He found the Incendiary and I saw him throw it away from the crowd."

Kai sucked in a breath.

"Indeed," Doctor Pinecrest said, mildly. "Many reports indicate his actions saved hundreds of people that day. Some still think it might have been a ploy."

It wasn't, I wanted to say, but bit down on the words.

"I don't," Pinecrest added, inclining his head at me. "For the record."

"If you insist. We didn't recover the other two Chimaera, in any case," Doctor Maral said. "They must have escaped. But studying this man alone has raised so very many questions."

"How different is his biology?" Doctor Pinecrest asked, leaning closer. I couldn't help but imagine Dirk with his ribs splayed, revealing his lungs and a once-beating heart. I shivered.

"Not significantly," Doctor Maral said. "Entirely the same internally. Just the addition of this . . . pelt. His muscles are denser than average, and his bones stronger. The brain structure is slightly different, perhaps. We're still consulting with a brain surgeon to return with his full report. The implications could be astounding."

Like telekinesis, I thought. *Or the ability to throw a Vestige sphere and have it sail further than any human muscle could propel it.*

Kai couldn't tear his eyes away from Dirk. My curiosity about him rose. He worked with Pinecrest, after all—what did he know of Chimaera? If I wanted to find out whether Pinecrest was involved with the blurred man, his assistant might be one approach.

My eyes caught on the stitches on Dirk's head from where his skullcap had been removed and put back. What had this man been like? How had he felt about being Chimaera, and what other abilities had he possessed? He'd tried to call for peace and been killed for it. Now doctors had taken his body, pulled it apart, and peered inside to discover what had made him tick.

To me, doctors had always been bogeymen—people hidden behind masks as they studied me, quantified me, and wrote about me like a specimen. I'd always imagined that was how they saw every patient—as a problem to be fixed.

"Will you use him for anatomy classes?" I asked, eying that Y-shaped incision. I'd never thought much about how doctors were trained.

"No. Can't risk students damaging the specimen," Doctor Maral said. "And there are many more observations to be made." He sighed. "We are desperately short, though. We should have one cadaver for every five or six students, but it's instead one for a dozen."

Doctor Pinecrest turned serious. "Don't turn to resurrection men."

Doctor Maral looked affronted. "Of course not. I would never."

My interest sharpened. I'd heard of resurrection men. They crept into graveyards to dig up fresh bodies, selling them to universities or anatomy schools. Doctor Pinecrest asking Doctor Maral not to use them was pointless, even I knew that: pretty much all universities employed resurrection men on the sly.

Doctor Maral worked the controls, and the four of us watched Dirk disappear back into the green liquid of the Ampula. This would be the last time I saw him. Wherever his soul was now, I wished him well.

"We did have one new corpse come in that we can use for anatomy labs," Doctor Maral said, brightening as we came back to the main morgue. "He's a little damaged, but he'll still prove useful. He's just here."

He gestured to another Ampula.

"May I see?" Doctor Pinecrest asked.

Doctor Maral humored him again, but from the first glimpse of the brown hair in the tank, I knew.

Alfred Deven. The body I'd watched the blurred man dig up from a grave rose from the liquid. The same features and muscled build. Around his wrists were the burns I'd already seen.

Doctor Pinecrest leaned closer, his brow drawing down. "Those look like electrical burns." He seemed truly surprised and didn't seem to recognize the man at all. Had he been in that room, or hadn't he?

Kai looked disturbed. "What could have made those marks?" he asked.

"I'm not exactly sure," Doctor Maral said.

"Curious." Doctor Pinecrest leaned back. "I assume this is the cause of death?"

"As far as we can tell," Doctor Maral said. "The rest of him is intact, and studying the burns will still be beneficial for the students, so we're grateful to have him."

"Where'd he come from?"

"He was dumped on the steps," the doctor said. "One of the nursing students found him first thing a few mornings ago, which must have been quite the shock. We haven't managed to track down his name, but the Constabulary eventually said we could keep him."

Did that mean no one had put together that he was the missing corpse from the Ashen Graveyard? My breath came faster, and I swayed on my feet. Without a word, I turned and fled the cool room, entering the blessedly warm and empty hallway. I slid down the wall and sat on the cool tile of the floor, head between my knees, trying to gain my air back.

The doors opened. Pinecrest walked toward me. "I should have realized this might be a lot for you to take in," he said. "You've just been dosed. I apologize."

"I'm fine," I said, not fooling either of us. Did Doctor Pinecrest know about the resurrection man in my dreams?

"That's a lie, but an understandable one. A reminder of our mortality is always sobering. You also saw Dirk when he was alive, if only briefly, which makes it harder. You know, when I cover the anatomy lectures here now and again, I actually urge students to name the cadavers."

My curiosity got the better of me. "Why?"

"Because that cadaver is their teacher as much as whoever's up on the lectern," he said. "They can't only study from diagrams in books, when the muscles are butterflied, bloodless, and pristine. Even wax models, intricate in their detail, aren't enough. Each body is subtly different. More than that, though, it'd be easy enough for students to discount who the corpse used to be, because they're often criminals. But no matter what they did in life, they were still someone who loved others and was mourned. The heart the students are about to hold in their hands like a mango once beat blood through the veins of a body, powering a life."

He was warming up, and I could just imagine him in a lecture theatre, speaking to a room of young men destined to be physicians.

"A doctor will never know everything that makes a future patient tick. You can see the moment it changes for the students—that very perception of what makes us human. A good practitioner's goal is to do whatever they can so the patient before them doesn't turn into a corpse."

His words hung between us, and I felt like a student caught under his spell. I'd come looking for answers, and while I'd definitely discovered a few things, I had no idea how it all fit together.

Pinecrest reached into his pocket and passed me a few coins. "Here. Take a cab home. I must stay here with Doctor Maral and Kai awhile longer, but I think you've had more than enough for one day. I hope you found it enlightening."

He turned around and paused. "By the way, I'll do what I can to keep my promise," he said. "I'll speak to the Steward about you performing for the Princess."

I nodded. "Maske will be delighted if it happens, I'm sure."

"It'll be one of my priorities this week. Travel home safely, and my apologies again if today upset you. I can sometimes forget how most people aren't hardened to the sight of death."

"I hope I never am," I said.

He gave me a bitter smile as I turned away.

13

STREET MAGIC

"A blink is all you need. A second of distraction, and you trick them with that precious moment. Magic is both the easiest and the hardest thing you will ever do."

**FROM THE SOON-TO-BE PUBLISHED MEMOIRS OF
JASPER MASKE, THE MASKE OF MAGIC**

That night, I told Cyan and Drystan everything that'd happened at the morgue. We spent hours looking at things from every angle. As soon as we came up with one theory, one of us would poke at it, and the picture would fall apart again. We'd given up, and I'd had a nightmare of Dirk floating in that tank all alone.

The next morning, we turned on our Glamours and did street magic. It wasn't the same after performing in the Kymri Theatre, but it was still magic.

We'd decided to perform in the merchant part of town. Rich enough that people would have spare coins to throw our way, but not fancy enough that Policiers would chase us off. I'd learned my lesson since we'd started performing and made sure we had a proper permit, just in case.

We set up our makeshift stage—an Arrasian rug—and set out the top hat for coins. We wore our full magician regalia: me and Drystan in our suits, Cyan in her Temnian sarong.

The air was loud with calls, the clop of horses' hooves, and the ceaseless footsteps of hurrying pedestrians. Nearby, a blacksmith's steady hammer rang against an anvil. Dust choked the air, and the sun beat down on the shop windows and the heads of people rushing past. From two streets over, we could smell the butcher's row: old blood, offal, and the smell of meat about to turn. Two young women, one blonde and freckled, and one dark-haired and brown-skinned, were walking down the street. They had no big bags, no children, and didn't seem in a rush.

"Excuse me," I called to them with a smile. "Would you care to see some magic?"

A pause. A shy smile in return from the dark-haired one, a skeptical raise of the eyebrow from the blonde. "All right," said the disbeliever, with a tilt of her chin as if to say: *impress me*.

"May I see your ring, just for a moment?" I asked the shy one. She wore a simple wooden band around her thumb. "I promise, it'll just be for a second, and then I'll return it to you, safe and sound."

She hesitated. "I don't know," she said in a slight Kymri accent.

"Here, you may hold my ring as insurance." I passed her a silver band. She took it and then slipped her ring off her finger and handed it to me. A few more people gathered. Cyan might have been pushing minds, just the slightest bit, to draw attention to our corner of the street.

A quick close and open of my fingers, and the wooden band was gone. The skeptic puffed up. "If you've stolen it—" she began.

"Never fear, miss. As I said, it'll be back in a moment. Now," I said, holding my empty hands wide. "Would you be impressed if the ring showed up in my pocket?"

"Yes," the shy one said.

"Well." I reached into my coat. I brought out a small wallet, opened it, unbuttoned a smaller pocket within, and revealed the wooden ring, chained to the wallet itself. I unclipped the ring and passed it back to her. "How about this?"

The shy woman gave a delighted laugh, and even the skeptical blonde was grudgingly impressed.

"Now, please pass me back my silver ring," I said, still smiling.

She reached into her pocket, but her fingers came up empty. She gazed at me with wide eyes.

Another quick flourish of my hands, and the silver was back on my finger. Both women clapped, along with several passersby.

We performed more sleight of hand as the crowd gathered. We fanned cards and guessed the one a punter chose, made other cards disappear and appear in pockets, on the bottom of shoes, or beneath hats. Drystan re-created his performance at the Elmbarks' on the Night of the Dead, telling a story of love and jealousy, having the right characters—the jack, the king, the queen—appear at just the right time.

For some of the tricks, we used our acrobatic skills—handstands, cartwheels, and flips. These impressed the audience just as much as the magic, and I spied one small child trying a cartwheel of his own. By the end of the show, our hat held plenty of coins. It'd help us buy food, as almost all our money was tied up in the sale of Taliesin's theatre and the repairs on our home.

We thanked everyone, took our earnings, and packed up our things.

"We made good time. And we're not far from Lily's apartments." Now that the dust of moving had settled, we'd been taking turns occasionally watching her apartment building while we decided what, if anything, we were going to do about her. Was she a potential ally, or merely a pawn of Pinecrest's? What was the significance of her son looking like the horned boy who had nearly ended the world so long ago?

Cyan went back to our rooms with the props, while Drystan and I went to a tea house that gave us a direct view of the entrance to Lily's apartments. It was here—a few weeks ago, at the very table where I now sat—that we had realized Lily Verre was the woman in the red dress I'd seen in visions before I'd fallen ill with my fever.

Our tea arrived. A Penglass dome to the right of the tea house cast the veranda in blue shadow. My eyes kept snagging on it. Penglass always called to me, especially on the night of the full moon. It was as if the Penglass emitted heat, and I wanted to unfurl in front of it.

Turning my back on the glass, I focused on the tea. "This is nice," I said, clinking my cup to Drystan's. "Like a date."

"A romantic date of spying on a Shadow with a Chimaera son who is courting our mentor." His mouth twisted, but he held up his cup in a sardonic salute before taking a drink.

"We don't have the time or the money for anything else, so I'll take what I can get," I said.

Drystan laughed. I took a sip. The black tea with a swirl of milk reminded me of my past life in Sicion.

After half an hour or so, Drystan nudged me with his elbow. "Luck's on our side, finally. There she is."

Lily came out, alone. She wore a hat wreathed with flowers against the early summer sun. We threw some coins on the table and followed her at a distance, shifting our Glamours to help disguise ourselves better. Using my elixir-enhanced powers, I reached out toward her mind. I wasn't anywhere near as good as Cyan, but I'd learned I could manage a little the first few days after a dose. Like Cyan, all I heard was an incessant chatter of noise. She kept it up whether or not she thought we were near, then. Where had she learned to shield herself, and what was she hiding?

A blink, and Lily was nowhere to be seen. It was a busy market, with thick crowds and stalls packed as closely as possible.

"Where'd she go?" I demanded.

"She's a damn sight better than Elwood, I'll give her that," Drystan said. "She successfully disappeared while wearing that ridiculous hat."

"Do you think she realized we were following her?"

His lips thinned. "Do you want my honest answer, or the one you wish was true?"

"Shit."

After a few minutes' fruitless search, we gave up and headed back to the Penny Rookeries. Yet on the way home, I kept turning my head to the left. I felt . . . something.

When I slowed down for the third time, Drystan asked me what the matter was.

"It's sort of like the heat or magic I feel from Penglass." I craned my head. "But this is different. It's like I'm drawn to a person . . ." Drystan met my eyes, and at the same time we whispered: "A Chimaera."

I followed the feeling, Drystan trailing behind. I caught sight of a young man, and something about the way he moved meant I couldn't take my eyes off him. He was young and slight, wearing a patched suit that was too large on him and a tall hat. When his face turned toward mine, I noticed his skin was slightly dappled across his nose and cheekbones. I knew, somehow, that if he took off that hat, beneath I would find short, fuzzed antlers, like a young buck.

"Sir!" I called toward him.

His head swiveled toward mine, skittish.

—*Wait*, I sent in my mind. *I'm like you. I just want to talk.*

He bolted. I started to run after him, but Drystan pulled me back. "If we've spooked him, I don't think he'll want to speak to us."

The young man in the top hat slipped into a large market crowd. As he disappeared from view, the warm blush faded.

"I . . . I sensed him," I said. "I knew what he was." Was this how Anisa perceived Chimaera—this glow?

Drystan rubbed his mouth. "Another side effect of Pinecrest's medicine, maybe. Still don't like you taking it one bit, but I suppose this is rather useful. What if you could find others?"

"Seems like that might draw myself—or them—right into danger." I tried not to think of the square at the Celestial Cathedral.

"Hm, that's definitely a risk. Let me or Cyan know if you feel it again, but don't go after anyone on your own, all right?"

I nodded. A headache bloomed at my temples, growing stronger with each step. By the time we reached our rooms in the Penny Rookeries, my vision was blurring, and it felt like ice picks skewered my temples.

Even on the other side of the door, I could sense burning in my mind like a flame.

—Micah— Cyan began as Drystan opened the door.

We froze.

Within our cramped lounge, Maske, Lily—her ridiculous hat set beside her on the sofa—and Doctor Pinecrest were having tea with a stiff and nervous Cyan. Ricket was asleep on Lily's lap. Traitor. Had Lily realized we were following her, even with our Glamours, and come straight here?

Maske couldn't contain his excitement. "Doctor Pinecrest has hand-delivered an invitation to perform at the Royal Snakewood Palace for the Princess. Can you believe it?"

"That's wonderful," I managed, but I knew my smile must have looked closer to a grimace. Now that I knew to focus on it, Cyan glowed like a coal, but I sensed next to nothing from Pinecrest except the faint warmth of his Vestige hand. That would mean he wasn't Chimaera . . . but then how had he spoken to me mind to mind?

Drystan was equally uneasy. We'd wear Glamours, and hopefully the Princess wouldn't invite many guests, but there was a slightly higher chance someone might recognize him as a member of the Hornbeam family. Cyan would feel like an outsider, but I knew she was keen for the coin. Maske looked as if Lady's Long Night had come early. I wondered if he might cry.

"Well," said Doctor Pinecrest, putting on his gloves, "I should probably return to the Palace and give them your acceptance. Thank you for the tea, and it was lovely to make your acquaintance, Mrs. Verre."

I barely managed not to scoff. Lily met my eyes, then glanced back at Doctor Pinecrest. "Oh, the pleasure's mine, I'm sure!" she said, falsely bright. "Good day, Royal Physician."

I walked the doctor to the door. Out in the hallway, he put on his top hat.

"Why are you doing this for us?" I asked, tired of dancing around everything. Perhaps I'd forgotten more of the etiquette my mother had taught me than I thought.

"As I said, it's not for you," he said. "Or not only. I'm doing this mostly for the Princess Royal. She's lonely."

"What's she like?" I'd only met her briefly just after the magician's duel. She'd been as excited as any other little girl. That night, she'd given us all emerald and diamond lapel pins. I kept mine safe in a little box in my bedside table.

"She's a jewel, our Princess. Whatever's in her future, it won't be easy. Pressure makes diamonds, after all. I just hope that she won't crack."

With those cryptic words, Pinecrest tipped his hat to me and made his way down the stairs.

I came back into the living room to find Maske pacing.

"Only half a week to prepare," he said, but his eyes were lit with glee. "A performance at the Royal Palace for Princess Nicolette Snakewood herself." He paused, leaning back in his chair. "They tell us to name a fee. Oh, gods. What should I charge?"

"I'd say double what you charged the Elmbarks' for the séance, at least," Cyan said.

Drystan whistled.

We all knew what this could mean. Not only would it be a good injection of coin upfront, but performing for the Princess would mean we were favored by the Royal Family. This would result in more séance and magic show bookings from the nobility throughout Imachara and the Emerald Bowl. By the time we were back in the Kymri Theatre, we'd be sitting pretty.

"There's so much to do," Maske said, rushing to his box room. He slammed the door, a bit of dust falling from the cracked plaster of the ceiling.

14

THE SHIMMERING GIRL

"Once there was a girl with dragonfly wings who soared above the world. Below her, she saw those who were happy or heartbroken. She flew further away and found wide expanses with no one at all save the animals, trees, rocks, and streams. She traveled all the way around the world, pausing to write down whatever she saw. When she eventually returned to where she'd begun, she showed no one her little journal. It was her version of the world, and she wanted to keep it for herself alone."

"THE DRAGONFLY GIRL," HESTIA'S FABLES

We went to the palace three days later, following the instructions sent by courier on sumptuous regal stationery.

The Steward sent a gilded carriage to the Kymri Theatre for us. We didn't wish them to know we were staying in the Penny Rookeries, and it wouldn't do to have something with the royal coat of arms appear in the poorest part of town with tensions as high as they were.

Maske, Cyan, Drystan, and I squeezed into it and enjoyed the rare luxury. I wished I could have brought Cyril, too, but his name wasn't on the invitation, and I didn't want anyone to see us together and risk making the connection between him and his missing sister.

The carriage jostled, the engine purring and smooth. Drystan, Maske, and I wore smart dark suits with green silk cravats, a color often associated with the Snakewood monarchy. We'd, of course, brought our Glamours.

Cyan kept glancing out of the window. She wore an Eladan dress of dark blue damask with a sash of matching Temnian green silk at her waist. She hadn't painted her face with the swirling Alder designs as she often did when she played Madame Damselfly, but she'd painted the lids of her eyes in silver.

We reached the Palace gates. The building was made of granite and marble. Penglass domes peeked from the slated roofs and turrets. There were so many windows that I couldn't even hope to count them all.

Every day in the Penny Rookeries, I saw thin beggars holding out hands for coins. We gave them what coppers we could spare, but we knew it was never enough. Hungry children played in alleyways unsupervised, and others, not much older, worked in factories twelve hours a day. Yet here, in one room of the Palace, there would likely be furnishings worth enough gold to feed everyone in that neighborhood for over a year. The Foresters were entirely right on that front.

As the carriage waited by the imposing metal gates of the palace, I leaned out of the window and looked back at the ruins of the Celestial Square. They'd cleared away the rubble, but the broken foundations of the Cathedral were like a scar on the city's face. Flowers lined the edges in tribute to those who had been killed. There were nubs of extinguished candles, and notes written by the victims' family members and other sympathizers were tied to posts, fluttering in the wind. There was talk of Imachara erecting a memorial statue and rebuilding the Cathedral.

The guards looked at our official invitation and then spoke through a Vestige communicator to the palace. After a long pause, the main guard nodded and opened the metal gate, letting the carriage through.

Even then, it wasn't a case of simply walking into the Palace. We were led to an alcove and asked to empty our pockets. Thanks to a little mental push from Cyan, they didn't notice Anisa's Aleph in my pocket. They patted me down and I told them that the binding corset beneath my shirt was for a problem with my back.

After we'd been searched, we were led into another room and asked to wait while our gear was unloaded from the carriage and examined. None of us said much, too aware that the guards lingered nearby. Despite it all, though, I was looking forward to seeing Princess Nicolette and having my first peek inside the Royal Palace. Here was the heart of the power of Elada. We might learn something useful, but I also hoped we could bring a young girl a little magic.

Finally, guards led us to one of the salons to set up. The room, of course, put even the Elmbarks' house or any estate in the Emerald Bowl to shame. Soft glass globes, tinged pale pink and orange, lent the room a dreamy glow. The columns around the dance floor were purest white, but the floor was a pale rose-tinted marble, with smaller tiles of a deep amber stone marking out the design of the Twelve Trees of Nobility. A large, twining Snakewood tree was ringed with a circle, surrounded with different leaf shapes like the hours of a clock: Snakewood at the twelve o'clock spot, surrounded by Ash, Balsa, Cedar, Cyprus, Ebony, Elm, Hornbeam, Oak, Poplar, Redwood, and Walnut. I noticed Drystan drifted over to stand on the Hornbeam spot, lingering for a moment before stepping away.

One end of the room housed a stage, smaller but more ornate than the one at the Kymri Theatre. We'd gone inside the Kymri to see the repairs two days ago, and it'd been grim. Here, all was pristine. More glass globes were suspended over the polished stage like clusters of pale grapes. Servants were setting out chairs, and we oversaw the seating placement to ensure that no one would be at an angle that might spoil the illusions.

We were experimenting with magic lanterns, and I mapped out where I could set up the contraption while remaining hidden. The servants lingered and watched, becoming our rehearsal audience, though of course we kept some of our secrets for the night of the grand show. They applauded at the end. Hopefully, this meant word of Maske and his Marionettes would spread throughout the Palace, and perhaps even some of the other servants would come to the Kymri when we were back up and running.

Near the end, after we were packing up, I caught sight of Princess Nicolette peeking around the door. She was with her nurse. When the Princess met my eyes she smiled, recognizing me. I gave her a wink, and she blushed.

As she turned, I caught a flicker and a flush of warmth. It was as if feathers of light emerged from her skin, then re-settled and disappeared. It reminded me of the shimmer when Anisa took over my body, or the glitch of a Glamour low on power. Cyan paused from where she was organizing wires, her head turning toward the Princess. The nurse noticed the glimmer, her eyes widening. With a frightened look in our direction, she ushered her royal charge away.

I met Cyan's eyes, reeling. Drystan and Maske hadn't noticed.

But we hadn't imagined it. The Princess was Chimaera.

• • • •

Our Penny Rookeries apartments looked all the tawdrier after the palace. Later that evening, Cyan and I filled Drystan in. I held Anisa's Aleph in my hand, still shocked.

"What does this mean?" I asked, as we clustered in the lounge. Maske was, as usual, back in his tiny workshop.

"Was the Princess wearing a Glamour?" Drystan asked.

I shook my head. "It was more than that. I felt it. A warmth.

Though it was maybe . . . different? Like hot chocolate instead of coffee." I didn't know how else to explain it.

"Curious, curious," Drystan said. "Well, there's little enough we can do about it now, is there? But it explains why the Snakewood Palace let Violet in when she appeared at the gates. Maybe we'll notice something when we're back for the proper show next week."

I rubbed my temples. It'd been long enough since my last dose that my energy was fading. "You're right. All we can do is push forward and hope luck gives us a break."

We went to bed, but I wouldn't say luck found me.

● ● ● ●

Under the cover of night, Timur's broken body drew the cart to a stop not far from the Infirmary. He had coated himself in dirt and grime and hunched his back to hint at a life of poor nutrition.

"Wait here," he instructed his two Kashura. One nodded, wordlessly.

The Infirmary was quiet at this time of night. The nurse took one look at his ruined face and visibly startled, then tried to hide it. He knew what she saw. There was a hole in his cheek and open sores deep enough to hit bone. She would think it a bad infection, but none of the medicine in this building would help him.

The nurse led Timur to a bed. She went to check his wounds, and, with a mental push, the blurred man made her believe she had done so before encouraging her to sit on one of the chairs in the corner of the ward.

—Sleep, he thought at her. Sleep, young healers and wounded. You all need your rest. His energy ebbed drastically.

Her head fell to her chest, her body sliding sideways into dreamland.

Timur approached his target. The man had been injured in the Celestial Cathedral attack but was nearly fully healed. Timur lifted one of his eyelids, revealing the brown iris, the pupil contracting in the sudden light. Like his first target, this man was generically handsome and strong from his training.

Inching closer, Timur took a syringe of the poison from his pocket and pressed it into the man's vein.

Timur made sure his mask was in place before stealing a doctor's coat from the supply closet and wheeling his prize out of the hospital.

"Come," the blurred man whispered to his Kashura as they loaded the body into the cart. "We must be quick."

With luck, this second body and the job it had held would serve Timur's purposes far better.

● ● ● ●

I awoke with a gasp. Drystan lay curled into a ball away from me. I had to shake him several times before he finally stirred.

"What's the matter?" he asked, his voice blurred with sleep.

"I had another dream," I whispered.

He put his arms around me. "Lord and Lady, you're cold as ice."

I told him all I'd seen. Cyan didn't come to us this time, but I sensed she was awake in the other room, listening in on our conversation.

"He stole someone from the actual Infirmary? Do you think he's working with the doctor?"

"I don't know."

"Should we try to warn the Constabulary again?" Drystan asked.

I shrugged. "It hasn't seemed to do anything the last two times, has it? I suppose we have to hope that whatever he's trying to do, it doesn't work again."

—*Go back to sleep*, I urged Cyan and she drifted away.

I pressed closer to him. He was so leanly muscled that heat radiated from him like a furnace.

My lips pressed to the square of his jaw, the small hairs at the base of his neck tickling my cheek. I always turned to him after nightmares, and he was always there to comfort me. As if, after dreaming of death, I had to remember that I was alive. He pulled me closer, and our shirts rucked up, our bellies pressing against each other.

I sat up, drawing him up with me and pulling off his shirt, running my fingertips along the tips and grooves of his muscles. He pulled off my shirt. My right breast just fit into the palm of his hand. We shimmied out of the rest of our clothes, leaving them in a heap on the floor. I'd learned so much about his body, and he'd learned much of mine, but I always loved discovering something new that would make him gasp or buck against me.

I was still so cold, but I let him melt me.

15

THE LILY

"Once upon a time, a mother's child was stolen by a Chimaera.

The mother had only turned from her babe for a moment, and when she glanced back, a Siren had him in her slick, four-fingered front paws. The creature might be shaped somewhat like a woman, but she had no hair. Her skin was smooth as a salamander's and orange as a sunset. The bridge of her nose was speckled with black spots like freckles. The child was wrapped in a blanket, and the creature wasn't touching the baby's bare skin, which was lucky, for all know that Sirens have a poison touch.

"Give me back my child," the mother implored.

The creature only stuck out its sticky tongue in response, as if testing the air. "You let him cry and cry. I have not slept for weeks with his caterwauling."

The mother grabbed for the child, but the Siren darted out of the way, and within a blink, she and the babe were gone.

The mother told the village what had happened, and people set off into the swamp to slay the Siren and search for the babe. Eventually, they gave up.

Six months later, the mother was hunting in the swamp when she heard a baby's cry. She followed it, and to her shock, her child was still alive. There was no sign of the Siren. It would be easy to simply pick him up and take him home. He'd been small and sickly, but now he was a smiling boy with wispy dark curls and fat cheeks. The tops of his fingers had turned orange, but he was obviously cared for.

The woman bent down and almost kissed him on the forehead, but she didn't let her lips touch his bare skin, for fear her changed child might poison her. In the end, she headed back the way she came, alone

> *Some might call her cruel, to abandon her child. Others might say she'd simply recognized that he was no longer hers, and it was better to leave him somewhere he would be better loved."*
>
> "THE SIREN CALL OF A MOTHER," HESTIA'S FABLES

We finally caught Lily Verre leaving her building with her son the day before we were to return to the Snakewood Palace for the proper performance. We were meant to be practicing for the following day, but Maske was tinkering away with the props we'd be using at the Palace. He wouldn't notice we'd slipped out. He'd been so busy, he hadn't seen Lily since she'd shown up at our apartment, though I could tell he was just as besotted with her as ever.

A middle-aged man in a bowler hat emerged from the apartment building a few minutes after Lily left her building. She wouldn't return from Pinecrest's for at least an hour, so hopefully we'd find something useful in that time. Cyan trotted up to the man, cursing herself for forgetting her key *again* and using enough of her abilities for him not to question it. Drystan and I slipped in after her.

Halfway up the stairs, a wave of exhaustion overwhelmed me. I stumbled. The timing of our heist wasn't ideal: my appointment with the doctor for my next dose was coming up. I rubbed my burning eyes and forced my feet forward.

Drystan took out his lock picks and set to work. As before, we turned on the Eclipse we'd briefly borrowed from Maske, since we weren't sure if Lily had a Banshee alarm. Better safe than sorry.

Drystan sighed in satisfaction when the lock opened with a little *snick*. The door swung inward. We crept inside, closing the door softly behind us. The haze of exhaustion was so thick I felt like I was moving through mud.

The apartment was dim inside, the sun through the window blocked by other tenements. Yet even though my powers were at their weakest, I thought I felt something in one of the other rooms. I sensed Cyan's echoing alarm as Drystan brightened one of the glass globes. I only had time to take in a nice, comfortable lounge before we froze.

Lily Verre sat on one of the two red leather sofas, legs crossed.

"Hello, you three," she said calmly, her voice edged in steel, with no trace of the flighty widow. "How kind of you to come calling."

• • • •

Lily arched an eyebrow and lifted her chin. "Sit down," she ordered.

Unsure what else to do, we obeyed, perching across from her on the opposite sofa. How had she gotten herself and her son back into the building without us noticing? That faint warmth must mean he was in the other room.

The apartment was filled with good-quality furnishings, but it wasn't as ostentatious as Shadow Elwood's place. My damp palms slipped on the leather of the sofa. Paintings of generic landscapes of rolling hills dotted with cows and sheep lined one wall. There was an empty desk of dark wood. A bookshelf lined another wall, but I couldn't read the peeling gilt titles. Nothing particularly personal that gave away anything about who she truly was.

Lily Verre spread her hands wide. "What now, my doves? You know what I am. I know that you know. Indeed, there's much knowing of things now." She smiled as if this was all terribly amusing, but I sensed the anger beneath.

"There's a damn sight more to discover, I reckon," Drystan said, and she shot him a look.

"When did you realize that we'd caught on?" I asked, my mouth dry.

"At first, I thought it was the time you followed me to the Royal Infirmary with my son. But it wasn't, was it? It took you until the café, just before you fell ill."

I went cold that she'd seemingly known every time we'd followed her. Had Pinecrest told her of my illness? "I didn't see your face, that first time."

"Ah yes. Always a good idea to step out with a good hood or brimmed hat. It's dramatic, fashionable, and helpful. Though I do like an eye-catching color now and again. Bad habit."

She smiled briefly before pressing her fingers to her lips, considering us. "I wondered if you'd accuse me then, give up the game, but you didn't. Found that curious. You've been watching me. Didn't take much to deduce that you'd try to sneak in when you thought I was otherwise occupied. Would have been useless, even if I wasn't here. There's nothing to find."

"What have you told Pinecrest about us?" I tried next.

Her eyes darted away, but not before I saw the flash of regret. "More than you'd like."

Drystan narrowed his eyes.

"Your son is here," I said, turning my head toward his door.

"Indeed he is." The hardness was back.

"How old is he?" Cyan asked, trying to soften her, a little.

"Seven," Lily relented. "Everything I do is for him."

"You used Maske to get closer to us," I said.

"Initially, yes. But he's a sweet man, and cares for me. And I for him. That's not a falsehood."

"He cares for the person you pretend to be around him," Drystan clarified.

Lily Verre flinched and changed the subject. "My son nearly died two years ago when he started to . . . change more dramatically."

When I'd seen him on the street, I'd only caught the briefest flash of scales green as beetle wings. His too-small, too-flat nose. Small horns poking from his skull and hidden by a scarf.

"He's Chimaera," I said. "In a different way to us. A Theri Chimaera instead of Anthi."

She nodded.

"But you're not Chimaera at all," Cyan said.

Her lips thinned. "Indeed, I'm not. When he grew sick, I went to the Royal Physician. I'd heard rumors that he'd studied birth anomalies on his sabbatical abroad. I thought Frey would die, but Pinecrest was able to save him. I was in his debt, and in return, he asked me for a few favors."

"You can't expect us to believe you're a recently turned Shadow," Drystan said, lifting an eyebrow. "You're better than Elwood."

At his name, her lip curled. "Indeed, I was a Shadow long before I ever met Pinecrest. And Elwood, well, I can't say I'm particularly sorry to see the end of him. He stole plenty of cases from me over the years and charged outrageously for shoddy work. I do know it was your doing that put him behind bars."

It was my turn to flinch.

"I've never heard of a female Shadow," Cyan said. Neither had I. And judging by Lily Verre's true accent, if this was it, she had been born to nobility or rich merchants. How had she become one?

"You wouldn't have heard of me under this name," she said. "I dressed as a man for years. You might recognize my old name." She paused. "Shadow Alban Verani."

My mouth fell open. Alban Verani had been one of the best Shadows in Elada, involved in high profile cases the Constabulary couldn't always solve. He'd been quite the mystery—no one knew where he had come from or much about him. He'd supposedly died years ago, though there were various theories: that he'd been murdered by the Eel of Imachara, the head of the illicit Lerium trade in the capital, or he'd made enough to retire from life as a Shadow. My brother had been the one to tell me of Verani's escapades when we were children. There'd even been a few penny novels written about some of his cases.

"You disguised yourself as a man?" I asked.

"Not exactly. I was raised as one."

She gave us a second to take that in before continuing. "Soon enough, though, I realized that wasn't correct. I might not have been born physically female, but I am a woman. It took me many years to admit it and let that side of me flourish. I continued dressing as a man because working as a Shadow was easier and safer in trousers, especially with some of the cases I took on."

Her face closed. "I tried so hard to make it all fit. I married a woman when we were both quite young. She guessed the truth soon enough, and when I told her, she not only accepted but celebrated it. Even found a doctor who was able to treat me and bring my body more in line with my mind." Lily trailed off, her face creasing in grief.

My mouth opened, then closed again. I'd heard of people who transitioned from one gender to another, but as far as I knew, I'd never met anyone else who'd done it.

"You didn't lie about being a widow, though, did you?" Cyan said, her voice soft with sympathy.

Lily shook her head. "I didn't, but the husband who left me riches was the falsehood. Andrea had a complicated birth. Our son was born with a caul over his face. They managed to save Frey, but not her." Her eyes clouded.

She bowed her head, gathering herself. After a minute, she continued. "If my son had died, I wouldn't have lasted the night. Yet he survived, I brought him home, and I carried on. He was tiny, but his cry was fierce. Around where the umbilical cord was cut, there was a cluster of small scales. Later, they fell off, but I kept them in a box."

She stared into the distance. "After my wife's death, I let Alban Verani die, too. My last case nearly killed me, and that was the sign to finally leave him behind and take cases where wearing skirts made more sense. They didn't pay as well, but I couldn't take the same risks."

"Verani isn't a noble name," Drystan said. "But your accent is nearly as posh as mine."

"I'm from standard merchant stock. Father was a cooper. I taught myself this accent a long time ago because of the doors it could open, and it comes naturally enough to me now." She let bits of the common accent break through as she spoke. My mother had scrubbed away her own working-class accent, too.

"I worked my cases," Lily continued. "Years passed. Frey grew, but his muscles remained weak. He was never able to walk, but he was otherwise healthy. I created my new life, and here I am."

"Is your name truly Lily Verre now?" I asked.

"Indeed it is," she said, and smiled faintly at our surprise. She shrugged. "Seemed easier to keep close to the truth, and I thought this would be a simple, temporary job like all the others. Turned out to be anything but."

We took that in.

Lily steepled her hands. "So now we come to the next stage: bargaining."

"We want you to stop reporting to him about us," I said.

She clicked her tongue against the roof of her mouth. "Not that simple, I'm afraid. I have to give him at least a little something every time I bring Frey for his medication."

"Frey needs regular treatments from Pinecrest?" I asked, my voice growing dry.

"Once a week, just like you. After the first dose, the seizures stopped. Pinecrest told me the medicine would slow the changes and keep him far healthier than he would be otherwise."

Something about the set of her shoulders made me think she wasn't telling me the whole truth. Cyan was solemn, but she fiddled with one of the ceramic beads in her hair. Drystan's eyes bounced between us.

"What do you know about the medicine?" I asked, rubbing the injection spot in the inner crook of my elbow.

"That it's part-Vestige, part-Lerium—which no, I do not like—and perhaps other ingredients. I know there's no way to get it anywhere else."

"You know more than that," Cyan said with certainty, echoing my own misgivings. "You've put something together. You started shadowing him, haven't you?"

Lily only stared at us.

"Is Pinecrest behind the Celestial Cathedral explosion and the attack on the Museum of Mechanical Antiquities?" I asked.

That shocked her into a sharp laugh. "Oh my, no, I don't believe he has a thing to do with that." Her gaze sharpened. "Why, do you?"

"You share, we share," I said.

Her eyes flashed. "You're learning. But yes, you're right not to trust Pinecrest. Whatever you've discovered or suspect, I still don't think you know what sort of man he truly is."

The skin of my face tightened at that.

Lily Verre rolled her neck. "For months, Doctor Pinecrest dosed Frey without asking for a copper in return. He lured me into a sense of complacency before he started asking me to take occasional cases for him, even though I was sure that was his goal all along."

She paused, swallowing. I sensed that for someone who traded in secrets, spilling them willingly was no mean feat. "They were always the same: tailing a subject and reporting my findings. They were usually children. It didn't take me long to realize that they were all patients that the Physician was dosing, just like Frey. And they were all... different."

"Chimaera," Cyan said.

Lily inclined her head. "Six months or so ago, though, my curiosity got the better of me, but I only put the pieces together recently. My investigation led me to a medical office in Imachara that specialized in prenatal and neonatal care. Every subject he asked me to follow had been treated there."

She raised her head and stared at us, her gaze a challenge. "Can you guess what I'll say next?"

"It was the same practice that your wife went to when she was pregnant with your son," I said.

Drystan stifled a gasp.

She nodded, slowly. "And there it is. Pinecrest wasn't the Royal Physician back when he started it, but he still owned the practice. Pinecrest himself was abroad at the time, so he didn't treat her directly, but..." Lily trailed off.

"But you think his practice might have done something to her," Cyan finished.

Lily inhaled shakily. "Yes. I can't prove it, but I believe that Pinecrest did something to Frey in the womb. Might not have caused his physical disabilities, I don't think, as something similar ran in my wife's family. But I do believe if Andrea had never gone to that practice, my son wouldn't have sprouted horns or scales. Perhaps that medicine slowed his initial symptoms, but now I suspect Pinecrest is instead speeding up the development of my son's abilities."

She met my eyes. "And he's almost certainly doing the exact same thing to you."

16

THE HORNED BOY

"It has been three months since my son, Brian Archer, went missing. I know what the Constabulary is implying: he was last seen standing on the shore of the beach, and many think he let the waves carry him away. But I know my son, and I don't think that's what happened.

My son is different. A few years ago, he sprouted short antlers, fuzzed as a new buck's, and his skin went dappled as a fawn's. After the Celestial Cathedral, we warned him to be careful: to always wear a hat to hide the antlers, to explain away the dapples as freckles. We knew people might hurt him. I think someone either took or killed him.

Every day, I pray that he'll be found safe. Every day with no news, the hope dims a little more. Please, I beg you, if anyone has seen a man who matches the sketch included with this article, help us find some answers."

EDITORIAL LETTER BY ROBERT ARCHER, THE DAILY IMACHARAN

Lily Verre nodded at our obvious horror.

"But . . ." I began. "I thought Chimaera were returning to the world naturally." That's what Anisa had implied.

"Perhaps some are," she said. "But I believe in my bones that Doctor Pinecrest somehow *made* Frey into a Chimaera."

"He told me someone left me outside his offices as a babe." My hands were shaking. What I wouldn't give to speak to Anisa properly just now, but she'd been dead silent for weeks, and I was afraid to use up another call. I was so exhausted that my nerves were frayed to tassels. "Perhaps my birth parents realized what he'd done and gave me back." My chest ached.

Drystan leaned against my shoulder as Lily's forehead wrinkled in sympathy. "The Royal Physician is experimenting on you, my son, and dozens of others, both here and on the other islands. I don't know why, for how long, or to what purpose."

My words dried in my throat.

"My mother . . ." Cyan began. "My mother was in Imachara for part of her pregnancy, and I know it wasn't an easy one. She could barely keep down water until she went to a doctor for treatment." She crossed her arms over her stomach and sat down on one of Lily's armchairs.

I didn't know what to say. Neither did Cyan. Even Drystan was struck silent. Why would Pinecrest do this? He was clearly not afraid of Chimaera, like Timur and his ilk. But to create and bring them back? Cyan was nearing twenty. Had Pinecrest been doing it that long?

"This is why you can trust me," Lily said, her voice shaking with emotion. "I'll never know if his actions resulted in Andrea dying in childbirth. Help me save my child from his influence, and I'll help you take him down. I'll delight in it."

Even though she'd proved herself a talented actress since we'd met her, I believed her.

Her gaze sharpened. "Now: your turn. Who do you believe is behind the attacks?"

The three of us exchanged a look. Cyan gave a subtle nod.

"Timur," I said.

"The Forester?" A line appeared between her brows.

I shook my head. "Not anymore. He left and took a few sympathetic people with him. They call themselves the Kashura."

I waited, but she didn't seem to recognize the word.

"And why are they attacking the city?" she asked.

"We don't know, exactly, but we do know that Timur hates Chimaera, and his goal is to destroy them."

Lily's mouth opened. Her eyes darted to her son's door, then focused back on me. "You've been wondering if Pinecrest was working for him."

"Yes," I said. "But if Timur hates Chimaera, and Pinecrest is the one creating them, then that wouldn't make much sense."

She exhaled. "A puzzle indeed."

"Mum!" came the faint call from the other room.

Our heads turned.

Lily smiled, faintly. "I suppose you may as well come and meet him properly." She went to the bedroom and opened the door. We followed her. In contrast to the lounge, the bedroom was cheery and colorful. I took in a bookshelf, plenty of toys, and framed childish artwork before I focused on the boy in the wicker chair next to a table, his scaled fingers holding a crayon.

Frey's flaking skin was gone, leaving him almost entirely scaled. His eyes turned to us. They were a luminous green in the dim light of the lounge. Even with my powers at their weakest, I felt his magic coming off him in waves.

"Hello, sweet," Lily said, her voice softening.

"Mum," Frey said. His voice was soft but sounded almost as if it had a built-in echo.

Like Anisa.

"I've finished," he said, proudly holding out his paper. Lily took it from him as if it were a precious illuminated manuscript. He'd copied one of the stories of *Hestia's Fables* about a salamander who stole a human child. Lily praised the illustrations he'd done in the corners. The handwriting and drawings were both better than I could have managed at his age.

Frey looked at us, wary but not afraid. "You two are warm." He pointed to Cyan and me. "You're cool," he said to Drystan, who shifted his shoulders uncomfortably.

"Frey, manners," Lily said. "This is Micah, Cyan, and Drystan. They might come around now and again. You needn't be frightened."

"I'm not," he said, but one hand went to his cheek, and he turned from us as though ashamed. How many strangers had he ever come across without being heavily veiled?

"Can I have more paper?" he asked.

Lily passed him a few more sheets. He picked up his crayon and bent over one, as though we weren't there. Lily rested her hand on his shoulder and kissed the top of his head. He didn't respond, but as we left the lounge, he looked up at us. I gave him a smile. One corner of his mouth quirked before he went back to his paper.

"He's shy," Lily said once we were back in the lounge. "You're the first new people he's met in quite some time. It's easier to keep him hidden. I have a Glamour, but it only lasts an hour and I'm not sure how much power it has left, so it makes even going to the park difficult."

"Are you his sole caretaker?" I asked.

"I have someone help me now and again."

"Who?" I asked.

She went cagey. "Not someone I trust, exactly, though he's good with Frey."

"Who?" I pressed again.

She met my eyes. "Kai Molleson. Pinecrest's assistant."

I exhaled, hard. "That way he can keep tabs on you both between doses?"

Lily inclined her head. "So he thinks, aye."

"Frey's powers are very strong," I said.

Lily nodded. "And only growing."

"What can he do?" Cyan asked.

"Telepathy," she said, with a nod at Cyan. "Telekinesis. The weather sometimes seems to echo his moods." Her features were pinched tight.

"Does he ever lose control?" I asked, thinking of Ahti.

"His abilities spike, sometimes, but he brings it all back when I ask." Her gaze was sharp. "Why?"

I wasn't willing to tell her about Anisa and her visions of the past. I didn't want to tell her that her son looked the spitting image of a Chimaera that had destroyed the world hundreds of years ago. But after seeing Frey properly, foreboding welled up in me. We'd been drawn to this boy for a reason. I felt it as certainly as if the spirits had whispered in my ears. If Timur hated Chimaera and knew enough of the past to know the name Kashura, then he'd likely be afraid of this one in particular.

"I've struggled to control my powers," I replied instead, which wasn't a lie. "I've learned some tips and ways to have a better handle on them. I could teach him the little bit I know, perhaps."

Her eyes shone. "Please."

We went back into the room. Frey glanced up at us, setting his crayon aside.

"Your mum has asked me to teach you a few tricks to control your powers. Would you like that?" I asked.

He shrugged. "Sure."

"All right, Frey. Close your eyes," I said.

He did as he was bid, showing the delicate scaling on the backs of his eyelids. I walked him through clearing his mind. He had trouble settling down, but when he did, the power that still sizzled around him calmed, as if settling deeper into his body.

"Yes," I said. "Yes. Whenever you are frightened or feel the energy escaping, come to this place. Block everything out. Right here, right now, you are safe. If the power ever feels like it's too much, imagine swallowing a star. You can bring it back into yourself."

"You sound like the dragonfly lady from my dreams," he said. I felt Cyan and Drystan stiffen behind me.

"Oh?" I said, lightly. "I've always liked dragonflies."

"She looks like a princess," he said, fiddling with a crayon. "With great dragonfly wings. She's nice. Haven't had that dream for a while, though." He looked sad.

I forced myself to reveal nothing.

"Carry on with your drawing, darling," Lily said. "Need to have a few more words with our friends here. But you did brilliantly, sweet."

Frey bent over his drawing again, making the Siren's skin an even more vibrant orange.

As we walked back to the main living room, I reached out tentatively to Cyan and Drystan, shielding my thoughts as best I could. —*What do you think?*

Cyan's lips thinned. —*Honestly? Everything she has said and shown us seems true, but it's hard to know whether she's being entirely truthful.*

Drystan nodded in agreement. He could hear us, but he couldn't speak back telepathically.

—*Do you think Anisa has visited him in dreams?* I asked.

—*Makes sense. She visited us, after all.*

Lily's eyes narrowed, correctly suspecting we were having a private conversation right in front of her.

Cyan held her hands out to Lily. "You've told us a lot, and we want to believe you. You know that there's an easy way to prove that you're telling us the truth. Cease that endless chatter and let me in."

Lily recoiled.

"Just for a moment," Cyan said. "I promise I won't go rummaging for anything you don't want to give me. But I'll be able to taste whether you're lying or not better than any Augur. We can't risk it."

After a long hesitation, Lily Verre rose, holding out her palms. Cyan took one hand, and I hesitated before grabbing the other. Drystan watched, knowing he wouldn't be able to follow.

Cyan's eyes rolled up into her skull until only the whites showed. For a moment, they glowed the bright blue of Penglass, and then her head slumped forward and images flowed through us.

• • • •

I lay in bed, one hand splayed over my wife's rounded belly. Andrea looked at me with half-lidded eyes. She had a heart-shaped face and strawberry curls.

"I can feel him kicking," I whispered in awe.

"He wants to meet you, Lily," Andrea said, closing her eyes and smiling softly.

A flash and I stood in a hospital room. Shouts surrounded me. Spots of red blood against white tile.

Hours later, I sat next to the bed, holding my son in one hand and my wife's cooling hand in the other.

I skipped through years, waking up to the sound of choking. Frey was having a fit. Fear spiked through me. A blink, and before me was the familiar sight of Doctor Pinecrest prepping a syringe. He gently pressed it to Frey's skin.

• • • •

Cyan pulled us back to the room. Lily's muscles were stiff, her shoulders hunched. She shook her muscles, relaxing when she realized we were no longer in her head. Drystan had watched it all, his lips pinched.

"All right," I spoke for the group. "We believe you."

"Good," she said, the word clipped.

Drystan's expression was clouded, and I suspected he wished Cyan had broken her promise and gone deeper. She had learned how to shield herself with a chatter of thoughts—could she have learned to press forward only the images she wanted to share? But I, too, sensed Lily was telling the truth. Most of it, anyway.

"What now?" I asked.

Lily smiled and leaned forward. "Oh, my sweet dears," she said in the affected voice she'd used when we first met her, before returning to her true cadence. "I thought you'd never ask. I'd like you to steal a measure of Pinecrest's medicine for me, if you please."

I opened my mouth to say we already had some from Shadow Elwood's apartments, but Drystan elbowed me sharply in the ribs, and my jaw snapped shut.

"I don't leave Frey alone with the doctor, so there's never been an opportunity. But Drystan, you go with Micah sometimes, yes? I bet you could spirit some away with those clever fingers."

She smiled sweetly at Drystan's sour expression. "I have a friend I trust who could analyze it. If I can identify the ingredients and find a way to recreate the formula, then we could break our dependence on Pinecrest and wean both you and Frey off of it," she said.

"No promises," I said, heading off Drystan's bristling. "But we'll consider it."

No need to tell her just yet that we already likely had a sample we'd stolen from her rival. Had Elwood lifted those vials, or had Pinecrest shared them willingly? We'd likely know.

There was a last secret I was curious enough about that I was willing to spill. "Did you know that the Princess is Chimaera?" I asked.

I'd surprised her for the second time. "What?"

"I sensed it when we were practicing at the Palace."

She whistled. "Then that means . . ."

"Yeah," I said. "If your suspicion is right, then there's a chance Pinecrest might have even experimented on the royal line itself."

"He wasn't the Royal Physician when the Queen was pregnant," Lily said. "He was abroad. But I suppose that might not have stopped him, or it means the previous Royal Physician was in on it, too." Her expression hardened.

"How can you stand it?" I asked Lily. "How can you look at him and be civil, knowing what he might have done to your son?"

"I honestly don't know," she said. "Sometimes I fear I'll snap and murder him for what he's done to my life and so many others. Like you, I have no choice for now, save to keep him close while I figure out what he's up to. Discover his weaknesses. And then take him down."

She looked at us. "I am truly sorry for lying to you and pretending to be someone I'm not. I know it'll take a lot for you to forgive that, if you ever can, but you do have an ally in me. You always have." Another pause. "I do ask that you not tell Maske what we discussed today."

"Does he know . . . about you?" I asked, unsure how to phrase the question.

One of her eyebrows twitched. "He knows parts of my past, but not that I'm a Shadow, that I have Frey, or that I know Pinecrest. I want to find a way to tell him the rest on my own terms. I didn't expect to find him, and I feel lucky to have him in my life. He doesn't deserve my lies. I know that."

"We won't say anything yet," Cyan said. "But I suggest you tell him sooner rather than later."

"I'll try." She stared into the distance for a minute, then tapped her lip. "Do you still have Elwood's Mirror of Moirai?" she asked.

I blinked. "Yes, though we haven't done anything with it."

She went to a cabinet and took out her own Vestige Mirror she'd secretly gotten me to touch at Twisting the Aces. The ugly frame was missing. "We can communicate through them, if we need to." She turned it on and walked us through how to do it. It wasn't only a map. Perhaps this was how Chimaera had communicated across great distances in the past. I'd seen portals in Anisa's visions. Vestige could do so much more than we'd ever imagined.

"Use it in case of an emergency," she said. "And I'll do the same."

I nodded, cautiously. "All right."

She led us to the door. "Thank you for trusting me today," she said.

As we made our way back to the Kymri Theatre, I kept thinking of Frey. No matter how bright and cheery that bedroom was, he was still a child locked away from the world, just like the Princess. Both Chimaera. And linking the two was Doctor Pinecrest.

17

THE HOSPITAL

"It's common practice for children to 'call upon the fairies' to help heal an injured friend. They will circle the injured party thrice, chanting 'sprites, take flight, we need your might to spite the blight!' Sometimes, a young one might kiss them on the forehead; a target for the fairy to know where to sprinkle their magic dust."

**A HISTORY OF ELADA AND ITS FORMER COLONIES,
PROFESSOR CAED CEDAR, ROYAL SNAKEWOOD UNIVERSITY**

Cyril was late. We were meant to meet at his favorite café by the university for lunch. I tapped my fingertips on the table, impatient. We didn't have long—I had to head back for magic practice by half past two.

With all the other students around us, it was strange to feel like one of them. I blinked in surprise when none other than Kai Molleson slipped into the empty seat across from me.

"Hello, Micah," he said, cheerfully. "Or would you rather I call you Anna?" His brown eyes were bright, his dark curls stuck up at the back, and he wore a thick woolen sweater despite the sunny day. His cheeks were flushed, warmth rising from him. He fiddled with a napkin, twisting it in his hands.

"Micah, please," I said, cautiously. I glanced at the door, but my brother hadn't arrived yet. "You're not here by accident, I suspect."

His eyebrows rose. "The doctor's right. You are suspicious."

That likely answered whether it'd been Pinecrest or Lily who had sent him. "Did you tell the good Doctor you'd met me before?"

"Nah," he said. "Not yet, at least."

"What do you want, Kai?" I didn't appreciate the threat.

He looked a little hurt at that. "I'm making an overture of friendship. I liked you, that day we met, and now I'm realizing maybe I was drawn to you because we have quite a lot in common." He opened his mouth to say something else, but my brother, of course, chose that exact moment to arrive.

"Sorry," my brother began, looking between us uncertainly. "Am I interrupting?"

"I was just leaving," Kai said, rising smoothly.

"Kai Molleson here is a medical student at the university," I said. Having etiquette lessons drilled into me meant I couldn't forget my manners. "This is Cyril Laurus, a . . . friend. He's just started studying law."

"Pleasure to meet you," Cyril said, shaking his hand. "How do you know Micah here?"

Too curious by half, my brother. "He, um, helped me out with a query a few months ago," I answered for him.

"Was happy to," Kai smiled at Cyril then made a show of checking his watch. "I'm so sorry, I'm late for an anatomy lecture. I'm sure our paths will cross again, Micah."

"Indeed, I don't think there's a way of avoiding it." My smile was tight.

Kai shot me a last look, gave a little bow to my brother, and left the café. I'd no doubt Doctor Pinecrest would know I'd visited Cyril by teatime.

"What's going on there?" my brother asked.

I hesitated. "Long story."

He narrowed his eyes. "Tell me."

We ordered of cream of mushroom soup and rarebit. The café was loud enough with student chatter that we shouldn't be easily overheard. I was still wary, but I had to tell him something.

"I first met Kai when I was trying to find out if Aenea, my partner on the trapeze, survived what happened our last night in the circus. I was getting nowhere, but he managed to charm the receptionist for me. Don't think he knew who I was, but our paths crossed again more recently . . . when I went to the university morgue."

"And you did that . . . why?" he asked.

"Doctor Pinecrest invited me."

His smile fell so quickly, I half-expected to hear it splat on the floor beneath the table. "The Royal Physician?"

Our soup arrived. I took a massive bite, and it nearly scalded my tongue. I took a gulp of water.

"There are a few things to catch you up on, I think," I said when I could speak again. My tongue hurt. I shuffled my chair a little closer and lowered my voice. "It hadn't felt right after . . . everything. I didn't wish to worry you."

"So, tell me now."

"I'm different," I began.

Cyril frowned. "Yes, I know."

"I don't just mean my anatomy. I was never sick growing up. Rarely hurt myself, and if I did, I healed quickly."

He nodded, slowly. "Yes."

—*It's even more than that.*

It took him a moment before he realized I hadn't moved my mouth. "Gene?" he asked, accidentally slipping back to my old nickname in his shock.

—*Please. This is hard. Let me get it all out. It's easier this way. No one else will overhear.*

He swallowed, his eyes still wide. "All right."

Our rarebit arrived, and we paused until the waiter drifted away.

I let loose more of my secrets. Cyril already knew most of what had happened in the circus and the duel with Maske, but I filled in the gaps I'd neglected. I told him of Anisa the Phantom Damselfly, her visions of the past, Chimaera, my illness and subsequent weekly visits with Doctor Pinecrest. I told him about Shadow Elwood and Lily. Of the blurred man and dreams of stolen corpses. All without ever uttering a word aloud. We must have made quite the pair, Cyril staring at me with no little fear, me gazing back at him, our food cooling between us.

I didn't share that Cyan was like me, as I figured it wasn't my secret to tell. But I finally laid the rest of it down and hoped it wouldn't scare him away.

"And there you go," I said aloud, weakly. I picked up my spoon and poked at my soup.

"This . . . is a lot to take in," Cyril said.

I nodded.

"It's hard to know where to start."

"Take your time."

Cyril's head was bent, and I stared at his crown of curly blond hair. Outside, people walked along the pavement, jackets unbuttoned in the warm weather, some of the women using parasols. My brother worried his big hands in his lap.

The waiter came over, not so subtly asking if we wanted anything else. The place was busy, and we were hogging the table. I shoved the last of my cheesy toast in my mouth, chewing vigorously as Cyril dug in his pockets for coins.

"I don't know how you've dealt with all of this," he said once we were outside in the sun.

My eyes filled with tears. I'd just told him impossible things, and despite everything, his first thought was how difficult it must have been for me.

"You're the best brother," I managed.

He gave a strangled laugh and held out his arms. I went to them without hesitation. Cyril gave such wonderful hugs. Firm, warm, and safe.

When he pulled away, Cyril shook his head. "What does it mean, though? How many of you are there?"

"We don't know. Sometimes I can sense them, but there must be so many more out there, who can do all sorts of things."

He grew still, eyes widening.

"What is it?" I asked, dread moving through me.

"You can speak mind to mind. Does that mean you read thoughts?"

"Not very well. Sometimes I can catch snatches of things."

"You should come with me to the hospital. To see if you could reach Mother and wake her up."

My mouth opened. Closed. The thought honestly hadn't even occurred to me. The day of the explosion, seeing her had been enough of a shock, and I'd locked away thoughts of her as much as possible.

Cyril looked at the clock. "We still have time before visiting hours are over." He grabbed my hand. "Surely it's worth a go."

I didn't want to see her. That one glimpse of her in her sickbed had been more than enough.

"Please, Micah," he said. "Please."

"All right," I said. "But let's stop by home, first. I should bring someone with me."

• • • •

The nurse, a round woman with a wide mouth and dark eyes, showed Cyril, Cyan, and I to the right ward before hurrying off to her next patient. The beds were still full of people recovering from the Cathedral and Museum attacks, but our corner was quiet. I reached up and pulled the privacy curtain around the bed with no small amount of trepidation.

My mother looked exactly as she had the last time I saw her. Shrunken. Subdued. I didn't sense anything from her. My brother hadn't asked questions when I'd fetched Cyan, but he'd already guessed why I'd brought her.

We clustered around the bed. Cyril pushed an errant strand of our mother's hair back from her face. He'd never dare do something like that if she were awake.

"Has Father been up to visit?" I asked.

Cyril's head bowed. "Just once, right after it happened. He keeps saying he'll come up more often but . . . well, you know how Father is."

Yes. Father was never there. Not even for his wife.

My fingers fidgeted, and then I steeled myself and took her hand. Her skin was papery and cool to the touch. The rosacea on her cheeks had calmed.

Cyril's hope was painted starkly on his face. I quested with my newfound abilities. It was like she was in the deepest sleep, or her mind was encased in Penglass. I could only slip off the sides. Letting go, I shook my head.

Cyan tried next. She took my mother's hand and closed her eyes, becoming still as stone. I sensed her reaching. A tiny line appeared between her eyes. The minutes ticked past. Cyril and I didn't speak for fear of breaking her concentration. Sweat appeared on Cyan's brow.

Eventually, she broke away, her eyes opening, gasping as if coming up for air. Her eyes glowed blue. Cyril couldn't stifle his gasp.

"Sorry," she said, shaking her head. "I thought I was close at one point, but she's in too deep. I couldn't reach her." She collapsed against the chair. "I'm sorry," she said again, her skin grey with exhaustion.

"Try again, Micah," Cyril urged. "Once more. Just in case."

I closed my eyes, even though I thought if Cyan couldn't do it that I had no chance. I came across that barrier again, smooth and hard. I smashed against it, but it was like I'd hit impenetrable glass. I stopped. My energy ebbed, and a headache pounded at my temples.

I thought of Cyan pushing her thoughts through that Shroud barrier by the Cathedral. I decided to stop trying so hard, and before I knew it, I'd melted into and *through* the mental block.

It was as though I floated in a void, darkness cut through with threads of blue, like Penglass. Up ahead was a shadowy figure: my mother, wearing her most fashionable dress, with her corset tight, her best bustle, those white gloves, and her favorite parasol. She meandered through the darkness as though strolling through the park on a summer's day.

—*Mother!* I called out.

She paused, then kept walking.

—*Mother!* I called again.

She turned toward me, her face blurred by blue light. She raised a hand, but hesitantly.

The blue light swirled, brighter and stranger. I blinked and my mother was gone. I was back on the outside of whatever barrier lay around her mind.

Cyril was above me, strands of blond hair falling into his eyes.

"I'm on the ground," I said, dazed.

"You fell off your chair," Cyan said, her worried face appearing next to my brother's.

My shoulder hurt. Cyril helped me back to my seat. "Anything?"

"Sort of." I told them both what had happened, keeping my voice low.

Cyan tried one last time, but after a few minutes, she came back, swaying slightly. "I couldn't get past the barrier."

"Have you ever come across anything like that before?" I asked her.

"Never."

Cyril slumped in defeat. "I knew it was a small chance," he said. "But I couldn't help but hope..."

Cyan gave us a sympathetic look.

—*If she's in that deep...* she began.

—*I know.*

My mother might never wake up.

18

THE SNAKEWOOD PALACE

> "The summer fete at the Snakewood Palace was one of the most incredible nights of my life, Tara. I wish you could have been there to see it, too. The food, the glass globes, the music, the magicians, and the gowns! It made our debutante ball at Sicion's ballroom positively pale in comparison. I still can't believe my luck. When no one offered for me after my first season, I thought I was doomed to spinsterhood. Now that I'm lady's maid to my cousin, perhaps here at court I'll find myself a husband after all."
>
> **LETTER FROM LADY WINIFRED POPLAR TO LADY TARA HAWTHORNE**

From the outside, you'd never have guessed a royal party would be underway that night.

I'd passed the Palace before during a night of celebration. Lights had glowed from every window, with music drifting down onto the streets, and more lights speckled through the trees of the grand promenade. But now, under the threat of attacks, all was seemingly quiet. The guest list was kept small and everyone subjected to the same rigorous security. We arrived early to set up before the guests arrived. Despite my nerves, I was excited. We had a strong act, an audience at the Royal Palace itself, and each other.

Doctor Pinecrest was one of the first guests to arrive. He was perfectly groomed, as usual. I'd seen him two days ago for my dose, and while it'd been difficult to shore up the fortifications of my mind, I couldn't risk him catching even the smallest stray thought. I wished I knew how to tear down his walls, unwind every secret coiled in his brain, and finally get to the bottom of this. Not even Cyan was brave enough to go digging around in his skull just yet, though.

"I'm looking forward to your performance," Pinecrest said to me. "I'm sure it'll be as fantastic as all the rest."

I hoped my smile didn't look as strained as it felt and told him we needed to finish setting up.

"Of course, of course. Break a bone, as they say."

I left him with relief. From behind the curtains, Drystan, Cyan, and I peeked out as several members of Elada's social elite entered the ballroom, sipping wine, nibbling food plucked from silver trays held by palace servants, and murmuring softly among themselves. I recognized a few of them. Lord Wesley Cinnabari, who had been at a séance we'd performed for the Lord and Lady Elmbark on the Night of the Dead near midwinter.

There was Lady Winifred Poplar—we'd been presented at our debutante ball together an age ago. She'd done well to have a position at court in the capital instead of still being in Sicion. There were a few younger girls I didn't recognize, around the Princess's age. In the middle of them was the Princess Royal herself, wearing a pink gown sparkling with crystals, her security guards never far away. She seemed subdued, quiet, barely speaking to anyone else. Her uncle, the Steward, dressed in a fine suit with the grand ribbon of his station across his chest, laughed and greeted guests. His grey hair caught the light, and he'd perhaps lost weight since we saw him at the duel. Was he stressed from the attacks?

Drystan suddenly stiffened.

"Fuck. I didn't think they'd be here," he whispered.

I followed the direction of his gaze and stifled my own gasp: it was none other than Lord Nigel Hornbeam. Drystan's father's features were so closely echoed in his son that it was like having a glimpse of him in the future—pale hair and eyes, strong jawline. Next to him was Damien Hornbeam, Drystan's younger brother.

"Are you all right?" I asked, resting my hand on his shoulder. "Do you want to sit this one out?" Even as I asked, my mind scrambled for an alternate show plan. We could do it without Drystan, but it would be far trickier.

"No," Drystan said, touching both the Glamour around his neck and the green velvet mask he'd wear over his eyes for reassurance. "I'm not all right, but he won't recognize me with all this. He'd never expect to see me here, so he won't."

With Pinecrest's elixir enhancing my gifts, I was even more sensitive to his emotions than usual. My throat closed. I held out my arms and he hugged me so tightly it almost hurt. I rubbed the space between his shoulder blades. I'd gone through nearly the same thing at the Elmbarks' when my mother and brother came. It was a strange parallel. Perhaps too strange. My gaze drifted over to Doctor Pinecrest. I'd suspected he'd meddled in the Elmbarks' guest list. Had he done so here, too?

I looked over Drystan's shoulder, and Cyan met my gaze in understanding. She wore the mask and the dress she'd worn to our one and only performance at the Kymri Theatre. She fluffed her skirts self-consciously. All three of us were wearing the emerald and diamond lapel pins the Princess had given us after the duel as a token of her favor.

"It's showtime," Maske said to us, and Drystan and I broke apart. "Everyone, to your places."

The music drifted to silence, and the final guests took their seats. I wore a fairly simple suit and dark blue mask, since I was mostly a stagehand tonight. Drystan tied on his own mask, and I adjusted it. It was a new one, with embroidered diamonds vaguely reminiscent of motley. I snuck a quick kiss on his cheek, and he gave me a wan smile.

When all was so silent you could hear a pin drop, Maske came onto the small but grand gilt-and-marble stage, wearing his customary tails, top hat, an elaborate cravat, and his velvet embroidered mask with a crescent moon and six-pointed stars. He'd be performing the bulk of the tricks tonight, while we had supporting roles. We were more than happy to give him the space to shine in front of nobility and royalty.

"Good evening. I am Jasper Maske, also known as the Maske of Magic." He paused for scattered applause.

"When I was a young lad," Maske continued, "my father was a woodworker, and his father before him, and his father before him . . . there was no magic to be had in my future . . . or so I thought." He paced the stage slowly, as if lost in memories.

I maneuvered the lantern, slotting in the small silhouettes Drystan had carved from flat pieces of wood and moving them slowly left to right, so a constant stream of shadows accompanied Maske's tale.

"I was working late into the night," he said. "Most of the time, my father created furniture to sell, but he always taught me that we should master true art, drawing something beautiful out from the grain. So I was carving a cat, looking at my little pet sleeping in front of the fire."

With easy sleight of hand, a little carved cat appeared in his palms. He made it disappear and then asked a member of the audience to stand and pat their pocket. The volunteer—the Treasurer of Elada—took out the carved figurine, incredulous, to scattered claps.

Maske sat down in a chair on the stage, pantomiming nodding off. "I was so tired that night that I fell asleep in the middle of carving. I was lucky I did not cut myself on the blade! At first, I thought I dreamed, for there in front of me was a great mage."

Behind the scenes, I crashed the cymbals, and Maske threw a powder that flashed bright green. When the smoke cleared, Drystan, nearly hidden by a huge cloak, appeared before him. I stepped away from the lantern, that part of my job finished. I flitted about, doing my other tasks.

"I am your great-great-grandfather, Jasper Maske," Drystan declared. Between the Glamour and his stage presence, no one else save me would notice the tension in his features behind his green and gold mask. We'd already agreed he'd pitch his voice differently and alter his accent, but it'd help disguise him further.

"You look a little young for that," Maske said, and the audience chuckled. "Either you lie, or I'm dreaming. My family has been naught but humble woodcarvers for generations."

"Are you so sure? The magic calls to you, doesn't it?" Drystan asked. "It sings to you, deep in your blood. It's always been there, and it always will be. All you need to do is unlock it, and you'll see your legacy continue."

Drystan twirled, his cloak flaring out behind him, showing his magician's suit. He levitated in the air and pressed his hands to either side of Maske's head, looking deep into his eyes. With another flash of smoke, he disappeared.

The rest of the story was Maske learning his "magic" and delighting the audience with his tricks. As it was a smaller stage, he couldn't perform as many grand-scale illusions as at the Kymri Theatre, but his arsenal of prestidigitation was impressive nonetheless. A shower of coins fell from his bare palms, even despite his rolled-up sleeves. He made a rose bush grow from a seed he planted, and water poured from a vase that appeared empty.

He disappeared into the spirit cabinet and reappeared at the back of the audience. I smiled to see it. It was one of the earliest tricks Drystan and I had learned, and though I hadn't liked being tied within the cabinet, the fact that Drystan had been crouched in the dark with me, close enough to kiss, had made it easier to bear.

Maske brought out Cyan, introducing her as his daughter. She beamed in delight. The silver paint on her forehead glittered like a tiara. He proceeded to teach her magic. I loved that we were using the falsehood of magic to weave in truth, and it was easy to see that ever since he'd learned he'd sired Cyan, Maske was determined to be a proper father figure to her. Peppered throughout the performance were card tricks of all sorts. Drystan joined me backstage briefly while Maske and Cyan flitted through the small audience. Maske took the lead. He asked one participant to throw the entire deck in the air and stabbed the chosen card with a small knife. Another card appeared within a block of ice, and still another in a woman's handbag on the other side of the room. Even I, who knew the truth behind every trick, couldn't help but be impressed by how easily he performed them. There was no hesitation, no awkwardness. Everyone knew it was sleight of hand, yet no one could catch him in the act.

Behind the scenes, Drystan and I pulled levers, provided sound effects, and did all we could to bring the show to life.

For the grandest trick, Maske and Cyan turned the small carved cat into a large, mechanical automaton of a lion. Maske had spent hours carving the wooden accents himself, piecing the bits of machinery and cogs together. The lion opened its mouth and roared before Maske passed his cloak over it, and it transformed back into the small cat.

After all the tricks were done, Drystan returned to the stage. "You see," he said, with a sweep of his cloak and a knowing glint in his eye. "Destiny cannot be denied. Your fierceness remains in you. A magician I was, a magician you are, and the legacy can continue as long as your family wishes it."

Maske and Cyan bowed to their "ancestor," and Drystan inclined his head in return. The curtains fell.

Everyone broke into applause, but my eyes didn't leave the Princess. The dark ringlets of her hair bounced as she clapped. I'd wanted to make her grin as widely as she had the day of the magician's duel. Job done.

The curtains parted again. Maske, Drystan, and Cyan held hands, raising them high before sweeping into a bow.

After the performance, we packed up our gear as the guests went to the grand ballroom for little cakes and drinks before the feast properly began.

"Even with the Palace as grand as all that, it's not quite the same as the Kymri Theatre, is it?" Maske asked. It'd still be another month before repairs were finished enough for us to move back in.

"I know," I said. We all did. "You still did brilliantly, though."

"It was certainly something," he said, positively bursting with pride. "Everyone played their part perfectly."

When we'd finished packing our bags, we mingled for a time in the ballroom. It was as grand as I'd imagined, the ceiling and walls painted with illustrations of Chimaera, the floor and pillars made of pale pink marble. The nobility came to congratulate us on the performance. The women's gowns were made of the finest silks or velvet, trimmed with lace or embroidered with gold and silver thread. The suits were of the latest cut and style, and some wore Vestige as lapel pins, the ultimate display of wealth. Even in our best magician suits, we were underdressed by comparison.

Maske glowed with the approval of the illustrious company. Cyan and I ate a few of the treats on trays and sipped sparkling wine. I quite liked the dates wrapped in bacon on little skewers. Drystan kept a wide berth from his family, but his eyes kept drifting over to them. Before long, some of the guests streamed into one of the banquet rooms for the main feast. Drystan visibly relaxed once the Hornbeams left. Maske had been invited to join, but not his assistants, which suited us fine. I was more than ready to go home to our shabby rooms.

The Princess tugged the Steward's sleeve and pointed toward us, rising on tiptoe to whisper something to him. The Steward nodded and she came toward us, accompanied by her guards. He left to join the feast. Doctor Pinecrest followed close behind the guards, his expression inscrutable.

Their footsteps echoed loudly in the now-empty ballroom. I smiled warmly at the Princess. She returned the gesture, but it was a little stiff. When I'd last seen her this close, she'd been missing a front tooth, but the adult one had come in. She looked at me and I felt a . . . *tug* at my magic. That warmth that was both like and not like when I sensed other Chimaera was back, stronger than ever. Cyan's lips tightened.

"The Princess and I wanted to congratulate you on a most excellent perf—" the doctor began and then stopped short.

The Princess had gone rigid, hands balled into fists at her sides.

"I'm sorry, Doctor," she gasped. "I've been trying to contain it all night, and I know we just reset it, but—I can't—I can't hold—"

Pinecrest ran toward her, but he was too late. The Princess fell to her knees, and her skin shimmered as it had the day of our rehearsal.

Drystan, Cyan, and I all froze. Around my neck, my own Glamour grew hot, and then there was a snap of pressure. Drystan's disguise was gone, as mine must've been, even though we had more than a quarter of an hour left on our illusions.

Guards surged forward, grabbing our upper arms in case we were a threat to the Princess.

I froze in utter shock.

The Princess lay on the ground, panting. The pendant of her Glamour swung from a gold chain around her neck.

She was no longer the girl with pink cheeks and dark ringlets. Instead, her skin was pale and tinged blue. Her black hair shone blue-green, like magpie feathers. Her features were sharper—the blades of her cheekbones, her brow, and the point of her chin. Her eyes were the blue of Penglass. She grimaced, and her teeth were sharp, the canines pointed just like Juliet's.

"Lord and Lady," Drystan breathed.

"Quick, to a side room," the doctor said. The guards made to stop us following, but Doctor Pinecrest waved them aside. "It's all right. Let them come."

Once we were safe behind a closed door, Pinecrest wasted no time. He knelt beside the Princess, taking a thin box very like the one we'd found in Shadow Elwood's apartments and opening it to reveal a single vial of a familiar medicine in a velvet tray. One of the guards left, probably to fetch the Steward.

"We should go—" I began, but the doctor silenced me with a look.

We watched in silence as the doctor tapped the air bubbles from the syringe and pressed the needle into the crook of the Princess's arm. Her head lolled back, and she panted loudly. Even her tongue was tinged faintly blue.

The medicine began to take hold. The lines on her forehead smoothed. She rested her head against Pinecrest's shoulder for a moment, gathering strength.

The Princess met our gazes. I kept my face blank. She had an ethereal way about her, even more so than Anisa. As if she were a strange, fairy creature from the illustrated storybooks I'd read as a child. Yet everyone knew that the fairies were based on the . . .

"Alder," I whispered aloud.

19

A ROYAL SECRET

"We have deduced from old writings and art that the Alder had blueish skin, pointed ears, and were taller and slimmer than most humans. They could be capricious, and many believe we see their nature reflected in fairy stories."

THE CHIMAERA MYTH, PROFESSOR CAED CEDAR,
ROYAL SNAKEWOOD UNIVERSITY

The Princess held the Glamour pendant in her long fingers, turning it over. "It's broken," she whispered.

"We have others," Doctor Pinecrest said, kneeling at her side. The Princess's brow furrowed, and she looked as if she might weep.

—*I can't cry*, she sent me, gesturing at her eyes. The pupils were too large, and the irises around them glowed like when Cyan accessed her powers. I shivered to hear her voice in my head. It echoed like Anisa's.

The guards stared straight ahead, as if they saw this sort of thing every day. Because they did. Both were brown-haired, tall, muscled, and so generically handsome they were hard to tell apart, save that one had brown eyes, and the other blue-green.

"I'm part-Alder," Princess Nicolette volunteered. "All of the Snakewood family is." She was only eight, but she sounded far older, as if in shedding her disguise she'd also left behind the persona of a young child. "Centuries passed and we started looking human again, just like you. But I look more different than my parents, or so my uncle says." Her strange features rippled. Her parents had died before she could even hope to remember them. "I've always had to wear these," the Princess continued, holding the broken Glamour in her hands. "I've always had to hide. It's a mask I can never take off."

If people found out the Princess was part-Alder, I'd no idea how Elada would react. Some might take it as proof of the family's continued right to rule. Others would react as well as they did upon the unveiling of Chimaera, especially with the growing anti-monarchy sentiment. The Princess could lose her crown, and maybe even her life.

The medicine had taken full effect on the Princess. Power emanated from her like a furnace.

"Are the other Alder really gone?" Cyan asked.

"As far as we know, we're the last," the Princess said. "But other Chimaera are returning." Her face creased in concern. "I hope the leopard and cyrinx Chimaera are all right."

"Juliet and Violet?" I asked.

"You know them!" She brightened.

"Only a little," I said, wishing I'd stayed quiet.

"I thought they were ever so nice. But I haven't seen them since . . ." She trailed off.

Since the explosion.

The door opened, and the Steward burst in, stiffening at the sight of the Princess freed from her Glamour illusion. The guards stood at attention. Their hands rested on the Vestige guns in their belts. I stepped closer to Drystan.

"What's happened here?" the Steward demanded, coming to the Princess's side. He was dressed in full formal velvet attire, the regent's crown heavy on his brow. As when I'd seen him after the magic duel, he reminded me slightly of an angry hound who wouldn't give up whatever was in his jaws. "And why in the world are *they* here?"

"Your Excellency," Doctor Pinecrest said, nodding at him. "When the Princess had an . . . incident in front of these performers, I thought it best to keep them close. I was about to call for you."

—*The Steward is wondering if he should kill us to keep the secret*, Cyan said. She sent the thought to both Drystan and me, judging by Drystan's tightened lips.

—*You maybe didn't need to share that with us right at this very moment.* I wanted to throw up.

"Don't kill them, Uncle," the Princess said, and I shot Cyan a look. Could the Princess could overhear us?

"Come now, Nicolette, we don't kill people," the Steward said, with that condescending tone people used for children. I wasn't sure I believed him. He looked pale, the skin of his cheeks doughy. "You three. Take off your masks. Let's get a proper look at you."

We did so, and I resisted the urge to crumple the velvet in my hand as he cast his eye over us. Without the Glamour or the mask, I felt utterly exposed.

"Your Excellency, they're entirely trustworthy, or I wouldn't have invited them here to perform for the Princess," Pinecrest assured him. "Micah Grey here is one of my patients," Pinecrest said, nodding to me. "Cyan Zhu may yet become one, as well."

The Steward gave him, then us, a sharp look. Great. The doctor had just unveiled me and Cyan as Chimaera to the most powerful man in Elada.

The Princess looked at us, her eyes wide. —*I knew you were different. You're like me, but not.*

"And this one?" the Steward gestured to Drystan.

"Drystan Hornbeam is not my patient, but I thought you might find him interesting nonetheless."

Drystan flinched, and despite the danger, I glared at Doctor Pinecrest. He only blinked at us serenely.

"Hornbeam?" the Steward echoed.

"Yes, Your Excellency," Drystan said, sweeping into his best bow. "Though I would be much obliged if you didn't tell my family. They aren't overfond of me, you see."

"Indeed, so I've heard." The Steward looked him up and down. "Most thought you had overdosed in a Lerium den long ago."

Drystan's polite smile froze to a grimace. "I've long left that vice behind, Your Excellency."

The Steward made a noise in his throat. "You," he said to one of the guards. "Fetch the Princess another Glamour."

The guard bowed and left.

"If you two are patients of Pinecrest's, what are your abilities?" he said to Cyan and me. I wilted under the power of that dark brown stare. This was a man who had run a country for years after his brother and his sister-in-law died in an accident. With a flick of his finger, he could change our fate entirely.

—*I wouldn't lie*, the Princess warned in our heads. *He's very good at knowing when someone's been naughty enough to lie to him, even if he doesn't have an Augur to hand. He knew when I only pretended to like the parma violets one of my cousins gave me.*

Neither the Steward, the guards, nor Doctor Pinecrest seemed to hear that thought. Interesting. Still, the warmth radiated off the Steward. Like the Princess, it was different from when I sensed other Chimaera. If he was Alder, too, though, it didn't run as strongly.

"I can read minds and sometimes cause others to do as I wish," Cyan said, swallowing.

"I can speak mind to mind, and I have been able to slow time or move objects," I added, hating how timid I sounded.

"Anything else?" the Steward said.

I licked my lips. "When I touch Penglass, it can glow beneath my touch. Cyan and I have both had visions of the past, or whispers from spirits about the future." I didn't tell him outright about Anisa. Perhaps some lingering enchantment of hers stilled my tongue. The remaining guard shifted, his hand inching closer to his weapon.

"And what have you seen of the future?" the Steward asked.

"Someone wants to hurt Chimaera and stop magic from returning," I said. "We think it might be Timur, the former leader of the Foresters. He was likely the one behind the attacks."

The Steward's eyes widened at that, but he didn't look entirely surprised, either. Perhaps our tip to the Constabulary did make its way to him, or his own investigations pointed that direction, too.

The other guard returned with a small bag, and he passed it to the Steward with a deep bow. The Steward opened it and put the new Glamour around the Princess's neck. She closed her eyes and concentrated. The blue tinge faded from her skin, and her hair lost its strange iridescence. Her cheeks rounded, and her build no longer seemed as frail. Her eyes transformed from eerie blue to a more normal shade of green, eyebrows appearing above them as if drawn on.

"That's . . . not how Glamours usually work, is it?" I managed. They usually had to be pre-programmed, and it took ages to get them right. When they were turned on, the new illusion settled over your skin in an instant, rather than almost . . . growing, as it had with the Princess.

"I can control it myself, even a little without the Glamour, sometimes," the Princess said. "It helps me concentrate, though. And thank you for not screaming. Once, a maid saw me, and she shrieked so loudly I thought my ears would burst."

The Steward's jaw tightened. I wondered what had happened to the maid.

"Do you feel better, Your Highness?" Pinecrest asked. "Any ill effects?"

"I'm quite all right, thank you, Royal Physician," she said, primly. "I am very hungry, though."

The Steward laughed, but it was hollow and didn't reach his eyes. "We'll return to the feast in a moment, my dear." The Princess's hand was lax in his.

The Steward nodded to us. "I thank you for answering my questions. Illuminating, to say the least. But I'm afraid if word of this reached those who are attacking the city, or leaders across the water, they'd would find a way to expose her. Us. And the Elada you know might very well crumble to dust in a heartbeat."

"I trust them, Uncle," the Princess said, her voice ringing with the same prescient certainty I'd heard sometimes from Anisa.

"Even so," the Steward said. "They've discovered a secret that could destroy us. I'm afraid we cannot let that stand. And if they're loyal to the Snakewood Crown, they will see the need for this, too." He reached into his pocket and took out a Vestige pendant. At first, I thought it was an Aleph, but it was smaller, with a stylized snake carved on its face. The eyes were as red as the rubies on the ringmaster's cane, and I shuddered.

"A Lethe," Drystan breathed, and I swallowed nervously. I knew that type of Vestige erased memories, but I'd never seen one before in person.

"Here." The Steward passed it to Doctor Pinecrest. "You've a better handle on controlling it than me. Take away the last quarter of an hour and then send them home. No real harm done, and I've learned something interesting about them, haven't I? Who knows? They may yet prove useful."

My heart was pounding. Cyan's nostrils flared, and Drystan looked poised to make a run for it.

The Steward glanced into one of the mirrors on the wall and patted his chest. With a shiver, I realized he must be wearing a Glamour, too. What did he look like, beneath the face of a standard middle-aged man with slightly sagging jowls and bright, black eyes?

Doctor Pinecrest held the Lethe, looking down at it regretfully. "I'm afraid needs must, you three. But I assure you, I'm well-practiced at this. The last few minutes will be gone, but that's all. The guards here consent to stare into one at the end of every shift. It's perfectly safe, I assure you."

I snuck a look at the guards, who gave no reaction. We couldn't refuse. The Steward and the Princess stepped to the side.

I couldn't even blame them. If I were the Steward, I'd have done the same thing. What if Timur found out? I shivered: Or what if he already knew? One of the guards shifted his stance. Both still had their hands on their weapons.

I grabbed Drystan's hand tight in mine, but he pulled away, volunteering to go first. Doctor Pinecrest fiddled with the controls. "Stare into the eyes of the Lethe, Drystan."

He swallowed, but he didn't flinch. The red eyes glowed brighter, reflecting in Drystan's blue eyes. It was done in a blink. Drystan stared ahead, vacantly.

"He'll come back to himself in a few minutes," Doctor Pinecrest explained. "Cyan?"

She stepped forward, but she couldn't hide how little she wanted to do this. Still, she stared into the glow of red. I caught the tilt of the Princess's head. Cyan stepped to Drystan's side, staring as vacantly as Drystan, but something was . . . different.

The Princess was staring at me intently.

"Micah," Doctor Pinecrest said, with a hint of regret. "Your turn."

I went to him, and he held the Lethe up to my face. This close, I could see every detail of the carved snake. It was a cobra, its hood flared, mouth open, showing fangs and the forked tongue. The red eyes glowed bright enough to drown out the world.

A moment later, it was done.

Yet I still remembered everything. The Princess, the Alder features, and every single word the Steward had said to us.

—I wanted you to remember, the Princess said silently from the corner. I chanced the shortest glance at her. Was there a flash of blue beneath the green? *I protected you and your friend Cyan from the Lethe. But you have to play the part.*

I stepped to Cyan's side, schooling my features blank and hoping the guards wouldn't realize how hard my heart was still beating or the damp sweat on my brow and palms.

"Perfect," the Steward said. "Nicely done, as ever, Doctor. Pop them back in the ballroom before they properly come to, send them on their way, and on we go. No harm done, I suppose." The Steward, the Princess, and the guards left. The Princess looked over her shoulder as she did so.

—Please don't tell anyone what I did, she sent. *I'll get in so much trouble. But I just . . . I felt you should remember.*

We stared blankly ahead. *—We understand*, I chanced sending.

—I'll ask for them to invite you back, she sent. *If you do, I hope you come. I did enjoy your magic show.*

With that, she was gone.

Doctor Pinecrest stepped forward, put on our masks, and switched on our Glamours. Following Drystan's behavior, Cyan and I let ourselves be moved as if we were dolls. I thought I caught regret on Pinecrest's face, but he'd done it to us all the same. Or thought he had. I could sense Cyan's mind working as quickly as mine.

We went back out into the empty ballroom. Behind us, out of

sight, Doctor Pinecrest clapped his hands, and Drystan blinked as if waking up from a nap. Cyan and I did the same.

Behind us, we heard footsteps. I turned, expecting Doctor Pinecrest, but he had slipped off. Instead, it was none other than Lord Nigel Hornbeam.

"Ah, the magicians!" he said, beaming.

I gave a little bow, and Cyan sank into a curtsey. Drystan was still a statue at my side, his eyes wide beneath his mask. Belatedly, he bowed too.

Nigel Hornbeam's brow furrowed before his lips curled in a faint smile.

"I'm not usually one for magic and trickery, but that was cleverly done. Perhaps we'll have you come perform for our son's birthday, if you're willing to travel down to Sicion."

"Thank you, my lord," Drystan managed. "I'm sure we'd be honored."

Nigel Hornbeam's smile widened before he carried on out to the terrace. He lit a pipe and stared out at the night.

"Drystan . . ." I began.

"I think I've had enough of palaces, nobility, and royalty for one evening," he said, curtly. "Haven't you?" He was unnerved at the sight of his father, but I also realized that what the Princess said was true: Cyan and I remembered, but Drystan didn't.

"More than you know," I said. "Let's go home."

20

FORGET YOUR WOES

"If the monarchy continues to bury its head in the sand and ignore the discontent of its people, there will be trouble. We cannot deny it any longer. While there have not been any large-scale attacks in Imachara since the arson of the Museum of Mechanical Antiquities, Forester protests are only growing, and small-scale fights and riots have broken out. Shop windows were smashed, goods stolen. Messages accusing people of being monarchists or Chimaera were scrawled across doors. There have been far more peaceful protests and vigils in the past, yet today, when I was present at one of them, the mood of the crowd was very angry indeed.

It has been months, and yet the Crown has not confirmed who was behind the attacks or seemed to make any real progress. Some claim it was the monarchy itself to distract from all the ways they are failing their citizens. Others believe the other islands of the Archipelago acted to destabilize Elada, though that seems unlikely. The rising prices have helped their coffers, sure enough. If I were the Steward, I would certainly be aiming to provide some concrete answers, or the speculations will only continue to grow both more ugly and more dangerous."

EDITORIAL, THE NICKEL DAILY

We said nothing on the carriage ride back to our rooms in the Penny Rookeries. Maske likely wouldn't be back until dawn. As soon as we'd closed the door of our room, Cyan and I interrogated Drystan on what he remembered. As far as he knew, we'd never left the ballroom before his father walked in. We immediately broke our promise to the Princess by telling him everything, with Cyan sending some memories to him to drive it home. He'd witnessed the truth, and he deserved to know what had truly happened in that room.

The disturbed expression on his face morphed into fear and nearly undid me. He blinked quickly, folding it away and speaking briskly. "Surely the Princess can't actually be Alder. Are you sure she's not simply a different type of Chimaera?"

I shook my head. "She felt . . . different. Her powers aren't the same. She's strong, though—very strong, and seems able to control it better than any of us."

"Alder and Chimaera. Fairy tales come to life." Cyan gazed into the embers of the fire in the grate. "Should we ask Anisa about this?"

I considered. "I really want to, but we only have a couple calls left of her power. She's never even whispered a word about the Alder returning, only Chimaera, so I'm not even sure if she'd know much more than us. Unfortunately, I think we're on our own for the moment."

Drystan exhaled unhappily.

"At least we told the Steward directly about Timur," I said. "If the Crown itself can't find him, then I'm not sure who can."

Cyan rubbed her temples. "Gods, I'm beyond beat."

So was I, despite being freshly dosed. We murmured our goodnights. Still, as we broke apart and Cyan went to her room, part of me wondered if I should have waited longer after the shock of seeing Drystan's father so unexpectedly.

Especially when, later that night, I woke to the sound of him crying.

I didn't know how long I'd been asleep. Drystan lay propped up against the pillows. He'd taken a bottle of port from the kitchen, and he'd made good work of it, judging by how little liquid remained. His nose and eyes were red, his cheeks damp.

"Drystan," I said. He drained the last of the port and set the empty glass on the bedside table.

I held my arms out, and he moved into them, hiding his face against my neck as if ashamed. He absolutely reeked of the sweet alcohol. He'd drunk in the circus at the bonfire, and he'd have the odd glass in the evenings here and there. Once, he'd bought us a bottle of horrible, cheap gin, and we'd sat on a pier and drunk it as we entrusted each other with the first of many secrets.

I knew from his past that he'd spent years running away from reality however he could, and he was careful not to pass a certain point. That night, though, he was properly sozzled. His tears dampened my neck as I stroked his hair.

"Did anyone ever tell you what happened to the orange clown in the circus?" he asked a few minutes later, his voice slurred. I could feel his lips moving against the skin of my throat.

I frowned. Whatever I'd been expecting him to say, it wasn't that. I searched my memory. "His name was Linden, right? And he'd been the former leader of the clowns before you. Don't think I know much more than that."

"Surprised people even gave you that much, really. After what happened, everyone was 'fraid to."

"What's the story?" I asked.

He sighed against my neck. "He got a bit big for his britches and got it in his head to start a mutiny. Against Bil."

I whistled. "And it didn't work, obviously."

"No, and I suspect I was part of the reason why. But that's the thing, see. I don't remember."

My breath hitched.

"Yeah. I put bits and pieces together, over the years. I think Bil somehow got his greasy mitts on a Lethe. Won it off a card game, maybe. Something about Linden's plan must have involved using it, but Bil must have found out. One day, Linden was simply gone, and Jive was the leader of the clowns. Not for long, though, as he was rather shit at it. It was easy enough for me to take over after that."

"And what happened to Linden?"

"Dunno for certain, but I think . . ." He paused. "I think Bil used the Lethe on him, but we all know Bil doesn't know how to do anything delicately. And if there's one thing a Lethe requires, it's finesse." He hiccoughed.

"You can't mean . . ." I trailed off.

"I think he probably took all of them, yeah." He exhaled, hard. "Or far too many. I've plenty of memories I wouldn't mind forgetting myself. But now, even realizing I'd lost a little sliver of my life . . ." He trailed off.

"I wish I could have stopped it," I whispered.

"If I'd been like you, I wouldn't have forgotten." He sniffed. "You and Cyan still have defenses I can't hope to have. Even with that, though, it wasn't enough when up against something Alder-made, was it?"

The silence between us stretched. What could I say?

"I wish the Lethe had lasted a few more minutes," he admitted. "Or I wish my father hadn't decided to go out for a smoke right then, to remind me of everything I threw away. Now Pinecrest evidently told the Steward of Elada my name, and he knows you and Cyan are Chimaera, and I've no idea what he'll do with that information."

I shivered. "Hopefully nothing."

"What if he's already told my father?" Drystan asked the darkness.

"Would you ever want to reach out to your family and reconnect?"

"They don't want me," he said, his voice harsh. "My father told me that very clearly the last time we spoke. I'm the rotten apple on the branch, and they pruned me off."

"I'm sorry." I stroked his back, unsure what else to say.

"Me, too."

His hands roamed my arms and along my collar bone, but I didn't let myself respond. I wanted to give him comfort, but not when he was like this. He sighed and let his hands fall. Eventually, his breathing slowed, and he drifted back to sleep. I kissed the top of his head, breathing in the scent of his hair. I closed my eyes against my own tears and tried to follow.

Thankfully, that night at least, I didn't dream of corpses.

• • • •

The next morning, my body was too heavy to move. My eyelids refused to stay open. I tried to sit up and fell back against the pillows. It was still a few days until my next dose, but my energy was already fading. I'd be all right once I was up and about again, at least until the day before I needed another vial of that medicine. Pinecrest had told me it wasn't too addictive at one dose a week, but I wasn't so sure.

"Are you all right?" I asked Drystan when he finally stirred.

His forehead creased as he rubbed the sleep from his eyes. "I have a bugger of a hangover," he admitted. "Feel like Saitha stepped on my head."

I hadn't thought of the elephant at the circus for a long time. I hoped Tym and Karla were looking after her well. "Aside from your head . . . how are you?" I asked, carefully.

Drystan shrugged. "My maudlin mood has passed, never fear. Let's go to breakfast. I need to drink my weight in water and coffee and eat some grease."

"Grease on its own? Delicious."

"A whole vat of it."

He helped me up and down the stairs to the kitchen. The others were already up. Maske was reading his copy of the *Nickel Daily*. The headlines pointed to rising Forester protests and the eyewatering price of flour. One that mentioned Chimaera caught my eye, and Maske handed it over when he was done. People had started accusing their neighbors of being Chimaera. A bakery had been burned because someone swore that the owner had eyes as yellow as the cyrinx people had seen at the Celestial Cathedral. The baker had survived, thankfully, but fled the city.

I set the article aside, disturbed. I'd seen a few stalls at the market advertising protection against Chimaera magic, and people wore small pouches filled with herbs and crystals. Superstition was only growing.

I made myself a cup of coffee, stirring the milk and sugar. Outside the window, we heard the Penny Rookeries awaken. Someone had chickens in their apartments—a rooster crowed. Maske brought out bread, butter, and preserves. He was in such a good mood he was humming.

"How was the feast?" I asked him.

"Absolutely marvelous. They had this one course with duck and redcurrants. It was so good I think I dreamed about it. And everyone was so kind about our performance. There'll be more invitations, mark my words. And the coin the Steward gave me means we'll likely be back in the Kymri Theatre a few weeks sooner, thank the Lord and Lady."

That bolstered us. I missed the theatre something fierce. We were too cramped here, and at the end of the day, it simply wasn't home. I tried to imagine Maske's expression if we told him that we'd had a private conversation with the Steward and discovered the Princess was Alder-descended. Cyan and I had decided it was better he didn't know, at least for now, but I didn't like keeping it from him. Made me feel like Lily.

"Go out and get some sunshine," Maske urged, and Drystan and I followed his orders. Lily still hadn't come clean to Maske, and we were beginning to feel complicit by not warning him about her, but at the same time, we couldn't quite bring ourselves to break his heart.

Outside, summer was truly unfurling. It was mid-morning, but the air was already hot and sticky. My clothing immediately itched and clung to my skin, and I could feel the sweat beneath my binder.

Drystan and I passed a grocer's. The ripe apples smelled so good that I bought two, and we ate them as we walked down the narrow, crowded streets of the Penny Rookeries.

The sun made the evidence of poverty even more stark, especially after our night at the Palace. None of the streets were properly cobbled, and we had to pick our way carefully so we didn't trip in divots or step in horse droppings. The faces I passed had smallpox scars and rotten teeth, and many were too thin from perpetual hunger. Others worked long shifts at factories, leaving before the sun came up and returning after it set, and could still barely afford a room in this part of town. Forester flyers were pasted on the lampposts.

We drifted closer to the docks. The air smelled of fish, both fresh and not so fresh, and their acrid guts. Stallholders hawked their wares and tried to entice us to purchase some shellfish or herring. I'd never been keen on fish to begin with and shook my head, continuing on. Drystan bought a small bag of smoked kippers, and I pulled a face.

"You're *not* kissing me after eating those," I said.

"You won't be able to resist my charms," he said.

"I will if you smell like campfire and fish. Sorry."

We laughed, and it was so good to simply walk through the streets, not thinking about performing, or politics, or portents. At another stall, we bought a bottle of iced lemonade and found an abandoned dock, finally sitting with our legs over the sides.

"It's like that night in the circus," I said, sipping the tart drink.

"No gin in this, which is probably for the best." He raised the bottle of lemonade and squinted into the sunlight. His hair shone bright gold, and even an hour in the sun would darken his freckles. I wanted to kiss him, but hesitated, feeling like I couldn't be physically affectionate while we were both dressed as men and hating that I had that pause. The fact that he did indeed smell of kippers helped. I settled for putting my hand over his and squeezing.

Drystan leaned back on his forearms, closing his eyes. I took the bottle from him and swigged.

"It's all building up, isn't it?" he asked. "The Princess. Frey and Lily. The protests."

He'd brought up all we'd tried to avoid for the last hour. I sighed. "Aye. Timur is still out there, and I can't help fearing he'll attack again before the Crown can find him. Anisa likely can't help us. I've sensed nothing from the spirits except dreams of Timur stealing dead bodies, and we still don't even know if his last experiment worked."

Drystan looked up at the brilliantly clear sky. "Indeed, it's like we're waiting for a massive storm to hit, and we think holding up an umbrella will stop us getting wet."

"Cheery," I said.

He stood and held out his hand. "Well, I don't think it'll break today, in any case. I don't want to mope about anymore."

He hauled me up, and we kept our hands clasped until the crowds grew thick enough that we didn't dare. My luck didn't hold two nights in a row.

● ● ● ●

The power drew me to him. I was lost in a rainbow of shifting hues. I was falling, yet without sense of a body or gravity. Far off, I sensed someone. A child, alone and afraid. His power spiked from him like lightning.

Another magic plucked at me, and it swept me away.

Somewhere else in the city, Timur's head rose, strong and hale in his new, stolen body.

"There is a horned one like the ancient monster," Timur said aloud to one of his Kashura. His new voice was deeper, though the Imacharan accent was the same. "I can taste his power. He'd be strong enough."

"Where?" a Kashura asked. "Can you find him?"

Timur clutched that stolen magic to him. It was trying to resist him, trying to keep this danger a secret.

—Show me, he commanded the magic. Show me, spirit.

Thanks to this being, Timur had seen how the world ended before. He'd had to sully his own soul, poison his body, and even leave his broken body and another corpse behind to gain that knowledge, but it had been worth it. Even now, the spirit fluttered in a corner of his mind, batting its wings uselessly as it tried to escape.

—No, came a voice from deep within Timur's skull, echoing in three tones at once. You will not have him.

Timur screamed in frustration, causing the other Kashura to cower.

—I will find the creature, Timur sent back. You might delay it, creature, but I will win in the end.

He stared at his Kashura. "The abominations of the past are returning, both by chance and by design, and they can't be allowed to reign unchecked. I will make sure it does not happen again," he said, tilting his new chin. "All we need is a little more time to put the pieces in play, and then the Archipelago will be free of Chimaera and Alder. We will create a better future for Elada."

"Yes," the Kashura called, bowing their hooded heads.

—Go to the boy, *the spirit said to me, his echoing voice desperate, and I sensed just how hard it was to give me even that.* Help him, or all is lost.

His words reminded me of the vision with Anisa and Matla. I plunged back into the colors—I reached—

● ● ● ●

I woke up with a strangled scream.

"What's wrong?" Drystan asked, half-rising from the bed.

Before I could tell him, the door to our bedroom opened.

Cyan was breathless. In her hands, she held Elwood's Mirror of Moirai, the glass glowing. "It's Frey. We have to go to Frey."

21

AHTI'S SCION

> "When I was six or seven, I used to walk through the gardens at my parents' house in the Emerald Bowl and thought the flowers were the perfect size to be teacups for fairies. There was a thicket, and I pushed through the dark green leaves, my feet sinking into the grass. One day, I didn't look where I was going, and the ground fell off sharply, down to a ravine. I slipped but managed to grab a root. I remember thinking how quickly all can change. One minute, you seem to be in a fairy's realm, and the next, you're hanging on, feet dangling. It took a long time to crawl back up, and my nightdress was stained. Mother berated me for it the next day."
>
> **FROM MICAH GREY'S INFREQUENTLY UPDATED DIARY**

We wasted no time, pulling on our coats.

"There's never a bloody break, is there?" Drystan complained.

"No, I'm afraid. Hold on," I said, darting briefly back into the bedroom and returning with Anisa's Aleph. "I have a feeling we're going to need to use one of our two last calls."

Cyan nodded. We slipped out of the door as quietly as possible. Maske was still awake, judging by the sliver of light around his door. With luck, he'd be fascinated enough by whatever invention he was working on that he'd never realize we were gone. He'd worry about us breaking curfew, and if we were caught by guards, we might be fined, arrested, or even beaten for our trouble.

"This could be a trap," Drystan said as we trotted down the stairs. "What if Timur is waiting for us?"

"Could be," I agreed.

"I don't think so," Cyan said, her jaw set. "I don't think he knows where Frey is. Not yet, at least."

We slunk through the streets as quickly as we could, darting into alleyways at times to avoid the notice of the night watchmen, but Cyan was able to nudge them away from our path.

It started to drizzle, the rain cool enough that I shivered despite the warm summer night.

When we arrived outside Lily's apartment building, Cyan sent a thought up and we waited anxiously for her to come down and let us in. Yet when the door swung open, it wasn't Lily who answered the door for us.

It was Kai Molleson.

The Royal Physician's assistant was still wearing his coat. His eyes slid over Cyan and Drystan. While he hadn't met them before, he obviously knew who they were. I took a step back, wondering if we should flee, even as I felt the warmth of Frey two stories above us.

"I didn't know what to do," Kai said, expression tight. "Frey was fine, and then he went into a fit and collapsed. I was . . . was going to go to Pinecrest first, but Lily begged me not to. Then I heard an echoing voice in my mind. The voice said to be strong, that you were coming."

I went cold at his words. Who had warned him? Anisa, somehow, or that strange spirit's voice from my dream?

Lily opened the door wider. Her hair was in disarray, her eyes round.

"Thank the stars," she said, practically dragging us inside.

We went to Frey's bedroom. The bright colors and drawings warred with the worry emanating from Lily. The low light glinted on Frey's green-black scales and the curves of his horns. The sheer *power* that emanated from his unconscious body was almost unbearable. Cyan and I took involuntary steps back.

"What's wrong with him?" Drystan asked.

"He's rupturing magic everywhere," I said. "The air is thick with it. He's losing control." I staggered again, my temples throbbing. If Frey had been a furnace before, now he was a forest fire.

Frey looked similar to Ahti, the Chimaera who had unwittingly nearly destroyed the world. I'd just had a dream where Timur was convinced that if Chimaera were allowed to return, then it might all happen again.

The smallest part of me wondered: what if he was right?

I took out Anisa's Aleph, holding it in my hands.

—*Anisa*, I said. *I call upon you. Come to me. We need your help.*

I flicked the switch and set it on the ground. It gave me a small sense of satisfaction to watch Lily and Kai's bone-deep shock as the smoke swirled into view and Anisa appeared. Her wings and body were even more transparent than before, as if a burst of wind would blow her away. The Phantom Damselfly went straight to Frey's side. Normally, it was difficult to tell what the Chimaera ghost was thinking or feeling, but fear radiated from her, and that scared me more than anything.

—*Dev, come here*, Anisa commanded, and, with a start, I realized she'd called me by the name of one of her ancient charges.

—*No time for doubts*, she said at my hesitation. *Take his hand. We do not have long.*

Outside, the skies opened, rain lashing against the windows. The gas lamps flickered. I took Frey's small hand in mine. The back of his hand was hard and scaly, and far too warm, but his palm was soft. His fingers tightened into a vice. I gasped. He leeched power from me, my energy flowing into him. Within moments, I was as poorly as I had been when I last needed Pinecrest's elixir.

The stuffed animals by the window rose into the air, spinning slowly around us. The books tumbled from the shelves, falling to the floor and then rising again, their covers flapping like birds' wings.

"He's hurting me," I gasped.

—*You must take control,* Anisa commanded. *It must be you. You are the Dev to his Ahti. You can swallow it like a star.*

"I . . . can't . . ."

Drystan darted forward. "Stop it!"

I half-fell onto the bed, still holding onto Frey's hand. A scream tore from my throat.

Drystan grabbed my hand, trying to pry me away from Frey, but as soon as he touched my skin, the power bleeding from me spiked, causing him to fly across the room. Drystan crashed into the wall before falling to the floor.

—*Only you can stop this, little Kedi,* Anisa said, her mental voice echoing through our skulls. *I can only guide you so much. Draw upon what you have learned. You must, or all is lost. Little bird, lend him your strength.*

Cyan clasped my other hand. Immediately, I felt more grounded. All too soon, though, she fell against me, struck by the same weakness as Frey stole power from her, too. I could barely see. I had no idea what Drystan or Lily were doing. My mind was full of swirling blue light.

"I have to get Pinecrest," Kai said, his voice far away.

"*No!*" Lily cried, the word echoed by the Phantom Damselfly.

I had to do something. Now. If I didn't, then Frey, Cyan, and I would die—and perhaps everyone within a set radius, too, if Frey's powers grew too strong. It would be like the attack in front of the Celestial Cathedral, or worse.

I stretched toward the whirlpool of Frey's mind. I swirled through the currents, trying not to fight against them too hard, or else I'd be swept away. Distantly, I felt Kai holding onto my hand and his strength flowed into me, too. He wasn't anywhere as powerful as me and Cyan, but the magic was undeniable, and it helped.

There. Off in the distance of my mind. A spark. A shining star.

—*Frey*, I called to him. *Frey Verre.*

—*Who are you?* His voice was high and wailing.

—*We've met before. I'm Micah, do you remember? You're frightened and your power has gotten away from you.*

—*I don't want to go back. It's better in here.*

The whirling colors were strangely hypnotic. The hues shifted until everything was varying shades of blue, like we were within a Penglass dome.

—*Your mother needs you*, I reminded him. *You don't want to worry her, do you?*

A pause. —*No.*

—*Come on, then.* It was as if I held out my hand, though where we were, we had no bodies and were only light.

It was like reaching for my mother at the hospital. He was too far away, or he was like smoke that slipped through my fingers.

—*Come on, Frey*, I said. *Reach toward me. You have to meet me partway so I can help you and bring you back to your mother. She's worried.*

Faintly, he connected. The swirling light around us slowed. I took the excess power into myself, swallowing it down. The bright, eye-watering blue grew dimmer until everything darkened to black.

● ● ● ●

Far off, Timur roared in frustration, no longer able to sense the Chimaera child. He twisted his magic viciously, and the spirit hidden within him whimpered in pain. He'd break this being down, and it'd give him the rest of its secrets, one way or another.

Until then, he knew what he had to do.

• • • •

Groaning, I raised my head. I felt like I'd been stepped on by a horse. Several times. And then kicked for good measure.

Cyan, her eyelids drooping, looked as awful as I felt. Kai wasn't much better. He was pressed against the wall, almost willing himself not to be noticed, his brown hair falling into his eyes. Frey looked at us, black eyes alert, as fresh as if he'd just awoken from a nap. That seemed unfair.

The bedroom was a mess, torn books and toys everywhere. The pictures had fallen from the walls, the glass shattered. I could hear the neighbors' frightened thoughts, wondering if there'd just been an earthquake. Outside, it'd stopped raining. Lily clung tight to Frey, resting her cheek against the top of his head.

Drystan dragged me to my feet and crushed me tight in his arms, too. I fell against him, hardly able to stand. I was as numb as I got after Anisa's visions or one of the bodysnatching nightmares. The edges of who I was blurred, still tangled up in Frey and that vortex of power.

"Are you all right?" Drystan whispered into my ear when I finally pulled away.

"I think so," I said.

—*I gave you some energy back*, Frey said, pulling himself away from his mother's embrace. The covers had fallen back, exposing his skinny legs.

If I was this poorly even with this help, I didn't want to think about how I'd be otherwise.

—*You'd be dead*, he added, answering the thought I hadn't sent him.

I sucked in a breath, but no one else caught his words. I still felt too exposed, too fresh. I clung to Drystan, hiding my face. The light hurt my eyes.

"Thank you," Lily said. "All of you. I don't know what you did, or how you did it, but thank you."

Frey looked at the Phantom Damselfly. "I remember you," he said in wonder.

—*Yes*, Anisa said. *From your dreams.*

"No, it was before that," he said, frowning. "It was a long time ago."

Anisa, for once, was taken aback. Her illusion flickered.

—*Ahti*? she asked, but he only frowned at her in puzzlement.

"How do we stop it from happening again?" I asked Anisa, my voice hoarse.

She tore her gaze from Frey and focused on me. —*You must help Frey learn to control his powers, or else be there to help him stop the vortex*, she said. *It is both to stop harm from befalling others, but also because, if it happens again, the blurred man will sense Frey's power and where he is.*

"Timur seems to have access to someone, like a spirit," I said aloud.

Anisa's expression went evasive.

"Anisa?" I pressed.

—*It does seem so*, she said, cautiously. *But it would seem he accepted the spirit into him permanently.*

Like I might have to do with her, when she ran out of power. I went cold. "In Pinecrest's front room. On his mantelpiece. He had an Aleph."

Lily's mouth opened. "I've seen that, too."

"As have I," Kai echoed, quietly.

Anisa stilled. —*Was it empty?*

"Yes, it felt like the one that used to house Relean," I said. "No one home. If that's the Aleph of the spirit now in Timur, does that mean they are working together?"

She flinched at the mention of her lost lover's name. —*That I do not know. There are plenty of empty Alephs scattered across the world. But if this Timur has access to a Chimaera like me, it might explain why Timur's body broke down and why he was able to use an Ampula to jump bodies.* She shook her head. *As you have experienced, when we blend, it is usually me who has control of your body, since I have better training and control over magic. Timur does not seem to have magic himself, which is why his human body broke down, so I am not sure how he could subdue an unwilling Chimaera phantom.*

"He seems to remember the past, and he's using that knowledge to find a way to destroy Chimaera in the present," I said.

Anisa stared at me intently. —*Even with all the work I'd done to train Ahti and Dev, it was not enough. But if you can manage it, then perhaps there is hope. We must not let Frey hurt anyone.*

"I don't *want* to hurt anyone," Frey said aloud.

Anisa smiled at him, almost sadly. —*Then that is a start, young one.*

—*Timur wants Frey*, I sent to Anisa and Cyan, privately. *He hasn't found him yet, but he wants him.*

Her face rippled, and her body went even more transparent. —*Then you must not let Timur find him. Take all I've taught you. Practice as often as you can. The next time you call me, remember: it will be the last. You must either let me join you permanently, where I may be able to help, or I will die. The choice is yours. I will not make it for you, little Kedi.*

She reached out to touch my cheek with a ghostly hand before disappearing back into the Aleph.

We all stared at it in silence, and I had more questions than answers. I raised my head, and my gaze caught on Kai. He'd just seen everything, and he worked with Pinecrest.

"Now," Drystan said, taking a step toward him. "Whatever are we to do about you?"

Kai hunched his shoulders. "I won't tell Pinecrest anything," he said, his voice hoarse.

"And why should we believe you?" I asked.

Kai met my eyes and straightened his shoulders. "Because I know what he did to me."

22

THE DOCTOR & HIS ASSISTANT

"The thing about addiction is that I know it's what will kill me. It won't be a carriage in the road, or a common flu, or the slow creep of cancer. Lerium will be my ruin and my end. And there's a strange, awful sort of comfort in that."

FROM THE ANONYMOUS MEMOIR OF A LERIUM ADDICT, DISCOVERED AND PUBLISHED POST-MORTEM

I blinked, surprised. At the morgue, Kai had seemed loyal to Doctor Pinecrest. I thought back to the time he'd cornered me at the café and the way he'd worried the napkin. What else had he been planning on telling me before he'd been interrupted by Cyril?

"Kai and I joined forces a few months ago, when we realized we were playing the same game," Lily said.

"It's why I didn't tell the doctor that I'd met you before the morgue," Kai said. "Or why I haven't told him how much Lily's put together. And I've shared next to nothing about Frey."

I felt it, then, subtle enough that I hadn't fully sensed that warmth before. He met my eyes, seeing I'd put it together.

"You're Chimaera," I said. "Tell us the rest of the truth, then, if you want us to believe you."

Drystan sucked in a breath, but Cyan showed no hint of surprise. Kai hesitated before taking off his coat. Underneath, he wore a bulky navy jumper. Awkwardly, he took it off, the shirt beneath revealing a body with a soft belly and a good amount of muscle across his shoulders. He took a deep breath and turned around.

Wings like a bat's spread from his back. They were a different shade from his skin, greyer, and small enough that, when folded tight across his back, they didn't create a noticeable bump. The membranes spread between the bones looked like soft leather, and the color changed from flesh to the same green as Frey's scales. When I'd first come to after my fever, I'd imagined bat wings behind Pinecrest's head. A warning from the spirits about this, or something else?

"You can't fly, I take it?" I asked. Had I felt a flush of warmth when I'd seen him at the restaurant? I couldn't remember. Had he been planning to tell me then?

"No. Far too small for that. They're vestigial." His mouth twisted at the play on words. "Beyond this, I don't have much magic at all. Pinecrest hasn't dosed me with his medicine, either, and I haven't asked him to."

"Pinecrest knows what you are?" Cyan asked as Kai shrugged his shirt and jumper back on.

"Of course he does. He saw my mother when she was pregnant. I put it together after Lily told me." His face darkened with real anger.

"How'd you start working with him?" I asked. I couldn't quite leave my suspicion behind, and judging by Drystan's scowl, he'd set down none of his.

"My mother and I lived in Imachara when I grew up, but we moved to Silken Cove when I was about eight. I came back and went to Pinecrest after I was accepted into medical school, claiming that I wanted to learn, and he took me in. He even helped fund my schooling and made sure I met the right people. I know why he really keeps me around: because I'm one of his experiments. But I don't trust him. I never have, and I never will."

Cyan stepped closer to him. "Can I check that you're telling the truth?" she asked, holding out a hand.

He stared at her palm, nervously licking his lips. He nodded. "I have nothing to hide." He took her palm and gripped it tightly.

Her eyelids fluttered closed. She only stayed long enough to discover what she needed before stepping back and opening her eyes.

"He's telling the truth."

Kai took his hand back, rubbing the skin. "Well. I hope that clears the matter."

"Can I have my chair?" Frey asked. We all looked at him.

Kai went to get his wicker chair and lifted Frey from the bed, settling him into the seat and tucking blankets around him with genuine tenderness.

It was unnerving how unafraid Frey was after his fit. But then, perhaps he didn't know how close he'd come to being lost. Frey reminded me of the Princess, in some ways. They both had to hide their differences, and by protecting him, Lily had also cut Frey off from the world, much like Nicolette. While I'd had my own secret during childhood, I'd been able to hide it easily enough, and had more freedom.

Cyan sat on Frey's bed, her feet drawn up under the skirt of her dress, her arms around her knees. Frey yawned, the light from the gas lamp glinting off his scales.

Lily looked at Frey, her face soft with a mother's love. "Thank you," she said. "I really thought I was going to lose him tonight."

"I'm glad you didn't." I still had no idea what it all meant. What if he wasn't able to control his powers, or I wasn't able to dampen them? I'd seen what happened when Ahti lost control. I shivered. What if Timur wasn't wrong, and Frey was a threat?

"You must all be tired," Lily said. "I won't forget what you've done."

We bid our farewells. At the door, out of sight of Kai and Frey, Drystan turned to Lily. He reached into his jacket pocket and brought out a small vial of the medicine we'd found at Shadow Elwood's. It barely contained a thimbleful.

"I think Pinecrest gave this to Shadow Elwood," he said. "I suspect it's the same elixir he's been dosing Micah with, though it's hard to tell. You think you know someone who might be able to test it, recreate it, and make more, right?"

She cradled it in her hand, as though it were precious. "Yes. Thank you," she whispered. "I'll send it to him first thing tomorrow morning."

"Are you sure you can trust him?"

She nodded. "I believe so. I worked a case for Professor Teak a long time ago, and he owes me a favor. He's known who I used to be all these years and never told a soul. If anyone can figure it out, it's him."

Drystan nodded. "Good. The sooner Micah and Frey can break free of Pinecrest, the better." He was the first one out the door.

We were silent as we returned to the Penny Rookeries, thankfully avoiding any watchmen. Maske's light was off, and Cyan confirmed he was asleep.

"Are you all right?" she asked me.

"I guess," I said. "You?"

"Tired, but I'll be better in the morning." She rubbed her forehead. "Good night, you two." Her door clicked shut behind her.

In our room, Drystan sat on the bed, staring blankly at the rug. He looked beyond haunted. "When Frey was hurting you, I couldn't do anything. I couldn't even touch you without being tossed across the room."

"He was so strong he could have thrown Karg from the circus," I pointed out.

"Even so," he said, clenching his jaw. "It wasn't enough."

"After I came back, I needed you, and you were there. That's not nothing, Drystan."

He nodded but didn't say anything else. We dressed for bed, and every line of his body was taut. He rolled away from me. After a moment, I curled against his back and wrapped my arm around his waist. He took my hand and held it against his chest. Eventually, our eyes closed, and we drifted to dreamless sleep.

●●●●

Of course, soon enough, it was time to visit Doctor Pinecrest again.

To say I was nervous to see him was an understatement. Drystan offered to come, but I waved him off, thinking it'd be easier on my own. This time, though, I'd asked to borrow Maske's Augur. He'd narrowed his eyes at the request.

"No, don't tell me." He cut me off when I opened my mouth to explain. "I'd rather have plausible deniability."

I'd snapped my mouth shut and put the Augur in my pocket, changing it to the setting where only I would know if Pinecrest lied. I'd done this once before, and he hadn't noticed it was on me. I needed all the help I could get as I faced the man who thought he'd successfully erased a few minutes of my memory.

After I knocked on his door and he let me in, Pinecrest left me waiting long enough in the lounge that I grew nervous. My hunger for the drug had grown over the last day, and I was positively ravenous. The Aleph I'd seen on my first visit was gone from the mantlepiece. My eyes darted to the cabinet of curiosities, but Pinecrest wore the square key for it on his person, and I was no pickpocket. Was it linked to Timur, or was it only a coincidence?

"Come on in, Micah," Doctor Pinecrest said, smiling at me warmly. "Apologies for the delay."

He took what felt like ages to prep the syringe. I watched the green liquid, silently willing him to go faster.

Finally, he set the needle against the crook of my elbow and pressed the plunger. The cold ice flowed through my veins.

When I was dosed, I was high but also heightened. My senses sharpened, the power answered my call far easier, and washed my fears away. I hated just how much I craved it.

My eyes fluttered open. Pinecrest was watching me.

"Better?" he asked.

"I suppose," I said, guarded, even as my insides sang. The only thing I liked less than being dependent on the drug was being reliant on Pinecrest for it.

The doctor tidied his things away and brought out his Vestige tea set. Usually, I demurred, anxious to get away from him, but that afternoon, I accepted my cup. The steam smelled of mint and a hint of rose.

"Did you enjoy our performance at the Palace?" I asked.

"I did, very much. The Princess keeps asking if you'll come again every time I see her. She's being very insistent."

Truth.

"Oh, I'm glad," I said. "I was sad to not be able to speak to her after the performance."

Pinecrest blinked twice quickly. "Ah, yes, I'm afraid the Steward whisked her off to the feast. She was quite put out about it."

The Augur made its little chirp, but Pinecrest didn't hear it.

"Well, we'd be happy to perform for her again, if you can pass that onto her and the Steward." I paused. "I worried that he'd dig into our pasts before he'd let us perform and discover that Drystan and I were the fugitives from the circus."

"He doesn't know that," Pinecrest said. The Augur was quiet. Well, at least there was that. Pinecrest had kept one secret back. There were so many other things I wanted to ask him, but I had no idea how to do it without giving away what I remembered.

"I noticed there weren't many children the same age as the Princess there," I said instead.

"Indeed. She's never gotten along particularly well with those the same age as her. I'm not sure she has any true friends," he said. The Augur was silent. "Everyone's instructed to be so careful around her. Perhaps because of the weight of the crown, she's mature for her age, and sees more than she might. Useful for a future monarch, but . . ."

"Less helpful for a lonely girl," I finished.

"Just so. The Steward encourages her to stay separate. It's safer, especially now. Tensions are rising in Imachara, and it feels like it's building to something."

The Augur didn't give a peep.

I took a sip of my mint and rose tea. It was steeped to perfection and just the right temperature. The mint reminded me slightly of my last night at my old house in Sicion, when I'd overheard things not even a Lethe could make me forget. I set my cup aside.

I peered at Pinecrest and recognized an expression I didn't expect. "You're *afraid* of the Princess. Why?"

He laughed. "Don't be ridiculous. I've no reason to fear her."

The Augur chirped his falsehood at me.

"I'm afraid of her uncle," he shared. Truth.

"Why?"

"He's an exacting man, and quite ruthless when he wants to be. If he makes an order, there is no option to refuse, no matter how much you might disagree with it."

Truth.

My heartbeat quickened. Was he hinting that he suspected I remembered what had happened in that side room in the Palace? He was staring into the flames, distantly, as if lost in a memory.

"Doctor Pinecrest?" I asked, and his head snapped up.

"Sorry, I was miles away," he said. "I covered an anatomy lecture at the University this morning, last minute, and I forget how tiring teaching can be sometimes." He quirked a corner of his mouth, but the half-smile didn't reach his eyes. "What is it?"

"Did you discover anything else about the Chimaera corpse?" I asked.

"Unsure," he said. A small chirp from the Augur.

"What does that mean?" I pressed.

He licked his lips. "His body seemed to hold energy. Magic, if you like. As if it was stored in the bones, the tendons, and the muscles. His body decomposed slower, and the glass globes of the morgue seemed to glow brighter in his presence, as if the very air was charged. But, gradually, it lessened, and his body behaved like a normal corpse."

I felt the skin pucker between my brows. I was hyperaware of my muscles, my bones, my eyes. Was I embedded with magic, and if I died, would it leak from me in a similar way? The morbid thought made me shiver.

"Gruesome business, I know," Doctor Pinecrest said.

He rose and gestured to the door. "You'll be wanting to head back, I'm sure. How are you feeling?"

I rose, and the room only tilted slightly. "Dizzy."

"It'll pass," he said, as he always did. "Oh, but Micah." He reached into his pocket and passing me a distinctive, creamy envelope. My fingers brushed his clockwork ones. "I took the liberty of speaking to the Steward again on your behalf. You and Maske's Marionettes are invited back to the Palace in three days' time for the Princess's birthday. I trust this pleases you."

"Thank you, Doctor Pinecrest." I clutched the envelope, suppressed a shudder, and fled.

23

THE NEEDLE

"Lerium is one of the most powerful drugs known to man. It was not consumed by the public until the last century. Before that, it was a sacred substance used only by priests in the remote mountains of Byssia. A foolhardy Eladan trekked through the mountains on his own and became trapped in a snowstorm. He would have died, had not a passing priest seen him shivering beneath a pine tree and taken him to their monastery. The priest may have later regretted his decision.

The priests had one of their ceremonies, and the Eladan, breaking their hospitality, stole some Lerium and tried it himself. The high was the best the man had ever experienced, and this was someone who sampled as many substances as possible. He brought the recipe back with him.

The secret was out. Within a matter of years, Lerium was no longer the exclusive providence of Byssian priests. But Byssians were very canny about it. They kept the recipe and the source of the drug secret, so Elada could not copy it. Though the drug has ravaged many in Byssia, Elada, and all the former colonies, at the same time, it has made Byssia incredibly wealthy.

Yet if that man had perished in the snowstorm, would Lerium still be the well-kept secret of the priests? Would all the people who have since perished from the drug still be alive? Very possibly."

**"LERIUM," PROFESSOR SHAWN TEAK,
ROYAL SNAKEWOOD UNIVERSITY**

We had even less time to prepare for our second performance at the Royal Snakewood Palace. This show was to be part of the entertainment for a masquerade ball, a celebration for Princess Nicolette Snakewood's ninth birthday. We were a last-minute addition thanks to the Royal Physician's influence.

The fee from our previous visit had paid for most of the Kymri Theatre's roof. With another payment of the same amount, we'd almost be in the clear. Maske was a ball of anxious energy, and he kept asking what we'd fix next in the theatre. "The kitchen? The gridiron? The mosaic in the hallway?"

"I don't know, this place has sort of grown on me," I teased him. "It has a certain charm."

"The hot water's stopped working, and every time we turn on the stove, we worry it's going to explode," Cyan said. "And there's mold in my room."

"Charming mold?" I asked. She pretended to throw something at me, and I pantomimed ducking.

Over the next couple of days, we heard Maske banging away in his makeshift workshop at all hours. He'd drag us into the lounge and have us map out a fight scene or spend entire days practicing.

Lily had set up our Mirror of Moirai, and it was beyond strange to stare into the reflective surface and see her staring back at me. I snuck off to Lily's with Cyan one afternoon to check on Frey and teach him the basics of what Anisa had taught me.

"Focus," I told him, Cyan at my side. Frey was restless, bored of practicing within a few minutes. We persevered. I helped him clear his mind and asked him to imagine building mental walls around himself, drawing the power closer to his chest.

Cyan shook her head in amazement. "He's done it. I can't sense anything from him at all."

Next, I tried to help him direct his power, instructing him to focus on one of his teddy bears. I attempted to demonstrate, but only really managed to give the teddy bear a sad wobble. Within a few tries, though, Frey levitated it and set it back down.

Soon, even Frey and his boundless energy flagged. He yawned, stretching his arms over his head. Lily brought some fruit for us.

"Frey's power seems stable," I said.

"But how long until it happens again?" Lily said, stealing a green grape for herself. "If we weren't tied to Pinecrest, I'd leave Imachara tonight. Hopefully, it won't take Professor Teak too long to recreate the formula."

"I could maybe give you another dose or two from our stash," I said, taking a slice of apple. "Then you could escape for a couple of weeks. Whatever Timur is planning, I think he means to do it soon."

She nodded. "Thank you."

"I'll bring it tomorrow, after we perform for the Princess," I promised, before heading back to the Penny Rookeries.

Maske, Drystan, Cyan, and I had managed to cobble together something good for the performance, but I was exhausted, even though I was only midway between doses. I, too, wanted to break my reliance on the doctor, and hopefully wean myself off of the drug.

"It's a brilliant routine," Cyan said as we clustered around our small dining table in our tiny kitchen in the Rookeries. "Don't fret."

"How am I supposed to not worry?" Maske said, pacing the cracked tiles. His voice was rough. "It went well last time, but that doesn't mean half a dozen things couldn't go pear-shaped."

"You'll have planned for each and every one of them," I reassured him.

"Your stew's gone tepid," Drystan pointed out, mildly. The three of us had finished our bowls a quarter of an hour ago, and his had congealed unpleasantly.

"I've no appetite," Maske said, his eyes bright, his cheeks flushed.

"My stomach's in knots. I've so much more to do." He made a gagging sound and ran to the bathroom. Distantly, we heard the sound of him retching.

When he came back out, looking green and miserable, Cyan pressed her hand against his forehead. "I think you're ill."

"I can't be," Maske croaked, his voice nearly gone. His eyes were wide with panic.

"Head to bed," Drystan said. "Maybe a good night of rest will keep you right."

His groan came out more like an indignant squeak, but the real sign he was feeling awful was that he didn't fight us and shuffled off straight to bed.

• • • •

I awoke in the middle of the night, alone. I lay on my back, staring up at the ceiling. I had the sense that I'd dreamed. I closed my eyes, trying to recall the details, but only had a sense of those same dark walls, the sound of dripping water, and . . . a flash of red?

I thought Drystan had gone to the toilet, but after about ten minutes, my restlessness grew.

I left the bed, my bare feet cold on the floor.

He wasn't in the bathroom. I reached out with my mind. Cyan was asleep, as was Maske. Drystan, strangely, was in the tiny box room we used for the storage of our magic kit. If he couldn't sleep, usually he'd go to kitchen or the small lounge and its banked fire.

I put my hand on the doorknob, frozen with indecision. I strained to read him and sensed . . . elation?

I'm probably going to regret this, I thought before pushing open the door.

For a moment, the room seemed empty aside from the covered

magical props, and I squinted. There, in the corner, Drystan held a needle of a vial of Pinecrest's medicine against his skin. He'd pushed it down, slightly, but the glass was still mostly full of green liquid.

"Shit." I darted forward, but he beat me to it, pulling the needle from his skin, the glass clattering to the floor, before he turned away from me and curled into a ball with a sob.

"Drystan," I said, my hand on his shoulder. "How much did you take?"

His head turned, his teeth chattering. "Not much."

"Why, Drystan?" My hands fluttered over him, unsure what to do. I had no idea how the medicine would affect him. What if even a small dose was poisonous because he wasn't Chimaera? What had possessed him to do this, without even warning me or Cyan?

Drystan's eyes opened and focused on me, his pupils completely hiding the iris.

"I wanted to see if it's like Anisa said. That if you have enough magic, you can sense the threads of the world," he said.

"And did you?" I asked, carefully.

A line appeared between his eyes. "Everything is made of light. The blue of Penglass, the orange of sunset, the red of blood."

I didn't know what to say. I felt my heart beating in my throat.

"I thought I saw him," he said, insistent. "Timur. The blurred man. He was standing on the shore, surrounded by rocks, looking at the waves. Above him there was this . . . pulsing red light? It was terrible being in his head. He's nothing but hate; he's all twisted up with it." He buried his face in his hands. "Lord and Lady, what have I done. I just . . . I wanted to be better than myself for a little while."

"Oh, Drystan," I said, stroking the hair back from his face. "But don't you see? I don't need you to be anything other than yourself."

"You do," he said, pushing me away. "I didn't do this for the high. You have to believe me. It wasn't for that . . ."

"Is this why you gave the sample to Lily?" I asked. "Because you wanted to have access to more? Have you taken this before?"

"No!" he said, the word forceful. "You were muttering in your sleep from a nightmare, and I couldn't wake you. I thought maybe it was Frey again, and you'd be trapped. And I was so desperate to do something, *anything*, that I thought . . . if it could give me power when I felt so powerless . . . then maybe it was worth it." He raised his head, his eyes bright, the pupils glittering obsidian. "And maybe it did. Maybe I caught your nightmare."

I wanted to chastise him, to show him all of my fear. But he was already punishing himself for what he'd done more than I ever could.

I opened my mouth. "I should take you to Pinecrest."

"No!" he said again, even more insistent. "I don't want to go anywhere near him."

"What if you've poisoned yourself, Drystan?"

"I took a small dose, much less than he gives you. I danced my way around Lerium long enough in my time to know it's not been too much. He'd just tell me to sleep it off, but then he'd know we have a stash from Elwood. Can't risk it."

"But you haven't taken Lerium mixed with mysterious, ancient Alder substances." I pressed my fingertips to his neck, but his pulse was steady. I saw no obvious signs of an overdose, but it's not as if I was an expert. I could take him to Kai, maybe, but I was pretty sure he lived in the university dorms, and I'd no idea how to sneak in there undetected.

"The high is already fading. I'll be fine by morning," Drystan insisted. He held his outstretched palm to the empty syringe. "How do you do it? Move things with your mind?"

Did the syringe twitch, or did I imagine it? He gave a groan of frustration. "No wonder they're so afraid of Chimaera," he said. "If I had taken more, what would it have let me do?"

I swallowed against the dryness of my mouth. His eyelids drooped, as if some of the energy was leaving him.

I drew him upright. "Come on. Come to bed."

Drystan protested weakly, but leaned against me. "Did you know there's no one like you in the entire world, Micah Grey?"

"Yes, I did. There's no one like you, either. We're all unique."

He stared off, thoughtfully. "Does it hurt? When Anisa steps into you?"

I felt the skin between my eyes pucker. "No."

"Does it frighten you?"

"Yes, of course. She takes control of my body."

He shook his head, as if casting off a fly. "If you call her again, you have to decide if you'll keep her."

I shivered. I didn't need reminding.

"I keep thinking about what she says about you. That you're going to be so important in what's to come. I think she's right." His voice was distant.

I paused, my fingertips going cold. "What do you mean, Drystan?"

"I can almost remember the dream. Something with the red light. Waves. Chimaera trapped in Penglass . . . ?" He trailed off and shook his head. "There are so many lives. Each with their own story. Their own joys. Their own sorrows." His expression fell. "You always see through me, Micah. Always see to the heart of it. And you're still here. You're not afraid."

"Why would I be afraid of you?"

"Because I've done terrible things. I was a terrible person," he said. The tip of his nose reddened, and his eyes filled with tears. "Maybe I still am. I swore I would never stick a needle in my veins again. I promised Maske, years ago, and then I failed under his own roof. I've disappointed him. I've disappointed you. I disappoint everyone."

The tears tracked their way down his cheeks freely.

"Stop this, Drystan," I said, trying to pitch my voice kind but firm. "I won't stand for you feeling this sorry for yourself." My tone was too sharp. "You've made a mistake. You learned from it. You moved on. You're not the same person you were when you first ran away from home, any more than I am."

He met my eyes, blearily. His pupils were smaller.

"You were one of my first friends in the circus, in your weird way," I continued. "Scared me half-senseless when you did that odd thing with your eyes."

That startled a laugh from him. He made his eyes vibrate in his sockets, just like he had the night I met him.

"Argh, I still hate it."

He laughed weakly, but he relaxed his eyes.

"I mean it," I said as he slipped back into bed. "When I told you who I had been before, you kept my secret. You saved my life. You weren't afraid that I was different. Do you realize how much that means to me? Ever since I can remember, my mother always told me that no one could accept me as I was. That I had to hide and change to be accepted. I'm so grateful to have you, to love you and have you love me." My outpouring of words sputtered to a halt.

Drystan broke down, weeping openly. I crawled in next to him and drew him closer. Cyan had woken from her slumber, and I sensed her alarm from her room.

—*He took a dose of Pinecrest's medicine. Read him*, I sent to her. *Is he in any physical danger?*

A pause. —*He's definitely affected by it, but it's fading. He doesn't seem at risk.*

I sensed her half-rise from the bed.

—*Stay there, please*, I told her. She drifted away but left the smallest tendril of concern behind.

We curled around each other, drifting off. Hours later, Drystan's eyes opened, the beautiful blue bloodshot. But he seemed himself again, more or less.

"You're still here," he whispered.

"Where else would I be?"

His breath caught in his throat. "Oh, Micah. I don't think I was capable of loving anyone as much as I love you."

I kissed him, and he clung to me. I held him until his breathing evened.

Once Drystan was asleep, I slipped from the bed, tucking the covers around him. Methodically, I went through our room, into every nook and cranny. Nothing.

I crept back to the bed and whispered in his ear: "Where's the medicine, Drystan?"

Drystan mumbled, but I couldn't catch it. I asked him again.

"Mmmh. You'll just hide it."

"Obviously. Where is it, Drystan?"

A brief, sleepy whine. A sigh. "Bookshelf in the lounge. Behind the history of Lerium." He laughed softly and then settled back into sleep.

I found the book and pulled it free. He'd given a sample to Lily and used the rest of that vial, but there were two left. My fingers shook as I held them. Despite everything, I was tempted to take an extra dose of my own, to have that extra power, so I felt stronger facing whatever came next. Somehow, I resisted.

I ended up sneaking into Maske's bedroom. He slept soundly. I found a cupboard filled with old, spare brass springs and cogs and hid the vials at the very back. I locked the cupboard and hid the key in another drawer. It'd mean awkward questions if Maske needed to access that cupboard, but judging by the state of the coils, he'd brought them "just in case" and he'd never actually use them.

I went back upstairs and crawled into bed with the boy I loved. I stroked his hair and watched him for the rest of the night. His brow furrowed, and he occasionally mumbled something. I wondered if he dreamed of the blurred man, and what he'd remember once he woke. Finally, his expression smoothed. I tasted magic swirling through the air like dust motes. The glass globe on the other side of the room briefly glowed before it dimmed and left us in darkness until dawn.

24

THE GARGOYLE

"*Attention: security throughout the Royal Snakewood Palace is to be doubled. Shifts are lengthening from nine to ten hours. Anyone willing to work extra shifts, please report to the Head of Security, and new vacancies will be posted imminently. Current guards are encouraged to recommend names of friends and family they can personally attest to being strong, capable, and trustworthy.*
In the Royal Snakewoods' name,
Palace Security."

PERSONNEL MEMO, ROYAL SNAKEWOOD PALACE

Sure enough, the next morning, Maske couldn't speak a word through his sore throat, and he was running a low fever.

He struck the pillow with his fist when we told him he'd have to stay behind. He couldn't very well narrate the show at the Palace without his voice, and the guards wouldn't let him near the Princess looking as sick as he did. He lay back in his bed, defeated.

In the kitchen, I made him a cup of tea while Drystan and Cyan leaned against the counter. Drystan was quiet and nursing a headache, and his eyes still glittered in a way I didn't like. I felt rough, both because my latest dose seemed to be waning faster than usual, and because I'd slept an hour or two at best.

—*Is Drystan all right?* Cyan asked me in the privacy of our minds.

—As well as can be expected.

She considered him. *—For all he thinks he's already done it, he needs to really examine his feelings. Reconcile his old life with his new one.*

As usual, she'd found a way to express it perfectly. Drystan hadn't quite mended the broken pieces of the various people he had been. The spoiled nobleman. The drug dealer and addict. The card sharp. The white clown in the circus, and now a magician's apprentice who had turned his life around. Despite all he'd done, he couldn't shed the guilt of who he used to be.

"I noticed something this morning," Drystan said, his voice uncharacteristically hesitant.

"What?" I asked.

He pulled up the sleeve of his shirt. There, in the crook of his arm, was a mark. Right where the needle had gone. I squinted, moving closer. It was as dark green as the elixir.

I rolled up my sleeves, but I didn't see any marks on my skin. "Maybe it left the mark because you're not Chimaera?"

"That's what I suspected." He swallowed. "You said Pinecrest speaks in your mind sometimes, but it's difficult for him. I bet if you looked at the skin of his elbow, you'd see a collection of marks just like this. I think he's human and he's dosing himself." He rubbed the mark, as if he could erase it, before rolling his sleeve back down.

I sucked in a breath. It made sense.

"I also expect if you or Frey went off the medicine, it wouldn't actually be too difficult. It doesn't seem to be as addictive as straight Lerium, at least not physically. I could tell that even from my lighter dose."

"But what about the fit I had? Or the fact that I feel so tired before treatments?"

Drystan thought back, his brow crinkling. He looked much better than he had this morning. I could tell that focusing on this problem was easier for him than having to face what happened last night. "The night we won the duel against Taliesin. Pinecrest was there, at the party afterward, wasn't he?"

"Yes," I said. "I spoke to him."

"Did he give you anything?"

My stomach turned. "A glass of wine. I had one sip."

Drystan nodded. "There you go. He pulled a magic trick of his own. Basic misdirection. Caused the fit, let you believe it was due to your health, and then started dosing you once a week. That explains why Cyan has had no symptoms."

"That manipulative bastard." I felt my nostrils flare. "What if I stop and do grow worse?"

"Well, then we have enough for a few doses to help wean you off." His jaw worked. "You hid them well, I hope?"

My mouth opened, then closed. I could only nod.

"Well . . . that will help for a while. Otherwise, I suppose we hope this friend of Lily's can figure out what's in it, and if need be, we somehow recreate the formula. But I think you could tell Lily to skip town, and Frey will be just fine."

"We'll send word," I agreed. "But do we go to the Palace without Maske?"

Cyan grimaced. "I don't know. It might be a good excuse not to go, after what happened last time."

"That's my thought. What if Pinecrest makes me forget again?" Drystan whispered, unable to hide his fear.

"I won't let him touch you," I promised, fiercely.

"Last night I thought I had all the answers of the world at my fingertips. Today I feel as blind as a newborn mole rat." His mouth twisted.

"The Steward doesn't know we were the fugitives from the circus, at least. Pinecrest unwittingly confirmed that much," I said.

Eventually, Cyan nodded. "I say we go."

Drystan grimaced. "I'll follow your lead, I suppose."

Cyan held her hands out. Drystan and I each took one and squeezed.

"We'll do you proud," I promised Maske when I brought him his tea. "Just rest and mentally spend the coin on repairs."

Maske gestured his thanks, even as his forehead was creased with frustration. By the time we left our rooms, he was in a deep sleep, his tea growing cold beside him.

• • • •

The air was thick with the threat of a summer storm. We stopped by Lily's long enough to tell her our theory before we went to the Kymri Theatre to wait for the royal carriage to pick us up. Like last time, we weren't about to send it into the Penny Rookeries. The outside of the theatre looked almost back to normal, and I stared at it hungrily. Soon, we'd be back, I hoped. Soon.

When the carriage arrived, the footmen loaded up our kit and we climbed inside. I didn't like the mistrustful looks people gave the carriage, with its royal coat of arms painted on the side. Later today, there was going to be a Forester protest in the Glass District that would march toward the Palace. Rumors were it might turn ugly. Soon enough, we arrived outside the Palace gates, its turrets stark against an overcast sky.

After the seemingly endless search through our possessions, we were led into the same room where we'd performed last time. We unpacked, painting our faces and changing into our costumes. We waited behind the curtains for the Princess and her guests.

The Princess wore a gilded mask and a dress of gold brocade and walked, stiff and proper, in front of a few girls closer to her own age. She settled at the front of the stage, rearranging her skirts. Cyan fed us the names of the masked girls we didn't know: Laya Oakbeam and Katharine Huckleberry. The last face of a young woman around my age I most definitely recognized: Darla Hornbeam. Drystan stared at his younger sister avidly.

Drystan tied on his mask. He'd chosen his green silk cravat for his suit tonight. I gave his shoulder a pat. Drystan would be narrating in Maske's absence, with me and Cyan performing. The show had been hastily re-designed to only briefly require a stagehand.

Drystan stepped out in front of the audience.

"A long time ago," he began, "there once was a Princess who lived in a faraway land. She had many friends, but sometimes she liked to be alone to watch the sun set and the moon rise."

The Princess shifted in her seat. We were drawing on one of *Hestia's Fables*. I found my thoughts drifting to Frey, wishing he could somehow be here tonight, too. I wondered where Lily would hide him and herself until it was safe.

"One day," Drystan continued, "she went to a tower that faced the west, as it had the best view. She hadn't climbed those steps in a long time, for, as a child, she'd found the gargoyle statues frightening. Yet one of them did not seem so fierce, so she stood beside it as the last of the sun faded."

With his foot, Drystan tripped a hidden lever, which caused a long swathe of silk to fall over the stage for just a moment. He tore it away, revealing Cyan and me in costume.

Cyan wore a Temnian robe, her hair freshly braided with beads. Her tin crown was studded with glass jewels, but under the light of the globes, it looked as fine as any coronet.

I was not so pretty. My skin was painted grey and my hair dusted white with chalk. I wore old, ripped clothing, likewise stone grey. I stared straight ahead. A gargoyle statue.

Drystan, behind stage, moved the glass globes to mimic sunset, and another silken cloth fell against the backdrop. This one was dark blue and dotted with stars, embroidered by Cyan and Drystan, as I was still rather hopeless with a needle and thread.

As the last "ray" of light left the stage, I shook myself awake, a small cloud of chalk rising from me. I stood on the low wall of the tower and stretched. My constructed wings rose behind me, fully articulated bat-like appendages made of metal, wood, and leather. They looked a little like Kai's, though bigger, and not bad for being made in two days.

Hopping down from the wall, I held up my hands to stop Cyan from fleeing the "tower."

"Wait, Your Majesty," I called. "I am called Petros. If you stay, I'll show you magic and tell you tales of such wonder that you have never heard. The world is wider and wilder than you could ever imagine."

Hesitantly, she returned, perching on the wall.

The magic show began in earnest. With prestidigitation, I made more of the carved wooden puppets I'd used in the lantern appear in my hands, the movements blending seamlessly with the tales I told the Princess of lands far away, filled with other Chimaera that I had flown to see. Behind stage, Drystan helped with sound and lighting effects. Soon, Cyan was laughing, no longer afraid.

When I finished, my character grew despondent. "I am enchanted," I said. "By day, I am hard as stone. By night, I come alive, but I cannot leave the top of this tower. I cannot fly." I shrugged my shoulders, and the constructed wings flapped. "How I miss the sky."

"Why were you cursed?" Cyan asked.

"Those in power think I mean them harm, though I'd do no such thing." I heard a couple of subdued gasps from the audience. We weren't meant to be overly political in our performance, and yet here was our unsubtle message, all the same.

"A wizard decided to trap me and was hailed as a hero for saving the kingdom from danger," I continued. "No one realized until it was too late that he was the monster, not me."

Cyan stood. "I know magic as well," she declared. "Perhaps I can free you, and you may take to the skies once again."

My eyes went wide with hope. "You would do that for me?"

Cyan closed her eyes, sifting through the audience's minds to find out which display would impress them best. She clapped her hands together, and the hidden chemicals she palmed sparked blue. Drystan maneuvered behind the scenes, and Cyan rose, held aloft on a strong, nearly invisible black wire.

She began to mutter in Temri, peppered with the odd bit of Alder. She clapped her hands again and, thanks to Drystan, the glass globes bloomed, as if lightning were in the room. Drystan created another boom of thunder. Cyan lowered herself to the ground, panting.

I sighed. "That was a lovely display, Your Highness, but it didn't work."

Cyan looked crestfallen. "Are you sure?"

"I am, my Princess. For look, the sun returns."

On cue, Drystan moved the glass globes so that the stage filled with soft oranges and pinks. I returned to my perch and settled myself back into my statuesque pose.

Cyan touched my shoulder and jumped back.

"So cold! As if made of stone!" she exclaimed. She stared at me in amazement before gathering her skirts and fleeing.

Another drop of the curtain, and then Drystan appeared back on the stage, taking up his role as narrator. In the wings, Cyan and I readied ourselves for the second half of the show.

"The years passed," he said, "but the Princess continued to visit the gargoyle at the top of the tower. As she grew from Princess to

Queen, she searched for a way to break the gargoyle's spell. For over time, they became close friends, and the gargoyle, with his centuries of experience, often gave her sound advice for her kingdom."

A pause, and I could imagine him slowly pacing the stage, making sure the audience was under his spell. "But sometimes, the Princess despaired—could Petros ever truly be set free? Could she undo the punishment he was wrongly given?"

Drystan disappeared with a flourish of his cape, leaving Cyan and me to take his place.

Cyan had changed into a dress with long, flowing sleeves. Her new crown rose high from her brow. She stood on stage, stiff-backed, as regal as the Queen she was meant to be.

"Over the years, I've searched far and wide," she said. To her left were several books which levitated thanks to more hidden wires, twirling slowly. We had gotten the idea from Frey's room after his magic attack. "I've emptied libraries and asked the greatest scholars and folklorists throughout the Archipelago about the myths of gargoyles. But no one knows anything that could break the spell. I'm so sorry, Petros." Her voice broke. "I don't know how to save you."

I turned my head and jumped down from the tower perch. "I don't think there is a way to free me, fair Queen. I have long since resigned myself to this fact. I am content to stay here, looking out on the horizon to protect you from evil, as long as you continue to visit me before sunrise."

Cyan shook her head. "That is not enough. I want you to be able to fly as I promised you."

I smiled at her sadly. "Your stories are my sustenance. For even if I were free, where could I fly to without risk of being shot from the sky? The world has changed so much since I was young. No, my Queen. I am where I need to be."

"Then I welcome you home, Petros," Cyan said.

At her words, the glass globes shifted to dark blues and purples. But the light that shone on me was all reds, oranges, and yellows. With another lift from unseen wires, I spread my wings out wide.

"The spell has broken," I said, delighted. I gave a short "flight" around the stage, lifted by wires, flapping the mechanical wings. The audience clapped as Cyan clasped her hands over her mouth in delight.

"But how?" she asked. "Why now?"

"I don't know. Perhaps the Lord and the Lady decided I had suffered enough. Or your acceptance was the key."

Drystan stepped out and finished the story. "Even though the gargoyle was freed, he stayed by the side of his Queen through all her long reign. He flew throughout the kingdom, protecting the borders. He became her adviser in earnest, though some still feared him and called him a monster. With the curse broken, the gargoyle aged. Decades later, when the Queen died, her gargoyle soon followed."

The glass globes brightened again, and the three of us bowed to applause. The audience clapped. The Princess smiled like the rest of them, but there was a small line between her eyes. The allegory was fairly evident: Chimaera, like the gargoyle, meant no harm. The Steward hadn't watched the performance, for he was entertaining in the masquerade for some of the guests in the grand ballroom, but I'm sure if he'd been there, he'd have scowled. He'd probably hear of it, and I wondered if we'd ever be allowed to perform for the Princess again.

I decided it was worth it.

25

UNMASKED

> "The nobility love nothing more than a masked ball. While they may be stiffly laced into their ballgowns or buttoned into their fine suits, the masks, like the Carnivale of the lower classes, give them a certain freedom. Liaisons can happen discreetly, and everyone will look the other way. While you cannot behave as wantonly as those in the Penny Rookeries, perhaps you can still bend the rules a little."
>
> **A HISTORY OF ELADA AND ITS FORMER COLONIES,
> PROFESSOR CAED CEDAR, ROYAL SNAKEWOOD UNIVERSITY**

After the performance, I'd found a washroom, scrubbed off the worst of the grey greasepaint, and changed back into my magician's suit. I tied my mask back on to fit in with all the other revelers for, this time, we were allowed to stay at the ball if we wished. The Princess had insisted on it, and it was her birthday, after all.

Music played from a quartet in the corner, and pairs swirled around the dance floor to a waltz. Outside the palace gates, many barely had enough to eat, while inside, people nibbled fine cakes and drank champagne. And here we were, among them. I might have lived in the Penny Rookeries for a few weeks, but I'd been raised closer to this than the slums. I felt abruptly embarrassed and more than a little ashamed. I glanced about for Doctor Pinecrest, but I didn't see the Royal Physician. Had his mask successfully disguised him from me, or was he elsewhere?

We hadn't had a proper dinner, so we sampled the various morsels carried around on trays or gravitated to the punch bowl. A few of the nobles tried to angle for our stage secrets, but Drystan and I demurred. The other merrymakers seemed faintly amused by us, as if our presence was a quaint indulgence. It rankled a little, but Drystan and I drew on all our etiquette training, and Cyan gently plucked pointers from our heads. A nobleman asked Cyan to dance, and she curtsied and let herself be swept away, the bell of her dress flaring like a tulip.

"You know," Drystan said, swirling his champagne in his glass. "I think I actually prefer the Penny Rookeries to all this."

I'd been feeling the same. We clinked our glasses together and took a sip, the bubbles bursting on our tongues as we watched the dancing.

The Princess found us a while later. Her eyes were bright behind the golden mask, and jewels glittered in her hair.

"Happy birthday, Your Highness," I said, and Cyan and Drystan echoed me.

"Thank you. Your performance was a most excellent gift." She dimpled at us.

—*How are you feeling, Your Highness?* I chanced asking her with my mind.

—*Much better than last time, thank you*, she replied, her hand drifting to where her Glamour hid beneath the fabric of her golden bodice. This close, I could see that the brocade had animals hidden in its design—stylized cats, bears, and deer with antlers.

—*I'm glad*, I said.

—*I've been wanting to speak to you*, she said. *Somewhere quiet.*

—*Lead the way, Your Highness.*

Her gaze flicked to the two guards lurking at the edges of the ballroom. —*Go to the same side room as before. I'll meet you in a few minutes.* She lifted her skirts. It was still unnerving to see a child who had just turned nine act so much older.

We followed her instructions, but it was slow-going, as more people congratulated us on our performance. Drystan was the one to turn on the charm and thank them. He was the white clown but now dressed in tails. Only I—and maybe Cyan—noticed how his gaze kept sliding over to Darla, Damien, and Nigel Hornbeam. While plenty of others were nibbling the fine cakes on display, Darla avoided them. She still had no sweet tooth, it seemed.

Finally, we managed to slip away into the side room. I'd been so addled last time, I'd barely taken in the gilded mirrors, the chandeliers, the sumptuous silken cushions of the furniture, and the Arrasian rug beneath our feet.

The door opened, and the Princess slipped in, flanked by the two guards. I recognized one with blue-green eyes from last time, but the other was a stranger.

She looked at Drystan, puzzled, for, as far as she knew, he remembered nothing.

"He doesn't remember, but we believe he deserves to see it for himself," I said to her.

The Princess took off her gilded mask, and then, with a sigh, she switched off her Glamour, revealing the blue-tinged skin, the dark blue hair, and the unnatural angle of her features. Drystan's eyes went round as saucers.

The guards stiffened, and she shot them a stern look. "It's fine, Marcus and Eric. I promise. You needn't even tell the Steward before you're Lethed for the evening. That's a direct order."

She stared at them so imperiously that I saw the makings of a future Queen.

"Yes, Your Highness," they murmured, but the blue-green-eyed one, Eric, didn't seem happy about it.

"What did you wish to tell us, Your Highness?" I asked.

She shuffled, and despite her different features, she suddenly seemed a child again. "I've been growing ill more often, and it's harder to keep the Glamour functioning. The doctor increased his dose, but I'm not sure if it's working or not. I keep having these dreams . . ." She trailed off.

"What do you dream about?" I asked, my heart hammering.

"There are other Chimaera around me. We try to break free, but we can't manage. We're in . . . glass?" She trailed off, frowning. "Then there's a bright light, red or maybe purple, and I wake up screaming. I've had it every night for the last week. Does it mean anything to you?"

I licked my lips. "I'm not entirely sure," I admitted. Drystan had a dream of pulsing red light and Timur standing on a rocky shore. I stepped forward and took her hands, speaking my next words to her mind-to-mind. Even if the guards were spelled to forget, I was still afraid to speak too openly.

—When we last spoke to your uncle, we mentioned a man named Timur, I said. *Do you know who that is?*

She looked at me, her blue eyes wide. *—Not really. I only know the Foresters hate the monarchy. They hate me.*

—They hate the crown and what you represent, not you as a person, I said, even though I knew I was partly sparing a child's feelings. *They hate that their lives are hard. But Timur doesn't work with them anymore, as far as we can tell. He was the one behind the Celestial Cathedral attacks, and we think he's planning something else. We've been trying to find out more and to stop him. Hopefully, your uncle has been looking for him, too.*

—I'll see what I can do, she said. *He never tells me anything, though. He always says I must wait until I'm older.*

Drystan's eyebrows were furrowed during this exchange, which had taken only moments. The guards stared straight ahead.

"Perhaps it's only a dream," I said, as if responding to what she'd last said aloud. "You should head back to the masquerade before your uncle or friends realize you're missing. It is your birthday, after all. Many happy returns, Your Highness."

Her smile was wan. She reached for the Glamour and turned it around in her hands. "It feels so much heavier. I wish I didn't need it."

We didn't know what to say to that. We watched as she grew the illusion over her Alder features as elegantly as she had the first time. Soon enough, she merely looked like a young girl in an expensive dress with jewels hidden in her hair. Reluctantly, she tied the golden mask back around her head.

The guards clustered near her. Eric looked back over his shoulder at us, and I couldn't read his expression.

We headed back to the grand ballroom, but I wasn't in the mood for more festivities. A sense of dread plucked at me, and though I trusted that intuition, I didn't know where it was coming from. I had a deep urge to get away from here, to go home.

"Something's wrong," Drystan said, his gaze darting between us. "I can feel it."

The Steward bustled into the ballroom, tension rising off him in waves. Behind him, guards streamed in, lining the perimeter.

"Honored guests," the Steward said when he reached the center of the ballroom, his voice carrying easily and bouncing against the marble. "I'm afraid we must cut short tonight's celebrations. We have just had word that people are breaking curfew, and a mob is aiming to march upon the Palace tonight."

I reached for Cyan's hand, and she sent her awareness out beyond the gates. With all the Vestige in the Palace, it was easier. Sure enough, we saw people streaming from apartment buildings, joining a throng.

Many held single candles, the flames illuminating their faces to show the ribbons tied around their mouths. It was a symbol of how they felt silenced by the curfew and the monarchy's policies. It was a protest organized by the Foresters.

"I must ask you all to go to guest quarters within the Palace now. No one can leave or enter the grounds tonight. With luck, this will be swiftly quashed, and you may all return to your homes first thing tomorrow morning."

Murmurs broke out among the guests. Half of my awareness was still out in the city. I felt some anger bubbling beneath the surface of the crowd. This protest was aiming to be peaceful, and while I didn't see anything resembling a mob, I suspected much would depend on how the Palace reacted to it. I didn't have high expectations that they'd do this without a show of force. It could very well backfire.

The Princess was gazing up at her uncle in open-mouthed alarm. I caught the barest shimmer on her skin. She was losing control of her illusion. Her guards loomed protectively behind her.

"Come, Your Highness," the guard, Eric, told her. "To your quarters. Now." He shot a look at us.

Other guards came toward Drystan, Cyan, and I, practically grabbing us by the elbows.

"Can't we just go home?" I asked. "We're only entertainers."

"No one leaves," the other guard, Marcus, said, stone-faced. "It's not safe, sir. Please, come with me."

Cyan narrowed her eyes at him. —*Leave us*, she instructed. *Leave us be.* I reached for my power, too, unsure if it would answer or what form it would take.

Their footsteps briefly slowed, but then there was a snap of magic, and they shook their heads. Cyan's influence hadn't worked. Had someone used an Eclipse nearby? I went cold, clutching my Glamour pendant, but it was thankfully still working. Even if I'd been able to keep my own spark of power, I couldn't exactly risk unveiling myself as a Chimaera in front of some of the most powerful people in Elada.

My head twisted, trying to figure out who had done it. But all was barely constrained chaos in the ballroom. The guards grabbed our elbows more firmly and marched us down the corridor. We reached a residential wing, and they practically threw us into a grand suite. At least they weren't separating us. I rushed toward the door.

"The Crown will update you once we've heard more," Eric said. He was close enough I could see his blue-green eyes were banded with copper. There was a dark spot by his iris. Something tugged at me, like a half-remembered dream. "Do not leave this room."

The door closed, and we heard it being locked from the outside. Drystan jiggled the doorknob, then bashed his fists on the door. "Let us out!" he cried. "You can't keep us here against our will!"

But they could, of course. Because this was the Royal Palace, and their authority here was absolute.

"What am I missing?" I muttered. "What am I missing?"

I kept thinking of the guard's eyes. The certainty spread through me as clearly as if the spirits had whispered it into my ear. It couldn't be. Could it?

"What?" Drystan asked, seeing something shift in my face.

"The spirit in Timur. The one that gives him access to magic and memories of the past. I've realized who it is, and whose body Timur stole."

Not long before the magician's duel, Anisa had taken control of my body long enough to fix Maske's automaton for the final illusion of our act. When Maske had caught us in his workshop, he had told us of the Vestige he'd lost to his old rival as part of the previous terms of the duel. Another Aleph, with a dragonfly man inside. Anisa had focused on him with an intensity that had almost frightened me.

—*His eyes,* she'd said. *Were they banded with blue, green, and copper? With a little dot of darkness, like the wing of a monarch butterfly, just here?* She had pointed to the bottom of her right iris.

"It's Relean. Anisa's Relean," I said. "He's the one within Timur."

Drystan paused in his frantic banging on the door.

Cyan stilled. "Lady," she breathed. "You might be right."

I paced the room, agitated. "When Anisa took control of my body, I always felt trapped in a corner of my mind. Not even Anisa put this together. But Timur somehow figured out how to do the opposite, to overpower a Chimaera ghost and keep him contained. And it's Relean," I said, breathing faster. "Timur's jumped to a new body after his original failed, taking Relean with him, but I bet this one will start breaking down too, if it hasn't already. I thought the Palace guard, Eric, was just sort of generically familiar. That's the body that Timur stole from the hospital ward. He'd been injured in the original Celestial Cathedral attack."

"So he took another body for himself," Cyan said, hushed. "Poor Eric, whoever he used to be."

"Exactly," I said, feeling sick at the thought. "He'd been there, watching us with the Princess, hiding right in plain sight."

Drystan whistled low. "It's a clever plan. I'll give the bastard that."

Cyan stared into the distance, her expression vague. I shook my head, still struggling to put it together. "He caught Relean, but doing so made him sick. Yet he learned enough of the magic of the past to cheat death itself."

"We have Relean's empty Aleph back in the Penny Rookeries, though," Drystan said. "How did Timur even do this?"

I shook my head. "I have no idea. But it doesn't matter. He's done it. Timur stole that body on purpose. To get close to the Princess. He's been at her side for weeks."

Cyan bent over, clasping her knees.

"Cyan?" I asked. "What is it?"

She didn't answer me. Her eyes were glowing blue, and her mouth slackened with the force of her vision. I reached for Cyan's hand, and the physical touch strengthened us. Drystan took her other hand, and I felt him drawn alongside us as the palace suite blinked out.

• • • •

The Steward was in a room with some of his closest advisors.

"We must stay calm," a man in burgundy velvet said. I thought I recognized Lord Balsa, one of the closest advisors to the Crown. "If we show too much force with the Foresters, it'll all go poorly."

"I've had enough of this," the Steward spat. "We must make a statement. We must show that the Crown will not stand for this level of insubordination."

We saw all this from the vantage point of Timur, hidden within Eric as he stood guard in the corner. I felt the pain of his body—the organs already straining against the magic contained within a vessel not meant to hold it. I could just sense Relean in a corner of Timur's mind, housed in the stolen body of the guard.

Timur stepped forward at the same time as a couple of the other guards. Timur had been hard at work. There were other Kashura in the heart of Snakewood Palace. He must have been laying this trap for years, recruiting them to his cause. They took out Vestige weapons, more advanced than guards usually had, that they had likely liberated from the Museum of Mechanical Antiquities. Ones that could fire bright beams of light, spelled so that they would never miss.

They started firing.

Timur grabbed the Steward before the regent could even react. He took out a knife, freshly sharpened this morning and tipped with a green poison I recognized from Anisa's dreams as Vitriol. Almost reverently, he slid it across the regent's throat.

"Free Elada," he whispered as the Steward fell.

● ● ● ●

The horror of those few seconds was enough to throw me back into my body. I put my hands against my own throat, fighting the urge to gag. Cyan and Drystan met my eyes, the whites showing around their irises.

The Steward and his top advisors were all dead or dying, and there was nothing we could do to stop it. I ran to the window, but we were on the fourth story, and I didn't see an easy way to climb down. Even tying bedsheets together for a rope didn't look promising. Someone would see us, and how many of the other guards were secretly loyal to Timur?

—Micah! Cyan! The echoing voice in our heads was strong enough to almost drive us to our knees.

The Princess. I had scattered impressions. She was being pulled by strong hands, her arms pinned behind her back, her Glamour torn from her neck. A bag was placed over her head, and she stumbled, nearly falling, before someone roughly hauled her upright.

—Princess! I sent.

—The doctor—he's the only one—I think he might be—

Her words cut off, and I felt the distant pulse of an Eclipse. Cyan and I were back in the suite, our powers dampened.

The sound of the doorknob rattling punctured the silence. The three of us banded together, crouching. I grabbed at my faulty magic again, hoping I would be able to hurl it at Timur or one of his Kashura guards if they were on the other side.

"Micah?" I heard a familiar voice call as the key turned in the lock. "Cyan, Drystan? Are you in there?"

Doctor Pinecrest. I wound my magic tighter. Had the Princess been warning us that he was involved?

"Don't attack," he said on the other side of the door. "Please."

The lock clicked and he opened the door, hesitantly. The spark was in my chest, but it flickered. I wanted to strike out with all my anger, but the fear and grief was so stark on his face that I hesitated.

"Come on," he said, gesturing. There was blood on his clockwork hand, and my eye was glued to it. "We have to get out of the Palace. We don't have long. Timur has killed the Steward."

"We know," I managed.

"Do you know he's taken the Princess?" he asked.

Our expressions must have answered that enough.

"She told me where to find you." His gaze was pleading. "Please, there's no time. We have to go."

The Princess had wanted us to find him. So, for better or worse, I didn't see any choice but to trust him.

"Lead the way," I said.

26

THE SPARK

"I haven't told fortunes since I left the circus. Sometimes, I'm tempted to spread the cards before I remember the blurred man's visions of the world on fire. Why did he visit me that evening, and what did I unintentionally reveal to him?

Every night recently, I dream I'm drowning in blue, locked within a Penglass dome. I hear others crying. Far away, there's a pulsing red light that shines purple through the glass. I'm sure I've dreamt of it before. It's like a clock, and I know that time is running out."

FROM CYAN ZHU'S DIARY

Doctor Pinecrest led the way, walking through the sumptuous corridors as if he had every right to be there. The three of us tried and probably failed to mimic his confidence. Our powers were not at full strength with the Eclipses being used somewhere in the Palace, but I sensed Cyan was doing her best to keep anyone from our path. I heard no alarms. Did anyone outside that planning room know what had happened yet? Had anyone survived? I didn't know how many other Kashura Timur had at his disposal. Enough to secure the Palace now that no one was ruling it, it seemed.

Doctor Pinecrest led us down to the lower levels until we reached a quiet storeroom. He moved a few sacks of apples and potatoes to reveal a trapdoor.

"Hurry," he said, pulling it up. "It's an old entrance in and out of the Palace. Hardly anyone knows it's here."

"How do you?" I asked.

He only smiled enigmatically.

Drystan went first, disappearing down the pitch-black drop. Pinecrest took one of the glass globes on the wall and passed it down to Drystan. Cyan followed, then me, with Pinecrest going last and shutting the trapdoor behind him.

"It's straight ahead," Pinecrest said. "You'll know when you're at the end."

The Vestige globe did little to light our way. We all hurried as fast as we dared. Down here, the dark stone walls reminded me a little of Timur's dreams and the morgue of the medical school. I heard a rat skitter somewhere, and I felt Doctor Pinecrest's gaze on the back of my neck. Our footsteps echoed.

A quarter of an hour later, perhaps, Drystan came to a stop. A sliver of light shone above us.

"Above your head, to the right, you'll find a latch," Pinecrest instructed.

Drystan opened another trapdoor. He hauled himself up before lending his hand to Cyan, and then me. I clambered up into an abandoned shop. It had once been a pharmacy. The wooden bar of the dispensary dominated one wall, its glass displays cracked. A few porcelain canisters still lined the shelves, neatly labeled with their contents. Yellowed letters and pamphlets lay clustered by the letterbox.

Pinecrest came up last. He locked the trapdoor. "Just in case," he said.

What would Timur do when he discovered we'd slipped out right underneath his nose? Unless my intuition to trust Pinecrest had been dead wrong, and the doctor was leading us straight back to him. We didn't have our Mirror of Moirai, so we couldn't contact Lily or Frey. Where was Kai? Was Maske safe in the Penny Rookeries? He was too far away for Cyan's powers to reach.

We left the old pharmacy. Overhead, the full moon shone like a magic lantern slide, and Penglass lit the streets more than the yellow gas lights. The crowds were thick. Many had torn off the ribbons over their mouths and were yelling, the countless flames of their candles wavering. I could just make out the tops of the Snakewood Palace's wrought-iron gates. They were barricaded by soldiers and guards. It would take so little for the anger within the crowd to spark to violence.

This wasn't our fight, not just now. The struggle belonged to Lorna Elderberry, the current leader of the Foresters, and the people on the streets. I could only fervently hope it wouldn't all come to blows. Pinecrest cut a path through the protestors, and we followed in his wake.

• • • •

Gradually, the streets grew less crowded, and we arrived at Pinecrest's apartment building. Griffin statues stood guard, as usual, their stone expressions severe. As soon as we were in the lounge, I rounded on the doctor.

"I think it's past time for you to share why you've been experimenting on unborn children for over twenty years, Doctor Pinecrest."

He blinked.

"On Frey, on Cyan, on Kai, and on *me*." My voice quivered with emotion.

"I was instructed to do it," he said, setting down each word as if it were heavy as iron, "by the Royal Family of Elada."

We stared at him.

"Why?" Cyan demanded.

He swallowed. "The previous Royal Physician had begun the experiment long before me. Chimaera were returning naturally in Elada, for reasons unknown, but in very low numbers. The previous Royal Physician discovered ways to help bring them back more frequently."

"Which am I?" I asked, my mouth dry. "A Chimaera born naturally or created to be one?"

"I honestly have no idea," he said. "I told you true. You were dropped on my doorstep. I've no answers for you there, I'm afraid."

I didn't know whether I was relieved or disappointed.

"Your mother stopped coming to the clinic and hid from us, Cyan, which is why you escaped my notice for so long."

Her eyes narrowed dangerously.

Doctor Pinecrest continued. "I returned to Elada when the previous Royal Physician grew ill, and I took up the title." He hesitated. "Over the years, I've grown increasingly uncomfortable with my role in this project. I knew it was wrong, but I wanted to learn the magic and science of it all. If I didn't do it, I knew the Crown would simply hire someone else, though that's a faint attempt at an excuse. I *did* indeed save several Chimaera whose powers were growing unruly. I saved lives, but I also caused harm. I know it's too late to undo my past actions, or to ask for forgiveness."

"You'll never get it," Cyan said, her nostrils flaring. "Not from me, at least."

My jaw clenched.

Pinecrest closed his eyes briefly. "I know you have no cause to believe me and every reason to doubt, but I wish no harm to Chimaera. For better or for worse, you are my life's work."

"Why does—did—the monarchy want Chimaera to return so badly?" I asked.

"The Steward convinced the King to begin the experiment. He believed that the more Chimaera in Elada, the more ambient magic there would be. That not only could their powers be harnessed—he hoped for soldiers, eventually—but that their presence could help rekindle dead Vestige. To my knowledge, he hadn't yet cracked that nut. My clinics were commandeered with the promise that I could succeed as the next Royal Physician of Elada if I complied. Early research was promising, and then I was sent away for a few years, both to see if rumors of Chimaera appearing abroad were true and to find more Alder-age elixirs to bring back."

Drystan crossed his arms, his face grim. I remembered the times Cyan and I had seemed to draw power from Vestige around us in times of emergency—the fight with Shadow Elwood on the darkened streets of Imachara, and backstage at the Royal Hippodrome when I'd stopped Taliesin from sabotaging our magic show.

"But if the Steward figured out how to recharge Vestige, or if this elixir became widespread enough that he could give even humans extra abilities . . . that would ensure Elada could become the most powerful island in the Archipelago again," I said, hushed.

"Yes."

"And when did you learn the truth about the Snakewood family?" I asked.

Doctor Pinecrest gave me a sharp look.

"Yes," Cyan said, unable to hide her smugness. "Micah and I remembered. The Princess herself interfered with your Lethe. We know she's Alder. The Steward, too."

His mouth opened, then closed.

"I learned on the first day I became the Royal Physician," he relented.

"Who is Timur, Doctor Pinecrest?" Cyan asked. "What do you know of him?"

"Timur Blane worked at the Palace for a time, in some bureaucratic middle-management job," he said. "I only met him once or twice before I went abroad. He was confident and had a certain mesmerizing charm, but I thought little enough of him, which was a critical error. My best guess is that he somehow accessed restricted archives and discovered both the secret of the Snakewoods and the Chimaera experiments. He left soon after—or was made to leave, I'm not sure—and grew the Forester movement to a larger, anti-monarchist organization."

"Then he was kicked out of there, too," I said.

"So many sources say, and I believe them. I've met Lorna Elderberry briefly, and she's not someone I'd want to reckon with."

"If Timur has access to an ancient Chimaera spirit, then he knows a lot about the past," I said. "What's he planning to do with it, though? Why does he need the Princess?"

Pinecrest's brow drew down. "What do you know of ancient Chimaera, Micah Grey?"

Before I could answer, Cyan's head rose. A knife of fear slashed through me at her expression. Was it the Kashura? Palace guards?

"It's Lily," Cyan said, her eyes wide.

"But she and Frey were supposed to be out of the city already," I said in dismay.

Doctor Pinecrest went to open the door, and Lily entered in a whirlwind. Her dark blonde hair was wild around her face, escaping her chiffon, and her cheeks were flushed. She pressed a knife to Pinecrest's throat. He held his palms up, trying to move back from the metal's edge pressed against his skin.

"This is all your fucking fault, Pinecrest," Lily spat at him. "They took my son. If you don't help me get him back, if they harm him, Lord and Lady help me—"

"Lily," I interrupted. "Tell us what happened."

Her head twisted toward me. "I'd gone to the Penny Rookeries to drop off some soup for Maske. I was just about to head back when I sensed something was wrong. Kai warned me—I heard him call you on your Mirror."

She brought our Mirror of Moirai from her bag and turned it on, propping it up so we could all watch the moving reflections coalesce into Kai's face.

"This is from half an hour ago," Lily said, voice tight.

"They're coming," Kai whispered, his eyes wide as he stared into the Mirror, his curly hair in disarray. "I'll try to stop them, but I don't know if I can. Go to Pinecrest, Lily. I know you don't trust him, but I think he's the only one who will be able to help. Him and Micah."

The door broke open, the wood splintering. Beside me, Lily flinched. In the mirror, Kai's head whipped to the right. Through the Vestige, I heard the high-pitched, frightened cry of a child.

Hooded figures streamed into the apartment, briefly caught in the reflection.

"No, don't you dare—" Kai said.

One of the hooded figures turned and reached a hand toward Kai, raising him from the ground and out of view. We heard the thud of him slamming into the wall.

I made a small noise in the back of my throat. This was the Kashura who had helped Timur raise the coffin from the ground in the graveyard. The one with Chimaera powers.

"Sleep," said a female voice. Even through the Mirror, I could tell the next word was cemented with magic. "*Sleep.*"

As Kai lost consciousness, one of the Kashura emerged from the bedroom, carrying a limp and unconscious Frey. His scaled hand dangled, and his horns caught the gas lamp light. They left.

The Mirror of Moirai showed only the upturned chairs in Lily's lounge before she reached forward to turn it off.

"The Kashura knew exactly who Frey was and where to find him.

And they knew I wasn't there." Her voice caught. "I raced home, but I was too late. Kai and Frey were both gone. I had to hope that they took both of them, instead of..." She trailed off, and I knew what she didn't want to say: she hoped they'd been kidnapped instead of outright killed.

"They took the Princess from the Palace, too," I said, and Lily gasped. "They want Frey and her for some sinister purpose. They're still alive, though. I'm pretty sure." Cyan nodded her agreement.

She relaxed ever so slightly.

"But they might consider Kai expendable," Pinecrest said, heavily. I sensed genuine fear from him for his assistant.

Lily tapped the Mirror of Moirai's controls. "I've had Frey touch this, so I'd always be able to find him," she said. "But he's not showing up at all, so they must have hidden him with an Eclipse. It's why I followed Kai's advice and came here instead of going after him. So where the fuck did they take my son?"

I swallowed. "We've had dreams of somewhere dark and cold, with stone walls. And Timur standing on a shore, with waves crashing onto the rocks."

"And there's always a red light," Cyan added. "Pulsing like a heartbeat."

Pinecrest stiffened, and I met his eyes. My gaze went back to the edge of the map, and a small island out in the water.

"Not like a heartbeat. Like a lighthouse," I said, my voice flat.

"The Royal Observatory," Pinecrest said, snapping his false fingers. "Of course. It's been abandoned as a research center since the salt wind proved terrible for the equipment, but the lighthouse still has a rather rare red Penglass globe at the top."

"That's it," I said. I'd stared out at that very light from the beach of the circus in Imachara a time or two on clear nights.

"No one goes out there these days, except for occasional maintenance, I'd expect," Pinecrest said. "What they're doing, though, I've no idea."

"Could you reach the Observatory with your abilities?" Lily asked Cyan.

She shook her head. "Too far, even with all of Pinecrest's Vestige around to help." I sensed the magic of the Doctor's artefacts in the cabinet of curiosities, like a lingering aftertaste on the tongue.

I brought Anisa's Aleph from my pocket. "I have someone who might be able to help."

Pinecrest's eyes widened in surprise and confusion. Seemed there was one secret he hadn't discovered, then.

"Micah, are you sure . . . ?" Drystan trailed off as I set down the Vestige disc.

"You know what that will mean," Cyan said.

Indeed, I did. My third and last call. Anisa would have to live on within me so she didn't disappear for good, and I might never be alone in my own mind again. I wanted that even less after what we had just discovered about Timur and Relean. She'd been powerful enough to control my body. Would she simply take me over?

"I don't think we have a choice," I said. I knew, without a doubt, that what Anisa was about to discover would break her ancient heart. No one else, save Lily, would be more determined to stop Timur. The Phantom Damselfly knew more of magic than any of us. We needed her. "Do you see any other option?"

Drystan and Cyan were silent. Doctor Pinecrest looked utterly mystified, and part of me was viciously satisfied by that.

"Anisa," I said. "*I call upon you for the third and final time.*" My magic sparked in my chest.

The Phantom Damselfly rose from the Vestige disc. She stretched her wings before focusing on me. She looked more substantial, as if she were a sputtering candle stub whose flame had found a last burst of wick.

—*Little Kedi*, she said, reaching for my cheek. I thought she'd step into my body immediately, but instead she rifled through my recent memories.

—*It cannot be*... she said, pulling her hand back as if she'd been burned. *How has the blurred man kept my Relean imprisoned within himself?*

"If you don't know, I doubt any of us do," Drystan said, his mouth twisting.

"A man opens his pocket watch, counting down the time," I said aloud. "He used that Isochrome Vestige to help control his magic. Could he have trapped Relean that way?"

—*Perhaps*, Anisa whispered.

"It doesn't matter how he did it: the fact is that he has," Drystan said. "We have to try and stop him."

—*Yes*, she said. She was growing more insubstantial by the minute. *But first: Micah, my time is running out. You must decide. Are you keeping me?*

My mouth opened, but no sound emerged. I swallowed, and nodded.

"Micah, are you sure?" Drystan asked again.

I wasn't, but what choice did I have? We needed her now more than ever. She'd saved my life more times than I could count by now—didn't I owe her the same?

"*Come to me, Anisa*," I said aloud, underlining the words with magic. "*Stay within me, Phantom Damselfly.*"

She stepped right into my skin, shimmering just like the Princess's Glamour illusion. I felt her meld deeper than she ever had before, as if she were twining around my very bones and settling deep in my marrow. For a moment, I worried she'd try and take total control, but this time, I could still use my body. We had blended. My magic danced across my skin, and with Anisa's help, I knew I'd be able to control it and do things I could never do on my own. I was her Aleph. The connection was more powerful than even taking Pinecrest's elixir.

"Stand in a circle and hold hands," I instructed, my voice echoing in two tones. I took Pinecrest's clockwork hand, and Cyan took my other palm. We stood in a circle, as if we were in a séance, and then we were off.

27

THE BLURRED MAN

"Hush, my child,
and fall to sleep.
Dream of wild worlds
and oceans deep.
Hush, my child,
and fall into dreams
of magic worlds
and bright sunbeams.
Hush, my child,
Let your troubles fade,
and save them for another day."

AN ELADAN LULLABY

Anisa, using mine and Cyan's magic, took our collective awareness out over the city, to the beach of Imachara, and swept out above the waves. It felt as though we were flying—I almost imagined wings fluttering between my shoulder blades. The lighthouse was a ruby beacon in the distance, drawing us closer.

Mist clung to the shore of the small, rocky island. One side was a steep cliff, with the Observatory perched at the top like a growth. The buildings attached to the lighthouse were made of the same dark grey stone as the cliff. Blue light shone through the windows, and up at the top of the lighthouse tower, the red continued to pulse. I knew that the Observatory building was on the site of Alder ruins. Other Penglass domes dotted the island, glowing under the full moon. A few rose from the shallow water around the island. Thankfully, we saw no guards on the coast. They were all clustered at the single-story Observatory.

It all spread below us like a stage, with us as invisible spectres. The Observatory was crumbling, the roof largely gone. The main atrium was about forty steps long and twenty wide and it, too, was peppered with blue Penglass: a large dome was integrated into one wall, with smaller domes around the edges. The old telescope still pointed up at the remnants of a constructed, non-Penglass dome, the metal rusted and corroded by salt, water, and wind. There was Timur, in the body of the Palace guard, changed into a hooded robe. Around him I counted twelve Kashura, their hoods finally pulled down to reveal the faces of strangers, mostly men and a few women.

One carried the unconscious Princess, another a limp Frey, and two had a very awake and struggling Kai. I was relieved to see him alive, at least.

The Anthi Chimaera's hands sparked with magic. Her hood was down, and I finally saw the face of the woman who had lifted a coffin from the ground and hurled Kai across the room at Lily's apartment. She was of average height, in her thirties, with hair in a severe black bun and round glasses. She looked more like a librarian than someone scheming to take down her own kind.

"What do I do with these two?" a man asked Timur, gesturing with his chin to the Princess and Kai. He looked like he might be another Royal Guard, but I couldn't be sure. Tall, muscular, salt and pepper hair.

"We'll put them in with the others," Timur said dismissively.

The others? *I wondered, sensing the echoing confusion and dismay from Cyan and the rest.*

Timur walked toward a large Penglass dome at the edge of the Observatory. He placed his hand on it, and it glowed just as the Penglass had blazed beneath mine. He traced a glyph, and I dimly remembered it from the vision with Anisa and Matla. When he finished, part of the blue glass turned transparent and became a door.

Timur had learned how to do something that was meant to be impossible since the Alder age: opening Penglass.

He stepped inside, and Anisa's awareness drew us all after him. With a jolt of horror so intense it almost brought me back to my body in Pinecrest's apartment, I realized there were already others inside: Chimaera.

The inside of the Penglass was all blue, with hexagonal holes like a honey hive. One of the Kashura dragged Kai inside and tied him up with the others. I wondered if the spirit trapped inside Timur knew we were there, watching.

There were perhaps a dozen total. Many were Theri, and therefore probably easier for the Kashura to target. I recognized Juliet, Tauro, and Violet among them. They were thin and dirty. Juliet and Violet pulled their lips back from their teeth, baring fangs, their wrists and ankles bound with rope. Tauro's great head was bowed—he didn't even look up. There was Jarek Lutier, the bear man I'd fought in the magician's duel. To my utter surprise, I saw Flora, the Taliesin twins' assistant. I'd had no idea she was Chimaera. Her dark blonde hair was matted and half-covered her face. One of the other prisoners had skin like an alligator. Another was feathered like Matla, but more corvid than owl. There was the antlered boy with dappled skin I'd seen in the market. The one whose father had begged for his safe return. I even remembered his name: Brian Archer. The rest all looked human—a portly man still wearing his baker's uniform, an elderly woman. I recognized the last Chimaera, too: the flower girl who had helped me up after my magic had overwhelmed me one day in Imachara. She sat hugging her knees, looking utterly terrified.

From the entrance, Timur considered his cache of Chimaera before letting it seal up again. How long had he been taking them, and what was he going to do?

Timur gestured to Frey. "His destiny, of course, is far more important."

He took his Isochrome Vestige from his pocket, opening it. Magic sparked along his palms. I noticed the fingers of this stolen body were already beginning to blacken at the tips, too. I felt a pulse of pain from Relean, and Anisa's grief wove through us. I wished we could do more, but we were only observers, as insubstantial as a wish.

With a strangled cry and another twist of power from Timur, the red dome shuddered and rose. It broke the remnants of the roof. The globe pulsed above us, turning slowly beneath the stars and the silver coin of the moon before coming to rest in the middle of the ruined Observatory.

The other Kashura watched the display, expressions slack with awe and devotion. Timur went to the red globe. He drew that same glyph, and once again the glass melted away to reveal an opening.

Back in my body, I could tell this vision was draining us all, but we had to hang on a little longer. We had to see.

The Kashura holding Frey hesitated before stepping inside. He placed Frey down before backing away in obvious fear. The red glass sealed itself, leaving the horned boy trapped inside.

"Tonight," Timur said, breathing hard with sweat pouring from his brow. "Two hands on Penglass in red, under the light of the full moon. All Chimaera must fall."

His words were an eerie echo of the prophecy Anisa had given me the night I'd met her at the circus. Timur's head turned in my direction, but whether he was aware of our presence or simply looking this way, I couldn't say.

Timur set his jaw and, with another burst of magic, raised the ruby globe back into the sky to rest at the top of the stone lighthouse tower. It was seventy-five feet high, with a cast-iron walkway at the top. Rusted metal rungs were hammered into the granite.

"All Chimaera must fall," the other Kashura echoed.

With a tug of our shared magic, the Observatory and the lighthouse disintegrated around us.

●●●●

We opened our eyes in Pinecrest's warm, comfortable apartment. It wasn't my first shared vision, but it was as disorienting as all the rest.

I staggered to the sofa, weakened even with Anisa's presence threaded through me. My powers were flickering despite her extra control, and the glass globes of Pinecrest's apartments dimmed. Cyan was grey, and Pinecrest, Lily, and Drystan also looked like they might be sick.

"This could be a trap," I said, staring at Pinecrest. "You could be leading us right to him, wanting us to add our power to Frey's and the other Chimaeras'."

The doctor held out his hands. "Cyan, read me. I'll drop all my walls, and you can determine the truth of what I say." His gaze was imploring.

"I won't say no." Cyan moved forward, touching his human and Vestige hands. Her eyes flashed blue before they closed.

She was not gentle.

Pinecrest stiffened, beads of sweat appearing on his brow. At one point, he staggered, barely remaining upright. I hadn't joined Cyan: partly because I was drained by the vision, but mostly because, curious as I was, I was afraid to go anywhere near that man's skull.

Cyan pulled away, her skin blanched. "He tells the truth, as much as he believes it. It's not a deliberate trap." Her face was so haunted—I wondered what else she'd seen in Pinecrest's mind.

"What is Timur doing with Frey?" Lily demanded. "And the Princess, and the others?"

I shook my head. "I don't know."

—*He's aiming to use the Chimaera he's trapped as power sources, I suspect,* Anisa said, and it was beyond unnerving to feel her sending thoughts from my own skull. Drystan's expression tightened.

Cyan hugged herself.

"What do you mean, Phantom Damselfly?" Drystan asked.

—*The Steward of Elada was correct. Chimaera* can *affect Vestige and Penglass in a way humans cannot. The domes are interconnected,* she said. *You may think of it like a web. Red Penglass functions differently.*

I had a sudden memory of Aenea, leaning close to a luminary shop near my old apartments in Sicion, her brown braid over her shoulder, staring at a cluster of glass globes, a rare red globe nestled among them.

—*That color Penglass was the material used for Alder ships,* Anisa continued. *It has always been an amplifier for power for those who know how to use it. One single red dome can connect to all the blue Penglass in Elada in the right hands. I suspect Timur is going to use Frey's power to connect to Penglass to target Chimaera. He would never have known how without Relean's knowledge or without access to someone as powerful as Frey. He might believe that containing the* horned boy in the red globe will be protection if his powers spike too much, but... She trailed off.

"But what?" Drystan prodded, grimacing.

—*Timur is grossly underestimating Frey's power, or his own ability to direct it with Relean's magic and the Kashura Isochrome.*

"So if Frey loses control?" Lily asked, pained.

—*Then the past will circle around again. Not only Chimaera will fall. We all will.*

The silence was loud as we absorbed her words. The first night Anisa spoke to me, she'd told me I was meant to help her save the world. I had tried to run away from it, but this had always been inevitable.

"Right. So how do we get to the Observatory?" Lily demanded. "How do we save my son and the others and stop this all from happening?"

She glanced at the grandfather clock in the corner of the lounge. It was already half past nine.

"I can get us there," Pinecrest said, straightening his tie and trying to regain his composure. "I have a warehouse near the harbor with many of my Vestige possessions, including a boat that should help us avoid detection."

"Fine," Lily rose. "Let's go."

"One last moment, please," Pinecrest said. "I do have a reserve of my medicine, and I offer it freely to anyone here who wants it. The vision drained me, so I can only imagine how it might feel for some of you. It would give you energy and power." He licked his lips. "I know after what you've learned, it may be the last thing you want, but there are at least thirteen adversaries on that island, and six of us, by my count."

"Unless we can free the imprisoned Chimaera," Drystan pointed out. "There were at least a dozen in there, and though they're weak, some would definitely join the fight." He set his jaw. "I want it. Oh, but I want it. But I'll not touch the drug."

"You don't need it," I said, unable to hide my relief.

"I know," he said, even as his face was pinched with a desperate hunger. He'd been hooked on Lerium for years and tempted by Pinecrest's medicine, but even with what we'd faced, he'd refused. Considering how deeply it'd affected him, it was also the wiser choice. He needed his wits and coordination about him.

"I know I should, but I won't touch it, either," Cyan said, firmly. "I wanted nothing to do with your experiments, and that hasn't changed."

Pinecrest nodded, not looking particularly surprised.

Lily also outright refused, as I'd suspected she would.

"I'll take it," I said.

Pinecrest opened his spirit cabinet and worked quickly, prepping the syringes as I'd seen him do so many times, calmly tapping out the air bubbles. I went first and resisted the urge to sigh in relief as the cool medicine hit my veins. Hopefully, this would be close to the last time I had to take it. But even with Anisa's extra power, it felt foolish to turn down the chance for more power with what we were going up against.

Pinecrest dosed himself, and indeed, when he bared the skin of his left arm, it was peppered with small green dots at the crook of his elbow. Some of the wounds looked infected, faint rings of rot surrounding them. He might not have a spirit in him, but clearly giving himself magic was exacting its own cost. Drystan flinched at the sight of them.

He closed his eyes, then opened them, his pupils blown. I hated seeing that same hunger echoed in his features that I'd felt myself.

Pinecrest rolled his sleeve down, showing no trace of embarrassment at the wounds.

"Are you ready?" he asked us.

"Yes," the others said, or nodded. In their faces, I saw fear and determination in equal measure.

"Let's save Chimaera," I said.

—And the world, Anisa whispered in our minds.

28

ACROSS THE WATER

"For centuries, it was assumed that all Penglass was blue. And indeed, almost all the domes are. The only exception is these few spherical red specimens. They have been found in very remote locations throughout the Archipelago. At first, it was assumed that these were simply large glass globes like we see in many homes. While the majority of Vestige lamps are clear or blue, other colors like orange, pink, yellow, and green are not impossible to find. Red is indeed the rarest.

While the discovery was momentous, we have been unable to determine the significance, if any, of the color and shape differentiation. Communication, perhaps? Is it a craft of some kind? Whatever their purpose, due to their steady, pulsing light that lasts for centuries, most red Penglass is currently used for lighthouses."

"VESTIGE," PROFESSOR CAED CEDAR,
ROYAL SNAKEWOOD UNIVERSITY

Outside Pinecrest's building, to our utter surprise, we found Maske. He must have heard Kai urge Lily to go to Pinecrest's, and so he'd come all the way across town from the Penny Rookeries. He was pale and peaky, and held a box beneath one arm. He glanced at Lily mournfully when he thought she wasn't looking. My heart sank. He might not have learned the whole truth, but when Lily had realized her son was at risk, I suspected he'd put together that Lily Verre was far more than the flighty shopkeeper at Twisting the Aces.

"I don't know exactly what is going on . . ." Maske held out the box to Cyan. "But I brought this for you. I hope these might help, in some way."

Cyan opened it. I leaned over and caught sight of Maske's Eclipse, plus the one I'd stolen from Taliesin, and even Maske's once most-prized possession: the other Aleph that had once housed a dragonfly Chimaera ghost.

"Thank you," I said, my voice thick.

"I only wish I could come with you, wherever you're going, but I'm afraid I'd be more liability than aid at the moment." His skin was sallow, and he was barely able to stand.

My heart warmed. We didn't deserve him. "You've done more than enough, Maske."

Pinecrest reached into his pocket and drew out a key. "Go to my apartments and rest, Mr. Maske. With luck and a bit of fate, we'll all be back by morning."

Maske's eyes shone with worry. "There are some magician's flashes and other bits in there, too," he said. "Whatever you're doing, perhaps you'll need a little misdirection."

I threw my arms around him and gave him a kiss on his clammy, fevered cheek, and Cyan and Drystan joined the embrace.

"Be safe," he whispered. "Be bold."

"One moment," Lily said. She drew Maske to the side and whispered something to him, and it proved to me how much she cared for him that she'd delay going after her son, even for a second, to apologize. As she pulled away, Maske gave her the saddest smile I'd ever seen.

It was difficult to leave him behind, but every second that passed was another second wasted. The streets were still too busy to hail a cab, so we headed down to the harbor as quickly as we could. The stony expressions of anyone we saw chilled me. Far off, I heard sirens wailing. I feared whatever might be happening at the Snakewood Palace. Around us, apartments were shuttered, but a few lights flickered in the gaps.

While I was frightened, I should have been beyond terrified. Shock, or Anisa's presence, had dampened my feelings. All I was focused on was getting out to that island and stopping the blurred man once and for all. Timur had an ancient dragonfly held against his will, but I had my willing damselfly.

Above us, the Penmoon glowed, full and watchful.

The docks were quiet. Pinecrest led us to a warehouse right on the water, unlocking the door with the same square Vestige key.

"I hereby invite you inside: Micah Grey, Lily Verre, Cyan Zhu, and Drystan Hornbeam," he said, formally. He motioned us in, and I felt the faint barrier of both a Banshee and a Shroud. I supposed Anisa needed no invitation.

Around us were remnants from the Museum of Mechanical Antiquities. Most artefacts were stored in pallets or wrapped in cloth, but I could taste the latent, ancient magic on the air.

Pinecrest went straight to a corner with a small iron safe. He opened this using his Vestige key.

"These should still have enough power," Pinecrest muttered as he took out three small pistols. They were much sleeker and smoother than non-Vestige ones and made of that same mysterious metal as Anisa's Aleph. They didn't need re-loading—the only danger was not knowing when or if they'd abruptly run out of the targeted pulses of light they fired.

"We're a couple short," Pinecrest said. "Who's best at shooting?"

"Me," Lily said, without hesitation.

"I've fired one or two in my time," Drystan said. "Unless you want one, Micah or Cyan."

"Not me," Cyan said. "Never liked them much, and I've other weapons." She tapped her temple.

"As do I," I said. "I've never properly been taught how to shoot. Not very lady-like, remember?" I had Anisa's control of my magic and my fresh dose of medicine, so I felt plenty powerful. The heady rush of it flowed through my veins.

Pinecrest nodded, keeping one pistol for himself and handing the other two to Lily and Drystan. He found a cache of Vestige knives and passed me a couple—one for my belt buckle and one for my boot. These I took, both for their sharpness and because we might as well take all the power stored in these artefacts we could get.

Pinecrest swiftly moved to another part of the warehouse and pulled off a tarp to reveal a small Vestige boat, its hull seemingly made of Penglass. Despite everything, I had a moment of awe. I'd never seen anything like it.

"Right," Lily said. "Before we set off, let's finalize something resembling a plan."

"Definitely," Drystan agreed. "I've some thoughts." He reached into the box of tricks and took out the Eclipses. "We already know these won't help against Frey if his powers properly activate—Micah will have to help there."

No pressure.

Drystan brandished one of the wands. "I was thinking perhaps Pinecrest and I could try to sneak close enough to set these off, so the Kashura's weapons won't work. I can set the range to be small enough that ours still will."

"Yes," Lily said. "I've this, too." She brought out a gun that was decidedly not Vestige. "But like we've said, we're still outnumbered." She glanced at Cyan and me. "Is there a way to free the Chimaera within the Penglass?"

"Anisa knows the opening glyph," I said. "She thinks that either Cyan or I should be able to do it."

"Show me the symbol now, then," Cyan said. "I can't quite remember it."

I reached over and clasped her hand, and Anisa traced the image in her mind thrice. With the Phantom Damselfly now within me, I wouldn't forget it.

"I think the only way for me to get to Frey," I said, "is to climb the lighthouse tower." I'd seen other Kashura at the base, and there'd be no way to reach that door without entering the main atrium and being spotted.

"Can you even climb it?" Drystan asked. "I know you've your aerialist training, but . . ." He trailed off. I understood his reticence. I was largely out of practice since the circus, and it'd be a tricky climb even with regular training.

"I spied rungs," I said. "And the stone bricks looked like they'd be deep enough to provide some holds if I really needed. I think I can get up, at least, but down will be another matter. Hopefully, the stairs inside are sound, and by the time I get Frey out, the rest of you will have dealt with the Kashura."

"Hopefully," Drystan said.

We looked at each other, all of us far too aware of the variables and the risks. We were merely this: a doctor who had experimented on himself, a few young people with varying levels of powers, and a mostly retired Shadow. We were facing a dozen Kashura, Timur, and a larger cache of Vestige weaponry. These were not great odds.

I found myself wishing we all had Alephs, so that if things went wrong, at least we'd have hope of being born again in another place and time. Instead, we were painfully mortal. Even Anisa, in a way, since she currently lived on through me.

"Come on, help me with this then," Pinecrest said, putting his hands on the craft. "It's lighter than it looks, but it's awkward. We must be quick. Best if as few people see us as possible."

Anisa whispered to me. I opened Maske's box of tricks and brought out the Eclipse that had once belonged to Pen Taliesin. I turned it on, twisting the base a certain way. The tip of the wand pulsed with a steady green light.

"Anisa knows this as an Acha rather than an Eclipse," I explained. "Used like this, anyone who glances this way won't notice us."

"Well," Pinecrest said, clearly taken aback. "That's indeed handy."

Drystan and Lily carried the strange boat out of the warehouse. The only sounds were the lapping of the waves and our footsteps on the wooden planks of the dock. Carefully, Drystan and Lily lowered the craft to the water and tethered it with a rope while Pinecrest re-locked the warehouse.

I wondered what was happening at the Palace on the other side of the city. I strained my ears. Perhaps I caught distant shouting, but that was all. One by one, our group climbed down the ladder into the bobbing copper and Penglass craft.

Pinecrest took his seat at the back of the boat and turned on the near-silent engine. We cast off the rope and the doctor angled around the other vessels until we made it out of the protected harbor and to the larger waves of the open sea.

On the horizon, we could barely make out the pulsing red light of the Royal Observatory. I huddled with Drystan, both the sea-salt wind and fear making me shiver. He held me tight. Cyan wrapped her arms around herself. Lily was looking at Pinecrest with narrowed eyes, as if she was considering tossing him overboard so we wouldn't have to worry about him potentially double-crossing us, even if Cyan had seen within his mind.

As we grew closer to the Observatory, I held the Eclipse aloft, praying it hid our approach. Luckily, Timur hadn't posted guards on the shore. They didn't have the numbers for that, and they clearly thought no one would ever follow them out here. We had to count on them underestimating us.

A larger non-Vestige boat was tied up to the ruins of an old dock that looked as though it could crumble into the sea at any moment. Carefully, we pulled up beside it.

—I remember this place, Anisa said, letting the thought carry to others. *From so long ago.*

"Was it an Observatory back then?" Drystan asked.

—Something like it. It's where we searched the stars. At the end, some of the Alder ships took off from this very island.

"What happened to them?" I asked aloud.

—I do not know. I would like to hope they survived and found another star. Another world.

"Despite how they treated you?" I remembered the punishment she had suffered after letting one of her charges die, and the fight with Matla to save Ahti so long ago.

—Not all of them were like the original Kashura. Like any people, they were a mixture of the marvelous and the terrible. Look at all they created, and all they left behind.

Pinecrest climbed out of the boat first. Lily checked both her guns. I touched the hilts of my knives for reassurance. The blue of the Penglass, the pulsing red of the globe above us that imprisoned Frey, and the silver of the moon bathed the island in shifting, eerie light.

"I'm going to make them regret ever laying a finger on my son," Lily said, her face hard. "Let's go give the godsdamned Kashura a piece of our minds."

She strode up the hill, holding the Vestige gun aloft, and the rest of us followed close behind.

29

THE KASHURA

"If there is one thing we have learned, it is that Penglass is indestructible. It survived the rising of the waters and the destruction of the Alder and the Chimaera. It has been here for centuries, and those domes will stand long after we are gone."

**A HISTORY OF ELADA AND ITS FORMER COLONIES,
PROFESSOR CAED CEDAR, ROYAL SNAKEWOOD UNIVERSITY**

I held the Eclipse aloft, its barrier surrounding the five of us.

Cyan straightened, her eyes widening as she gazed toward the Observatory. "There's a lot of Vestige here. I can feel my powers strengthening. Can't you?"

I looked up. "It's partially all the weapons they have. But it might also be the Penglass itself." The power of both the standard blue and the red sphere washed over us in waves. I suspected an Eclipse would be as useless against it as it was against Frey's powers. Magic, which was always difficult to control and predict, felt even more unknowable here.

"I don't like this," Drystan muttered.

"Me neither," I replied.

Please keep them safe, I whispered to the spirits, unsure if they heard me.

We circled the Observatory, crouching low and ducking behind rocks to hide ourselves. A light mist spread across the island, dimming the moon and providing better cover. A few cold drops of rain splattered onto the backs of my hands and the top of my head. We spotted two guards outside the main entrance to the Observatory and crouched behind an outcropping.

Drystan held a finger to his lips, taking out his Eclipse and creeping toward the guards. His circus training came in useful here—he moved silently, and he pointed the wand toward the two guards. He'd set the range to be small, so he had to be close before he activated it. Their hoods were down, the cloaks open to reveal the armor of Royal Guards. Both were in their forties, with the usual Eladan coloring of dark brown hair, lighter brown eyes, and lighter skin kissed by the Eladan summer sun.

As soon as the guards were in range of the Eclipse, Drystan's palm flashed red with the flares we'd used in our illusions. The guard's heads turned toward the light, pointing their hopefully useless guns in his direction.

Lily didn't hesitate. Two quick shots of her near-silent Vestige gun, and the guards fell.

Cyan let out a small sound, quickly stifled. We'd both sensed them die like candle flames snuffed out. I suppressed a shudder as Lily took the guards' Vestige guns and holsters. She held one out to me, but I shook my head, so she gave it to Cyan instead.

I spied a structure tucked against the outer wall that had once held the generator and pointed to it. It was wide enough for all of us, and we'd be able to reach a small, glassless window.

We clambered up and, sure enough, we had a good view of the

ruined Observatory's atrium. Everything was largely as we'd seen in our shared vision. The Kashura were dwarfed by the wrecked telescope and the largest Penglass dome, which housed the kidnapped Chimaera. It and the smaller structures dotted through the Observatory glowed brighter than I'd seen on any Penmoon. Two Kashura still lingered near the base of the lighthouse tower. My eyes went up, up, and settled on the pulsing red globe before drifting back to the blurred man.

Timur almost seemed to be in a trance, his head tilted back toward the full moon. The Kashura around him were eerily still, waiting for whatever was going to happen next. Tempting as it was to start shooting, each of the remaining Kashura had fully charged Vestige weapons out of range of our Eclipses, plus we had another added complication.

"Timur put up a Shroud," Cyan said, hushed.

The filmy iridescence surrounded him like a bubble. Both Vestige pulses and normal bullets would simply bounce off.

"Well, that's complicated our plan," Drystan said, keeping his voice low. "Even an Eclipse can't shut that off easily, either."

I tasted the strange magic on the air and felt Anisa clamping down on the spark of energy in my chest, ensuring no jagged spindles of my powers escaped. My abilities seemed to be drawn to the red Penglass.

"Two Eclipses might be enough to pierce it, though," Pinecrest said. "If we activate them at the same time on opposite sides?"

"That might work," Drystan tapped his lip. "Worth a try, anyway."

"Drystan, you should try to get to that smaller Penglass dome there," Lily said, pointing. "Doctor, you aim for the one closest to where the sentries were. I'll stay up here, as I've a good vantage point, and once the Eclipses are set off, I'll start firing."

She spoke with the confidence of a Shadow who had run numerous jobs. Pinecrest checked his watch. A little more than half an hour to midnight. We took a last look at each other.

"I'm going to start making my way over to the tower and climbing the far side," I said. "Cyan, come with me so you can stop at the other side of the dome."

She nodded.

"Wait until I've gotten Frey out of the globe if you can," I said to the others. "The element of surprise is all we've got. With a little luck, this won't take long." Especially if Anisa could help me meddle with time.

"We'll try," Lily said.

"For Chimaera," I said. "And everyone."

"For Chimaera," the others echoed. "And everyone."

All of us, save Lily, crept back down.

I stole a moment to press my forehead to Drystan's. "Don't be stupid," I whispered.

"Back at you." He rummaged in the box of Maske's tricks.

"Here," he said, passing me a small bag. "Chalk."

"Thank you," I said.

Cyan and I circumvented the outside wall, crouching low. I was all too aware of the sheer drop of the cliff at my left.

The back of the largest Penglass dome had been built into part of the exterior wall. Time had crumbled the stone around it, so there was a gap. We risked glancing through it. Timur and the others were still in their trance. While the Shroud was a complication, it likely did help hide our presence. The Kashura hadn't yet realized that two of their guards were dead, for instance.

Cyan put her hand to the opaque Penglass. While it hadn't particularly responded to her touch before, sure enough, thanks to the full moon, the outline of her fingers glowed.

"Wait until I give you the signal or there's no other choice," I said.

If she went in now, some of the Chimaera inside might panic and give us away.

"I know," she said. "Go."

The lighthouse tower wasn't far. Up close, I balked. The rungs were badly rusted. I had no rope, no harness, no nets. It'd be more dangerous than any aerialist act. I felt Anisa draw my magic to do her best to slow time as I dried my palms along my trousers, before reaching into my pocket and chalking my hands.

I began to climb.

Even with the chalk, the rungs were slippery. I couldn't rush it, but I also couldn't hesitate too long, or I'd burn through my strength, and my grip would give out. I held my magic lightly. From this angle, I couldn't see what the others were doing. The climb was harder than I'd suspected. Twenty feet or so up, one of the rungs was missing entirely, and I had to cling to the grooves of the crumbling mortar, my fingers cramping. I held my breath until I could stretch up for the next one, all my weight on my big toe wedged into the crumbling mortar.

Soon enough, I made it up to the most difficult part of the climb: the overhang of the cast iron lower walkway. The rung was within reach of one of the supports, just. To make sure I had a proper hold required a dynamic move. In other words . . . I'd have to jump. No rope. No trapeze. No net.

If the metal crumbled, or if I missed, even if Anisa was somehow able to help slow my fall, I'd injure myself far worse than when I'd tumbled from the gridiron of the Kymri Theatre. I heard muffled, distorted sounds from the atrium below, but I couldn't risk glancing down.

"Here goes," I said.

I swung out and up, launching myself from the last rung with all my strength and throwing up my right hand. My throat closed in fear, knowing my body was in mid-air, beholden only to the power of my muscles. My fingers closed around cold metal. I hung on as hard as I could, my legs dangling, my heart pounding, the ground too far away for my liking. If I'd misjudged by even an inch, I'd have fallen.

With a grunt, I brought my other hand up for a second hold.

My shoulder muscles screamed as I swung my legs until I could hook my heel and haul myself up with brute strength to cling to the bottom of the walkway. I dragged myself over the banister of the fence and took a moment on all fours, panting. Between the concentration needed to climb and being closer to the red Penglass, I felt time speed back up.

—*Micah!* Cyan's mental voice was sharp with fear. It might not have been the first time she'd called out for me.

I heard shouting and begging, no longer distorted. Cyan sent me scattered images: the Penglass had opened on the other side before Cyan went in. She'd started drawing the glyph, but her hands were shaking so badly she kept having to swipe and start over.

I glanced down and froze.

A Kashura was dragging Brian Archer, the antlered Chimaera, toward Timur. They passed through the Shroud barrier.

"Tonight, we fulfill our destiny," Timur said, and his voice carried even up to the top of the lighthouse. The Chimaera twisted desperately, fear making him panic.

Anisa and I reached for the magic coiling in my chest, but the Penglass above me was so powerful that I kept losing hold of it. I dragged myself up to the second walkway for a better view and to get closer to the horned boy trapped inside the red glass.

"We have already learned that even a single death can help charge a defunct Vestige," Timur said, his voice carrying enough to reach me.

I realized, with horror, that meant they'd already sacrificed a few to rekindle the weapons they'd stolen from the Museum of Mechanical Antiquities.

I'd never hated anyone more than I hated that man down there and those foolish enough to follow him.

"Tonight, we need only feed the Penglass a few more corrupted souls," Timur called. "I have read the scrolls the royalty hid from us. I have seen into the past. A Chimaera child powerful beyond measure exists with the power to save the world or trigger its end. Set him off in a certain way, however, and channel his powers, and all Chimaera shall fall alongside him. When I feed the energy of these Chimaera to blue Penglass, the boy's magic will expand, multiply, and obliterate every Chimaera for hundreds of miles. Only my loyal servants, sheltered by my side within this Shroud, will survive. Tonight, we can end the threat once and for all. Elada will no longer be held back by an Alder monarchy, and humanity will finally flourish."

Timur raised a knife coated with Vitriol. The poison that would kill Alder or Chimaera.

"No!" I cried, too late. Timur had already nicked Brian's skin.

Dimly, I sensed Drystan get into position behind one of the smaller Penglass domes, and Pinecrest the second. They signaled to each other, switched on the Eclipses at the same time. There was a pulse, and my heart lifted, then fell.

The Shroud held.

Lily, thinking the Eclipse had done its job and desperate to save the antlered boy, fired her Vestige gun, but the shot bounced harmlessly off the Shroud barrier.

Brian fell to his knees, gasping. She'd never have been able to save him, and we'd lost the element of surprise.

"We're under attack!" Timur called, pushing the dying Chimaera into the nearest Penglass dome. Brian glowed with light as his body touched the glass, and I watched in horror as it *consumed* him. Within moments, he was gone, leaving only a glowing outline behind him. I bit down on a cry of grief.

More Vestige gunfire erupted, bright streaks like lightning streaking across the atrium, fizzling against the Shroud.

—*Do something*, I sent Anisa. *We have to do something.*

—*Reach the globe. Stop Frey*, she said.

Frey had woken up, alone and afraid. My own magic was sprawling, my awareness bleeding out across the island despite Anisa's influence, but it was nothing compared to Frey's powers activating.

—*Leave them to their roles and take up yours*, Anisa said. *You are the only one who can stop him.*

The sacrifice of the Chimaera had activated the Penglass somehow—thin lines of power emanated from the red sphere above me to the blue domes around the island, disappearing into filaments that spread beneath the waves and toward the city across the water.

I climbed onto the metal cage around the floating red globe at the top of the lighthouse. Once, it'd likely housed beautiful glass windows to refract the red Penglass globe's light and push it further out to sea. I could make out Frey's outline and his pointed horns within the sphere because he was *glowing*.

I stretched out my arm, but I couldn't reach the glass's surface, much less draw the glyph. No choice: I'd have to make another leap from the metal cage onto the top of the sphere. It'd take every bit of my acrobatic skills to pull this off.

I climbed higher, panting. From the sounds, Lily, Drystan, and Pinecrest were still firing their weapons down below.

I finally chanced another glance down. The Kashura couldn't fire from within the Shroud, but emerging from its protection left them vulnerable. A Kashura fell, and another was clipped in the shoulder.

Drystan's hands sparked with flares, trying to distract and briefly blind our enemy. There were still far more of them than us.

I couldn't sense Cyan. Did that mean she was inside the dome? Could she release the other Chimaera in time?

Pinecrest sprinted in the direction of the Penglass, and I heard the shot of a gun. My magic left me so psychically exposed that I felt the echoing slash of pain sizzle across my shoulder blades, as if I'd been the one shot instead of him.

Timur stood in the center of his Shroud, his head turning up toward the light. He must have spotted my outline or sensed my abilities.

—You are too late, Micah Grey! Timur shouted at me using his stolen magic. *You were always going to be too late. The world will remember that I was the one to save them from monsters.*

I'd no idea if anyone else was injured aside from Pinecrest. Cyan hadn't managed to release the Chimaera. I soon discovered why.

The Kashura Chimaera had found Cyan and dragged her through the gap in the wall and away from the dome, a hand clamped over her mouth so she couldn't command him to sleep. Cyan hadn't managed to finish the glyph. The other Chimaera were still inside, ready to be sacrificed to the surrounding Penglass.

If Timur's plan worked, that Chimaera Kashura would fall, too. Did Timur believe he had protection within that Shroud, or was he willing to risk himself if it took us all down with him?

I reached the top of the metal cage and swung my legs over, until I was standing on the inside of it. The sharp edges of the metal nicked my palms, and the red globe hovered below me. I shrank my awareness back to my body as best I could, drawing my magic around me like a cloak. I had to focus. Frey's fear was so strong, so overwhelming, I wanted to scream. Even if I landed this perfectly, I remembered how easily my brother had slipped from the top of a Penglass dome much wider than this. Below the red, I could just make out the hollow tower of the lighthouse and a half-ruined staircase spiraling around its edge. No escape that way.

Tensing my muscles, I gathered my courage. I had to believe Timur was wrong, and Anisa was right. I had to believe the spirits were on our side. I'd put my faith in myself beneath the big top, and now I had to believe both in Frey and myself.

I jumped.

30

RED GLASS

"*Professor Shawn Arbutus, a classics linguist, spent much of his life translating Alder scrolls on various subjects. He was the first to identify a different faction of Alder called the Kashura, who seemed to regret creating Chimaera and believed this mistake should be undone. Clearly, they succeeded, but did they destroy their own kind in the process?*"

"THEORIES OF THE ALDER,"
A HISTORY OF ELADA AND ITS FORMER COLONIES,
PROFESSOR CAED CEDAR, ROYAL SNAKEWOOD UNIVERSITY

Time stretched and twisted. My stomach dipped just like every time I'd swung on a trapeze. Muscle memory took over. I trusted my body to know how to position my feet, how to move my arms. I couldn't think, I could only *feel*.

From that height and with the force of my propulsion, I should have smashed onto the surface of the red dome. Yet instead of speeding up, I slowed down until I drifted as gently as a feather on a breeze. My feet grazed the dome, and I held my arms out for balance like I was on a tightrope, my muscles straining. When I felt as though I wasn't about to slide off, I very carefully came down to my hands and knees. I couldn't believe I'd actually managed that move.

I held my breath and began to trace the glyph Anisa had taught me. My fingertip left a glowing streak of light as beautiful as the time my brother and I had perched on a dome in Sicion. Anisa's presence grew stronger, as if she hugged me from behind and rested her chin on my shoulder. I imagined her taking my hand, guiding me true.

I put the last swirl on the glyph. The red around me brightened, dissolved, and I fell through.

Time was still fluid. I twisted and managed to avoid landing on Frey before sliding toward him.

He was curled into a ball, his arms over his head, his horns just visible. His whole body was still glowing. His magic was so strong it felt as if it might sear the skin and muscle right from my bones. My own power was answering, my heart aflame.

—*Frey*! I sent to him mentally, Anisa helping me. *Frey, can you hear me?*

He grimaced in pain, revealing his pointed fangs. He didn't answer. He was lost.

My awareness split. Down below, Lily fired at Timur, but once more, the shot bounced harmlessly off his Shroud. His hands were raised, the rot now reaching the second joint of his fingers.

Frey screamed, his muscles stiffening. The sound echoed in the glass sphere until I worried my eardrums would burst. I clutched him, cradling him against my chest.

I sensed the atrium below again. A Kashura fired at Drystan, who dodged behind a dome just in time. The Chimaera Kashura still had a firm hold of Cyan.

The blue Penglass prison glowed brighter than all the rest. The Chimaera inside were weakening as the glass siphoned their power. Juliet sagged against Tauro. How long did they have until they were consumed, too, and what would all their collected magic do to Frey?

Frey's powers glowed brighter, stretching further, dragging me along with him. His magic was refracting through the Penglass on the island, in the water of the harbor, until he reached the domes in the city. I sensed the links between the Penglass, and near-invisible lines connecting to pinpricks of light throughout Imachara. I knew that each and every small star represented a Chimaera. A life.

—*I don't want to hurt them!* Frey cried. *I don't want to hurt you!*

I opened my watering eyes, seeing only the red inside of the sphere. Sweat dripped down my face. Every nerve was on fire. A flash of lightning was just visible through the glass, spidering across the sky too slowly, and thunder boomed deep in my chest.

I gasped, my lips cracking with the heat. The scales on Frey's hands were hot enough that they burned me, but I didn't let go.

—*I'm here*, I told him. *I'm here. Let me in.* Anisa had told me that I was meant to be the Dev to his Ahti. The only one who could balance his powers. But how? We were both burning bright, but I couldn't dampen it. I couldn't swallow it down.

—*Focus*, Anisa instructed.

Frey twisted in my arms. I sensed the island shuddering like an earthquake, magic pulsing through the air.

—*Frey is just as strong as Ahti, and he broke the world*, Anisa said in my mind, her fear hitting the back of my throat. *Do you see the cost of Frey trying to hold it all back? He's just a boy, and he can't do it alone.*

Hairline cracks branched across the inside of the sphere like more lightning. I sensed some of the smaller Penglass domes below had echoing fissures.

Penglass, a substance meant to be indestructible, was breaking.

—*Even last time, this did not happen*, Anisa said. *Micah, you must stop him, you must bring him back. If you don't . . .*

I opened my chapped, bleeding lips, the horror spreading through me. The hairline cracks were glowing brighter.

"Then they'll explode," I whispered.

I'd witnessed what a tiny Incendiary had done to the Celestial Cathedral. If all the domes nearby detonated . . . no one would stand a chance. Timur had hoped to kill Chimaera, but he'd end up killing countless humans, too.

Frey's powers were affecting the weather, the earth, the air. Centuries ago, Ahti's magic had triggered the seas to rise. If that happened again . . . there would be no Archipelago. There might be no land at all.

Down below, even Timur seemed to realize his critical error. Now that his plan had begun, though, he couldn't stop it. Any control he thought he could exert over Frey with his Vestige pocket watch and his stolen dragonfly was futile. He'd triggered arcane artefacts without fully realizing what he was doing. If the Penglass exploded, magic would rip through his Shroud like it was wet paper.

I clutched Frey closer, bringing my lips to his ear.

"Frey," I said again, with my mouth and my mind.

"I can't," Frey sobbed aloud. "I can't stop it. It's too much."

—*Then let me in, Frey. Let us help you.*

He turned his head and buried it in my neck, throwing his thin arms around me. With a cry, he dropped his walls and sucked me into the maelstrom of his magic.

The last time he'd lost control, I'd been trapped in a swirling vortex of blue. This time it was red, blue, and purple. I heard a howling wind, and I was surrounded by bruised clouds and distant pinpricks of stars. Magic hummed, reverberating in the glass. Our shared awareness left us as open as an exposed nerve.

Each of those stars, I realized, was a person. Visions slammed into both of us. Throughout Imachara, Elada, and across the sea, Chimaera froze. Hundreds, thousands—so many more than I'd ever imagined.

A man in a dark room, his skin rough as an elephant's, his ears large, his fingers short, blinking blearily in the dim light. A woman with hair like a lion's mane, her pupils slit like a cat's, her lips dark against her tawny fur. A child with feathers sprouting from the backs of his arms. Somewhere hidden was a warm lagoon. Inside swam three Chimaera with gills at their necks and fish tails instead of legs. Elsewhere, I saw a creature with the head and torso of a man, but the body of a horse: a real centaur. In a jungle, a cyrinx paused, one paw raised, yellow eyes glowing in the darkness. So many others who did not have Theri features but hid powers like mine and Cyan's. Twin girls my age who could turn invisible. A Byssian man in his home, surrounded by his family, who could tell when someone lied.

So many who might be different from humans but still loved, dreamed, and hoped.

—*Pull back from them, Frey*, I said. *Let them go to keep them safe.*

I felt the edges of time peel back.

Frey and I were inside a cobalt Penglass dome in a very different time. Frey was himself, but he was Ahti. I was me, but also Dev. I felt Anisa and Relean in another room as distant, reassuring presences. They had loved us so deeply, so unconditionally, and done their best to protect us. Ahti and I were using our magic in tandem to lift glass globes and circle them around our head in an orbit. If the one's power sparked, the other drew it back, until we knew we could keep those globes spinning indefinitely. Our abilities kept in perfect balance. Complete.

Centuries ago, we'd been separated, and we hadn't been able to stop the old world from shattering. But as the past faded and the present came back to the forefront, as an Anthi and a Theri Chimaera, we had a chance to stop it all from happening again.

I felt the unnatural wind on my cheeks. I was there with him, every step of the way, urging him back to himself. I lent him what strength and control I could. I kept my emotions steady to balance out his spikes. I was an anchor, or a counterweight. There, cupped within the red glass globe, I felt Frey cast off the first star. Another.

Another. As each tendril and filament snapped, he was able to disconnect from nearby domes

If Dev had been there with Ahti, all those years ago, they could have been like this. Together, perhaps we could right that ancient wrong. Yet part of me knew that, there on the island, the Penglass was still drinking the kidnapped Chimaeras' powers, threatening to upend our tentative balance. We had to get them out before it was too late.

I sensed Anisa drawing my magic to us, able to help Frey with his task while I pulled back enough to have more awareness of my surroundings.

I opened my eyes. Frey was glowing, but so was I, as if we were both lit up by the magic in our hearts.

Carefully, so carefully, I broke off a spindle of magic for myself.

Working off instinct, I sent the spike of energy out of the sphere toward the Chimaera Kashura like a lightning bolt. The woman shrieked and flinched, and that was all Cyan needed. She wrenched her face free, opened her mouth, and shouted a word in Alder, her magic flaring. The Kashura dropped like a stone. I couldn't tell how many were left.

Cyan sprinted the few steps to the Penglass dome, frantically finishing the glyph. Timur shouted, chasing after her, but he was too far away. She drew the glyph, and it opened for her.

She wasted no time, drawing her Vestige knife and cutting through the bonds as quickly as she could, freeing the Chimaera.

Violet emerged first, transforming mid-run from a woman to a cyrinx, the dark purple fur sprouting on her skin and her eyes brightening to gold. She snarled, digging her claws into the earth as she launched herself at a Kashura. He barely had time to scream before the sound cut short. Jarek Lutier followed, bristling into a great bear, fighting at Tauro's side.

One by one, the others followed. Even the little flower girl who had helped me up from the snow near the Royal Infirmary last winter bent down to take a fallen Vestige weapon with shaking hands and fired toward a Kashura.

As the Chimaera had their vengeance, Drystan darted out from a nearby dome. I sensed what he was aiming to do. The Penglass was sucking all the ambient magic out of the surrounding Vestige. Everything was weakening—even, finally, Timur's Shroud.

The Princess emerged last from her Penglass prison. She'd lost the jewels in her hair, her golden brocade dress was ripped, and she was barefoot. There was no Glamour, no illusion, and her Alder features were on full display. She looked up at the dome, and I sensed her reaching out for us. I stretched, as if clasping her metaphorical hand, and there was a muffled pulse of power that shook the island.

Drystan raised the Eclipse as if it were an ice pick and physically stabbed the Shroud around Timur as the Princess took a bit of our magic and fed it to the Vestige wand. Most of the power ricocheted, the recoil of it shoving Drystan back, but with us working together, the Eclipse made the smallest crack in the Shroud's defenses. It *popped*.

Timur stood there, shocked at the sudden exposure.

He roared and turned, lashing out with magic. The flash spread out from him in a whip of blue light; Drystan rose into the air and slammed to the ground.

I wanted to cry out, but I was afraid of distracting Frey and Anisa as they worked on unpicking Frey from the constellation of Chimaera minds. I was half with him, half with the Princess Nicolette, and wholly terrified.

Timur stumbled toward Nicolette, gathering his magic in his palms again. If he was going to go down, I realized, he wanted to make sure he took down the last of the Alder monarchy with him. In that moment, despite the Princess's power, I saw only a scared girl, quailing under his fury.

Just before Timur reached her, a silver flash of metal flew through the air. At first, I worried it'd missed, or the Shroud had repaired and protected him again, until Timur stood and stared down at the knife sticking out of his stomach.

Across the cracked flagstones, Pinecrest sagged, his clockwork hand outstretched. Despite his gunshot wound, he'd dragged himself along the ground, leaving a trail of dark blood behind him, until he grasped the knife Timur had used to cut the antlered Chimaera. The blade tipped with Vitriol poison.

Timur's mouth opened, the wound in his torso smoking.

Frey's powers were almost back within himself, the last tendrils between the Penglass weakening. With a burst of my own magic, Anisa and I helped him swallow down the last star.

My ears rang in the sudden absence of power. The storm above had calmed. I could no longer sense anything outside of the red glass. I blinked, holding a boneless, limp child in my arms, struggling to cling to consciousness myself.

I felt a sudden, horrible lurch. For a moment, I feared it meant the domes were already too damaged. I felt the red glass globe rise, just as I'd seen in our vision before we crossed the water.

This time, though, it wasn't Timur doing it: it was Princess Nicolette Snakewood.

She raised her arms. The glass globe left the broken metal cage of the lighthouse behind, rising until it must have looked like a second blood-red moon in the sky to those below.

With control, the Princess navigated the sphere with Frey and I inside. We landed in the center of the atrium with a shudder and the red sphere split right down the middle.

I picked Frey up and stepped out of the Penglass on shaking legs.

The Chimaera had subdued or killed the rest of the Kashura. Lily ran up to me, and I passed Frey to her. Distantly, I saw Drystan rise to his feet, and I wanted to sob with relief to see him largely unharmed by Timur's magic.

I stumbled, and I was so weak that I relinquished control and let Anisa step to the fore. Part of me wondered if she'd ever cede my body again. We vibrated with a hatred and a determination so pure I could do nothing but stay out of her way. Using my frame, she stalked toward Timur.

He tried to scrabble away, but he couldn't even raise himself onto his elbows. The stolen guard's corpse was alive, but only just.

We knelt at Timur's side and ripped the Isochrome from his hands. The blackness had spread across his palms, the flesh desiccated and skeletal.

"Please . . ." he gasped. "Mercy."

"*You shall find none here*," Anisa said with my mouth, our voice echoing in three tones at once. I suspected my eyes glowed as Cyan's did when she used her powers. Anisa took Relean's empty Aleph from my pocket and leaned close to Timur's face. There were those eyes, banded blue and copper, with the monarch butterfly dot by one iris. Relean's eyes.

Behind us, Cyan stepped forward, kneeling at my side and taking my hand, knowing what Anisa and I needed. Together, we dove into Timur's consciousness.

In that instant, we knew him. He hadn't always been consumed by hatred. We rifled through his memories. He'd run away from a terrible home, driven enough to work his way up in the royal household, until he saw too many instances of corruption to ignore.

One night, he'd caught a glimpse of the Princess with her blue skin and learned that Alder had been here all along. He dug deeper and discovered that Chimaera were both returning naturally and being deliberately brought back by the Steward's experiments. Timur's purpose had crystallized: to stop them, however he could.

One night, he'd gone to a magic show at the Spectre Theatre. Taliesin hadn't been able to sense or hear Relean, not that the dragonfly man would have helped him as he had Maske. Relean had sensed Timur in the crowd that night, curious about a man who knew of Alder and Chimaera. Timur had suspected something magical and gone back the following night with the Isochrome he'd already had in his possession, using the Vestige mechanism inside to help trap the unsuspecting ghost in his mind. He'd already learned the secret of the Alder and the Monarchy, so once he learned more of the past, his determination to take them down had only grown.

Out there on the island, Timur had hoped that the Shroud would protect him, but he'd known there was a very real chance that, even though he believed his soul was corrupted by a ghost, he might have been destroyed alongside the other Chimaera if his plan had worked. The risk was worth it to him. Whoever he'd been before, whatever softness was left in him had long since burned away. The blurred man was also a hollow man. There was nothing left now but his hatred.

Anisa batted Timur's petty concerns away until she found the kernel of magic in the corner of his dying mind, fluttering weakly, like a butterfly that had been half-crushed in a palm.

—*There you are, my beloved*, Anisa said, but I sensed her growing dismay. *But you're fading so fast.*

I threw the pocket watch over my shoulder without looking, and the Princess caught it.

—*Now*, Anisa instructed.

She twisted her magic, and I felt the Isochrome activate. I'd known the Princess could affect Vestige, like stopping the Lethe from working on us, but I was still dimly amazed. At the same moment, Cyan, Anisa, and I dragged Relean from Timur's dying mind.

Relean's magic flowed into the Aleph, but it was too low on power. Relean began to flicker.

—*It's not enough. We're losing him,* Anisa cried out, the power of her grief and fear intense enough to bring those around us to our knees. *I cannot lose you again. Relean! Please, stay with me!*

My eyes streamed with Anisa's fear. Her love for him reverberated across the island, but Relean was still fading.

"Little bird," she called. "*Will you take him? Please?*"

Her mouth opened, but she shook her head. "I'm sorry," she said. "I can't."

Anisa gazed pleadingly at the other Chimaera and the Alder, but they either didn't fully understand what was being asked, or had the same fear as Cyan. Nicolette was only a child—it didn't seem fair to ask her. Beyond that, while we were reasonably sure Relean was on our side, it did not seem wise to house a Chimaera within the future monarch.

"Please," Anisa said. "*Please, after everything, we cannot lose him now.*"

Drystan stepped forward. "If I took him, temporarily," he said. "Would it be safe for me, as someone non magical? Could we find a way to get him out, just as we will try to free Micah from you? Would Relean know how?"

Anisa and I looked up at him. "*Yes, yes, I believe, you would be safe for a few days before the magic caused you harm. My Relean knows more of the old ways than even me. I believe he could help. You would do that, pale jester?*" she asked in that echoing voice.

"For you, no. But for Micah, I would do anything," he said, and Anisa and I gave a sob.

"*Take the Isochrome. Say the words, pale jester. Hurry.*"

The Princess passed it to him with wide eyes. Drystan turned on the Isochrome with shaking fingers. I told him what to say.

"Come to me, Relean," Drystan said. "Stay within me, Phantom Dragonfly."

The echoes of Relean rose from Timur, swirling in delicate light. Drystan's eyes didn't leave mine as the magic settled into his skin. Trapped within my own body, I watched in awe and horror as Drystan's blue eyes shifted hue, becoming greener, banded with copper. A little dot appeared in one iris. Relean's eyes. He staggered with the feel of Relean's magic within him, but he stayed on his feet.

Timur gave one last choke. His once-again brown eyes went distant as the light left them. We had managed just in time.

My back arched. Anisa's triumph burned through every nerve and tendon, and I had no reserves left. Drystan and Relean came behind me, his arms closing around my shoulders.

"*Thank you,*" Relean whispered in Drystan's voice. "*Thank you.*"

—*You better let him go*, I thought at him, and Anisa allowed the thought to pass to him. *You can't keep him. He's mine.*

Relean's eyes glittered from Drystan's face. My head turned, and I caught sight of Pinecrest's body. His false hand was outstretched, his eyes open and unblinking.

The doctor had frightened me, and I'd never trusted him. At times, I'd downright hated him. But I remembered the faint curl at the corner of his lips as he turned the carriage towards the university hospital. The moments of almost gentleness, and his insistence that he had cared for me and all of his Chimaera charges. Despite everything he'd done, I let out a small sob, my eyes stinging with tears. In the end, when it'd mattered, he'd done what was needed, and I was grateful to him for that.

Half of the Kashura had died, and one or two of the smaller domes had shattered, pieces of glowing blue scattered across the stone. Kai was limping badly, but I watched him help Juliet to her feet. Jarek Lutier and Tauro had tied up the remaining Kashura. Violet, still in cyrinx form, circled them menacingly, growling low in her throat. Flora stared ahead, shocked, her arm around the flower girl's body. The man with the alligator skin had died as well. The rest of the Chimaera, both here at the Observatory and throughout the Archipelago, had survived.

"We did it," Drystan and Relean whispered in my ear. "We did it, my love."

I managed to stay conscious until we got the Chimaera and bound Kashura back into the larger craft. Frey, the Princess, Lily, and Kai took that one. Drystan, Cyan, and I took the smaller Vestige boat.

Nicolette's head turned toward the city, her expression apprehensive. What did she sense out across the water? What would we be returning to?

I looked up at the bright moon above us, the waves rocking the boat until my eyes fluttered shut.

31

AWAKENING

"The Alder created us, perhaps, yet they never let us know their secrets. When the world broke, they left. They've been gone long enough for history's axis to turn again.

Any clear night, I look up at the stars. I wonder if they will return one day. One way or another.

And sometimes, I swear, one of the stars brightens in response to my thought, or my wish. Whichever it is."

PROFESSOR CAED CEDAR'S
UNPUBLISHED NOTES

I awoke in the Royal Infirmary. Well, more accurately, *we* woke up in the Infirmary. I lifted my hand, wriggling my fingers before letting it fall. At least I could move my body again, even if Anisa was still curled up in a corner of my mind.

What happened on that island came back to me in pieces. The stone of the lighthouse beneath my fingertips. That leap onto slick glass the color of blood. The feel of Frey in my arms, his skin and scales hot enough to burn as we connected with every Chimaera in the Archipelago. The *thwip* of gunfire, the snarls of Chimaera finally freed, picking off the Kashura like prey. The star in my chest, swallowed down. Pieces of glowing Penglass, and a dragonfly ghost freed from a fading, blurred man in a stolen corpse who had fallen into Drystan's body. I realized the full impact of that, and my heart squeezed. Would we be able to get Relean out in time? Where was he?

I was in a nearly empty ward. I later found out that privacy was courtesy of Princess Nicolette Snakewood. Frey was in the other bed, sans Glamour, with Lily at his side. He was awake and raised a scaled hand to me in greeting. I returned it, still coming back to myself. My magic was thrumming behind my ribcage, though more faintly. I sensed two royal guards stationed outside.

—*Are you all right?* I asked Frey.

—*Yeah. I think so. Thanks to you.*

I shook my head. —*You did most of the work. I just helped nudge you in the right direction, and Anisa guided you.*

He shook his head. —*I was lost, and you found me. Thank you.*

I smiled at him, faintly. —*You're welcome.*

Every part of me hurt, and a headache pulsed at my temples. A moment later, a nurse came into the empty ward and spied my labored movements. I recognized her as the one who had treated Cyan and me after the Celestial Cathedral attack. Did she remember me? She gave me a dose of laudanum and urged me to drink two large glasses of water. Next, she took my temperature and pulled up one of my eyelids to look at the whites of my eyes.

"You're making a remarkable recovery," she said, her eyebrows rising a little in surprise. Her eyes darted to Frey and his scales, then back to me.

"They're both rather remarkable," Lily said. The nurse left.

Lily came over to me, brushing my hair back from my face. "You saved my boy. I owe you a life debt, Micah Grey," she said, her voice shaking. "Anything you need, if I can provide it, it's yours."

I smiled sleepily at her as the medicine took hold.

• • • •

When I next came back to myself, a warm hand held mine.

Drystan was asleep in a chair pushed close to my bed; his neck was at an awkward angle. His skin was pale, and he had dark circles under his eyes. Frey's hospital bed was empty.

As if he sensed my gaze, Drystan's eyes opened. The whites of his eyes were bloodshot, and the sight of Relean's irises staring back at me unnerved me anew.

"Are you all right?" I asked. "Are you in control, Drystan?"

"Yes, it's me. Relean is being, ah, polite. I'm doing better than you, I think." He smiled at me, and I sensed the relief washing over him.

"Do you feel all right?"

"Yes," he said. "A little tired, but otherwise fine. Relean assures me we have some time, and that he has some ideas of how to get both him and Anisa out of us. He says my taking of that dose of Pinecrest's elixir might have actually primed my body to be able to withstand his magic without it being as much of a shock to my system. At least my awful mistake wasn't entirely futile, though I'm not planning to repeat it."

I blinked at that. "How long was I out?" I asked.

"Two days." He looked closer at me. "It's strange, isn't it? That neither of us are alone."

I felt Anisa's overwhelming rush of love towards Relean. Still, I didn't wish to speak about our ghostly passengers, and they both held back, letting us have our moment.

"Everyone's all right?" I asked.

He nodded. "Yes, or near enough. Quite a few cuts and bruises, and Kai's shoulder and ankle injuries were nasty. Overall, though, nothing too serious, thank the Lord and Lady. Most everyone's at the Palace just now. The Princess is making it her mission to spoil them all."

I closed my eyes briefly. "That's good. What happened after we came here? Tell me everything."

He did. It'd been an eventful couple of days. The Penglass brightening so alarmingly had helped interrupt the protest. Lorna Elderberry, the new leader of the Foresters, had stepped in and helped prevent the crowd from turning into an all-out riot. By sunrise, it had returned to a vigil.

The Princess had shared the truth with the public: that Timur had killed the Steward and the Council in the hopes of a coup. She said that the Foresters had nothing to do with them and would never have wished for that violence.

The next day, she had invited Lorna Elderberry to the Palace and had a meeting with the Foresters, Juliet, and Violet, though Drystan didn't know what the outcome of that had been. It must have been strange for Lorna Elderberry to have a meeting with a child who was so young but spoke seriously and maturely about various elements of government. Evidently, Nicolette had shown her true face and communicated that she wished to change the monarchy's role in Elada. To be one voice of many.

The Princess's other main goal was for Chimaera to be able to live openly. Even if the Kashura at the Observatory were all dead or imprisoned, I was sure there'd still be plenty of people throughout Elada and the Archipelago who would rail against those of us who were different. Still, it was a start.

"She wants to throw us a parade," Drystan said with a twist of his mouth.

"Gods, no."

He chuckled. "I told her you'd say that. She demands we all at least accept a medal."

"Fine. If she must. Privately."

His mouth stayed quirked. "She's also asked that Frey come live with her at the Palace, and I think Lily will agree to that. They've already struck up quite the friendship, by all accounts."

"That's good," I said.

Drystan's half-smile faded. "When we went back to the Palace . . . I ran into my father," he admitted.

That got my attention. "Oh?"

"'Oh' is about right." He gave me a rueful look. "I was still covered in soot, dust, and not a little blood, so of course that was when he recognized me." He gestured to his eyes. "Though he didn't seem to notice this, at least. Would have been awkward."

"And how'd that go?"

He exhaled hard through his nose. "No tearful hugs or falling to our knees or anything. My family's all moved to Imachara, and he's invited me for a visit, which I've tentatively accepted. So not bad, all told."

I'd no idea if this meant they'd publicly claim Drystan as part of the Hornbeam family again, or if he'd want that, but it was still a first step. I took his hand and squeezed. "I'm so glad. Really."

Drystan squeezed back. "Me, too. I think."

My head fell back against the pillow. "When can I get out of here?"

"Tomorrow, the doctors say. You can go back to the Kymri Theatre. It's all fixed now. We can go home."

I briefly brightened at the thought, but then I sighed. "We'll still have plenty of other messes to sort through, though, won't we?" Relean and Anisa were at the forefront of those.

His lips brushed my forehead with a kiss. "Aye, indeed we do. but we'll get through them together, my love."

As I faded, I saw Drystan's expression shift, and I knew that Anisa and Relean would have their first proper conversation since they'd been reunited. I drifted away, leaving them to their reunion.

• • • •

My mother called my name.

I tried to respond to her, and though my voice echoed in the mist, I couldn't find her.

She called again. I saw her figure, a dim shadow in the grey. She came into focus, and she was facing away from me. She was dressed impeccably: tight corset, a fine bustle, and a full skirt of black crinoline and silk. There wasn't a hair out of place in her greying chignon. I never knew why she always seemed in perpetual mourning save for the white of her gloves.

She turned, the jet-black necklace swinging, and gave me the brightest smile I'd ever seen on her features, as if she were truly delighted to see me.

"Oh, there you are."

• • • •

The next time I woke up, it wasn't Drystan at the side of my bed, but Cyril.

"Hullo, sleepyhead," he said, but he looked at me with enough trepidation that I wondered just what he'd heard about the events at the Royal Observatory. "I asked Drystan if I could be the one to pick you up."

"Hullo, Cyril." I was grateful to see him.

"Are you all right?" he asked.

"Battered and bruised, but already on the mend." I sat up. "Desperate to be home."

He hesitated. "I've come to ask a favor before you do."

Anisa's intuition flared within me. "Mother woke up, didn't she?"

He looked at me oddly. "She did, yes. She's still here, just a few floors above us."

My tongue was stuck to the roof of my mouth. I glanced up, as if I could see through the ceiling.

"Will you speak with her?"

"Why would I?" I asked, carefully.

"It's just that . . . she still thinks you're dead."

I felt a complicated pang of regret. "Tell her I'm not then, if you like."

"Do you not think . . ." He trailed off before continuing. " . . . it would be good if you did speak to her? Even for a few minutes. For both of you."

I said nothing.

"I could come with you, if you like."

"No," I said. "No. It'd have to be just me and her."

I realized there was plenty I wanted to say to my mother, though I doubted she'd want to hear any of it. But sitting on that resentment and not having that last confrontation had been eating away at me in countless little ways. Drystan had taken a step with his family. I owed it to myself to do the same, whatever happened. No more running away.

I sat up and swung my legs over the side of the hospital bed. "Do I have any clothes or anything?" I wasn't about to face her in a hospital gown with my arse bare to the wind.

His face broke out in a smile. "Of course. Drystan gave me some."

Half an hour later, I'd cleaned myself up. Drystan had chosen one of my favorite suits. The jacket and trousers were dark brown, the waistcoat was burnt orange, and my shirt cream with just a hint of lace. I tugged at my cuffs nervously as I took a deep breath, feeling my Lindean binder against my ribs. The thing that unnerved me the most about my reflection was my eyes: the change was subtle, but they were closer to blue than hazel, due to Anisa's presence in me. Would my mother notice?

Cyril walked me to the door of Mother's ward. He squeezed my shoulder. "I'll be down in the waiting room. All right?"

"All right," I echoed, faintly. My brother left me, his footsteps echoing down the corridor. Anisa retreated, giving me what privacy she could.

Tempted as I was to flee, Drystan had taken a step to heal his past. I couldn't run away anymore, no matter what version of my mother was on the other side.

I pushed open the door.

My mother was in one of the beds by the window, propped up by pillows, looking out over the buildings to the courtyard garden. She was much changed from the pristine version of her I'd seen in my dream. She wore no cosmetics, and the light through the window illuminated every line on her face, every grey hair, and the dark smudges beneath her eyes. Her skin was slightly jaundiced, and her form diminished. She didn't look at all like the mother I'd once feared.

At the sound of my footsteps, she turned. Her eyes fixed on me like a magnet to a pole. I slowed my steps.

My mother took in my suit, waistcoat, jacket, and polished brogues. My hair was a bit long, the auburn curling around my ears. My hands fluttered nervously before settling in my trouser pockets. I'd been afraid that as soon as I'd been pinned beneath her gaze, Micah would fade and leave only a frightened Gene behind. Yet I was secure in myself, and I knew I looked like a young man to her, even if I still had echoes of her daughter's face.

"I'm still dreaming, aren't I?" she said, her hand going to her throat. "You're a phantom sent to haunt me."

"Hullo, Mother," I managed. "I'm afraid I'm no ghost." I wasn't about to tell her I housed one in the corner of my mind, though.

"I did dream of you, didn't I?" Her eyes were slightly unfocused; she was still on a mixture of medication. The skin on her arms was slack from lost muscle. Gone was the imperious woman who had ordered me to finish my embroidery or stop tugging at the collar of my dress.

"Perhaps you did. I don't call myself by my old name," I said, not wanting to hear it on her lips. "I go by Micah Grey now."

"Micah Grey," she repeated, diffidently, and it felt beyond strange to hear her say it.

I took a deep breath and jumped into it. "I know what you were going to do to me."

She looked away, unable to meet my eyes. "The next morning, I realized you must have overheard me and your father, and it was why you left. I recognized my plan might have been . . . hasty."

"*Hasty*? How could you even have considered operating on me without my consent, even for a *moment*? To not give me a choice?"

She licked her lips. "I thought . . . I thought it would be easier."

"For me? Or for you and the family's reputation?" My voice was shaking.

She closed her eyes, her brow wrinkling, before she forced herself to meet my glare. "I wanted you to have prospects. A future. I was afraid the Hawthornes would recant their offer. It wasn't an unfounded fear." Her fingers worked at the cloth of her thin hospital coverlet.

"It was cruel. Evil, even. I don't say that lightly."

She flinched as if I'd struck her. "I was wrong. I'm sorry for it."

I blinked. I wasn't sure I'd ever heard my mother apologize for anything. Yet here were the words, or as close to them as she was capable. Even though I'd fantasized about this moment plenty of times since I climbed out of Cyril's window, I didn't quite know what to do with it now that it had passed.

"I don't know if I can ever fully forgive you," I admitted. "But I do thank you for saying that."

She bowed her head.

When I was small, I'd thought my parents were nearly perfect beings. But I'd discovered that they were just as flawed as everyone else. My father, too distant and detached, unable to stand up to his wife even when he knew she proposed something egregious. My mother, hiding behind the power and prestige she'd fought so hard for, pushing away the real things that mattered. Dosing herself with drink and laudanum, seeking numbness. I ran away, and Cyril was the son and heir, caught in the middle of it all. We were a broken family, and I didn't think our puzzle pieces would ever fit together.

"You never let me know you," I said. "Not really. I was never sure if you actually wanted me, especially when I found out the Royal Physician had given me to you. I always felt a burden."

She swallowed, hard. "You were wanted. You are."

I wanted to believe that. And on some level, I did understand her fear. To try and protect me from a cruel and unkind society, she'd been cruel and unkind under the guise of caring.

"I still can't believe you're alive. I thought . . ." She trailed off. "Where did you go?"

I couldn't tell her about the circus, and I didn't even want to tell her about the Kymri Theatre or reveal that I'd been hidden away at the Elmbark séance. "I made my way. Despite everything that's happened to me since I climbed out that window, becoming Micah has been the best decision I've ever made."

Her head rose, and her cheeks were wet with tears. "We could try again," she said, meekly. "Perhaps?"

"If we did, would you openly claim me as your son?" I asked.

Her mouth opened, but no sound emerged. Her gaze flicked away, and that was answer enough. After all that, she still hesitated. It hurt, but not as much as I expected. She wished she could be different, and I supposed that counted for something.

"Goodbye, Mother," I said, but there was no bitterness in my voice.

"Goodbye . . . Micah," she whispered.

I went to the door, and we stared at each other for a moment, not speaking. I gave a nod, not sure exactly what I was signaling, and I left her.

Out in the hallway, whatever Cyril saw in my face, he decided not to press me about it. It'd been hard, but maybe speaking to my mother had started mending the crack that had been in my heart since I'd put my ear to the door of the study that night in Sicion. Holding onto the pain didn't serve either of us.

Maybe one day, I'd reach out again. Maybe by then, she'd be brave enough to love me openly. But if she wasn't . . . I realized I would be fine. Better than fine. I still had my brother. Anisa said nothing, but I sensed her reassurance and comfort flow through me like a hug. She'd been mysterious and frustrating and odd by turns, but in a way, she and Maske were more my parental figures than Lord and Lady Laurus had ever been. I had Drystan, Cyan, and all the other people who didn't simply tolerate me but loved me just as I was. Without compromise.

"Take me home, Cyril," I said.

32

LIKE CLOCKWORK

"The Alder and Chimaera seemed particularly interested in the mechanisms of time. So many of the automatons tick like metronomes and play on loops. Plenty of Vestige are watches that never need rewinding. Their time ran out, but the seconds, hours, and years beat on."

"VESTIGE," PROFESSOR CAED CEDAR,
ROYAL SNAKEWOOD UNIVERSITY

Cyril and I pulled up to the Kymri Theatre just before noon. The roof was fully restored and freshly slated. The columns had been repaired and repainted, along with the entire exterior, the colors fresher and brighter than ever. The broken windows had been replaced. It was as if they'd never been damaged at all. I walked up the steps, remembering the first time I'd seen the Theatre, glorious even with the peeling, faded paint.

When I tapped that familiar brass knocker, Maske swung open the oaken door and greeted me with a wide smile before sweeping me into a hug. He smelled faintly of oil—he'd been in his workshop.

I pulled away from his embrace and stepped into the hallway, the mosaics of Chimaera staring down at me. The kitchen was bright, with a new stove and shining copper appliances. Ricket was gulping down food from her bowl. Maske put on a cup of coffee, and my eyes settled on Drystan where he sprawled in his usual seat next to Cyan. She smiled at me, underpinning her expression with a pulse of warmth from her mind. She still looked tired, but much better than expected after all that had happened to us.

Drystan's blond hair was sticking up a bit at the back, and I couldn't resist the urge to smooth it down and run my fingernails through his scalp. His eyes closed in pleasure.

"Hey, you," he said. But I sensed the slight unease when he looked into my eyes and we both knew we weren't alone.

"Hey."

Maske poured coffee into mugs and placed them on the table as Cyan set out the sugar and creamer. I made my coffee just as I liked it and relished the first sip.

"So . . . now what?" I asked, breaking the silence. It was unreal to be sitting in a warm kitchen, clutching the cup of coffee in my hands, as if the battle at the Observatory had never happened.

"Now . . . we take back our lives, I suppose," Cyan said. "We need to find a way to free Anisa and Relean from your bodies." She looked nervous at that, and I also sensed a hint of guilt that she hadn't stepped up to take Relean. I understood why she didn't, though.

"First we heal from our wounds," Drystan said with a confidence I wished I felt. "We perform stage magic. We watch the world change in front of us."

"I do think I want a nap," I said. The others laughed.

"There's one matter of business you might want to see to first," Maske said. "You received a letter from a solicitor yesterday. The late Royal Physician's solicitor."

I sucked in a breath.

"We debated opening it," Drystan said. "We showed great restraint, but we're all desperate to know what it says."

Maske passed me the envelope, and I looked at it in trepidation. Part of me wished they had peeked so I could have some warning of whatever was inside.

I broke the seal and took out the letter. A Vestige key fell out, and I recognized it immediately. The others watched me curiously as I read, though they didn't crane their heads to look. Cyan didn't even try to brush my mind to read over my mental shoulder. I read it twice to make sure it was real. Anisa echoed my surprise.

"Well?" Drystan demanded.

I looked up at them. "It seems . . . Doctor Pinecrest changed his will a few weeks ago. He left all his Vestige . . . to me."

Maske sucked in a breath, and Drystan's eyes widened. I shook my head.

"Why would he do that? He barely knew me." My voice was flat with shock.

"Who did he actually have in his life?" Drystan asked. "We saw those marks on his skin. He knew dosing himself so often was making him sick, and that his own time might have been running out."

I swallowed. "He never mentioned family, or friends to us, did he, I suppose."

"I think his life was his work. So, in that case," Maske said, voice soft. "You were, for better or worse, the subject of his experiment that he knew best. If he had to leave it to someone, then it seems he decided on you."

I kept staring at the typewritten words, emotions tumbling through me: I was baffled, suspicious, touched, and it was all stained with a complicated welling of grief.

Cyan whistled low. "Well, damn, Micah Grey. Whatever his reasons, the result is the same. You're filthy rich."

• • • •

Two days later, Drystan, Cyan, Maske, and I stood outside the warehouse by the harbor. I squinted in the bright afternoon sunlight. I held Pinecrest's square Vestige key in my hand, and my rucksack was slung over one shoulder. I'd gone into the warehouse alone yesterday—well, save Anisa, of course, who I couldn't escape, but I wanted the others here for this next step.

I'd never have been able to go up against Timur without Anisa's help at the Observatory. Yet she knew, of course, that I didn't want her in my body for the rest of my life. I, of course, had always known how much she'd craved feeling alive again, to be housed within a solid body. If Pinecrest hadn't passed me my unexpected inheritance, we might not have had a choice in the matter.

But now, perhaps we did.

Relean and Anisa had spent hours speaking to each other, with Drystan and I eavesdropping within our own bodies. They believed they could each be called out once more to transfer them somewhere else. After centuries, Anisa had the love of her many lives back. Today, we might be able to reunite them properly and free ourselves.

As the new owner, it was my role to officially invite Cyan, Drystan, and Maske through the Shroud and Banshee barriers of the warehouse. The doors shut behind us as the glass globes brightened, and Anisa, Relean, Drystan and I located the potential answer to our predicament.

I led the others to our discovery. They gasped, as shocked as Anisa and I had been when we'd first seen them the day before.

Pinecrest's two Ampula vessels, a match of the ones I'd seen in the morgue. And they weren't empty.

"Lord and Lady," Maske breathed.

While the clockwork woman's head had been displayed in the Museum of Mechanical Antiquities, that little story on the placard about how she'd been found had been a lie, or else Pinecrest had discovered the rest of her later. Her body was complete. A tall woman, her proportions similar to Anisa's damselfly body, minus the wings. She was hairless. In the other Ampula was her match: a clockwork man, perfect save for the fact that he was missing a hand. That, too, had been given to me as the most macabre bit of inheritance from the Royal Physician of Elada. I had it in my rucksack.

The clockwork pair hovered in the Vestige of their liquid glass coffins like the bodies I'd seen at the medical school. The liquid was opaque enough that they almost looked like real corpses. Almost.

I'd already told the others our plan: to transfer Anisa to the clockwork woman, and Relean to the clockwork man.

"Would that work?" Drystan had asked when we'd spied the Ampula. "Is it safe?"

"Relean and Anisa seem to think so," I'd said. "But we have to try." Drystan had darker circles beneath his eyes, and I was afraid he wasn't telling me if Relean's magic was starting to affect him or not. I kept finding myself checking his fingertips, searching for signs of darkening.

Maske helped me connect wires from the other Ampula to my temples while Cyan assisted Drystan with his. The magician muttered under his breath the whole time about how he couldn't believe he was seeing not only one clockwork person this close up, but two. He'd created a clockwork automaton for his grand finale, but of course, that had paled in comparison to the Alder-age ones.

I couldn't pretend I wasn't terrified. Even Anisa wasn't fully confident, much as she tried to hide it. After all, she had moved from a human body to a clockwork one in the past, but that body had been grown especially for her, without another soul inside. Timur had used an Ampula to jump bodies, but Eric, the poor Palace guard, had died in the process. Would Drystan? If he did, I would never forgive her.

The four of us in two bodies had discussed it for hours the night before in the confines of my skull, but in the end, I'd decided to trust that she would be able to disentangle us safely and leave me intact in my own body, and Drystan in his. Cyan would try to help if we ran into complications.

They had said this should work. Theoretically. I had to trust that the Damselfly and the Dragonfly would know what to do.

"Here we go," I said.

Drystan was pale but determined. He didn't like the thought of the Phantom Damselfly and her Dragonfly lover being ghosts in our shared life going forward any more than I did, even if he had been able to house Relean indefinitely. While I was fine sharing my magic with Frey, Cyan, Anisa, or even the Princess, my body and my mind deserved to be mine, and mine alone.

I moved closer to the tank, breathing shallowly. The clockwork bodies floated, unmoving. Anisa guided my fingers along the Ampula's controls. They lit up at the same time, humming, and I tasted magic on the air as the glass globes around us dimmed, then brightened.

Behind me, Cyan, Maske, and Drystan were hushed with awe and fear. It felt almost as if we were in a church and these Ampula were the altars. The clockwork bodies arched as the Vestige whirred. The tops of the tanks opened, and the bottoms rose until the false bodies emerged from the water, glistening. Once out of the greenish liquid, the bodies looked far less human with their transparent false skin and brass gears at the joints. Their faces were serene and empty.

"Maske?" I asked. "Give me the hand, please."

He bent down and opened my pack—it was the very one the other clowns at the circus had stolen not long after I'd joined. Drystan had searched it and learned I was a runaway noble, just like him.

Maske took out Doctor Pinecrest's clockwork hand and gave it to me. I felt the whisper of his lips against my cheek. "Break a bone," he said instead of wishing me luck, like we were in a theatre.

I shuddered at the sight of the clockwork hand's cold, slack skin as Maske attached it to the stump. As soon as it was screwed in, the faint seam in the false skin disappeared.

Drystan stepped back. I adjusted the wires at my temples. I was trying to put on a brave face, but fear was choking me.

Anisa and I and Drystan and Relean pressed the final button on our Ampulas at the same time.

Blue, green, and purple magic rose from the Alder-age metal. The same shimmer played over the surface of my skin. The Phantom Damselfly untwined herself from my bones, my muscles and tendons, and the grooves of my mind. I could just imagine her, dragonfly wings catching the light, the skirt of her simple dress twirling about her legs, her dark blue hair streaming behind her. With a feeling like a sigh, she left my body behind, the colors of her magic travelling down the wires before settling into the clockwork woman.

Cyan hovered, her magic at the ready. I worried I would be forced to follow or dragged along after Anisa. In the end, I didn't need Cyan's help. I stood tall, holding back, secure in my sense of self and my body, desperately hoping that Drystan and Relean were doing the same.

I opened my eyes and met Drystan's blue ones. His normal irises, with no trace of Relean's copper and monarch butterfly dot. He was clammy with sweat and barely standing, but he was alive.

We had uncoupled. I was Micah Grey. She was Anisa, the Phantom

Damselfly. He was Drystan, and only Drystan, Relean equally separated. I disconnected the wires from my temples.

Both Vestige life-size automatons were glowing, and magic was even thicker in the air. The artefacts in the warehouse hummed. The moment stretched, or perhaps time slowed.

As one, both bodies breathed in and out. Blue crystals at their hearts lit up and began to pulse.

I pressed a palm flat against my chest, feeling my own breath. Maske's mouth was open in unrestrained awe. Drystan startled back, and even Cyan stiffened. The clockwork bodies arched, their mouths opening and closing, but they weren't in pain. Their magic was melding with the incredible, impossible technology created by the Alder once upon a time.

The last of the swirling colors faded back into that false skin before their bodies slackened.

In tandem, their eyes opened.

They struggled to sit up, growing used to their new bodies. Liquid dripped from their skin, and their hearts still glowed as if . . . as if they'd swallowed stars. They were utterly unaware or unbothered by their nakedness. They blinked, turning to look at each other, and their expressions melted to ones of such tenderness, such love, that I abruptly felt like we were intruding.

"Anisa?" I whispered. "Relean?"

Their heads swiveled, their unsettling gazes landing on me. Anisa's eyes were the brilliant blue of a clear, afternoon sky. Relean's irises were the match of the ones I'd seen staring out from Timur's stolen body's, hardened with hatred, and Drystan's face, softened with love. Now, they were inscrutable.

"Little Kedi," the clockwork woman said in Anisa's voice. It was the first time I'd heard her speak aloud without using my mouth.

I moved closer to her. She reached out and cupped my cheek as she had in her ghostly form so many times before. I felt the touch.

With effort, Anisa and Relean rose. I'd brought them simple clothes, and they wrapped these around their clockwork bodies. Already, they moved as smoothly as well-oiled machines.

Relean smiled at me faintly. "Thank you," he said. His voice was deeper. "I'd hoped the dreams I'd sent would help. And they did. You freed me."

Part of me was still afraid of him. Yet more understanding passed over me in a wave. Relean had done what he could while trapped within the blurred man. Some of Anisa's messages from the spirits had, in fact, been warnings from this ghost, whenever he could break free from Timur's control, even if only for an instant.

Relean's head turned toward Maske. "Hello, old friend."

Maske was gaping like a fish. "Hello . . . Relean."

Relean reached out his hand, the one that had lived on Pinecrest's body for years, and clasped Anisa's palm. It'd taken all of us to defeat Timur. Anisa, Relean, and their knowledge of the past and magic. Me and Frey and our symbiosis at the top of the lighthouse. Cyan's powers, and the other Chimaera Timur had stolen. The Alder Princess and her control over Vestige. Drystan, Lily, and Pinecrest. Even Maske giving us his Vestige and a few magic tricks had made all the difference.

I gave Anisa and Relean two Glamours, and they slid them over their false necks with reluctance, along with the clothing we'd brought. Like the Princess, they didn't have to program the Vestige—their skin grew less transparent, and hair sprouted from their skulls. Anisa's was blue-black and fell to her waist, as it had in Damselfly form. Relean had soft waves of a matching shade that reached his shoulders. They were still a bit too tall, moved that bit too gracefully. They were so preternaturally beautiful it was almost alarming.

Wordless, we left the warehouse. I locked up behind me with Pinecrest's key. I still wasn't sure what I'd do with all the other Vestige, but I figured I had some time.

With that, four magicians and two phantom ghosts in clockwork bodies headed back to the Kymri Theatre.

33

HOMECOMING

"Home. A nebulous concept, far more than the stones we build around us and the slates we put over our head. It's where we feel safe. Where those who love us dwell. Sometimes that's not a physical place, but a state of mind."

FROM THE EARLIER WORK OF PHILOSOPHER ALVIS TYNDALL

Maske decided not to rush straight back into performing, giving us a chance to catch our breath.

Relean and Maske spent hours in his workshop, tinkering with new innovations. Anisa spent a surprising amount of time with Ricket, who took to her rather quickly. She reveled in her new senses, eating whatever food she could get her clockwork hands on, smelling perfume, or walking through a crowded marketplace with Cyan, Drystan, and me. She marveled that if she spoke to anyone, they could hear her.

One evening, I passed through the theatre and caught Anisa and Relean dancing onstage to unheard music. I watched them a while. The steps were unfamiliar, but not the way their fingers tangled and how they looked into each other's eyes.

A few days later, the clockwork couple bid us farewell.

I'd half-expected it. I'd seen Anisa with a distant, wistful stare. In recent days, they'd both grown restless.

"Our journey with you is finished, for now," Anisa said, with those eyes that blinked just a bit less often than they should. "We wish to travel to all corners of the Archipelago, to see how the world has changed." I knew her well enough by now to catch the excisions and elisions. I also knew directly asking her would get me nowhere. She'd either tell us where they were really going, or she wouldn't.

"Will you ever return?" I asked.

Her gaze was mysterious. "Perhaps."

We gave them supplies and enough money for passage to Byssia and spending money when they arrived. Still, seeing Anisa and Relean dressed in travel clothes and with packs slung over their back was unexpectedly emotional. Maske had gone out with Lily. I also suspected the magician had partly fled the difficulty of a longer goodbye. The former Shadow and the magician had decided to begin their courtship again, without the lies, though Maske's trust would be slow to heal.

"Oh, my little Kedi . . . how much you've grown." Anisa reached out her hand and touched my cheek.

I leaned into her palm.

"Before we go," Relean said to Cyan, Drystan, and me as Anisa pulled away. "We are willing to show you one last thing, if you desire to see it."

"What?" I said, with no small amount of apprehension.

Anisa smiled beatifically. "The true secret of Penglass."

• • • •

We walked through Imachara, the stars shining overhead. There was no longer a curfew, and it was early enough that the public houses were open, their light and the sound of conversation, music, and laughter spilling out onto the cobbles. It was early days, but the city slowly seemed to be returning to normality.

Anisa and Relean brought us to a Penglass dome the size of a small house on the beach, not far from where the circus had once camped. It glowed, though not as brightly as on the night of the full moon. No one was near, but a few bonfires burned in the distance. Anisa raised a fingertip and drew the glyph. Enough of the glass melted away. She and Relean stepped inside, and we followed.

I had only seen the interior of Penglass in visions, aside from the red globe. I could see echoes of the past in here—this felt like an old common area, with alcoves where there had been seating, and twining stairs that led to another room above. Yet there was no furniture, no other evidence of whomever had once lived here, whether they were Alder or Chimaera. It was extraordinary, to stand somewhere no one had entered in thousands of years, but this was not a secret, at least not after Anisa's visions of the past.

The walls had the same hexagonal shelving I'd briefly glimpsed in the dome that had imprisoned the Chimaera on the island. Anisa lifted her hand to one, drawing another glyph, and they *opened*.

It took me a moment to realize what I was seeing. Cyan gasped softly, and Drystan leaned forward.

Alephs. Countless Alephs, neatly stacked on top of each other.

"Yes," Relean said, picking one up and holding it reverently. "While most of the Alder fled for the stars, there was enough notice that a small percentage of Chimaera managed to save themselves."

"So this means . . ." I trailed off.

"The Chimaera of the past could indeed return," Anisa confirmed. "Most of these are very low on power, and they would emerge as ghosts, as Relean and I did. We'll look for more clockwork bodies and wake up a few, or perhaps we'll find a way to regrow bodies like the

Alder once did. But yes, modern Chimaera will keep returning, and as magic rekindles, the ancient ones might, too. Probably not soon, maybe not even within your lifetime, but one day. This is why we're leaving. To see what can be done."

I picked up an Aleph. The Alder script twined over the Vestige metal. It hummed faintly with magic.

"What will that mean, for the world?" I asked.

"That it will change," Relean said. "How, there are too many ways to say. Life is nothing but change, after all, and we believe the world having a little more magic, a little more wonder, is no bad thing."

I had to hope they were right. I tried to imagine Imachara populated with Theri Chimaera living openly. People with dragonfly or owlish wings. No one needing to hide scales or antlers or anything else that set them apart. It didn't seem like such a terrible future to me. I set the Aleph back, gently, and Relean did the same.

"Sleep well," Anisa murmured to them.

We stepped back out onto the sand, the Penglass closing behind us.

There, on the beach, we said our last goodbyes. Anisa whispered something to both Drystan and Cyan, though I didn't catch the words.

When she came to me, she rested her lips on my forehead.

"This was all meant to be darker, little Kedi," she said. "Some of the visions the spirits showed me . . ." She trailed off. "I thought more of us would die, out there on that rock in the middle of the sea. But it was you, little Kedi. Your hope, your determination. I truly believe you changed the fate of the world far more than I did."

I swallowed. Her words were meant to be kind, but their undercurrent left me uneasy.

"It was an honor to share your life and mind with you for a

time," she said. "I hope our paths cross again. Farewell, Micah Grey, my little Kedi."

Anisa and Relean waved one final time, and they walked away from us, hand in hand, leaving a trail of footprints in the sand.

●●●●

Drystan kept his palm clasped in mine as we climbed the stairs to the loft.

The space wasn't exactly as it'd been before, but it was close enough. Ricket was already curled up on the bed. The evening light shone through the restored stained-glass dragonfly window.

I lay down, and Ricket meowed softly at the disturbance.

Drystan lay next to me, tucking his arms behind his head. His shirt rode up, showing a sliver of white skin dusted with blond hair. I slipped my palm into the gap and rested my hand on his heart.

"How are you feeling?" he asked.

"Better now that I'm alone in here," I said, tapping my temple. "What about you?"

"I'm a hero who helped save the world, even if no one really knows that. I'm absolutely grand."

I laughed softly.

"How's your magic?" he asked.

I considered. "Fainter, now that Pinecrest's medicine is largely out of my system and Anisa is gone." Lily had decided not to give the elixir to her Professor friend, in the end. We'd all agreed that it was too risky to allow the drug to become widespread, considering it was so dangerous to humans and, though it increased Chimaera powers, it had a different type of risk. She'd helped Frey and I wean ourselves off with the last of Elwood and Pinecrest's supply. It was rough going initially, but soon enough, we were free of it.

"I think I'll still be able to use my magic without it, but it will be weaker." That, to be honest, was fine by me.

He stared up at the ceiling. "I've been having odd dreams."

I rose on my elbows, fighting down a flare of alarm. "How so?"

"Oh, nothing concrete, really. I can't suddenly fly or make objects levitate, or anything like that. But . . . I don't know. My dreams are more vivid, like I'm peeking into peoples' lives."

"Maybe you are," I teased, even as my heartbeat sped up a little. "Is it from the drug?"

He shrugged. "I don't know. It was only the one dose. Maybe it's proximity to you and Cyan, or housing Relean for a time. Anisa said magic is coming back to the world." He smiled, faintly. "I don't mind the dreams, anyway."

"What have you seen?" I asked.

"This and that," he said, mysteriously, sounding exactly like the white clown I'd met my first night at the circus.

I shifted a little on the bed. Drystan's hands stroked the hair back from my face, his fingertips dancing down my neck. We'd kept our distance when we hadn't been truly alone. My body had felt numb after all the events of the past few days, but at his touch, it came alive. Every inch of my skin tingled, and my stomach dipped with desire. I reached up and drew his lips to mine, kissing him fiercely. His mouth opened and I met his tongue with mine.

My fingers fumbled at his belt as he unbuttoned my waistcoat, and then my shirt. He pulled it open, and I wriggled free, throwing it to the floor. His shirt joined mine, and his fingers made quick work of my Lindean corset. We shed the rest of our clothes, and it felt like it had been ages since we'd last been this close. I pressed him to the bed, my skin against his.

Drystan gasped as my hands moved lower, and he gripped me close. My kisses trailed down his neck and chest. I didn't close my eyes, and neither did he. We drank in every detail as we fit together, finding our rhythm. We started leisurely until we raced to the crest, and beyond.

After, we lay in bed, spent and sleepy, our limbs heavy. Ricket curled up behind my knees. As I rested my head on Drystan's chest and listened to his heart beating like clockwork, I knew I was exactly where I wanted to be.

EPILOGUE: CARNIVALE

"Carnivale, also known as the Day of Fools, or Summertide, is a tradition that you can find within some villages, or poorer parts of town. The nobility may hold masked balls for the occasion, but among the lower classes, celebrations are more uncouth. Historically, in feudal times, Carnivale played with the notion of topsy-turvy. Social order can be upended—the poorest peasant might dress up as a king or queen, and hierarchy is flattened. The star of the celebration is the fool or jester, and several dress up in motley for the occasion, their bells and chimes ringing as they don gruesome Chimaera masks to tell ribald jokes.

It is considered good luck to disguise yourself for the duration of the festival. It can be a time for trysts, rendezvous, and letting instincts rule over logic. It is a time of magic."

**A HISTORY OF ELADA AND ITS FORMER COLONIES,
PROFESSOR CAED CEDAR, ROYAL SNAKEWOOD UNIVERSITY**

Drystan, Cyan, Maske, and I bowed, hand in hand, as the curtain fell to applause in the packed Kymri Theatre.

It was the matinee show, and we'd be skipping our evening performance for the Summertide Carnivale. I peeked through the curtain, impatient for the ushers to empty the theatre so we could join the other revelers. Over the past year, we'd transformed the space even more, courtesy of strong ticket sales and Doctor Samuel Pinecrest's generosity: new chandeliers, reupholstered seats, and fresh gilt paint on the columns. We'd hired more stagehands and no longer had to scrub it all down from top to bottom ourselves.

Maske took off his cloak and star-studded mask, beaming. "Another fine show. It does feel somewhat the end of an era, though, doesn't it?"

"Or the beginning of a new one," I said.

"Quite right, my dear, quite right." He nodded before ambling off the stage.

Still, I knew what he meant. Recently, we'd decided to expand our offerings—we'd already installed a permanent trapeze, but as of next week, we were going to transform the magic shows into more of a variety act or small-scale vaudeville. When the dust had settled and I had assurance from Princess Nicolette that no one would be searching for us in connection with Bil Ragona's death, I'd reached out to some of the circus performers. I'd successfully nicked the Kymri tumblers, Dot the contortionist, and I discovered Bethany the Bearded Woman did a fine comedy routine that left us all in stitches. We'd have the grand opening the following week.

"Are you lot ready yet?" a familiar woman's voice called from the wings. "Carnivale is in full swing."

"Hold on, hold on," Drystan groused. "I've got to get changed."

"Me, too," Cyan said, and they briefly left me alone with the finest act we'd poached from Alan Nickleby's vaudeville show.

A few months ago, I'd nervously told Drystan my plan, and to my extreme relief, he'd been all for it. My promise to Anisa was no longer in effect, I decided, now that I'd saved the world and she was somewhere far across the sea with Relean. Drystan had come with me to the Crescent Amphitheatre, both of us dressed up in our finest suits. My heart had hammered behind my ribs as we'd sat, side by side, and watched Aenea step onto that stage for the finale, dressed in green just like the first time I'd seen her beneath the big top. We'd watched her fly, a fairy of the trapeze once more.

When we hovered by the stage door after the performance, I nearly ran off half a dozen times before she finally came out, a coat pulled around her shoulders. She froze, staring at us like we were apparitions. Those keen, brown eyes darted between Drystan and me. And then, like the sun coming out from behind the clouds, she'd smiled.

Her expression in the Kymri was a little more hesitant. We hadn't spent much time one-on-one since I'd told her everything. For that had been her stipulation for leaving Nickleby's and joining our show: no more secrets. I'd held nothing back, her eyes going wider with every word as we hunched in the library of the Kymri Theatre.

"You were sloppy on that last double spin," she said.

I winced. "You caught that?"

"'Course I did. Thought I taught you better than that."

"You did."

"Damn straight." Her eyes crinkled. I knew, beneath that braid, she had a scar on the back of her head from Bil. It gave her headaches, sometimes, but aside from that, she'd made a full recovery. Step by step, like creating a new trapeze routine, we were rebuilding our friendship.

Cyan appeared, wearing a fresh sarong of Temnian silk. She and Aenea got on well, as I'd suspected they would. She held a tablecloth and her tarot cards in one hand, and I raised my eyebrows at them.

She shrugged a shoulder. "It's been a minute since I read a fortune. Fancied doing it tonight." Perhaps she no longer feared what future they might show her.

"Nice, Madame Damselfly. Where's Drystan?" I asked.

"He said he'd meet us down there."

"Let's *go*," Aenea said, tugging my wrist, and I let her lead me.

● ● ● ●

The street outside of the Kymri Theatre was filled to the brim with revelers.

People had erected food carts and a wooden stage, and Carnivale was well underway. The air was thick with the smell of roasted potatoes with garlic, onion, and butter. Someone passed me a clay mug of ale. Another stall sold sausage rolls at a discount, and a bakery offered free biscuits in the hopes of more regular customers. Growing up in Sicion, I'd never experienced anything like this—Mother had usually taken us out to the Emerald Bowl to avoid the crowds, and we'd go to some stuffy masked ball at one of the estates.

On the stage, a group of men and women played fiddles and drums. Cyan peeled away from Aenea and me, setting up at an empty barrel to read fortunes for free. The Kymri Theatre kept us so busy that we'd retired from séances.

More people arrived as the afternoon lengthened and the streetlamps lit. We were surrounded by people from all walks of life: well-to-do merchants, the odd noble in plainer clothes, factory workers, or rougher folk with missing teeth or ancient navy tattoos on their forearms. It was bad luck to pickpocket at Carnivale, and even the greediest of thieves tended to take the day off.

I spied Maske and Lily chatting animatedly with a middle-aged couple I didn't recognize, Frey in his wheelchair at their side. He wore a scarf over the lower half of his face, and most people probably thought his scales and horns were one of the many Carnivale masks rather than his true features. I sensed other Chimaera like fireflies dotted through the crowd. I was drawn to a cluster and soon found Juliet, Violet, and Tauro. Aenea made an exclamation of delight at the sight of them.

The music grew more boisterous. I danced a jig with Aenea, Violet, and Cyan.

"Where's Drystan?" I shouted breathlessly over the sounds of the crowd and the fiddles.

"You'll see!" Cyan called back before whirling away.

I fought my way through the crowd back toward Maske, Lily, and Frey. Kai and Cyril had arrived, and I greeted them enthusiastically. Only Princess Nicolette was missing, but even in disguise, she'd never be allowed to come to something like this. Sunset tinged everything orange and gold.

I heard the bells first. A path cut through the crowd, making room for the Parade of Fools. The Fools wore outlandish outfits—instead of motley, most wore strips of brightly colored rags added to normal clothing. All of them wore Chimaera masks, most of papier-mâché, the features twisted like gargoyles. Bells strung from their wrists, waists, and ankles jingled, somehow both merry and ominous. People clapped and stamped their feet. The music changed to an older style, the drums growing louder. The Fools scattered into the crowd, pinching an arm, telling an off-color joke, or generally causing good-natured trickery.

I recognized Drystan immediately, of course. I didn't know where he'd gotten a hold of his Chimaera mask, but it looked like a particularly ugly toad. With a start, I realized he was wearing his old, ruined clown's motley from the circus. I thought he'd thrown it out, but at some point, he must have repaired it and sewn brightly colored patches over most of the old white and pale pink. He moved with that same smooth grace I'd seen countless times beneath the big top. He worked the crowd, urging them to move back and create an open space on the dance floor, and flipped and twirled as if he'd never left the circus ring.

Cyan, Maske, Aenea, and I hollered as loud as the rest of them. Drystan stuck his hands by his ears as he mocked people nearby, waggling his fingers and blowing raspberries behind his mask. He pushed another Fool to the ground with infectious exuberance and cartwheeled over him to the shocked delight of the audience.

He caught sight of me and danced over, sweeping a bow as elaborate as any courtier.

"Care to dance?" he asked behind his mask. I was dressed as a boy, but on Carnivale, it didn't matter.

I laughed and took his hand, letting myself be carried away. Though we waved our arms and I pulled faces to get into the spirit of it all, our steps fell into a classic waltz. Old habits die hard. Drystan led, and I followed, his hand around my waist, and I had far more fun dancing around with him in his hideous mask than I'd had at my debutante ball.

The party lasted well into the night. Above, the stars shone, and the Lady of the Moon looked down on us. I laughed so much I nearly lost my voice. It reminded me of the bonfires and dancing after the circus.

Human and Chimaera alike, wild and free, we danced to the beat of the drums.

A Conversation with L. R. Lam

Did you always think you'd take Micah to the Royal Palace? What was it like, writing about that setting?

I knew I wanted each volume to draw on performance in some way, so *Pantomime* was the circus, *Shadowplay* stage magic, and *Masquerade* court magic. Micah started in a privileged part of society and had seen most levels except for the heart of the nobility: royalty. Considering Micah and his friends are living in the poorest part of town for most of this book, the Palace became an even starker contrast. I enjoyed the chance to show more about the government and royal family secrets.

Can you share how you felt about Micah's development in this novel?

Micah continues to come of age in *Masquerade*. This time, he has to face the challenge of Pinecrest and his medicine. Addiction and temptation are big themes in this book. Anisa's powers are curtailed so he's having to do things more on his own, which gives him more agency. He still isn't perfect and makes mistakes, but he's always trying his best. He's learning to trust himself and his abilities, to stick up for what he believes in, and to lean on those around him.

What made you decide to show flashes of the blurred man's plan through Micah's dreams? How might the novel have been different, if we didn't have those glimpses into the blurred man's plot until the end?

As those who read the old version of *Masquerade* know, that subplot previously served an entirely different purpose, and re-writing that was one of the larger changes in this edit. The old version had much less about the blurred man's motivations until the very end of the book because I hadn't figured out an elegant opportunity to share them. I also changed and deepened his motivations and how he had the knowledge to enact his plan, in general. It was one of the many instances where I could see how I've leveled up as a writer in the decade since I wrote it the first time.

How have you revised this book, from its last edition?

Beyond the dream snatching subplot shifting, the underlying structure stayed similar in the first part of the book—I wasn't moving things around as much as I did in *Pantomime* and *Shadowplay*. I think I made the politics and macro concerns about Eladan society a bit more nuanced, since I've lived through the last ten years of increasingly alarming world events (though it was hilarious/dismaying that in the old version of *Shadowplay*, Timur at one point said he wanted to 'make Elada great again.' I wrote that line in 2013! I deleted it as it's far too jarring now). I realized I wasn't very happy with the old version of the climax—everything happened a bit too neatly, I saw some plot holes, and it was over with too quickly. I also realized there were opportunities to bring in some characters we'd seen before, like the other Chimaera, and to have Micah rely more on the acrobat skills he learned in the circus. I deepened the revelations about Penglass, and in general felt I ended things on a stronger note.

What was your favorite scene to write?

As with the other volumes, I always enjoy the magic performance chapters, as well as the softer, tender moments between characters. I usually struggle a bit more with action sequences, but I'm pleased with how I edited and improved the first explosion chapter, for example. I also like the newer scenes I added to the denouement.

Reading Group Guide for *Masquerade*

1. Did you trust Doctor Pinecrest? Did you think Micah was right to trust him?
2. Chimaera, Vestige, and other long lost magic returns to Elada in this novel. Is there any old magic or folklore you'd like to see 'returned' to our world?
3. If you were Chimaera, what power would you most want to have? What would you want to look like if you were Theri Chimaera?
4. If you were Micah, which three times in the story would you have asked Anisa for help? Do you agree with the times he chose?
5. What was your favorite instance of magic in this book?
6. What was your favorite chapter?
7. How about your favorite line or scene?
8. What did you think of the ending?
9. What was your favorite twist? Did you see any of them coming?
10. What was your favorite book out of the whole trilogy, and why?
11. How do you think Micah has changed, since we first met him in *Pantomime*?

ACKNOWLEDGEMENTS

I first dreamed up *Pantomime* while filing at my first job after I moved from California to Scotland back in December 2009. I'd already started another manuscript that took a different direction with an older Micah as a detective solving crimes, but I thought I'd try writing from the point of view of Micah as a teenager joining the circus. I'd planned a short story, and here we are, a trilogy and several tie-in novellas and short stories later (*The Vestigial Tales* are available on Kindle). There are so, so many people to thank who helped me along this long and bumpy road.

The first person I told about the book was my husband. He's listened to me talk through plot problems and been with me through all the highs and lows. Craig, I'm so lucky to have had you in my life since I was fifteen.

I also wanted to take a moment to commemorate Mowgli, my Bengal cat that we sadly had to say goodbye to after nearly sixteen years while I was doing the line edits for this volume. He'd been there since I was drafting *Pantomime*. Every time I unboxed a final copy of a book, he was crawling into it. He spent many hours in my lap as I wrote, or distracted me with his yowls. I picked him up and squeezed him when I got good news, or cried into his fur if I had the opposite. He unfortunately went at a time when I really needed him. I miss him desperately, and the flat is far too quiet without him.

Thank you to my mom and ever-stalwart cheerleader Sally Baxter, and to Erica Bretall, Shawn DeMille, Wesley Chu, Lorna McKay, and Mike Kalar, who were early readers on the previous versions of all three books. Cheers to Joseph Morton, J. B. Rockwell, and Corinne Duyvis for their time and excellent comments. Thanks to Katharine Stubbs and Kale Levin, readers of *Pantomime* who ended up being beta readers for *Masquerade* and giving insightful notes. More appreciation to Laya Rose for all your awesome fan art starting way back in 2014—I love that now we have collaborated on merchandise for *Dragonfall* through Kingdom of Threads in a full-circle moment.

Thank you to Arcady Wolf, C. J. Henderson, and Sasha Strangfeld for reading the new versions of *Masquerade*. P. M. Freestone, thank you for being my rubber duck when I got a bit tangled up while we were writing at the library—the ending of this book is what ended up changing the most on this pass. Kit Briarson, merci for all the lovely social media posts, and a general thanks to my friends who cheered me on and offered emotional support: Hannah Kaner, Beck O'Leary, Callum Howell, Alyssa Blair, L. D. Lapinski, Katie Gage, Dhonielle Clayton, Kate Dramis, Amy Plum, Noelle Harrison, Becky Sweeney, Seumas MacDonald, Anne Campbell, Ariana Weldon, Patrick Guaschino, Kieran Faulkner. More thanks to Linden A. Lewis, Cat Hellisen, Eris Young, Nick Binge, David Bishop, Ally Kersel, Sam Eastop, Elle Macray, Jay Martin, Emily X. R. Pan, Emma Törsz, Sophie Burnham, Kim Curran, Amy McCulloch, Elizabeth May, Samantha Shannon, Marvellous Michael Anson, and Sarah Rees Brennan. Thank you to everyone in the ESFF Discord and the in-person writing group led by Megan Lederman. Thank you to my local café and everyone at Argonaut Books and the many wonderful bookstores who supported my work, both in Edinburgh and beyond. Thank you to Kat Safras and everyone at Barnes & Noble.

On the publishing side, continued gratitude to Aranya Jain for editing, Betsy Wollheim, Molly Powell, Laura Fitzgerald, Eugenia Woo, Ben Schrank, Laura Bartholomew, Kate Keehan, and everyone at DAW/Astra and Hodderscape. Thank you to Lean Spann for copyediting. I remain thankful to Amanda Rutter, who saw the promise in *Pantomime* way back in 2011, and Julie Crisp for doing the same in 2014. My gratitude to my new collaborator and champion: Safae El-Ouahabi. I look forward to seeing what we do together!

If I've forgotten anyone, a million apologies.

Last and not least, endless thanks to everyone who has taken the time to read and review these books. The series had yet another chance because of my readers' love for my books, and you've helped me keep writing many times when times were tough. That's why this book is for you.

Thanks for meeting Micah Grey and his friends and finishing his tale, or revisiting to see how it's changed in this reimagination. I hope he stays with you and that you might consider spending a little more time in my made-up worlds.

YOUR NEXT GREAT READ IS JUST A FOLLOW AWAY!

DAW

DISCOVER GROUNDBREAKING NEW AUTHORS AND UNFORGETTABLE CHARACTERS FROM @DAWBOOKS ACROSS ALL SOCIAL NETWORKS.

FOR BREAKING NEWS, EXCLUSIVE CONTENT, AND DEALS, SUBSCRIBE TO OUR NEWSLETTER AT:

ASTRAPUBLISHINGHOUSE.COM/SIGN-UP-FOR-EMAILS